THE TEMPLE
OF THE
THREE WHISPERS

BOOK THREE:

MISPLACED IN
MYSTERIA

BRIAN HARMON

The Temple of the Three Whispers
Book Three: Misplaced in Mysteria

Copyright © 2024 Brian Harmon
Published by Brian Harmon
Cover Image and Design by Brian Harmon

All rights reserved.

ISBN: 978-1-945559-26-6

Don't miss these other great books by Brian Harmon!

The Temple of the Blind series:

The Box (Book I)
Gilbert House (Book II)
The Temple of the Blind (Book III)
Road Beneath The Wood (Book IV)
Secret of the Labyrinth (Book V)
The Judgment of the Sentinels (Book VI)

The Temple of the Three Whispers series:

The Lady of Cedric's Cove (Book I)
Circles in Hermes' Footsteps (Book II)
Misplaced in Mysteria (Book III)
The Denselands (Book IV)
The Impassible Wall (Book V)
The City Beyond Memory (Book VI)
The Keeper's Dollhouse (Book VII)
Priestess of Ruin (Book VIII)
The Temple of the Three Whispers (Book IX)
Whispers in the Murk (Book X)

The Rushed series:

Rushed (Book 1)
Rushed: The Unseen (Book 2)
Rushed: Something Wicked (Book 3)
Rushed: Hedge Lake (Book 4)
Rushed: A Matter of Time (Book 5)
Rushed: All Fun and Games (Book 6)
Rushed: Something Wickeder (Book 7)
Rushed: Evancurt (Book 8)
Rushed: Relic (Book 9)

Hands of the Architects trilogy:

Spirit Ears and Prophet Sight (Book 1)
Pretty Faces and Peculiar Places (Book 2)
Broken Clocks and Amber Threads (Book 3)

For Christopher

Chapter 1

"It'll be a laugh," insisted Brandy. "You know it will."

"I'm sure it will," replied Albert. "Assuming we can find it." The directions on the brochure had led them beyond the city limits of Wevenwert and out into the wilderness of Tennessee. The road was narrow and winding through the densely forested mountain terrain. There were other cars on the road with them, but not quite enough to stave off that eerie feeling of isolation.

They checked out of their hotel a little before eleven on the final day of their honeymoon and then had lunch together. It was a long drive back to Briar Hills, but Brandy had one last stop she wanted to make before going home. Something she found tucked in with all the other brochures in the Lucianna Mysteria's lobby that morning. Something distinctly different from anything else they'd ventured out of the intimate privacy of their hotel room for.

"Come on," she prodded. "How often are we going to get the chance to check out a *sex museum*?"

"Before today, I didn't know there *was* such a thing." He wasn't sure about this. It sounded a little skeevy, if he were being honest. He was a tiny bit embarrassed about the idea of actually walking into such a place. But she insisted it sounded hilarious.

"Of course there is. There's the Museum of Sex in New York City. And the Leather Archives and Museum in Chicago. And the Hollywood Erotic Museum. People are fascinated by sex. I mean it only makes sense, really."

He glanced over at her, one eyebrow raised. "You just looked those up on your phone today, didn't you?"

"Maybe. There should be a turn-off coming up on the right." She was squinting through her glasses at the little map on the back of the brochure and playing with her ponytail. "Looks like this road curves to the left and the road we want branches off to the right a little and then curves straight." She let go of her hair as she spoke and made a gesture with her hand to illustrate.

Like everything she did, Albert found it adorable. Was it weird that he was still so enchanted by her after all this time? They'd been together almost six years, now already. And yet he couldn't stop stealing glances at her as he sat behind the wheel. She looked so amazing in her short skirt and sleeveless white blouse.

Of course, it didn't hurt that he knew she wasn't wearing anything under those clothes. He thought she was just being playful when she told him she didn't pack any panties for their honeymoon, but all week, she'd been flashing him naughty little peeks everywhere they went. And if anyone out there thought *that* never got old…well, they were absolutely right. The mountain sunset views were nothing compared to the ones his beautiful bride kept sneaking him.

Six years ago, when they were still strangers, the two of them were lured into the steam tunnels underneath Briar Hills University by a mysterious box and key. There, deep below the earth, hidden from the eyes of the modern world, they encountered an ancient labyrinth containing, among so many other strange and fantastic things, a room filled with erotic statues that made them lose all earthly control. They tore each other's clothes off and engaged in crazed, unbridled sex. To some, that probably wouldn't sound like the worst thing that could happen, but it was actually quite terrifying for both of them. After all, they were stripped of their senses and reason and reduced to little more than lust-fueled animals. They could have hurt each other. At the very least, they could've ended up resenting each other. They could've *hated* each other. It wouldn't have been hard, after all, to view what happened down there as *rape*. Fortunately, it worked out in the end. It turned out they rather liked each other. And not just as casual lovers. They very quickly became best friends. They fell in love. And now, finally, they were happily married. But sometimes he couldn't help wondering if that room hadn't changed them somehow… Was it really normal to be *this* sexually attracted to someone? Was it simply that they just happened to both have *very* active libidos? Or did that room do something to them that night? Did it change them into what they were now?

He supposed it didn't matter. As long as they both felt the same way. But he sometimes wondered what he would do if she ever grew tired of him. What if she lost interest in him while he still lusted after her? He wasn't sure he could stand it. What an absolutely depressing ending that would be to an otherwise incredible love story.

"There it is!" chirped Brandy.

Ahead of them, just as she described, the road curved to the left and a small, gravel drive branched off to the right and then turned sharply to the left and continued straight on into the woods.

"No sign," he observed.

But she only shrugged. "It says 'now open' on the brochure. It's probably still new."

He turned off the paved road and drove deeper into the woods, feeling a little bit like the dumb character that always got himself killed at the start of every horror movie.

"Maybe we'll get some *inspiration*," she said. She glanced over at him, the tip of her pink tongue sticking out of the corner of her mouth in a mischievous grin.

"What, like *hillbilly style*? Like doggy style, but we're drunk off our asses on moonshine and wearing floppy hats and wading boots?"

This made her laugh. "Where the fuck do you come up with stuff like that? You're so weird sometimes!"

"You like me weird."

"Yes, I do. You crack me up."

Ahead of them, the forest opened up. He could see a grassy parking lot and a building of some sort waiting for them. "Is this it?"

"We followed the map," she reminded him.

The building revealed by the parting foliage as he continued forward was little more than an old wooden cabin set back into the woods with a covered porch stretched across the entire length of the front. There was a neon sign in the shape of a busty, naked woman in one window and two mannequins wearing leather bondage gear standing by the entrance. A large sign mounted on the roof of the porch displayed the words "SEX MUSEUM" in huge, bright pink letters.

He parked on one side of the lot and squinted out at the scene before him. "You *sure* this is the place?"

"I think it *might* be," she laughed. Between her husband's silliness and the absolute *absurdity* of the place, she couldn't seem to stop giggling.

"No cars," observed Albert. They appeared to be the only customers.

"Good. We'll have the place to ourselves."

"But what about the people working here?"

Brandy wasn't concerned. She was already stepping out into the Tennessee heat. "There's an open sign on the door. *Somebody* has to be here."

That was true. And the lack of cars didn't mean anything. Maybe employees parked around back. Or maybe they carpooled and someone was out getting lunch. It really wasn't worth thinking too much about.

He stepped out of the car and glanced around. The air was alive with the sounds of the forest. Birds and cicadas sang their endless songs. And he could faintly hear traffic droning somewhere in the distance.

As he looked out across the weedy lawn, he caught just a glimpse of a gray and white cat prowling through the trees.

He closed the driver's door of the Mustang and followed his stunning wife to the porch, where she paused in front of one of the lewdly dressed mannequins, looking it over.

She turned and gave him another of her mischievous grins. "What do you think? Wanna see me in something like that?"

He looked it over, picturing it in his mind. "Sure," he decided. "But I like the ones you showed me in the hotel better."

She pressed up against him, still grinning. "Oh yeah?"

"They were more revealing."

"Hm... So I picked good, then?"

"Yes. You did."

She kissed him. Then she wrinkled up her face in a childish sort of pout. "I'm bummed our honeymoon is almost over."

"I know, right? We have to go back to having sex all the time at *home* instead of in a *hotel room*."

She laughed and gave him a gentle push. "It's not about the *sex*," she told him. "You only get one honeymoon. It's special."

"*Every* day I spend with you is special," he told her.

"Awe." She tugged on his shirt, pulling him closer, then kissed him again, longer this time. "You're such a suck-up when you're trying to get laid."

"I'm not trying to get laid. I just adore you."

"Awe." She kissed him much longer this time, savoring him.

Again, he found himself wondering if that strange, pornographic chamber they were trapped in did something to them, if it altered their brains somehow, making them like this. But every time he looked in her gorgeous blue eyes, his heart swelled so much he could barely breathe. And *that* wasn't lust. He loved her so much he could barely stand to be apart from her. It didn't have to be sex. Holding her hand... Caressing her knee... Rubbing her back... Running his fingers through her hair... He just wanted to be *touching* her. And every moment *she* spent touching *him*, even the *briefest* of moments, like when she plucked a piece of lint from his shirt or brushed away an eyelash or even just bumped her thigh up against him in a crowded room, was pure *ecstasy*! He couldn't get enough of her. He was *addicted* to her.

If that was what the sex room did, then it was the best thing that ever happened to him. He wouldn't trade a single moment with her in all this time, not for all the other pleasures in the world.

She playfully tugged at his lower lip a little as she pulled away. "I love you."

"I love you too."

She let go of his shirt and gave him another of those naughty grins. "Let's go inside," she said, biting her lip.

She could probably get him to do almost *anything* when she

bit her lip like that. It was almost as sexy as it was adorable. And she knew it.

He opened the door for her, but paused a moment before following her inside, his gaze drifting out toward the dense forest. For just a second or two, he felt as if something were off about this place... Something he couldn't quite put his finger on...

But the sensation faded as quickly as it came.

He shrugged it off and stepped inside.

Chapter 2

"Holy shit!" gasped Brandy. She pressed one hand over her mouth, trying to hold back the giggles that were bubbling up inside her.

"Holy shit, indeed," agreed Albert.

The moment they stepped through the door, they were confronted with no less than a four-foot-tall, three-dimensional, full-color anatomic model of the human vagina. It was standing right in front of the door so that it was the first thing you saw, whether you wanted to or not.

"Glad they're easing us into it," he said as he stared at the biggest clitoris he'd ever seen. "Jesus Christ..."

Brandy couldn't stop laughing. She turned and looked at him, her wide eyes screaming, "Is this for real?"

"That's a *lot* of pussy," he said, sending her into another fit of giggles.

The sign over the model asked in great big, shameless letters, "DO YOU REALLY KNOW HOW TO PLEASURE HER?" while smaller signs pointed out the various places one should pay close attention to and offered a variety of suggestions for interacting with each indicated place.

"Just... Wow."

Brandy regained control of herself and grinned at him. "Mine's cuter, right?"

"*So* much cuter," he assured her. "Yours is adorable. *And* it fits in my car. Bonus points, there."

Again, she broke into a fit of giggles. She couldn't help it. It was just so completely absurd. What kind of person even came up with something like that? Much less put it on display!

He glanced around. There was a counter on the right, preventing them from going that way. Behind it was a small, empty space, gloomy, with only a single dim ceiling fixture illuminating it and heavy black cloth draped over the walls. It looked like the place where you were supposed to pay to get in, but there was no register or cash box or even a tip jar. The counter was completely empty. He'd expected to at least be charged for entry before they were allowed to see anything. Was this place free to visit?

To the left, a pair of dark red partitions separated the space into a narrow hallway lined with enlarged vintage photographs of men and women engaging in all manner of sexual acts. Beyond that, in the corner against the far wall, stood a glass case with what appeared to be a variety of old sex toys.

He looked back at the door, frowning. He was a little distracted by his bride's flirtatiousness on the porch, so he might've missed it, but he didn't recall seeing a sign warning that this was an adults-only establishment. What if some kid wandered in here? Shouldn't there at least be some kind of lobby you entered through before they surprised you with something like a gargantuan vagina? Shouldn't someone be here to check their IDs?

He looked up into the open rafters overhead. There were wires and hanging lights and ventilation, but no cameras that he could see.

The place smelled funny, too. Sort of musty, which he supposed wasn't surprising for a museum. But it also smelled like a strange mix of old leather, cheap plastic and other things he couldn't quite place.

"Come here." Brandy pressed herself up against him and snapped a selfie with the giant model in the background.

"Seriously? We needed that?"

"Yes. We needed it." She turned her head and snapped a second picture, trying to get a better angle. "Come on, this is fucking *hilarious*. Don't you think it's hilarious?"

"It is," he agreed.

"Nikki's going to laugh herself into a coma when I show her these."

"I bet she will."

She turned and eyed the model one last time. "Things I

didn't know I needed to check off my bucket list: one giant cooter. Check."

Albert chuckled. This place was weird, but at least she was having fun. He loved it when she laughed.

"Good afternoon."

Surprised, both of them turned to find that a young woman had appeared on the other side of the naked counter and was standing directly under the light, her dainty hands clasped in front of her. She was wearing a revealing, black leather teddy with a tiny skirt that appeared to be entirely decorative because it covered nothing. She had matching studded leather bracelets and choker. Her hair was raven black and tied into long pigtails with prim, straight bangs and little wavy locks that dangled down on either side of her face. Her long nails were also black, as were her full lips. Her skin, however, was strikingly pale, almost white in contrast. And her eyes, as blue as the sky, seemed to shine from the gloom of her long, black lashes and stark eyeliner. She looked like a pretty little vampire standing there in the gloom.

"Welcome to the Sex Museum," she said, her voice and expression virtually emotionless, as if she were nothing more than a realistic robot. But those pretty eyes drifted back and forth between them as they spoke, as if studying them. "Please take your time and enjoy all that Master's gallery has to offer."

Albert and Brandy exchanged a surprised look. Did she really just call it "Master's gallery"? What kind of kinky theme was this place trying to pull off?

"I'll be happy to answer any questions you might have about any of the exhibits," she informed them, managing to sound not at all happy to do any such thing.

"Do I pay you here?" asked Albert, still confused, "Or where do I…?"

"There is no charge," the scantily clad greeter informed him in her deadpan tone.

"Oh… Okay."

"Nice," said Brandy.

"You're on the VIP list. Master has been expecting you."

"Huh?" said Albert. "I don't think we're…um…?"

"Enjoy the gallery," said the woman. Then she turned and disappeared through a doorway hidden behind the black curtains.

"Okay…" That was kind of weird. "We were expected?" How could anyone have been expecting them? It was only by chance that Brandy found the brochure in the hotel lobby.

But she only giggled again. "It's just a gimmick. Everybody who comes in the door is probably an expected VIP. The brochure looked like they only recently opened. They're probably trying to drum up business with free tours and a kinky character greeter. Seems like you've got to be creative these days to start a business."

He supposed she was probably right.

"I told you this place would be a laugh! Let's see what else is here." She turned and strolled through the aisle of vintage photographs. "Old timey porn," she said, nodding. "Solid. I can dig it."

Albert pushed the greeter from his mind and followed her, his gaze washing over every photograph. There were dozens of them. Most were of ordinary couples in various sexual positions or of women simply posing naked by themselves, but several depicted three or more people thoroughly enjoying each other's company. And some were as whimsical as they were lewd. In one, there was a woman having sex with a man dressed as Santa Claus. Another depicted a man pleasuring two women wearing witches hats and fake warty noses. And one seemed to be an entire *Alice in Wonderland* tea party scene, complete with Alice, the Mad Hatter and the White Rabbit as well as both Tweedledee *and* Tweedledum, neither of which he recalled even *being* at the tea party, much less doing…*that*…with Alice.

(Maybe it was in the deleted scenes that came with the Blu-ray.)

He looked back and forth, scanning the entire display. "I can't help thinking that all these people are most likely dead now."

She glanced back at him, surprised. "Morbid much?"

"Sorry."

"I mean you're not *wrong*," she decided. She wrinkled her

nose at a couple who were probably in their early thirties when the picture was taken and wondered how many years had gone by since that day. "Just…morbid."

"I'm just saying, you know, think about it. What if these are the only pictures that still exist of any of these people?"

"Wow… That's a depressing thought."

"Yeah. What if one of these pictures was literally all that was left in the world of you?" He pointed at one of them. "And you're doing *that*."

She tilted her head to one side and considered it. "Well *I* couldn't do that. I don't even *know* that many clowns."

Albert chuckled. He supposed she had him there.

She walked past the photographs and glanced briefly over the display case with the old sex toys. "Antique dildos," she observed. "Because why not?"

"Why not?" he agreed.

More display cases lined the wall next to the sex toys. There was an exhibit about the evolution of sex in primitive humans. There was an "Illustrated History of Prostitution." Another contained a collection of fertility idols from various cultures. (Those were kind of neat, he thought.) And one was an entire cabinet filled with nothing but *whips*. There was even a display about the history of *cartoon porn*, of all things, complete with a little television screen playing a silly animation starring a slutty princess engaging in a series of exaggerated sexual encounters as she wandered around her castle.

"Check it out," said Albert. "An *exhibit* on *exhibitionism*. Clever."

"And the complete history of the *breast implant*," added Brandy. "The world totally needed *that*."

They turned the corner and found a display of erotic body jewelry, including several photographs and a plastic penis with a large number of piercings inserted through it.

"Ouch…" said Albert, wincing at the very sight of it. "No thank you. Didn't want to see that."

"I work with a girl who has one of those," said Brandy, pointing at one of the pictures.

"Really?"

"Remember Britney?"

"Oh…" Albert stared at the image for a moment, distracted. "Huh," was all he could think to say. He *did* remember Britney. She was an attractive young woman with a sweet, girl-next-door kind of face. Not the sort of person who immediately jumped to mind when the subject of erotic piercings came up. He wasn't entirely sure how he felt learning that she had one of *those*… There was something arousing about knowing such an intimate detail about someone. But there was also something a little bit embarrassing about it, too. It made him feel like he knew a dirty little secret about her, like some pervy peeper. He was probably going to feel awkward the next time he saw her. "How does something like that come up in conversation?"

"I don't even remember," she laughed. "But she told us all about it one day. Wasn't a bit shy."

"Huh," he said again.

She stared at the display a moment, thoughtful. "You think I should get a nipple pierced?"

He stared at the picture, surprised. "Uh…?"

She grinned that mischievous grin again, the tip of her tongue peeking out from the corner of her mouth, then bent toward him and tugged down the collar of her blouse, flashing him her bare chest underneath. "You like shiny things, don'tcha?"

"I like *you*," he told her.

She stood up straight, still grinning. "Well don't get too excited." She glanced at the photographs again. "I seriously doubt I'd ever be brave enough to do something like that."

"It *does* look painful," he agreed.

She nodded and crossed her arms over her chest. "Yeah, no thank you."

"Yeah."

"Maybe if I were *really* drunk."

"I could see that."

They lingered a moment longer, looking over the photographs, then moved on.

Beyond the body jewelry case, the wall was adorned with a collection of frilly handcuffs, iron shackles and leather restraints, along with more erotic photographs, modern this time, in full color and high definition, depicting women and men bound and gagged. There was a large television screen displaying a slideshow all about the history of S&M.

Opposite these stood several mannequins, each of them dressed in sexy lingerie from various time periods. Brandy thought most of them looked *very* uncomfortable.

They walked past the mannequins and through a beaded curtain, into a room filled with glass cases displaying all manner of sexual paraphernalia. Albert looked around, feeling a little overwhelmed. He didn't think he'd ever seen so many things that vibrated in one place before. "Why the hell are some of them attached to *power tools?*" he gasped, staring at a large, plastic penis attached to the blade holder of what appeared to be a reciprocating saw. "Who dreams up this stuff?"

Brandy took another selfie with the absurd device in the background. She couldn't remember the last time she giggled this much. She was so glad she found that brochure this morning in the hotel lobby. This was even more fun than she imagined. "Nikki's seriously gonna shit when she sees these."

"I think *anyone* would if they saw that thing coming at them," reasoned Albert, sending her into another fit of laughter. "*I* almost did."

The next area looked like something he might have found in an actual art gallery. There was artwork on the walls that looked like it might be very old, depicting all manner of nonsensical sexual things. He saw a painting of a woman running from a flock of winged penises. Another depicted a group of naked women lying drunkenly about the feet of a winged devil with a raging erection. And a third was of a tortured-looking man lost in a labyrinth of stone walls with breasts growing out of them.

There was also a marble statue of a beautiful woman that looked like it could've come straight out of ancient Greece, except she was lifting her dress and exposing herself in a very unladylike manner. And there was a copper statue of a man who appeared to be stooped over and contemplating his own grossly exaggerated genitals.

And because the space apparently needed something else, there were a dozen flaccid stone penises mounted to the wall.

Albert stopped and stared for a moment at an etching of three men with penises for heads who seemed to be unable to decide which way to go at a crossroad. He couldn't decide if there was supposed to be some sort of deep and thought-provoking meaning behind the image or if the artist simply thought all men were idiotic dickheads who refused to ask for directions.

Brandy paused in front of a six-foot-tall, illuminated poster-board mounted to the wall. "'Masturbation,'" she read as yet another giggling fit came over her, "'Are You Doing It Right?'"

He looked up at this, confused. "Who the fuck's doing it *wrong?*"

Her giggles exploded into hearty laughter at this. "Oh my god!" she gasped.

"Seriously! How do you fuck *that* up?"

She laughed so hard she snorted and then clasped her hands over her mouth and blushed, embarrassed.

He dropped his voice several octaves and, in a bad, uppity British accent, said, "*Truly* proper masturbation requires only three things: a tool belt, a rubber ducky and a jar of Helman's brand mayonnaise."

"You're going to make me pee myself!" she wheezed.

In the same goofy voice, he exclaimed, "*That's* how you know you're doing it right!"

She grabbed a handful of his shirt and buried her flushed face against his shoulder, pushing up her glasses in the process. "Oh my god! You have to stop!"

He chuckled and wrapped his arms around her. He really loved making her laugh like that. He wished he could do it more often.

She caught her breath and reached up under her glasses to wipe the tears from her eyes before straightening them. "You're so silly. I love you."

"I love you, too."

"I hope you're enjoying all that Master's gallery has to offer."

They turned to find that the leather-clad greeter had appeared among the half-naked mannequins behind them. She was standing exactly as she was before, her back straight, her chin up, her small hands still clasped together in front of her. Now that she wasn't behind that counter, they could see that she was also wearing a pair of black leather, knee-high boots with very tall heels and laces running all the way up the front, adding to that slutty vampire look she seemed to be going for.

"Yes," said Brandy, embarrassed. "It's very…" She glanced at the huge display board again. "…*informative*," she finished, barely containing another fit of giggles.

"I'm so happy to hear that," she replied in a tone that didn't sound particularly happy at all. "Master has extended an invitation for you to visit our most exclusive gallery." She nodded toward a curtained doorway leading into the back of the building. "He's prepared a demonstration for your enjoyment."

"For *us*?" asked Albert. "Are you sure you don't have us confused with someone else?"

"Quite sure, yes," she replied without hesitation.

"I told you, it's all a show," whispered Brandy. "Just go with it."

"The lights inside come on automatically," she informed them. "Master hopes you find it…*pleasurable*." She gave them that strangely forced smile again and then turned and walked away.

"She is *so* over-the-top!" giggled Brandy as she watched her walk away. Then she tugged on his shirt again. "Let's go see what's in there!"

Chapter 3

It was dark when they stepped through the curtain, but just as the strange greeter told them, the lights came on as soon as they'd taken a few steps into the room.

They were in a short corridor with a low ceiling, lined with wall-mounted information boards and glass cases. All of the light was focused on the items on display, leaving the rest of the room bathed in atmospheric gloom.

Albert started forward, looking over the items in the nearest cases. There were little bottles of lotions and oils, along with little information plates that gave detailed descriptions of each one. There was a display of crystals, each one accompanied by a card that revealed their unique properties and energy. In another case was a collection of odd-looking jewelry, including strings of strange-looking beads, necklaces of irregularly shaped jewels and coils of something that looked unsettlingly like human hair. Yet another was filled with curiously shaped sex toys and a pair of suspiciously unclean-looking lace panties.

He found himself hesitant to read the little note cards placed in front of most of these things. He wasn't sure he wanted to know what some of them were. Several of those jewelry pieces appeared almost...*anatomical*...

He turned his attention instead to an old book sitting on a podium between two of the displays, open to a page with graphic illustrations of sexual acts. A variation of the famous *Kama Sutra*, perhaps?

Brandy skimmed over one of the information boards. "'Sexual *magic*'?" she read. "That's a thing?"

He leaned closer to the book and found that there was writing in addition to the erotic illustrations, but it was in a language he didn't recognize. The plaque beneath it described it as a sexual *spellbook*.

"'Sexually charged energy'..." she read, "...'visualization of one's goal'...'utilization of sexual power'...'leading to manifestation within the physical universe'... Huh." She turned her attention to the next board. "This one's about 'brain activity during sexual stimulation and orgasm.' *Very* scientific," she chided. She moved on to the next. "'Rituals for Aligning Sexual and Spiritual Energy.'"

"People really believe in this sort of stuff?" he wondered.

"We're not exactly ones to talk about something being unbelievable," she reminded him.

She had a point. No one would believe in the Temple of the Blind, either. Or in Sentinel Queens. Or man-eating night trees. But *magic*? There was no such thing.

At the end of the corridor, bathed in darkness, was a set of double doors.

Albert glanced around. There were no signs. No arrows instructing them to "go this way" or even telling them where the exit was, which seemed like kind of a safety hazard.

But Brandy didn't hesitate. She walked up to the doors and pulled one of them open. As soon as she did, the lights in the corridor faded. Surprised, he hurried forward and grabbed her hand, not wanting to be separated as the darkness swallowed them.

"Creepy," whispered Brandy.

"No kidding. This doesn't seem safe."

"It's like they're putting on some sort of show or something."

Albert wasn't sure he wanted to see any kind of *show* that related to anything he saw on his way in here.

They stepped through the doorway and into the darkness. He couldn't see anything, but it felt like they were in a much larger space now. And it seemed colder.

"Shouldn't the lights be coming on now?" wondered Brandy. There was a brief echo to her voice, as if the room they were in were empty.

He pulled her a little closer to him. He didn't like not knowing what was going on. "Hello?" he called.

Something was in front of him, he realized. He sensed it there. A large shape was blocking their path. Carefully, he reached out and felt it, something cold and hard and smooth.

From somewhere overhead came a loud burst of static followed by a man's voice: "Sexual energy is sexual power."

Brandy looked up at the ceiling, her eyes wide, straining to see through the darkness. Was this the kinky greeter's "master" she was talking about? It wasn't a very attractive voice. It was sort of gruff. There was something about it she didn't think she liked very much.

"One only needs to know how to harness sexual energy in order to wield that power."

"Is this about the proper way to beat off again?" wondered Brandy.

"God, I hope not," grumbled Albert. He certainly didn't want to see *that* kind of demonstration.

"There exist places in this universe, very ancient places, very *powerful* places, that were designed to utilize and channel this very energy."

One by one, all around them, a series of lamps flickered on, dimly at first, so that the sudden glare wasn't blinding, allowing them to see with perfect clarity the horror they'd walked into.

"Oh god no!" gasped Brandy, her heart leaping with sudden and overwhelming terror.

"That's impossible!" shouted Albert.

Shades of gray materialized from the black, revealing vivid human shapes all around them, frozen in time like so many of the photographs in the previous rooms.

At their feet lay an all-too-familiar stone woman, naked and screaming and clawing at the floor in silent ecstasy as an equally familiar stone man forced himself between her spread legs, his face contorted into a vulgar mask of lascivious greed.

More statues loomed behind them, vulgar scenes of sexual deprivation, madly lusting people caught in acts of unbridled fornication. There were dozens of men and women, all of them naked and crazed with uncontrollable carnal desires. A literal orgy of cold stone stretched out before them. They were even coming out of the walls.

It was the sex room, exactly as it looked six years ago, when they had no idea that such a place existed, that cold stone could have the power to rob them of their senses and make them do the things they were about to do.

Brandy snatched off her glasses and turned away. "Don't look at it!"

Albert didn't need to be told. He'd already turned away from the stone obscenities and was moving toward the door they entered through.

But there was no way out. The door was still there, but there was no handle on this side. They were locked in the moment they let it close behind them. He banged his fist against it, knowing it was pointless. Who was going to come to their rescue? There were no other customers in the museum. It was only the two of them, the kinky greeter who sent them into this nightmare and perhaps the one she called "master."

They were trapped.

Chapter 4

"How can this be here?" gasped Brandy.

It was a good question. He didn't have an answer for it. The sex room was a part of the Temple of the Blind, which fell apart when they opened the doorway at its summit. It was *gone*. *All* of it. Collapsed into itself. He was almost buried with it as it came down. If it hadn't been for Andrea... Well, he didn't like to think too much about that. But the fact remained that even if the sex room had somehow survived the collapse of the temple six years ago, why the hell would it be in a backwoods sex museum in Tennessee? They were nowhere near the Temple of the Blind!

"*Albert...*" she whimpered, her voice tinged with fear. She was clinging to his shirt, her face pressed against him, hiding her eyes from those wicked statues.

"Don't panic," he said, speaking as much to himself as to her. "We know how this place works! We just can't look at it! It doesn't affect us if we don't look!" But even as he said this, he found himself inexplicably looking back over his shoulder at it all.

She nodded, her face grinding against his chest as if she meant to burrow into him. Yes. Don't look. That was how it worked. They could cross the freaky emotion rooms inside the temple if they just kept their eyes closed. She was even able to cross the hate room just by taking off her glasses and navigating with her poor eyesight. The mysterious power of the statues seemed to be tied in some way to their lifelike detail, at least in part. Blurring all that detail was enough to keep the emotions they depicted from overtaking her. Keeping her eyes closed protected her from the effects entirely.

But she couldn't help herself. Some part of her brain convinced her that they weren't alone here, that there was something behind them, something hidden among the vulgar statues, something *dangerous*. She looked. It was only a for a second, but she looked. And she could feel the room's strange power. It was like a sudden breathless sensation deep in her chest. A warmth that spread through her belly and down between her legs. A strangely *desperate* longing deep inside her.

Her glasses were off. She was clutching them in her hand. But that wasn't going to be enough. Simply blurring those statues was enough for the hate and fear rooms, but it wouldn't defend against *this* emotion. She was inside this room twice that first night. Once on the way in and once on the way out. The first time she didn't know. She looked at everything, took in every detail with wide-eyed ignorance, soaking in the strange power even as it took her over. The second time they passed through it, she found that she remembered all the details from the first time. It affected her just the same. They ended up succumbing to its bizarre power again.

It was only the following year, when she gave her glasses to Nicole, who'd never seen the statues, that they finally managed to pass through the sex room without indecent incident. Nicole had no memories of this place, so hindering her eyesight with Brandy's glasses was enough. But Nicole wasn't here now.

Albert squeezed his eyes closed and pressed his fingers hard against his eyelids. What was wrong with him? Why would he look? He knew what would happen if he let these images in. Their only hope was to keep their eyes closed.

But if you close your eyes, you won't see what's coming for you.

Startled at the alien thought that forced its way uninvited into his mind, he looked again before he could stop himself, his gaze darting to a perfect likeness of a buxom woman in the throes of an intense orgasm. She was only half visible, the rest of her seemingly hidden behind the wall, as if she were in the process of clawing her way into the room. She was only stone, and yet her lustful expression was so *lifelike*. Her lips seemed so soft. Her eyes glistened. Her full breasts seemed to yield to the inevitable pull of gravity, curving downward, perfect and round, motionless, and yet seductively swaying, her plump nipples standing out.

He jabbed his fingertips against his eyelids again, harder this time, hard enough to see colors blossom from the black, and yet the image of those breasts remained burned onto his brain. His body felt hot. His stomach was twisted and burning. He already felt himself reacting to the unwanted emotions flooding his senses.

"*What do we do*?" squealed Brandy.

"There were *two* doors in the sex room," he recalled. He looked out across the chamber. He did it automatically, without thinking. He couldn't even remember taking his hand away from his eyes. Obscene details flooded in, each and every one like a punch in the gut. A great, aching longing exploded repeatedly inside his belly, like a series of bombs, and he forced his eyes closed again. "Maybe there's another way out of this one, too."

"If they locked this one, they would've locked the other one too!"

"Maybe…" he agreed. That was the likeliest outcome. If this way was blocked, why wouldn't the other way be as well? "There was always a way out in the temple, remember? Maybe we're just supposed to go out the other way."

"This isn't the temple!" she snapped. "There weren't any *doors* in the sex room! Just open door*ways*!"

She was right. This *wasn't* the Temple of the Blind. This was some stupid sex museum out in the Tennessee boonies. He couldn't wrap his head around how or why this could possibly be here, much less have any idea what the intentions were behind it.

Brandy thrust her shoulder against the door, frustrated. "That slutty little *skank*! *She* told us to come in here!"

Yes. The half-naked, leather-clad greeter. She called this room their "most exclusive gallery" and said that her "master" had "prepared a demonstration" of some kind. There were so many questions circling around in his mind. Who was she? Who was her mysterious "master"? What were their intentions? And of course there was the biggest question of all: how could the sex room be here? And for what purpose?

A thought crossed Brandy's mind, as vividly as if she were watching it play out before her eyes. One of those nasty hounds that lived deep in the depths of that temple, foul-mannered things covered in upright scales like razor blades, each one slashing back and forth like an oscillating saw, designed to slice anything it touched to pieces. If someone could bring back the sex room, perhaps they could bring back a hound. And now she imagined that one was creeping up behind them, its deadly scales stilled while it stalked its prey, almost ready to pounce!

She looked back again, convinced that it wasn't merely her wild imaginings, that the monster was really there, very nearly within striking distance. But there was no hound. There was nothing but cold stone. But the imagery within that stone was just as dangerous.

She was staring at a couple caught in the heat of passion, clawing at one another, their bodies so realistic that she thought she could see the sweat glistening upon their faces.

The man was rippling muscles and long, flowing hair. How did one even go about sculpting hair like that? She could see individual strands standing out from his head as it was tossed back and forth with the violence of his thrusting.

The woman's leg was lifted high in the air. She could see where their bodies met, the stubble of her pubic hair, the slit of her sex, the base of his manhood half submerged inside her...

She squeezed her eyes shut and let out a strangled whimper. "I can't!" she cried. "I can't go through there again!" Her body was burning up. Her heart was pounding. It was hard to catch her breath. "Don't make me do that again!"

Albert didn't know what to do. Of course he didn't want to make her go through that again. But what were they supposed to do? These doors were solid. They weren't getting out the way they came in. They should at least attempt to check the other door.

At the very thought, however, he peeked in that direction and met the stone gaze of a woman frozen in a scream of pleasure, her mouth open, her pert breasts thrust toward him.

Why did he keep doing that?

He pulled Brandy closer to him, willing himself to calm down. But he could feel his body reacting to the perversions of the room. He was breathing heavily. His heart was racing. His stomach was twisted into a burning knot. And he already had a throbbing erection.

"Keep your eyes closed," he told her. "We'll move in that direction. I remember the way." He could recall almost every detail of this room from their first visit. He dreamed about it sometimes. It was like a permanent tattoo etched into his brain. He couldn't unsee it if he wanted to.

"That's all it takes," she whimpered. "Just our memory of it… It'll get to us. Like that second time. When we thought we knew how to beat it…" She shook her head against his shoulder, her tears soaking into his shirt.

"That was when you walked through it *nearsighted*," he reminded her. "The third time, when Nicole had your glasses, we walked through it blind. We were fine. Just keep your eyes closed. I'll get us out of here."

They just had to go to the other side of the room. That was all. They'd check the other door. If it was open, they'd face whatever was waiting on the other side together. If it was locked… Well, he didn't really know *what* they could do if they were still locked in. But he knew that this room couldn't harm them as long as they kept their eyes closed.

They'd just make their way to the other side. To the far end of the room… Where the stone orgy culminated in a great pile of bare flesh…where men and women were clawing at each other as they struggled upward, trying to reach something unseen, something beyond the room's ceiling.

He didn't *need* to see any of it. He could remember it all with vivid clarity. Every detail came rushing back to him.

"Hang onto me," he told her. "Keep your eyes closed. I'm going to move toward that other door. Nothing here can hurt us if we don't let ourselves see it."

She nodded against his shoulder. He was right, after all. They couldn't just stay in one place. This wasn't just some random thing they happened upon. They were lured here somehow.

It couldn't be a coincidence that the sex room was here. They were literally the only two people alive who knew what it looked like.

Slowly he turned, eyes closed tight, and started forward, one arm stretched out before him, guarding against probing stone limbs that were more than happy to give him a hard jab if he dared get careless.

He focused his thoughts on a single point, just a single stone hand stretched toward him, and began walking. It should only be a few steps forward…about chest height…

Somewhere around here…

Open your eyes.

He couldn't seem to help it. His lids parted just enough to glimpse the stone hand he was reaching for, hovering just above his own searching fingers, allowing him to grasp it. But it also let in the rest of the statue…the lustful expression…the silent cry of ecstasy…the slight curves of her hips…

He squeezed his eyes shut again and stood there a moment, feeling a wave of vertigo pass over him.

"Albert…?" whispered Brandy, concerned.

"Just orienting myself," he assured her. "Keep your eyes closed."

She nodded. Of course she'd keep her eyes closed. The last thing she wanted was to lose control again like that first night.

But another odd sensation of panic swept through her, convincing her that there was something there, something that needed to be seen, something *dangerous*. Her eyes seemed to open on their own. Fortunately, her face was still pressed against Albert's shoulder, blocking her view of most of the room. But there was a space between the right side of her face and his shirt. Through that crack, in her peripheral vision, she could see things. Vulgar things… Strangely *intriguing* things… Things that sent urges racing through her mind and tingling sensations deep inside her…

No! She closed her eyes again and pressed herself even closer against him. Her heart was racing so fast now…and so was *his*…she could feel it as she embraced him…deep inside his chest...as his strong arms held her...as his heavy breath blew through her bangs...

This time yesterday, they were making love in their hotel room... She felt his heart racing then, too... It was racing for *her*...

She wanted that again. Right now. She wanted it so badly...

She squeezed her eyes closed and let out another whimper. Why was this happening again?

Albert was moving. He held onto the stone hand, using it like a compass, calculating the path forward. There was a man stooped over in front of him, his back turned, his muscular legs bent. Once he let go of the woman's hand it should only be about five steps and he should lay his hand right on the man's bare butt...

(The guy probably wouldn't mind. He didn't seem terribly picky about the other three people groping at him.)

Open your eyes.

Again, his eyes fluttered open. Again, the filthy scene flooded his senses. Again, he felt his body react. His heart skipped a beat. A great heat spread through his lower body. And his underwear seemed to become another size smaller.

Was that a voice he was hearing inside his head? Or was it only his own frantic mind playing tricks on him?

He didn't understand how this room worked, how mere statues, no matter how incredibly detailed and lifelike they were, could force them to do those things. He didn't even understand how such a place could be built. How it could be *designed*. What he *did* understand was logic. He loved puzzles. He loved solving mysteries. He studied computers and coding in college and became a web designer. He knew how to break down complex problems into simple steps. It was how he was able to find the map six years ago. It was how the Sentinel Queen lured him there.

But the Sentinel Queen was dead. The Temple of the Blind was gone.

Yet *someone* arranged this. He didn't think for a second that this was a coincidence. Like Brandy, he'd realized that there was simply no way that the two of them, the only people alive, so far as he knew, who'd actually seen this entire room, should stumble back into it in a place like this.

Logic told him that this whole thing was set up somehow. Someone *meant* for them to be here today. But *who*? And why *now*? Why *here*? On their honeymoon, no less?

His hand brushed against a smooth, stone surface.

Target acquired, he thought. *We've found the butt.*

From here, he thought he should be able to see the door. It was just past the final statue. That great mass of clawing, struggling bodies clambering all over each other, trying to reach some just-out-of-sight thing. But of course he had no intention of actually looking. That would be stupid.

Open your eyes.

He opened his eyes and found himself gazing at the mountain of stone flesh before them.

What the hell was wrong with him?

He squeezed his eyes shut, but not before registering the fact that the other doorway was just like the first. The doors were heavy and solid and firmly shut, without handles, with no means of opening them.

They were trapped down here.

"*Albert...*" Brandy was practically panting now. She was pressing her body against him, *grinding* against his thigh, her hands closed into tight fists around the fabric of his shirt. He could feel her glasses digging into his ribs as she clung to them.

"Just breathe," he told her, unsure what else to say. "Focus only on your breathing." But he was one to talk. He was pulling her against him, his hand buried in her hair, clutching at her.

He *wanted* her.

There was a pain blossoming in his head, the beginnings of a throbbing headache, but its intensity didn't match the aching in his loins.

This was their honeymoon. They'd spent the past four days immersing themselves in romance. And every intimate moment they'd spent together was rushing back to him now, in perfect, vivid detail, the entire trip condensed down into a single moment of pure *passion.*

He couldn't control himself…

Open your eyes.

Brandy turned her head and looked out at the orgy at the end of the room, at the bodies groping at each other. So much overlapping pain and desperation and desire!

Open your eyes.

Albert looked at it, at all the men and women struggling to reach whatever was up there. They were clawing at each other. They were *trampling* each other. In their desperation for whatever they wanted, they were literally *killing* each other…

And he could feel himself filling up with that same mad desire.

Look at her.

Both of them lifted their gazes upward, to the woman at the top of the pile, her face a mask of crazed yearning in spite of the pain she must have been in, in spite of the scratches and bruises and the fact that one of her fingers was bent at a painful angle, her eyes bulging with desperate wanting.

What was it she was reaching for? What was up there, hidden by the limitations of the chamber's ceiling? What weren't they seeing?

Brandy pushed him against the statue and kissed him hard. She yanked at his shirt, impatient, then clawed at the fly of his shorts.

He wanted to tell her to calm down. He wanted to tell her to close her eyes and take a breath. But he couldn't help himself. He was already yanking at her blouse buttons.

This wasn't right. It wasn't safe. Someone was probably watching.

But none of that seemed to matter. His shorts flew off into the statues. Her skirt followed. Then his shirt. His underwear.

Somewhere inside, they were screaming. This wasn't right. This was madness. But they couldn't help themselves.

He pushed her up against one of the statues and she let out a sound that was something between a terrified whimper and a breathy moan. The sound of it simultaneously startled him and aroused him. He wanted to ask her if she was okay, if he'd hurt her, but he also wanted to make her make that sound again.

She reached up and grasped two fistfuls of his hair and pulled him against her, kissing him hard, shoving her tongue into his mouth.

Somewhere deep down inside, she wondered where her glasses had gone, but it felt so unimportant right now.

He squeezed her naked breasts.

She thrust her hips against his thigh, grinding that part of her against him.

The gray world around them blurred as they met each other's aggression.

It was different this time. They could both feel it. It was more intense. It was *hotter*. It was more *visceral*.

They clawed at each other. They pushed and shoved. Albert seized her wrists and tried to pin her against the statue, but she wrenched one hand free and snatched at his manhood, pulling on him even as she thrust her face into his, forcing her tongue into his mouth again.

They didn't even *sound* human. Somewhere inside, Brandy could hear the noises they were making. Grunting and moaning and *growling*, as if they really had been reduced to wild animals.

It was mortifying! And yet, it was also *exquisite*!

They fell onto the floor, their bodies entwined, their flesh slick with sweat, their hearts hammering together like pounding machines working at their very limits, threatening to melt down.

Like the first time they were here, it didn't end when one of them reached orgasm. Those didn't matter. Their bodies kept going, thrusting and grinding and pumping, forcing themselves desperately onward, even after thunderbolts of pain began shooting through their bodies from the exertion. Pain didn't matter. This room…why it was here…who brought them here…*why*… None of that mattered. All that mattered was the raw, fiery desire that filled their bodies.

They didn't notice the lights fading around them.

They didn't see the figure standing in the shadows, watching them with keen interest.

All that existed was desire…until darkness swallowed them whole into its empty, black belly and exhaustion finally overcame them.

Chapter 5

Albert groaned and opened his eyes. The world around him was blurry. He felt sweaty. His muscles ached. His knees and elbows felt bruised. His head was positively pounding. And everything was red.

Why was everything red?

He blinked, confused, and forced himself to focus. The *room* was red. He was lying on a large, four-poster bed in a spacious, but dimly lit bedroom, wrapped in a tangle of silky scarlet sheets. Curtains of matching red tulle were strung between the tall bedposts in a curious sort of canopy while much heavier and darker crimson curtains blocked out the windows. The walls were painted a deep wine red with garish gold trim. Even the shades on the wall sconces were red stained glass.

He stared up at the ceiling, where a strange, classically styled mural depicted a sprawling garden filled with naked people engaging in all manner of sexual activity.

Right... It was coming back to him. The kinky sex stuff... The museum... And then the sex room that was supposed to be gone forever with the rest of the temple...

Brandy was safe. That was the most important thing. She was right there, asleep in his arms, naked but unharmed.

They were *both* naked. Where were their clothes? At some point she'd found her glasses, he realized. They were back on her face and seemingly undamaged. And she was still wearing all her jewelry. But just like the first time, everything else was gone.

Unlike the first time, however, they hadn't awakened in the sex room. They'd moved. The question now was where were they? What was this place? And how did they get here? Had someone brought them here while they were unconscious, or had he lost the memories of whatever happened following the unexpected return of the temple's sex room?

He looked around, wincing again at the aching in his skull.

The bed's headboard was mirrored. And there were more mirrors mounted on the walls on either side of them. There were leather restraints with feathered shackles hanging from all four of the curtained bedposts, which was more than a little disconcerting. And there were framed pictures of people lounging naked on every wall. There was an antique wardrobe on one side of the bed and on the other side were shelves stocked with bottles of massage lotions, lubricants and brand-new sex toys still in their packaging. There was a faux bearskin rug on the floor and a jacuzzi tub big enough for at least four set into one corner of the room, surrounded by more mirrors. A red and gold sofa and armchair, perfectly matched to the curtains and the trim, sat against the walls in the other corner. On a little table between these seats stood an ice bucket with an unopened bottle of champagne and two glasses.

It looked like some sort of sketchy roadside adult motel. The sort of place where you paid by the hour and probably brought home STDs as souvenirs.

He pulled Brandy tight against him and kissed her. "Wake up," he whispered.

Her eyes fluttered open. For a moment she looked so peaceful there, her lips spread into a happy little smile, just like when they woke up together at home. But then the memories of the newly revived sex room came rushing back to her and her eyes flashed open, terrified.

She pushed herself up onto her hands to look around, but winced at the pain the motion sent through her head. "Ow! What the *fuck*? Where are we?"

But he didn't have an answer for her. He'd never seen this place before. There were three doors, each set in a different wall. The one on the right was open, revealing only a bathroom. Did one of the others lead back to the sex room? He hoped one of them was an exit.

"You're in Master's VIP guest suite," replied a familiar

voice.

Brandy's face twisted into a baffled expression as she looked down at the messy sheets.

Albert lifted them and peered under to find the museum's leather-clad greeter there, no longer clad in *anything*, seemingly dozing, apparently using his lower belly as a pillow, her pert breasts mashed against his naked thighs.

Brandy's jaw dropped open and she immediately turned her accusing gaze on him.

"This is the first *I'm* seeing of this too!" He wasn't sure how he didn't notice her there right away. She was literally weighing him down. But he supposed waking up in a strange and somewhat *icky* looking room after being tricked into entering an impossible sex room would throw off anyone's skills of observation. He hadn't noticed where Brandy's body ended and the greeter's body started.

The naked greeter opened those remarkable blue eyes and looked up at them, first at him, then at her. She didn't look ashamed in the least to be found naked and snuggling with a stranger in front of his wife. "Are you still enjoying Master's gallery?"

"No!" snapped Brandy. "I'm not! And you are *way* too close to my husband's dick!"

The woman didn't seem the least bit intimidated by her. She didn't cringe. She didn't flinch. She didn't flee the bed. In fact, she blatantly looked down at that part of him, as if she hadn't been aware of it until Brandy brought attention to it.

He felt a flash of embarrassment at the unexpected attention, but he wasn't sure what to do about it. He couldn't jump out of bed because she was lying on his legs. And he couldn't cover up because she was under the covers with him. But he couldn't remember ever feeling so uncomfortable in his entire life.

Then, ludicrously enough, she reached out and *touched it*. She lifted it with her dainty forefinger and thumb as if it were a curious toy she'd found lying around, surprising him and making him jump.

"Whoa!" he yelped.

"*Hey!*" shouted Brandy.

He shoved her hand away and covered himself as best he could with a fold of the blanket.

The woman still showed no reaction. She looked up and met her gaze. "You didn't mind sharing him with me last night."

"*What?*" She turned her wide eyes on him again.

He stared back at her, just as shocked. They did *what?*

"She's joking," said a man's voice from the left doorway.

Brandy let out a startled, "Eek!" and yanked up the sheets, covering herself.

Albert tried to pull a stray corner of a sheet over himself, but it was tangled up between him and the naked greeter and wouldn't quite reach.

The man in the doorway was short, pudgy and very old, with pasty skin covered in ugly moles and blotches. He had a scruffy start of a gray beard and what little remained of his hair was long and greasy and unkempt. He was wearing a silky robe that appeared to be several sizes too small for him. It barely covered his great, saggy ass and didn't quite close all the way in the front, so that his doughy belly and hairy chest were mostly visible. He was staring at them through a pair of very thick, oversized glasses that made his bloodshot eyes look huge.

"Dolly's not allowed to do harm to my guests, per the express details of our agreed contract," explained the creepy looking old man. "And that goes for anything that might cause irreparable damage to an otherwise happy marriage."

The greeter—whose name, it seemed, was Dolly— rolled her eyes like a spoiled child and stretched. "So *boring,*" she complained. "You never let me *play…*"

Albert couldn't seem to find a free corner of the sheet to hide himself, so he grabbed a pillow and shoved it into his lap instead. "So we didn't…?"

"You've both been asleep since you passed out in my special exhibit. She moved you to this room. That was all."

"Then why is she *naked?*"

"Master likes me naked," said Dolly. Then, in a whisper:

"He makes me."

He stared down at her, surprised. What kind of twisted relationship did these two have?

Brandy was staring at the ugly little man, distracted. "I've seen you before..." she recalled. She pointed at him. "At our reception. You were in the crowd!"

"And what a lovely affair it was," he replied. "You looked stunning."

"Fucking...?" She felt a shudder pass through her as the reality of the fact sank in. Why was he at their wedding? Was he stalking them?

"Who are you?" demanded Albert, trying not to sound intimidated just because he was butt naked under his pillow.

"Right. We haven't had our proper introduction yet, have we?" He cleared his throat and said "Dolly, dear? Do your job, please."

The woman uttered a deep, long-suffering sort of sigh, then slid off the bed and walked to the middle of the room in front of them. Still naked and unashamed, she lifted one arm toward the old man and said in a tired tone, "Presenting the Foremost Expert of the Erotic Arts, the Undisputed Master of Emotional Magic, Calligrapher of the Human Heart..." She sighed a disgusted sort of sigh before adding, "The Sexiest Man Alive..." She shuddered a bit at having to say that part and made a gagging face. "Lyle Shanzer, the Shaman of Wevenwert."

"Seriously?" said Brandy.

"He is, unfortunately..." groaned Dolly.

"Where are our clothes?" She pulled the sheets tighter around herself and scooted backward on the mattress. She didn't know what this guy's deal was, but he sounded like a first-class pervert and she intended to keep her guard up.

"Master had me put all your belongings in your car," replied Dolly as she plopped her naked butt down in the armchair.

Their car? What good were they going to do them there? "Well go get them, you stupid skank!"

"Can't," she replied, clearly unfazed by either her tone or the insult. "It's not there anymore."

"What do you mean not there?"

"Please," said Shanzer. "Indulge me just a moment of your time and patience. I'll explain everything. I promise you're in no danger here."

"Then why'd you steal our clothes?" countered Brandy.

"I didn't steal them," he informed her. "You threw them away yourselves. And my little Dolly was kind enough to put them in your vehicle so you wouldn't lose them."

"You know what I meant, you freak!"

"Besides," he went on as if she hadn't shouted at him, "being naked was useful to help ensure you didn't storm out of the room before I've had my say."

She glared down at the sheets she was covering herself with. There wasn't really anything stopping her from just taking it with her. But she'd definitely rather not have to flee the building in only a bedsheet. And then there was Albert, who was wearing only a pillow... (Although it'd serve him right, cuddling with that little goth slut in his sleep... They hadn't even been married a week yet!)

"What was up with that room back there?" asked Albert.

Lyle Shanzer, Shaman of Wevenwert, Boaster of Stupid and Almost-Certainly-Self-Appointed Titles, gave him a sleazy sort of grin, revealing a mouthful of crooked and discolored teeth in the process. "It wasn't the first time you've seen that room." It wasn't a question. This man clearly knew things about them. "You've experienced its power before."

"How do you know that?" snapped Brandy.

"I saw it," he replied, as blunt as he was ugly.

"*What?*"

"It was almost six years ago now, wasn't it?" He lifted his hands with a pompous sort of flourish and clapped them together three times. "An absolutely *outstanding* performance. Such raw emotion! Such youthful energy! Such free, uninhibited, *carnal lust!*"

She stared at him, horrified, her entire face flushing red. He was really *watching* them that night?

"I'm a huge fan," the old creep went on. "I've replayed it

hundreds of times."

"Ew! You make it sound like you have it on hidden camera!"

He pushed his mouth upward into a sort of thoughtful frown and gave his head a little wobble. "Not a camera, precisely, but very much the same principle, I suppose."

Her mouth fell open in a shocked expression of horror and disgust. He couldn't be serious…

"He *does* like to watch," groaned Dolly.

"*Oh my god!*"

"But how is it *here*?" pushed Albert. It was disturbing to imagine the gross old troll watching what they did in that room six years ago, but there was nothing they could do about it. He wasn't even the first person who told them they saw it. Beverly Bridger claimed to have seen them in her dreams the night it happened. He'd always known it was possible that others had been looking in, too. He probably shouldn't think too much about it. Instead, he was much more concerned about the fact that someone had apparently *resurrected* the sex room in the back of a sex museum in Tennessee. "That room doesn't exist anymore. It was buried forever."

Again, Shanzer flashed that slimy grin. "Do you really think so?"

"I watched that whole place fall apart. I was damn near buried *with* it. Even if it *is* still in one piece, it's under a mountain of rubble in another universe somewhere."

"And you're quite sure that was the only one of its kind?"

Albert stared at him, lost for words. More than one sex room? The idea was horrifying.

The sleazy shaman turned and gestured at the bottle on the table. "Champagne?"

"What do you want with us?" demanded Brandy.

"No champagne? You sure? It's the good stuff, I assure you."

"*Why are we here?*"

He sighed and turned to face them. As he did, his ridiculous robe shifted. The view was anything but inspiring. Both of them grimaced and looked away. "You're here as my esteemed guests, of course."

"We didn't agree to be your guests!" Brandy snapped. "You kidnapped us! You and your slutty little...*whatever* she is!"

"Basically his slave," replied Dolly. "He does terrible things to me. All the time. It's a living hell."

Brandy stared at her. She couldn't tell if she was being sarcastic or serious. Her expression never changed.

"There are two answers to your question," relented Shanzer, completely ignoring Dolly's worrisome accusation. "Depending on which version of your question you're asking."

She scrunched her pretty face up, confused. "What?"

"First, the reason why you're here, at this precise point in time in your lives, in the greater scheme of all the things going on in the universe *right now*. Why *any of us* are here. Why *all of us* are here. *What you're meant to do.* The answer to *that* question is very simple. You're here because it's *time for you to be here.* It's time to finish what you started six years ago."

Albert and Brandy exchanged a fearful look.

"Finish it...?" said Albert.

"We *did* finish it!" shouted Brandy. "We opened the stupid door!" She did it herself, in fact, with her own hand. And nearly lost everything in the process!

"You opened *a* door," Shanzer corrected her.

She stared at him, horrified. "No..."

Somehow, the pervy creep managed to look sympathetic as he said, "I'm afraid so. That was only the beginning. And now the next stage in the cycle is underway."

Brandy was shaking her head. "No... We refuse! We're not going through that again!"

"You won't have a choice. Believe me, trying to avoid it will only make it worse. It's already started. Events are already in motion. There's no stopping it. That means things will be turning their eyes on you, some of them *terrible* things. They'll be looking for you."

"No..." She turned and looked at Albert, pleading with him.

He could see tears shimmering in those beautiful eyes and the sight of them broke his heart, but he didn't know what to say. This guy was a creep, but if he was telling the truth about another door, then he probably wasn't lying about them not having a choice in the matter. "Like those phone calls," he said at last. "The ones that just kept coming. No one on the line, but those intense memories of the temple filled our heads."

She made a pitiful face and then lifted the sheet and hid behind it. "This *sucks!*" she cried into the fabric. "I *just* got married! Why does it have to happen now?"

"I'm sorry," said Shanzer. And he *did* sound sorry. He almost sounded human, even. "But the next gear in the Keeper's machine is turning. These are *his* rules. And *everyone* is subject to his rules."

"The Keeper?" said Albert, surprised.

"You know him?" asked Brandy as she emerged from behind her sheet again.

"Oh yes. I know about him. I've glimpsed him in my visions a few times. He's spoken to me. He's great and ancient and wise beyond imagining. He's in charge of the cycle that's kept our species alive for countless eons. Very impressive." Then his expression soured. "But he's an ugly little thing. Flabby. Wrinkled. Pale as a corpse. *Disgusting.* Not sexy in the least." As he said this, he propped his fists on his hips and shifted his weight. The motion spread the robe open again and made both of them look away in disgust. "He's positively *grotesque.*"

"You're one to talk!" shouted Brandy. "Put some pants on!"

Shanzer glanced down at himself, at the parted robe, but didn't make a motion to close it. He only returned his lecherous gaze to her and smirked.

"Master is a disgusting, shameless pig," sighed Dolly.

He didn't seem at all fazed by the insult. In fact, he gave an indifferent sort of shrug, as if to say, "I am what I am."

"So it's *his* fault we're here?" said Albert, as he studied the mural on the ceiling. "The Keeper?" The last time he saw the Keeper was after they'd opened the doorway, just before they were reunited with Wayne. (He was, indeed, an ugly little monster, but he wasn't sure that point was particularly relevant to this matter.)

"This is about *him*, yes," confirmed Shanzer. "He sent me a message recently. He tasked me with finding you."

"Why *you?*" asked Brandy.

"That's the second version of your question, isn't it?" He took a step forward, those great, magnified eyes sweeping back and forth between them. "The reason you're *physically* here…in this specific place…at this very moment…with *me*. And the second answer is just as simple as the first: I'm the only one who can prepare you for what lies ahead."

"By kidnapping us and stealing our clothes?" snapped Brandy.

"No. By showing you the truth about what *really* happened in that magnificent chamber that night."

They looked at each other, twin expressions of confusion reflected on their faces.

"What do you mean what *really* happened? What are you talking about?"

He grinned that nasty grin again. "I'm talking about *magic*."

Chapter 6

"Magic?" scoffed Albert.

"What, you mean like all that weird shit you had on display?" asked Brandy.

"*Precisely* that kind of magic," replied Shanzer.

"I don't believe in magic," Albert informed him.

The shaman laughed an ugly bark of a laugh. "But you'll believe in parallel worlds? Psychics? Telekinesis? Zombies? *The Keeper?*"

"Well…" Again, he glanced at Brandy. "I mean, not until I saw them with my own eyes, I guess."

"Fair enough," said Shanzer. He turned and strolled across the room and seated himself on the couch, his thighs spread casually apart, like some rude passenger taking up more than his fair share of space on the subway. "Manspreading" was the word for it, Albert recalled, and it wasn't remotely pretty.

Brandy groaned and looked away from the shriveled monstrosity dangling below the shaman's exposed belly fat.

Dolly rolled her eyes. "If only there were magic to make Master less repulsive."

"Tell me," said Shanzer, ignoring her again. Those great, magnified eyeballs remained fixed on Albert. "What do you *think* happened that night when the two of you entered that chamber for the first time? How do you explain the effect it had on both of you?"

Albert looked up at the muraled ceiling again, as if admiring the art, though all he cared about was looking at anything other than the repulsive display sitting in front of him. "I don't know what happened. I have no idea how that place works."

"Yes, but surely you have *ideas*. You have *theories*. I've studied you. I've seen how your brain operates in these kinds of situations. You like to rationalize all the strange things you saw down there. So humor me."

He frowned. He didn't like the idea of anyone claiming to know how his brain worked, much less *this* disgusting creep. It was almost as much of an invasion of privacy as being watched that night. Just how did this pervy shaman know so much about them? "I guess..." He shook his head and sighed. "I guess it almost has to be something subliminal. Something written into the likenesses of the statues, maybe. Because they only affected us when we could see them, which would rule out any kind of airborne pheromone, if there even is such a thing, or some kind of mind-altering audio tone or...anything else like that, I guess... Unless there were *multiple elements* working together to instill the desired behavior...elements that only worked when *all* the ingredients were combined..."

Shanzer nodded eagerly. "Very astute reasoning, yes. Go on."

"Okay... I guess...different parts of the brain are responsible for different aspects of our mind and body. It's all electrical impulses and chemicals. So it's reasonable to assume that something about those statues *targeted* the part of our brains responsible for our sexual desires."

"Sure."

Albert leaned forward a little. This subject had always interested him. He loved talking about the mysteries of the temple. But he didn't bring it up very often. He didn't want to upset Brandy or their friends by dredging up any of those old nightmares. But now that he was being asked, there was a subtle excitement rising inside him. "But science isn't even close to knowing everything about the human mind. There are so many things we don't understand yet, so many possibilities. I've thought before that it could even be something triggered deep in our memories, tapping into the most primal of our emotions. I don't know if there's any such thing as a kind of...*ancestral memory*...passed down in our DNA..."

Shanzer was nodding. "Very good." He leaned back on the

couch and propped his elbows up on the back of the sofa, revealing even more of his disgusting anatomy.

Albert remained careful not to look directly at the unattractive exhibitionist.

"You're not far off, actually. The statues in those chambers are like snapshots from the distant past. Those were real men and women, captured at the precise moment of absolute sexual peak. They aren't merely a visual representation. They actually *contain* the memory they're based on. And within that memory is that *sexual energy*. It saturates every atom of the stone they're crafted from. It *radiates* from it."

Albert nodded. His gaze had become distant. The shaman repulsed him, but this information he was sharing…it *intrigued* him. He could almost grasp the idea of it. Now that he was thinking about it that way, it almost explained the feelings those statues gave him. It wasn't just that he could see that couple engaged in that activity. It was as if he could feel *exactly* the physical and emotional pleasure they must have felt in that moment. He'd always thought it was the perfection in the statues' details that did it, like the way a really good artist could portray expressions and gestures that could make you relate so perfectly with the scene they were painting. But while a painting might be capable of instilling feelings of peacefulness or sadness or even eeriness, there'd never been such a thing as a painting that made two strangers so horny they'd lose all their inhibitions and tear each other's clothes off. Not as far as he knew, anyway. As much as he'd tried, he just couldn't wrap his head around how something like that might work. He'd even tried researching the subject, but wasn't able to find anything concrete. In fact, he couldn't even figure out how to put it into words to search for it.

"Human beings give off energy," explained Shanzer. He leaned forward, mercifully closing his legs in the process, and propped his wrists on his knees. "And human *emotions* determine the characteristics of that energy. And different kinds of human energy can be interacted with in different ways. In the case of *sexual* energy, it can be both expelled *and* imparted onto others. There are people out there who possess a natural affinity for sexual energy. You may think they're 'charismatic' or 'charming,' or even just 'hot,' but the truth is that they naturally produce more sexual energy, which other people can sense and react to, even if only on a subconscious level. All emotions work this way, defining the characteristics of the energy each human being produces, shaping the way they're perceived by those around them, effectively defining a person's personality and, in many ways, the reality in which they live."

Albert frowned as he processed this. "So...this is one of those 'the world is only what we perceive it to be' kind of things?"

"In many ways, yes." Shanzer scooted forward and sat on the edge of the seat. (Albert and Brandy both made a mental note to not touch those cushions. *Ever.*) "Now let's discuss the two of you."

"What *about* us?" asked Brandy, pulling her sheet a little tighter around her body. She still didn't understand what this creep wanted with them, much less why they needed to be naked. She certainly wasn't comfortable with this topic.

"Both of you are naturally *very* proficient with sexual energy. And you feed off each other in a very unique way. You practically *ooze* sexuality. It's the reason you've always had so much sex. Why you never seem to get tired of each other's bodies. Why you sometimes can't wait until you're alone and sneak off somewhere quiet to be together, even for just a moment."

Brandy blushed visibly at this. "Oh my god! How long have you been spying on us?"

"I told you he likes to watch," Dolly reminded her. Then she made a lazy "jerking off" gesture with her hand to illustrate.

Brandy grimaced and turned away. "Ewww..."

"It made it easy for that chamber to get into your heads," Shanzer went on as if he didn't hear them. "You were extra sensitive to that energy. And each and every one of those statues is imbued with a *tremendous* amount of it. It set those emotions into overdrive, so strong that they overrode all your inhibitions."

"So that's what happened...?" muttered Albert. He could pretty much follow along with that, but...sexual energy? Really?

It all sounded so hard to swallow. "Does that mean we were the only ones in danger of losing control in that room? The others would've been fine?" It was something he'd always wondered.

"Not at all. Any of your friends would have lost control walking into that room unprepared. The raw output of sexual energy would have been overwhelming to almost anyone's senses. There's no telling what those statues might have done to them. There's no telling what it might have done to the two of *you*. I'm sure you already know you're not the same people who went in there that night."

Albert and Brandy exchanged an uneasy glance. They'd wondered so many times since that night if their experience in that mysterious chamber had changed them.

"It definitely unlocked something inside both of you," Shanzer explained. "It's not a *bad* thing. Not in your case. You both are clearly very happy together. I'd wager that it even helped bond you together. Some people would have drifted apart if only because of the trauma brought on by frightful memories of that place. But like I said, you two already possessed a natural aptitude toward sexual energy, even if you weren't aware of it before that night."

Brandy wasn't sure what to say to that. On one hand, he'd just confirmed something both of them had theorized since that night six years ago. They *had* been changed by the sex room. They *were* different people than they were when they went in. But not in a frightful way. The idea that those statues had merely unlocked something that was already inside them…something that had brought them closer together…it was actually sort of reassuring.

Was that why she never felt this way about anyone *before* Albert? She'd had other lovers before him, but she never felt this way about *them*. In fact, sex had never satisfied her much at all before Albert.

"And being who you both are," Shanzer went on, "you fed as much of that energy back into that chamber as it fed into you. That's the only reason you were able to unlock the way through the labyrinth."

Albert shifted his weight. His legs were beginning to fall asleep under him. "Wait. What do you mean? Unlocked how?"

"I mean that if the two of you had never lost control in that chamber, the way forward simply wouldn't have existed. You'd have found nothing beyond that next doorway but a dead end."

He shook his head. "That makes no sense. How would us *screwing* in that room change the layout of the labyrinth?"

Again, the old shaman leaned forward on the couch and replied, "*Magic.*"

He reached up and rubbed at his eyes. Again, they'd circled back to this. Sex magic? He couldn't wrap his head around *regular* magic.

"Well," added Shanzer, "in all honesty, 'magic' is a bit of a broad term. It would be more accurate to keep calling it what it is: sexual *energy*. Energy comes in a great many forms, many of them still utterly unknown to modern science. In fact, the more *modern* science gets, the *farther* they get from the whole truth. Science is merely the natural side of things, after all. We human beings, all life as we know it, the natural world, the whole of the observable cosmos. That's *nature*. There's also the *supernatural*. Supernature is everything that exists *beyond* life. It's death. It's the great hereafter. Ghosts and spirit planes and everything that lies on the other side. And all the things out there that don't precisely fit into either of those two categories belongs to the realm of the *unnatural*. It's actually quite complicated."

"No shit," grumbled Brandy, confused.

"My point is, there are lots of different kinds of energies out there that *science* doesn't recognize but are perfectly real. Psychic energy. Spiritual energy. *Magical* energy. And of course emotional energy. Just to name a few." He turned those leering, magnified eyes on Brandy now. "You saw my exhibit about sexual magic. You browsed over the information boards on display. Magic is, at its core, a specific type of energy. But *using* magic is all about utilizing *other* forms of energy. Therefore, it varies wildly depending on what energy you're manipulating. Sexual magic is only *one* form it takes. And utilizing magic is entirely about transforming that energy into a visualized, manifested outcome. That means that real magic is often no different than stage magic. It only *looks* like magic because we *call* it that. That first night in those tunnels, when you let yourselves be overwhelmed by those emotions—"

"We didn't *let* anything happen!" snapped Brandy.

"—when you *acted* on those emotions," he went on as if she never interrupted him, "you fed your own energy back into that chamber, which activated its programming to unlock the way forward. In essence, you two were the first *key* on the path to the doorway."

"Well that's just *stupid*," she grumbled. "And what's the point in even telling us all this?"

"Because whether you want to or not, you're both headed back into that unspeakable darkness that's haunted your nightmares all these years. There's going to be more locked doors waiting for you along the way. And you won't be able to rely on the doorway's caretaker to hold your hand this time."

Albert stared at him. The doorway's caretaker... He was talking about the Sentinel Queen, who claimed to have guided their hands throughout much of their journey last time, first giving him the box and then offering subtle hints when he became stumped. But she was dead now. They wouldn't be receiving any of her help ever again.

"Whether you believe in it or not," Shanzer went on, "all these things exist. And it's the *only* thing that's going to open the way forward." He stood up and finally cinched his robe tight. "You two are about to learn how to utilize all that sexual energy. And I'm going to be your teacher."

Chapter 7

"You can't be serious," scoffed Brandy.

"I'm always serious about sex and magic," the pervy shaman informed her. "Now pay attention. The first thing you should know is simple, but absolutely *crucial*. Sex magic isn't what you think it is. You don't just get naked, hump and then shout some magic words. Most of the time, there's no actual sex involved at all. It's all about the *emotions* involved. It's about harnessing that unique *energy*. And *anyone* can do it. You don't even need a partner, although it's better with one, obviously. Lots more fun, believe me."

Brandy looked over at Albert, an uncomfortable expression on her face. Were they really going to have to sit here naked and listen to this creep lecture them about something as ridiculous as *sex magic*?

"What you need to remember," Shanzer went on, "is that magic is about *willing* your intentions into the world around you. And I'm not talking about making stacks of cash appear at your feet or causing someone you hate to drop dead. You can't make drastic changes to the world or the people in it. More often than not, that'll create a sort of butterfly effect. And when contradictions start adding up, the spell falls apart. So you have to start very small and very precise and work your way up. For example, you can change the *perception* of the world and the people in it. You can change your *own* perceptions. You can make yourself see what's been hidden. By starting small, you can do things you never imagined." He paused a moment and swept those great, bloodshot eyes back and forth between them. "One could even recreate a very specific location from a person's past, from nothing more than their own memories of that place."

"The sex room..." realized Albert. Was that how he did it? Was it not even real? Was it just some kind of magical manifestation? Or an incredibly realistic hallucination?

The old man grinned that slimy grin again. "It won't be easy, but you both have a natural talent for it. It's no coincidence that it was the two of you who ventured into that labyrinth first."

He looked over at Brandy. She still looked miserable. She didn't want this, and he didn't blame her. He didn't really want to go through any of that again, either. It took weeks for his arm to heal after that last adventure. What might he break this time? Or worse, what might he lose entirely?

But there was also something else, deep inside him, that he didn't quite dare to acknowledge. He had so many questions after he came back last time... Was this his chance to finally find those answers?

"I have some things for you," said the Shaman. "I'll be back in a moment." He turned and strolled to the door he entered through. "There are clothes for both of you in the wardrobe. Feel free to get dressed." Then he closed the door behind him and was gone.

"I really hate that man," sighed Dolly.

Brandy gathered the sheets around her, slid off the bed and hurried to the wardrobe. But she frowned when she opened it. "He wants me to wear *this*?" Hanging there was a skimpy red party dress.

One pillow covering his front and another covering his naked butt, Albert stepped up beside her and peered in. There was a tuxedo hanging there for him. It didn't look remotely practical, but there was nothing else in there.

"There's no underwear," observed Brandy.

"You weren't wearing underwear when you arrived," Dolly reminded her.

"Shut up, you."

Albert had been wearing underwear but he didn't see any for him, either. It looked like they were *both* going commando now.

She pulled the dress out of the wardrobe and looked at it in the light. "Seriously?"

"It's appropriate attire for the evening," Dolly assured her.

"How is this appropriate?" asked Albert. He looked back at her and was startled to see that she'd hiked one slender leg up over the arm of the chair she was sitting in. In that position, from this angle, there was nothing at all left to the imagination. He quickly turned away, but not before Brandy saw what he saw.

"I swear to God, if you get a boner with her in the room, I'll break it in half!"

"I'm minding my own business!"

"Whatever!" growled Brandy. She dropped the sheets around her feet and lifted the dress over her head.

For a moment, he caught himself staring at her, her slender body exposed to him as she stood there in nothing but her glasses, the curves of her familiar breasts, the glint of her bellybutton ring, the perfect V-shape where her torso met her lean thighs, so perfectly fair and smooth where she'd kept herself cleanly shaved throughout their honeymoon…

It wasn't fair. That was *far* more arousing than the weird stranger flashing her goods across the room, but getting turned on now would land him in the doghouse for sure! He was starting to have flashbacks to walking around naked in those dark tunnels with Nicole…

Unable to dress while holding the pillows, he tossed them aside and quickly grabbed the pants off the hanger before his betraying body could commit a damnable offense.

Brandy tugged the dress down into place, then turned and looked herself over in the mirror. "This dress is stupid! You can see my butt crack!"

"Just barely," said Albert as he *quickly* fastened his pants and reached for the shirt. He stared at her as she examined herself. She looked good in it. *Really* good. It hugged her beautiful body perfectly. It had a plunging neckline that revealed the inner curves of her gorgeous, pert breasts. And it was *very* short, revealing all of her lovely legs. She looked like she'd just stepped off the red carpet. Or right out of his greatest dreams. "It looks…sort of familiar…" he added, his gaze washing over her sexy bottom. "I think I saw one like it somewhere not too long ago…"

"That creep did this on purpose," she growled. "He's playing dress-up with me. *Pervert*."

"Probably," agreed Dolly. "He makes me wear *all sorts* of humiliating things."

"*You* put some clothes on, too!" she snapped.

But Dolly ignored her.

Albert buttoned up his shirt and then examined what was left. Socks, dress shoes, tie and a jacket. He grabbed the socks and shoes, but he wasn't bothering with the tie or jacket. It was late July in Tennessee out there. And he wasn't trying to impress anyone.

There was a pair of matching red high heels. Brandy snatched them off the shelf with another groan. "Oh sure. This is *exactly* what I was thinking I'd wear the next time I had to crawl around in sewers and run away from man-eating hounds. This guy's an idiot."

She slipped her feet into the shoes and then turned and looked at herself in the mirror again. The rest of her didn't match the dress at all. Her hair was a mess. Her makeup had all worn off. And was it any wonder? She did, technically, just roll out of bed.

While she took down her disheveled ponytail and ran her fingers through her hair, trying to look a little more presentable, Albert finished tying his shoes and stood up straight. Immediately, he was surprised by a pair of slender arms wrapping around him from behind.

"I like you," decided Dolly.

"Hey!" shouted Brandy. "Bad skank! Down!"

But Dolly ignored her again. She pressed her naked body against his back, laid her chin on his shoulder and gazed at him. "Can I give you a little advice?"

"*I've* got some advice for *both* of you!" warned Brandy.

Albert felt her lips brush his earlobe and her breath danced across his cheek as she whispered, "Don't trust that man."

He pulled away from her. "What?"

She stood there, still naked, still unashamed, facing them both. "He's a monster. He makes me do awful things. Disgusting, humiliating things." She set those blue eyes on Brandy. "He'll do the same to *you* if you let your guard down. You'll see. He's *evil*."

"I didn't realize you were so unhappy," said Shanzer as he entered the room again.

Dolly clasped her hands together in front of her again and stood up straight, like she did when she was working in the museum. "I was only joking with them, Master." It was difficult to see through that expressionless doll face if he'd even surprised her.

"By all means," pushed the pervy shaman, "if you're not satisfied, we can cancel our contract. Go our separate ways."

"That's not at all necessary, sir. I was only playing with our guests."

"No, no. I couldn't bear the thought of you feeling as if you're being treated unfairly."

"No, Master."

"Perhaps these two would like to take you in."

"Please, Master." Her emotionless façade had begun to break. There was true fear welling up inside her.

"They'd probably feel much better taking you away from here now that you've told them—"

"*Please no!*" she shrieked. Her eyes had grown huge with fright. A tear slid down one cheek.

Albert and Brandy stood staring at her, shocked. What did they just witness?

"Very well," relented Shanzer, turning away from her.

Dolly sank to her knees, her face twisted with a strange fear. She was visibly trembling.

The shaman turned his attention to his guests without acknowledging the poor girl's obvious distress. "Sorry for making you wait. You should take this with you." He held out a pocket-sized, leatherbound book with yellowed pages for Albert to take. "Some basic guidelines for what sexual magic is, how it works and how to utilize it, along with some beginner spells you can practice when you have time. *If* you have any time," he added.

Albert flipped through the book, curious. "So...*Sex Magic for Dummies?*"

The old man chuckled at this. "Sure. Call it what you like. It's yours now. Consider it a gift from teacher to student."

He frowned at one of the pages. "I can't read most of this..."

"It'll reveal more when you're ready for it."

"Weird..." said Brandy as she looked over his shoulder at the alien-looking scribbles scrawled on the page. Neither of them had ever seen anything like it before. It wasn't any language either of them recognized. It was difficult to even discern whether it was meant to be read horizontally or vertically. There didn't even appear to be spaces to indicate words.

"And you'll be needing *this*, of course." He held out a familiar chain with an odd-shaped golden medallion hanging from it.

"That's..." Brandy stared at it, surprised. "Wasn't that in your box?"

Albert nodded. "At home, yeah. In the back of the closet." It was the mysterious artifact they found on their way up the burning mountain. It was hanging around the neck of a one-armed skeleton hidden in a little recess near the original temple entrance.

"I took the liberty of returning your vehicle to your home. You won't be needing it."

"My car...?" said Albert. All the way back in Briar Hills?

"And while I was there, I collected this for you."

Brandy wrinkled her nose. "Ew! You were in our *bedroom?* Gross!"

"You're welcome," said Shanzer, ignoring her.

If he'd really taken his Mustang to their apartment, retrieved this from their bedroom closet and returned...just how long were they asleep? What time was it?

"Take it. It's no coincidence you ended up with it after you opened the first doorway. It was left on that mountain specifically for you to find. You're going to need it."

Albert took it from his hand and looked at it. It wasn't really a medallion, he didn't think, but that's what he kept calling it, because he wasn't sure what it was. It wasn't ornate at all. It looked like something a child might have made. It was a mostly flat, oblong piece of what he was fairly sure was gold, with a hole on one end for the chain to pass through. One side was blank. The other side had an unusual symbol etched into it. He suspected it was significant from the moment he first glimpsed it. Later, when they finally reached the top of the blazing mountain and the final chamber where the door was hidden, the meaning of the symbol came to him, as if forced into his conscious thoughts. Probably by the Keeper, himself. It meant "devil." And it revealed to him the identity of his enemy, the old man who gave Wayne the means of escaping the Wood, the old man who schemed to keep them from opening the door, the old man the Sentinel Queen claimed was the devil, himself.

He wasn't the devil, though. Not really. Those were only lies he used to scare people. But he wasn't quite human. Humans might sometimes possess incredible powers, they might even be able, he supposed, to eventually possess the kind of telekinetic powers he used to construct that monstrosity of corpses. But humans didn't live the kind of long life he'd lived. And humans certainly didn't survive being *burned alive*.

"What do we do with it?" he asked.

"That's for you to figure out on your own," Shanzer informed him. "Consider it your final exam. I'm confident you'll pass."

Albert wasn't so sure. He looked down at it. It was just a hunk of gold with that weird symbol carved on it. It probably wasn't even real gold. He couldn't fathom what he could possibly use it for.

He stared at it, his brain slowly ticking away at the fact he'd been presented.

The pervy shaman stood there a moment, looking Brandy up and down. "You look positively ravishing, my dear."

She looked him right in the eye and said, "You think I give a shit how you think I look?"

This made him chuckle. "Yes, you'll do quite well, I think."

Then he turned and looked Albert up and down. "You'll do," he decided.

"Thanks," he grumbled. He stuffed the book and the medallion into his pants pockets. "So what now? You going to teach us *magic*?" He couldn't help sounding sarcastic when he used the word. He just couldn't quite wrap his head around it. Magic? The Temple of the Blind used *magic*? That sounded like such a lame copout. He'd spent years pondering how the things in that place worked, and this fat toad was just going to appear one day and tell him it was all just *magic*? That was like watching an entire television series, following along with every detail, expecting some grand, brilliant revelation, only to discover that it was all just a dream.

It sort of pissed him off, if he were being honest.

"*Now*," said the shaman, "you're free to go."

"What?" said Brandy, confused.

He gestured at the second of the three doors, the one that had remained closed the whole time. "That way, please." Then he gave her that lecherous grin again and motioned at the door he'd entered through, "unless you'd like to take a personal tour of my bedroom suite, of course."

"In your dreams."

"Perhaps," he agreed, and something about the look on his face made her shudder with revulsion.

Albert took her by the hand and started across the room, but he paused before opening the door. "But where are we supposed to go if you took away our car?"

"You'll figure it out," promised Shanzer. "It's all part of your training. Your first lesson begins immediately."

"Ugh…" groaned Brandy.

"Oh," said Shanzer, "and I meant what I said. If you'd like to take my mouthy little assistant off my hands, feel free to keep her."

Dolly was still sitting slumped on the floor, her head hanging. Now she sat up straight, her eyes wide with fresh fear. "No! Master please—" But her words cut off as soon as he lifted his hand.

"It's up to *them*, now," he told her, "not me."

Brandy stared at the young woman, confused. She looked so young. And what kind of awful life must it be to have to call a slimy creep like this "Master" all the time? There was something dreadfully wrong about the relationship these two had. And yet there was genuine terror in her eyes at the prospect of being taken away from the shaman. She was staring back at her now, shaking her head, begging her not to do it.

"Is this some kind of test?" asked Albert. He, too, wasn't sure what they were supposed to do. On one hand, Dolly had said awful things about this man. But on the other, he hadn't seen any actual proof that any of it was true. And then there was that undeniable fear in her otherwise emotionless face at the mere suggestion that he break their contract.

Shanzer considered the question for a moment. "Is it?" he wondered. "I suppose it could be… But it doesn't really matter one way or the other to me. Do you want her? No paperwork. No ritual. All you have to say is 'yes' or 'no' and it'll seal the deal. Choose 'yes' and she'll belong to you. Mind, body and soul. Her contract with me will be permanently severed. She'll never have to see me again."

"Just a contract…?" considered Brandy. If it was only a contract they were talking about, wouldn't it be better if she said yes? Couldn't she just immediately *cancel* the new contract and set her free?

But Dolly's expression suddenly turned sinister. She glared at her, blue eyes blazing, and growled, *"Don't you dare, bitch!"*

Brandy actually took a step backward. "No!" she spat back at her, almost without thinking. It was something about that look in the girl's eyes. There was actual *hatred* there.

"Very well, then," decided Shanzer, sounding completely indifferent. "I suppose I'll keep her a while longer."

Dolly slumped back onto the floor, a relieved sob escaping her.

"Go on now," he urged. "Be on your way. Good luck. And remember, magic can open doors that can't be unlocked."

"Sure," said Albert. Still clinging to Brandy's hand, he fled the room and closed the door behind them.

"That is a *seriously* toxic relationship!" whispered Brandy.

Chapter 8

Albert had half-expected to find himself back in the sex room after leaving the garish guest suite. It seemed like the sort of cruel trick the sleazy shaman would play on them. At the very least, he expected to find himself back in that perverted museum. Instead, they were standing in a carpeted hallway lined with more of those red, stained-glass sconces and decorated with more paintings of naked people.

"This guy is *way* too into bare tits," grumbled Brandy as she tugged at the ridiculously short dress.

"Is this his house?" wondered Albert. Where the hell was the museum? How long were they out after they passed out in that fake sex room? Was it even the same day? He scratched absently at his lower belly and shrugged off an unpleasant sort of shudder. "I feel gross just being under the same roof with those two."

"Serve you right if you caught something from that creepy whore," she grumbled.

He shot her a dirty look. "Nothing happened."

"*Better* not have."

"Let's just get out of here already."

The guest suite was located near the end of the hallway. It was one of eight identical doors, four on this side of the hall, two on the other side and one at each end, all of them closed, none of them marked. Judging by the shaman's creepy invitation, at least one of the other rooms on this side of the hall were part of his bedroom suite, which was somewhere he definitely didn't want to go exploring. The rest might be more guest rooms, which wouldn't get them any closer to leaving. The most likely way out was the adjacent hallway, located in the middle of the opposite wall, between the two doors. They walked in that direction, unwilling to linger for fear that the Pervert of Wevenwert might change his mind about letting them leave.

"Do you think we did the right thing back there?" asked Brandy, looking back over her shoulder as they rounded the corner. "Leaving that girl, I mean?"

This hallway was considerably longer than the first, with more closed, unmarked doors. But the far end appeared to be open, which was promising.

"You saw the look she gave you," he replied. "You ask me, she's as crazy as that bug-eyed boss of hers."

She supposed he was right. There was no telling what they might've gotten themselves into if she'd said yes. But she hated the idea of leaving *anyone* at the mercy of that disgusting creep.

Albert slowed down and cocked his head, listening. "Music."

"And voices," added Brandy. Wherever they were, there were people here. Were they somewhere public? There were no room numbers or nameplates on any of the doors. It looked like a private residence, though not anything they'd likely ever be able to afford…

The music and murmur of conversations grew louder as they approached the end of the hallway. A very large room loomed ahead of them. The music and voices seemed to be coming from there.

Albert felt a nervous knot tightening in his belly. He had no idea where he was, who those voices belonged to or what the pervert shaman expected them to do here. The only information he'd allowed them was that their first lesson had already begun. He hadn't been in control of anything since he stepped inside that ridiculous museum and he didn't care at all for how helpless that made him feel.

Was this really about the Temple of the Blind? Was there really another doorway? Were they really about to go hurdling headlong back into that five-year-old nightmare?

They stepped out onto an open balcony circling a room roughly the size of a high school gymnasium with several large and very expensive-looking chandeliers hanging from the high, domed ceiling. Directly in front of them was a grand staircase leading down to a large open space decorated with fifteen-foot-tall marble statues of naked men and women, huge, indoor flower beds overflowing with tropical flowers, trees and ferns, and a great, bubbling fountain spilling into a pool of bathing granite nymphs. There were several dozen people in formalwear mingling around the room or grazing between four long tables covered in an elegant display of fancy food and wine.

"What the fuck?" blurted Brandy.

Albert stood there a moment, looking down at the party. Dolly was right. The clothes in the wardrobe *were* appropriate attire. Every woman in sight was wearing a sleek, form-fitting evening dress and every man was wearing a fancy tuxedo, many of them having forgone their stuffy jackets and ties, just as he'd decided to do. They really did fit right in.

Except that nearly half of the people down there were wearing masquerade masks for some strange reason...

"Where are we?" Asked Brandy, adjusting her glasses as she took in the unexpected scene below.

"Welcome!" exclaimed an energetic young man dressed in an all-white suit and sporting long, sideswept bangs dyed bright yellow. He'd emerged from a room off the balcony on their right, carrying an empty silver tray. A waiter, perhaps? "You must be the newlyweds. Congratulations on the nuptials!"

They glanced at each other, confused.

"Um...thank you?" said Brandy.

"We were expected, then?" asked Albert.

"Of course!" he replied, sounding amused. "*Everyone* at Mr. Shanzer's parties are expected."

"So this *is* his place?" said Brandy, looking around, surprised. She had no idea being a perverted creep could be so lucrative...

"It's invitation only," explained the waiter. "These parties are *literally* impossible to crash."

Albert gazed down at all the dressed-up partygoers. It certainly looked like a lavish affair. But somehow he didn't think this guy was complimenting Shanzer's security team. *Sex magic...* he thought, pondering. *Manifesting your will into the universe...* Was that really a thing? What did it mean? What would be the scope of such a possibility? He supposed to someone with that kind of power, making his home impossible to sneak into would be child's play.

Your first lesson begins now, he thought, recalling those ominous words the shaman sent them off with. What in the world did he expect them to do?

"Help yourself to some refreshments in the grand entrance hall," invited the waiter, gesturing at the tables spread out below them "The bar is on the left at the foot of the stairs. It's open bar all night long. And by all means, feel free to mingle. There's nothing to be shy about." He walked past them and headed down the stairs as he added, "We're all the same here."

Brandy watched him go for a moment and then pointed after him. "What did he mean by that?"

"No idea."

"I'm *so* not in the mood to party right now," she grumbled as she looked down over the crowd of people below. She couldn't help tugging at the front of the ridiculous dress, paranoid that the people down there would be able to see right up the stupid thing from that angle.

Albert reached into his pockets and withdrew the book and the medallion. "If that weirdo wanted to kill us, he had more than enough opportunity. Instead, he gave us these, told us he was going to teach us about sex magic and sent us here... So what does he want us to do?"

"He can crawl off somewhere and *die,*" she snapped. "I'm not doing anything for that creep."

He held the medallion up and let it dangle from his hands as he examined it. It looked exactly the same as it always had. He still couldn't see how it would be useful for anything. Unless they were meant to sell or trade it, he supposed. But that didn't feel right somehow. "It feels weird," he said, watching it as it slowly turned before his eyes. "Like...now that I'm holding it again...it's almost like I'm relieved to have it. Like I never should've left it at home."

She stared at it for a moment, her eyes narrowing. "Great," she said. "Next you'll be having conversations with yourself in a puddle and calling it your 'precious.'" She snatched it from his hand and slipped it over her neck. "Let's get the fuck out of here already."

"Something tells me it won't be that easy."

They made their way down the stairs. Brandy clung to his arm with one hand for fear that the unfamiliar heels might trip her up. With her other hand, she kept tugging at the front of the dress, half-convinced that every step she took was flashing peeks of her most private things at anyone who might happen to look up at them as they descended.

(Stupid slutty dress!)

They reached the bottom of the stairs and paused at the base of the first statue. It was carved from white marble and depicted a large, muscular man (naked, of course) standing with his face lifted to the heavens as two naked women with folded angel wings on their backs clung to his naked thighs, their awe-struck gazes fixed not on his face, but on his blatantly exposed and somewhat generously proportioned genitals.

"This guy *seriously* only has one thought on his brain, doesn't he?" said Brandy.

Another waiter in a white tuxedo strolled past them, carrying a large tray of food. This one had a luxurious and perfectly trimmed beard complete with an immaculately shaped handlebar mustache. "Enjoy the party," he said cheerfully.

"Thanks," said Albert, trying to be polite.

Brandy felt a slight shiver pass through her. "I'm getting a seriously weird vibe from this place."

He took her by the hand again and continued across the room, weaving through the sparse crowd and circling around the fountain. He observed the people they passed on their way.

There were two couples standing together, chatting. Both of the women were wearing masks, but the men hadn't bothered. All of them turned their gazes on them as they passed by and seemed to take a moment to look them up and down, as if measuring them.

In fact, a lot of people were turning their gazes toward them as they passed. Did these people know they didn't belong here? Were they intruding on something private? They were, after all, strangers here, regardless of whether or not the waitstaff knew who they were.

"I don't like this," whispered Brandy, tugging at the dress again. "I can't explain it, but there's something different about these people. It feels *really* uncomfortable when they look at me."

Albert nodded. She'd always been a pretty good judge of character. If she met a guy she didn't like, even if she couldn't quite explain why, he almost always turned out to be some kind of creep. She even had a knack for knowing when someone was lying to her. But he didn't think she needed any special talent to get a bad vibe from these people.

Then again, not everyone was paying attention to them.

Near one of the refreshment tables, three women were sipping wine together. By the flushed looks on their faces, they'd been there a while.

On a garden bench in front of one of the flower beds, two middle-aged men were sitting together, one on each end, as if they didn't know each other, staring off in different directions. They were completely silent, not moving, as if they were stuck in a waiting room instead of at a party.

The entire perimeter of the room was occupied by little sitting areas with comfortable-looking chairs and sofas, separated by latticed partitions for partial privacy. Many of these were occupied by two or more people enjoying drinks or engrossed in conversation. In more than one, he could see couples kissing.

"That waiter said this was Shanzer's place…" he recalled. "This is supposed to be *his* party? Does that mean all these people know him? And they all came here *willingly*?"

"I guess if you have enough money to throw around, *anyone* can make friends." Ahead of them was a wide double doorway leading into what appeared to be a smaller entryway or foyer. The front door waited beyond. As soon as she saw it, she picked up her pace, practically dragging him along.

Albert's gaze was drawn to the windows as he crossed this next room. There was a fat tabby cat curled up on one of the window sills, its big, green eyes following them as they walked. But it was the darkness behind the curtains that drew his attention. It was still only about lunchtime when they arrived at the museum. But when Dolly was teasing them about having participated in some kind of unsolicited three-way, she said, "You didn't mind sharing him with me last night," suggesting that it was already Friday morning. Was the sun not up yet? What kind of party was going on at that sort of hour? "What time is it?"

"I don't know," she growled. "The pervert took my phone. I swear to God, my purse better still be in the car when we get home."

How much time passed while they were sleeping off the effects of the sex room? If it was already dark, then they'd lost at least eight or nine hours, even if Dolly was lying about there having been a "last night" at all. That might've been enough time for Shanzer to retrieve the medallion, but it was a really long time for them to have slept. They weren't out that long the *first* time they were trapped in the sex room. Were they drugged? And where were they? In that kind of time, they could have been moved almost anywhere. Were they even still in Tennessee?

Brandy let go of his hand as they neared the front door and grasped the handle, but it was locked tight. "Figures," she grumbled. She pulled aside the curtains and peered through the glass. There was no porch light on out there. Nor were there any streetlights that she could see. Everything was utterly dark. Only the internal lights through the curtained windows cast any illumination, reducing the entire outside world to a few shallow pools of glowing deck boards and a bare glimpse of a polished railing.

"You won't be able to leave."

They turned to find another waiter standing in the doorway behind them, this one a broad-shouldered man with short-cropped hair and several piercings.

"Shanzer's magic has sealed all the exits. No one gets in or out until after the party."

"And how much longer is this party going to take?" demanded Brandy.

"It's hard to say. Sometimes they go on for days."

"*Days*?" she glanced at Albert, shocked. "What the fuck kind of party goes on for *days*?"

"The kind of party where time, space and reality become distorted, transposed and intertwined."

Albert shook his head, confused. "What, like you say you're just gonna have one drink and you wake up three days later in Mexico with a donkey and a stripper named Gerald?"

"No." The waiter walked toward them, crossing the room. There was something off about him. He wasn't nearly as polite as the last two. But even more so, there was something not quite right about his face. "The kind of party that literally transcends dimensions. The kind of party that rewrites the very world around you. The kind of party where people are often changed forever…or sometimes cease to exist entirely."

As he drew closer, Brandy grasped Albert's arm and crowded closer to him. "His eyes…" she whispered.

He saw it, too, more clearly with each step the waiter took. He didn't *have* eyes. There was only a blackness where they should be.

"It's the kind of party where people who don't know what they're doing can find themselves stranded at the far reaches of the universe, where reality deteriorates into existential chaos and unspeakable things prowl the toxic waves of Oblivion."

Albert wasn't going to even try to understand any of that. "Doesn't *look* like that crazy of party…" he observed instead, glancing at the well-dressed partygoers mingling in the next room.

"Because it hasn't started yet."

"Oh…"

"When *does* it start, then?" asked Brandy.

"In less than twenty minutes. The ritual begins at the stroke of midnight."

Midnight? So it wasn't early morning out there, it was still evening. Either Dolly *was* lying about "last night" or they'd lost even more time than he'd realized and it was almost Saturday.

But Brandy was more concerned with another part of the waiter's reply. "Ritual?" she glanced at Albert, confused. "As in magic? *Witchcraft?* Like Captain Pervo was going on about?"

"Of course," replied the waiter. "Shanzer *is* one of the Seven Mages of Magreech. His magic is unparalleled." Then he sort of sneered. "Although there is, admittedly, no accounting for his personality."

"Okay…" Brandy looked back at the locked front door, frustrated. "So how the hell do we get out of here?"

"Unfortunately, I doubt you're meant to leave before the party gets started. If he's added you to the guest list for one of these events, then he's the only one who can let you leave. Like it or not, you're going to be forced to partake in his extravagant celebration of depravity and debauchery."

She wrinkled her nose. "Well *that* sounds awful. You mean this is some kind of *sex party?*"

"An oversimplification, but not inaccurate."

Albert glanced past the waiter again. "You mean all those people are here for…?" He recalled the way those two couples seemed to size them up as they walked past them.

"Ew…" groaned Brandy. "What are we supposed to do?"

"I can't pretend to understand a mind like his, but it seems to me that Shanzer means to force you to learn his personal school of magic. A sort of trial by fire. If that's the case, then the only way to leave this building will be to play whatever twisted game he has planned for you."

Remember, magic can open doors that can't be unlocked, thought Albert. Was that what the shaman meant by that?

"It may not be possible to leave before the party starts, but once it does, time won't be on your side. The longer you remain in this house, the less likely you are to ever leave it with your mind, body and soul intact."

Brandy spat a very unladylike curse, frustrated.

"Who are you?" asked Albert. Or perhaps he should be asking *what* instead of *who*, since those weren't the eyes of a human.

"My name is Warner Harr. I speak for the Keeper."

"The Keeper…?"

"Oh, I've got some messages you can pass on to *that* little freak!" snapped Brandy.

"I don't have the answers for you," said Warner. "But the Keeper entrusted you to Shanzer. And the Keeper doesn't make mistakes. Shanzer must have given you a way to succeed."

Albert thought about it a moment, then he reached into his pocket and withdrew the book. "You mean this?"

But the waiter blinked and frowned. In an instant, his eyes had become human. He looked back and forth between them, then glanced around at his surroundings, looking confused. "I'm sorry, were we talking about something?"

He stared at him, puzzled. "Warner?"

"Who? No, my name's Tanner." His mannerisms had completely changed. He was suddenly much more soft-spoken and friendly. "What were you saying just now?"

"You...don't remember?" asked Albert.

He put on a polite smile. "So sorry. Sometimes things like that happen. Mr. Shanzer's parties are known for that."

Albert and Brandy glanced at each other again. What the hell was going on in this place?

"As long as I'm here," said the displaced waiter, "can I get you anything?"

Chapter 9

Albert and Brandy left the foyer and set out across the entrance hall again. Now that they knew what kind of gathering was taking place, it was impossible to miss how many eyes were crawling over them as they moved through the room. They weren't being judged, they now understood. They were being *browsed*, like items on a store shelf. These people were shopping for partners.

"How much longer do you think we have until midnight?" asked Brandy as she stopped and looked around.

"No clue. The dirty old creep isn't much for clocks. I haven't seen one anywhere."

She groaned, frustrated. "I don't like this…"

"Which part? The fact that we're at a sex party, the black-eyed monster thing or the ritual of depravity and debauchery he was telling us about?"

"*All* of it. I mean, what the fuck's going to happen at midnight?"

Albert glanced across the room at a man with two women hanging on him, all three of them wearing strange, ornate masks. "Oh, you know what? I think I've seen this one! Everybody breaks out in 'The Time Warp,' right?"

Brandy groaned. "Don't even *try* imagining me in fishnets right now."

"No promises."

There was a lounge off the corner of the room on one side of the foyer and a leisure room with pool tables on the other side, but there were people gathered in both of them. She stopped, her mouth pursed and her teeth clenched. She didn't want to go where other people were. She wanted to get as far away from everyone as possible.

As she turned back to face Albert again, however, a woman in a glittery gold evening gown slid between them, so close to him that their noses were nearly touching, practically pinning him against the ferns.

"Hello there," the woman purred. "You'll do nicely." She appeared to be in her fifties, but it was difficult to say for sure. She'd obviously had a lot of work done over the years. Her face had that somewhat pinched look of someone who spent money on such things. She had long, almost-certainly dyed blonde hair, immaculate makeup and huge, barely covered breasts that were far too perfectly round and gravity-defying to be natural. Her body was toned just right and her exposed skin was a veritable art gallery of tattoos. She dangled a key in front of him, then placed it in his hand. "Top of the stairs," she told him. "First door on the right." She reached up and gave his cheek a brief caress. "And *don't* bother being gentle," she added before turning away.

Albert stood there, frozen in place, staring at the woman, an expression of bewilderment and mild horror painted across his surprised face, her room key still dangling from his fingers.

Brandy stepped into the space the woman just vacated, her mouth wide open in a "how dare you!" expression that he didn't think he quite deserved.

What the hell did *he* do?

"And bring your cute friend," added the woman, giving Brandy's butt a firm squeeze.

She let out a startled, "Eek!" and twirled around, but the woman was already strolling off, probably to pass out more keys.

Her face flushed, Brandy turned back to Albert, snatched the key out of his hand and threw it into the flower bed. Then she grabbed his hand and dragged him away.

"You know there was no way in hell I was agreeing to that, right?"

"You took the key, didn't you?"

"I wasn't going to use it! And you were invited too, remember!"

"As if! Some *Real Housewives* wannabe skank…"

"Where're you going?"

"The bar. I need a drink. And the *pervert's* paying for it."

She pulled him across the floor, managing to glare at every woman who dared to look at her husband along the way.

How did they end up at a fucking *sex party*? This was *not* on her honeymoon itinerary.

Albert wasn't sure what to do at this point. He had no interest at all in that woman, but Brandy was pissed. And he didn't blame her. He'd be pissed, too, if one the men here had walked up and propositioned *her* like that. And then there was that business with the sex museum greeter turning up naked in bed with them… That didn't look good for him, either. This was their *honeymoon*. Technically, he guessed… If it was really almost midnight, then it would've been over by now if they'd actually made it home… But they barely made it past the city limits of Wevenwert. And their honeymoon couldn't be over until they were safely back at home…right?

She dragged him through the open door and right up to the bar, where she demanded a margarita.

Albert's drink of choice was usually a whiskey sour, but he didn't think he wanted anything very strong. He hadn't eaten since lunch, after all. And he wasn't certain that the shaman and the slutty goth chick hadn't drugged them. The last thing they needed was for a couple drinks to go straight to their heads at a place like this. There was simply no telling where they might wake up next.

The bartender was an attractive woman with big, brown eyes and long, black hair with a streak of bright red running down one side. She handed him his beer with a bright, flirty smile that naturally made Brandy glare at him again.

Careful not to even look at the pretty bartender, he turned and glanced around the room at the people mingling. Were they all really here for a sex party? How much work must it have taken to gather this many perverted people into one building?

And yet, as he glanced down at the far end of the bar, he saw that there was a Siamese cat bathing itself on the last stool, looking perfectly at home, as if this place were *always* filled with well-dressed strangers looking to get freaky.

According to the pervert, this was supposed to be about the Temple of the Blind. Or rather, whatever came *after* the Temple of the Blind. *It's time to finish what you started that night six years ago...* But this wasn't anything like the way everything started back then. They weren't sucker punched in some skeevy adult roadside attraction. They were lured into those tunnels with the box.

Where was the box? Where were the cryptic clues? Where was the tantalizing mystery?

In the end, they never even really did anything back then. Everything was orchestrated for them. They were mere puppets, playing along with the Keeper's twisted game. All they did was follow the script that had been written for them.

He remembered feeling so used after they came home. Everything they went through was a lie, after all. Like those hours they spent mourning the deaths of their companions, only for them to both turn up alive again. It was like a cruel joke, a mere pantomime pretending to be reality, all for the twisted amusement of that creepy little Crypt Keeper knockoff.

How did they go from creepy steam tunnels, ancient labyrinths and the Sentinel Queen to raunchy museums, sex wizards and swinger parties? This was just *stupid*.

Brandy noticed that the friendly bartender handed her margarita to her with a noticeably less flirty smile. Somewhere inside, she knew it was because she probably looked about as friendly right now as a debt collector for the mob, but she chose to assume the pretty little bitch was scheming to seduce her husband because that was just the sort of mood she was in right now.

It wasn't fair. Why today? She supposed it was better than their *first* day in Wevenwert... At least the pervert waited until they were ready to go home. But still...

"I hear congratulations are in order," said an old man two stools down from them. He was dressed up, like every other man in the room, including the stuffy jacket and tie, with thick, white hair carefully combed back. He was leaning forward on the bar, slumped, weary looking, staring down at his old fashioned, not even looking up. "The happy newlyweds."

Albert glanced over at him. "Thanks," was all he could think to say. Why did everyone here know who they were?

"I was married a few times," the old man went on. "Best years of my life, each time. And I've been around a *long* time…"

Again, he glanced over. He didn't look *that* old. Late sixties, maybe. At most.

"Outlived 'em all," he sighed.

"I'm sorry to hear that. It must've been tough."

He nodded. "Every time."

Albert's gaze lingered on the old man. He looked sort of familiar. Had he seen this guy somewhere before?

"It's what happens as you get older. You lose more and more of the people you love."

Cheerful, he thought. *The life of the party, right here.* But he didn't say anything. He felt bad for the old man.

"If you're *really* unlucky…" He lifted his drink to his lips and stared out into space for a second or two before continuing: "…you live long enough to find yourself all alone. Sometimes over and over again…"

He glanced over at Brandy as she took a sip of her margarita, her eyebrows raised as if to say, "What's up with this guy?" He was seriously putting a downer on her pissed-off mood.

Albert wasn't sure what to say. What was a sad sack like him even doing at a party like this? Weren't all these people supposed to be here to get laid?

Brandy leaned closer to him, her voice hushed. "What are we going to do? It's going to be midnight soon."

But he didn't have an answer for her. He didn't know what to do. He took a swig of his beer and then pulled the book from his pocket and flipped through it. Most of the pages were illegible. He still had no idea how he was supposed to use it if he couldn't read it.

The old man took a long sip of his drink. Then he stared at it again. "I lost a lot of friends that night."

Albert looked over at him and frowned. Was he still talking

to him? Nobody else seemed to be paying him any attention.

"Their whole world was ripped apart... Everything... Every life... Every *soul*..." He shook his head. "All gone."

He looked over at Brandy, but she only shrugged and went back to her margarita.

"I blamed you, of course. I mean, it *was* your fault."

Was he talking to the drink? Did he get drunk and cause an accident or something?

But the old man turned his pale, blue eyes on the two of them. "*You* opened that door."

Albert sat up straight, his heart leaping as realization finally dawned on him. "*You!*"

"What?" gasped Brandy. "Who? What's going on?" She'd never seen the man sitting in front of them in her life.

Albert didn't recognize him at first, either. For one thing, he looked at least ten years younger than the man he faced that night. For another, the last time they spoke, he'd been burned alive, reduced to little more than a charred corpse.

It was the old man from five years ago. The one who pretended to be the devil and tried to stop them from opening the door.

"You never did answer my question."

"What question?" demanded Albert.

The old man offered him a tight smile. "Do you really think you can face Oblivion?"

Chapter 10

Do you think...you can face...oblivion? Those words drifted back to Albert from the depths of his memories, spewed like fetid smoke from the charred lips of a walking corpse. It was the very end of that long, long night, when the blackened remains of the old man staggered out of the darkness of that black tunnel. He turned his dead, soupy eyes on him and asked that question.

He didn't understand what it meant at the time. And he didn't understand it now, either. But it occurred to him that it wasn't the first time he'd heard that word tonight. The thing that called itself Warner Harr said something about it, too, he recalled.

...where reality deteriorates into existential chaos and unspeakable things prowl the toxic waves of Oblivion.

Then the old man looked back down at his drink and shrugged. "I suppose it's still a little too early to be asking you that, though, isn't it?"

"How are you...?" asked Albert.

"...no longer well done?" he finished without looking at him. "I got better. I always do. It's why I've been around so long."

He stared at the old man. Apparently, being burned alive was surprisingly good for one's complexion if you possessed the unnatural ability to heal from such a thing, because he really did look at least ten years younger than he did when he stepped out of that swirling monstrosity of broken corpses, maybe even closer to twenty.

But then again, this man had been alive for hundreds or thousands of years. Maybe tens of thousands. The Sentinel Queen told them so. He'd been around throughout human history, interfering and scheming, building his fearful devilish reputation.

The bartender handed a cocktail to a plump, middle-aged woman in a dress that barely contained her bountiful bust and then turned to face them. "Lucas Kneede," she sneered.

The old man still didn't bother looking up from his drink. "Hello Warner."

Albert and Brandy turned, surprised, and saw that the bartender's pretty brown eyes had gone completely black, just like the waiter whose real name was Tanner. Did this Warner Harr, whatever it was, just jump from one body to another like some kind of cheap science fiction movie monster?

"Why are *you* here?" demanded Warner. It was the bartender's voice, but her tone was exactly as it was when he was speaking through Tanner. Something about the way the words were formed, the very distinct subtleties in pronunciation and the pace of the words were eerily the same. It wasn't like watching one actor mimic another. It was strangely eerie to listen to.

"I was invited."

"Why would Shanzer invite *you*?"

"Good question. I wondered the same thing, myself." The old man—Lucas Kneede, apparently—turned those pale blue eyes on Albert again. "The last time we met, we didn't exactly part on good terms."

"Something about if we ever crossed paths again…" recalled Albert.

Kneede nodded. "We're not allies in this. The Keeper is my enemy. And so are his *tools*. Shanzer knows this. So I'm not sure what the sleazy bastard expects me to do here tonight."

"Tane's dead," said Warner. "Don't tell me you intend to keep fighting for his lost cause. Or is someone else holding your leash these days?"

"What?" asked Brandy. This was confusing. What were these two even talking about? "Who's Tane?"

"Don't mind us," said Kneede. "Bad blood."

"Janon Tane was a key part of the cycle's process," explained Warner. "But he became convinced that he could do a better job than the Keeper and tried to sabotage it. The results were disastrous, to say the least."

"And now a *filthy product* of that disaster *lectures* us about it."

"I make no excuses for where I began," growled Warner. "At least I became something *better*. Something that fights *for* the living things in this universe."

"At the cost of *how much* suffering?" His voice remained calm in spite of these accusations. "The good of the many out-weigh the good of the few, is it?"

Brandy leaned closer to Albert and whispered, "What the fuck are they talking about?"

But he could only shake his head. He had no idea. Clearly there was history between these two.

"It was under Tane's instruction that he interfered with the opening of the first doorway five years ago," explained Warner. "Something along the lines of, 'Play the Keeper's game, but don't let them open the door'? 'Kill them all if you have to'? Does that about sum it up?"

"Spoken like all the great liars throughout history," sneered Kneede. "You and the Keeper both. Only the parts of the truth that suit you."

"And you should know better than anyone. 'Father of Lies' and all. *Hypocrite*."

"Drama much?" muttered Brandy as she took another sip of her drink.

Kneede wasn't really the devil. Albert figured that out five years ago. He only pretended to be the devil to frighten and manipulate people. But the fact that he wasn't what he pretended to be didn't mean he was harmless. This old man possessed incredible psychic powers, for starters. He could move thousands of objects simultaneously with his mind, enough to surround himself in a tornado of broken zombies and transform himself into a giant corpse monster.

But he wasn't so clever as to not be fooled himself.

Albert didn't know what was going on, but he clearly remembered that last interaction between the old man and the Keeper, two monsters standing face-to-face in the darkness of that tunnel. He replayed it in his head again as he sat there. Kneede asked the keeper a single question: "How…?" And the Keeper had replied with two questions of his own: "Shouldn't you already know? Aren't you familiar enough with deceit and lies to figure it out for yourself?" *I don't like being used*, he thought, remembering the last words the old man spoke to the Keeper that night. It seemed clear, even then, that Kneede was somehow mislead. In the end, he was just another of the Keeper's unwitting puppets, just like the rest of them.

But there was more to the story. Perhaps *much* more. What was it Kneede said when they first sat down, before he recognized him? Something about people dying? What the hell did *that* mean?

"What do you intend to do here tonight?" Warner demanded again.

Kneede looked up from his drink for the first time in a while, meeting those empty black eyes. He even managed a sinister sort of sneer. "Who knows? Maybe nothing. Maybe I'm just here to watch."

Warner stared at him for a moment, the bartender's pretty face twisted into an expression of scorn and distrust. Then she blinked and her eyes were human again. Her expression melted into a much softer one of brief puzzlement and slight disorientation. Then she smiled at the old man. "Anything else I can get you, sir?"

"Thank you, but no," replied Kneede, as if he'd seen Warner Harr come and go a million times before—which he probably had, given the confrontation that just took place. They clearly had a history. Then, as the bartender turned away, he glanced over at Albert again, one white eyebrow lifted. "I'd be ready if I were you."

"Is that a threat?"

Kneede smiled. "No. Just some friendly advice. I'm guessing you've never been to one of Shanzer's sex parties before, have you?"

Brandy stared back at him over her drink, those bright blue eyes big and concerned. "Um… No. We haven't."

"Don't say I didn't warn you."

Before either of them could ask him what he meant by that, a loud chime rang through the room, like the tolling of a great church bell.

Behind them in the bar, and throughout the building, there was an excited murmuring of voices and muffled cheers.

The bartender sang out, "Midnight!" and as the second bell tolled, she twirled around. Her white waitstaff uniform erupted into a flash of smoke and fire around her and, when she was facing them again, she was stark naked but for the little bow tie and the belt from which her cleaning towel still hung.

Albert sat gaping at her, too surprised to think of anything else to do, until Brandy clapped her hand over his eyes.

Startled out of his stupor, he snatched away her hand, spun around on the bar stool and looked around the room.

The other waiters wandering around were just as naked and unashamed. He caught just a glimpse of Tanner's pale butt as he strutted past the doorway. And they weren't the only ones. *Everyone* in the bar was stripping down.

It wasn't an awkward process, either. No one was fumbling with their buttons or tripping over their pants legs. Evening dresses slipped to the floor effortlessly. Dress shirts popped open with ease. Pants were dropped and left behind in a single step.

No one had any underwear to get in the way. Everyone was ready to get started.

"Oh god..." gasped Brandy as she watched a handsome older gentleman with Sean Connery looks at a table right in front of them step out of his dress pants, his considerably-larger-than-average equipment on full display. Her very brain seemed to short circuit a bit at the absurdity of the scene and she found herself unable to tear her eyes away for a moment.

Before the fourth midnight bell had tolled, the filthy shaman's obscene festivities had already begun. Everyone but the two of them and Kneede were already naked and very few people were bothering to even leave the room. Women were lying back on tables, spreading their thighs on stools or simply sinking to their knees on the floor. Men were bending over them, sliding under them or grasping them from behind.

"And now we're in the middle of a cheesy porno," grumbled Albert between the fifth and sixth tolls. "Fantastic."

"If you two need anything," said the bartender as she leaned over the bar, her pert breasts resting on the polished mahogany surface, "and I mean *anything*," she added as those pretty brown eyes swam down Albert's body and back up again, "don't hesitate to ask, 'kay?"

"Uh…thanks…" said Albert, his gaze drawn to her pink nipples like space debris pulled into a black hole. He couldn't seem to stop them.

Brandy grabbed his arm and dragged him off the stool, nearly knocking him to the floor in the process.

"Careful!"

"What do you think you're looking at?"

"Don't snap at me! I saw you looking at James Bond's junk, too!"

"I was not!"

They emerged from the bar only to find that the party was going on *everywhere*. There was a couple making love on the stairs. Two women were pleasuring a man on one of the benches. The drunk women were entertaining each other at the feet of the well-hung Greek god and his starstruck angels. There were bare feet and a pasty white ass sticking out of one of the flower beds. And there were at least enough people to form a baseball team frolicking naked with the nymph statues in the fountain.

By the time the twelfth bell tolled, the entire house had erupted into one gigantic orgy.

Chapter 11

"Look what you've gotten us into this time!" snapped Brandy.

"How is this *my* fault? *You* wanted to go to the sex museum, remember? 'It'll be a laugh,' you said!"

They were hurrying down a long hallway leading off the entrance hall, searching for somewhere comfortably apart from all the lewd partygoers, but every room was occupied. There were people copulating in the kitchen and in the dining room. Even the guest washrooms and closets had become settings for all manner of pornographic activity. There was an entire gallery already full of obscene paintings, sculptures and photography, but now there were also at least two dozen naked men and women writhing on the floor.

There was even a couple going at it right in the middle of the hallway!

"There isn't enough Purell in the world to cleanse this house!" groaned Brandy as she eyed a large, sweaty man with entirely too much body hair sprawled atop a petite brunette who looked as if she were being slowly crushed to death beneath his formidable bulk.

Not everyone was engaging in sex, though. There were quite a few people who appeared to be content to just masturbate while watching others doing it, which, oddly enough, Brandy found even more perverted than the people who were actually participating.

At the very end of the hallway was a sunroom filled with plants and a half-dozen naked people. There was an exit here, but like the front door, it was sealed tight. Albert considered attempting to break one of the many windows, but he was sure that it would do no good. The perverted shaman would've thought of that. Either the glass would prove impossible to break or something would physically prevent them from leaving through them.

He might have tried it, just to see what would happen, but he didn't see anything heavy enough that wasn't uncomfortably close to someone naked and uttering obscene noises. Were there this many people in the building *before* it turned midnight? It didn't seem as crowded when everyone was still upright and decent.

"We've got to figure out what the pervert wanted us to do," he decided. "He called it our first lesson… Did he say anything else that might be a clue?"

He glanced over at Brandy, but she wasn't looking at him, she was staring wide-eyed and fascinated at two very attractive men in the midst of breathless lovemaking.

"Hey!"

She jumped and twirled to face him, her face flushing bright red. "*What?*"

"Forget it." He grabbed her by the hand and led her back the way they came. "Come on."

She nodded, but she glanced back once more as she hurried away, still blushing.

"This isn't like the sex room," he said, thinking aloud. "Seeing all these people isn't making us like them. It's just…" He glanced over to see a man in the midst of intense intercourse, his face contorted absurdly and making loud, pig-like grunting noises. "…*uncomfortable*," he finished. "There's no logical reason he'd dump us in here just to watch us run around looking disgusted. So what does he want us to do?"

There was a quiet stretch of hallway between the gallery doors and the entrance hall. Albert led her to one side, against the wall, out of the way of anyone who might happen by, and stopped. Here, he took out the book Shanzer gave him again. Only the first four pages were legible, and none of what was written there seemed to make much sense. There was a page and a half of tiny handwriting with no punctuation or spacing ex-

plaining once again what sexual energy was and how it was possible to utilize it, pretty much as he'd explained it to them back in
that guest room, but without any actual directions for doing so.
There was another full page about manifestation of will and cen-
tering one's inner thoughts and clearing one's head of distrac-
tions and impurities… It sounded like a bunch of new-aged self-
help nonsense to him.

Did the old pervert expect them to sit down in the middle
of a giant orgy and *meditate*?

Brandy crowded closer to him and browsed the open pages.
"'Spells are not cast with words, but with intentions,'" she read.
"'Visualize. Anticipate. Materialize.' What the fuck does *that*
mean?"

Albert shook his head. Even if he could manage enough
concentration to wrap his head around this stuff, he wouldn't
know what to do with it. Was there a "get me the hell out of this
disgusting sex party" spell?

A strange sort of shudder swept through the building
around them, sending them momentarily off balance. At the
same time, they both felt a brief and subtle wave of vertigo.

"What was that?" asked Brandy.

"Felt like the whole foundation shifted." He turned and
looked around. He couldn't quite put his finger on it, but he felt
as if something had changed.

He stood there a moment, waiting to see if it would happen
again. When it didn't, he turned his attention back to Shanzer's
book.

"'Belief in the process is a crucial element to all spells. If
you cannot believe yourself capable of casting the spell, the spell
cannot be cast.'" He frowned. "How the hell do you believe you
can do magic if you can't prove to yourself you can do it?"

"That's confusing," agreed Brandy.

Two naked women emerged from the dining room and ran
giggling and squealing past them, into the entrance hall, their
oversized breasts bouncing obscenely. A moment later, a man
wearing only a cowboy hat came running after them, laughing
like a madman and shouting, "For Massachusetts!" for some un-

fathomable reason.

Brandy watched the man's pale butt disappear around the corner, a bemused look on her face.

"Private joke?" guessed Albert.

"I'm surrounded by perverted lunatics…" she muttered.

"Look at this," he said, pointing at a scrawled line in the book. "'Magic isn't glittery and shiny. Nor is it fast or grand. It's invisible. It's miniscule. It's changes in the tangible universe at the most minute level. The sick magic user doesn't banish his illness with a curse. He meticulously changes the sickness *and himself* in order to become healthy again.' I almost understand that, I think…"

"At least one of us does…"

"He was talking about that before, remember? About how we couldn't just conjure wealth or make someone we hate drop dead."

"I wasn't really paying attention. That guy was the human equivalent to sewage."

Somewhere in the art gallery a woman let out a loud, orgasmic scream.

"I'll have what *she's* having," muttered Brandy. It was one of her favorite jokes. Something she'd blurted out countless times while out drinking, whenever she heard someone let out a drunken squeal or scream that could be perceived as even remotely sexual. But she immediately made a face at herself as she realized what she'd just said. "Wait… No I won't!"

"It's like anything else, really," he went on. "You don't snap your fingers and there's a skyscraper. You have to clear the land, lay the foundation, construct the frame, piece by piece. Plumbing, wiring, ventilation, networking. Walls, windows and doors. It takes time, planning and resources." He looked up from the book and met her eyes. "Magic must work the same way."

She nodded. "*Or* the guy who wrote that's an insanely demented pervert creep who just gets off on screwing with people."

He shrugged. "Maybe both. I mean, *the Keeper* sent him."

"According to the pervert, himself," she reminded him.

"And Warner."

"We don't even know *what* he is…"

"Kneede and that black-eyed thing didn't get along at all," Albert reminded her. "The enemy of my enemy?"

"Isn't necessarily your friend," she countered. "Crocodiles and lions don't exactly get along, but they'll both eat you if you give them half a chance."

"I suppose… But what choice do we have? I'm open to suggestions here."

But of course she didn't have any.

The last legible page contained only one line. "'The key to opening it lies in opening yourself,'" he read aloud. "And we're back to making no sense again."

"I'm telling you, the guy's a toilet brain."

Again, the world seemed to tremble. Another shudder swept through the building around them, making them clutch tighter at each other. This time, Albert *heard* it. A soft groan seemed to snake its way through the building around them, moving from the entrance hall outward, toward the sunroom.

When he looked in that direction, something seemed off. The hallway seemed longer, somehow, the ceiling higher. Were there more doorways than there were before?

Somewhere, in another part of the building, someone let out a long, piercing shout. This one didn't sound like the woman in the gallery a moment ago. It didn't sound orgasmic. Nor did it sound frightened or angry. It sounded strangely triumphant. And as soon as it touched their ears, another of those strange, dizzying trembles swept through them.

"What's happening?" whispered Brandy.

Albert stared at the distant doorway of the sunroom, at the creeping branches that weren't reaching into the hallway like that a moment ago, at the strange mist that was rolling across the floor from the open kitchen door. "Magic…" he sighed. "Magic is happening…"

Chapter 12

Things were changing. The very building seemed to be growing around them. It was as if all the sexual activity were *feeding* it, making it swell. There was another hallway between them and the sunroom that wasn't there before.

He turned and walked back to the new intersection and peered down it. There were other doors there, but none that looked like an exit.

"We just came from that way," said Brandy, impatient.

He glanced back at her, confused. "*This* way?"

"*Yeah*. It was locked, remember? They're *all* locked. That creep has us trapped here."

Locked? He looked down at that far doorway again. A memory seemed to bubble up from somewhere deep down. A luxurious reading room with big windows and a cozy fireplace and several very comfortable-looking chairs, all of which were occupied by horny partygoers.

Except that never happened… Because they never went down that hallway… Because it didn't exist until a moment ago… So what was he remembering?

"Are you okay?" asked Brandy.

It was a good question. He wasn't entirely sure. Something was wrong here. Why did he have two different memories of the past few minutes?

But before he could think of an answer, another of those vertigo-inducing shudders swept through the building.

Albert leaned against the wall to steady himself. Brandy clutched at his arm.

When it had passed, he looked up to see that the new hallway was even longer than before. There were two more doors.

"Do you see that?" he asked.

"See what?"

Why couldn't she see the changes that were going on around them? What was Shanzer doing to them?

He started to turn away from the new hallway, but he paused as something caught his eye.

No... That wasn't quite right. Nothing caught his eye because there was nothing there. It was the same hallway he was looking down before. But there was *something*... He was sure of it. Something...*significant*...

"Albert?"

Something was happening, but he didn't have enough information to process it. And they couldn't just stand around. If the Shaman was capable of changing the very building around them...if he was capable of altering their very *memories* along with it...then there was no telling what else the creep was capable of. He took her hand again and hurried back toward the entrance hall.

His thoughts were racing now. These contradictions... Which memory was wrong? It could just as easily be that the hallway had always been there and the memory of it and the reading room *not* being there was the false one.

Was Shanzer trying to drive him mad? Was that his goal? Or was it that old man? Was Lucas Kneede behind this, instead?

This was frustrating. How was he supposed to know what to do? He needed a clue. "That Warner guy...or whatever he was... I wish he'd come back here and explain some of this crap to us!"

Brandy looked into the kitchen as they passed the doorway. The people in there had smeared themselves with what appeared to be all the ice cream sundae toppings in the pantry and were engaging in very unsanitary activities on the counters and floors and even in the sink... "If I were him, I don't think I'd be too eager to borrow any of the bodies here right now."

"You've got a point there."

As they approached the doorway leading back into the entrance hall, another of those dizzying shudders swept through them, this one much bigger than all the ones before it. They stumbled and fell against the doorframe, clutching at each other. And when it had passed and they stood up and stepped through the doorway, they found that it was no longer the entrance hall. They were standing in the doorway of a fancy library. The walls were towering mahogany bookshelves. There was a large antique desk and chair in the middle of the room. There were reading chairs and sofas arranged around it, all of them occupied by naked people.

No one was practicing proper library etiquette, he noticed. Books were strewn everywhere. There were drinks spilled on the side tables. And no one was being the least bit quiet. They were moaning, grunting and even screaming.

It would've been impossible to do any studying in there.

Besides, it appeared that all the books here were erotic fiction, pornography and better sex self-help manuals.

There was definitely a running theme to the perverted shaman's home décor.

Albert turned and looked back the way they came. This was an entirely different hallway. Where were they?

And yet, even as he tried to wrap his head around somehow being transported to another part of the Shaman's dirty mansion, he found himself recalling glimpses of a series of events. Of rushing *through* the great hall and past the stairway…

But that didn't happen.

Did it?

He recalled passing two women in leather masks who invited them to help "discipline" them. And there was a man crawling around on all fours wearing only a dog collar and a leash who told them that he was a "good doggy." And there was a much older woman standing in an open doorway, dripping with jewelry but without a stitch of clothing to cover her slim and rather wrinkled body who assured them she'd take "*very* good care" of them if they'd join her "little party."

Did that really happen? Why did it feel like he was remembering two different timelines? Was he blacking out after each of those weird tremors and running on autopilot?

He fled down the hallway, away from the library, still clinging to Brandy's hand.

Or was he fleeing *back* down the hallway? Was he moving forward into a new place, or backtracking? God, this was confusing.

Ahead of them, a man and a woman emerged from what looked like a large closet or storage room, both of them naked and disheveled, their hair a mess, and passed them on their way to the library.

He wasn't terribly keen on the idea of going into that closet where those two had clearly just finished some probably very unhygienic business, but it might be their one chance to hide from this icky party, so he steered Brandy in that direction and stepped through the darkened doorway.

But he came to an abrupt halt when he realized that the couple hadn't been partying alone in here. There was another couple still enjoying the space.

"Oh wow!" gasped Brandy.

The couple didn't stop what they were doing. It was difficult to tell whether they even noticed them.

"Sorry!" Albert tried to hurry on, but Brandy didn't move when he pulled at her hand.

She was staring at the scene before them, wide-eyed, distracted. She pointed. "See that...?"

He looked back again. "Yeah. Kinda can't miss it."

"We've never done *that*..." she said, still pointing.

He glanced at her, then back at the people before them again. He tipped his head to one side, considering it. "No, we definitely haven't."

Her eyes still wide, still pointing, she said, "We should try that sometime..."

Again, he glanced at her, a surprising tingle washing through him at the thought. "Uh... Sure."

"When we get home..."

"Yeah. Whatever you want. First thing." He tipped his head to the other side and frowned. "I might have to stretch first."

"Uh huh..."

"Come on!"

This time, when he tugged at her hand, she let him lead her away. But she kept staring until they were past the doorway and out of sight.

Another dizzying shudder washed over them and suddenly they were back in the entrance hall, standing in front of one of the flower beds looking out across the crowd of people splashing and frolicking in the fountain.

Albert clutched at his head as he grappled with a fresh wave of memories that weren't there a moment ago.

What was happening to him?

"You okay?" asked Brandy.

"I think so..." He blinked at the soaked partygoers as if all the craziness were nothing more than a bit of dust in his eyelashes and might just vanish if only he could bat it away. But the lewd scene didn't change, so he turned and started back toward the foyer and the front door.

"What are you doing? We just came from over there."

"What?" He looked back and forth, confused. "When did...?" But even as he was asking the question, he remembered crossing the house again. He remembered finding that the party guests had spread to the foyer. He remembered that the front doors were still very much locked.

And yet he also remembered that they did no such thing. They were walking down that last hallway and felt one of those odd shivers and then they were just here.

Which memory was real?

What was happening?

"Albert...?"

"Why's it only happening to *me*?"

She gave him a confused frown. "Huh?"

"What are we even doing? It's pretty obvious we can't get out."

"You said you wanted to go upstairs and find somewhere quiet to take another look at the book."

He cocked his head to one side. "Oh yeah... I remember that... Or I *think* I do..."

"Are you okay?"

He shook his head. No, he wasn't. He felt like he'd taken too many turns on a carnival ride. His stomach was knotted up. He felt nauseous.

"Let's sit down," she said, gripping his arm and leading him around the flower bed. There was a semi-private spot here at the end of it, a little space where there was a gap between the lush leaves and where none of the lewd partygoers were doing all their dirty things directly in front of them. A low brick wall formed the base, wide enough to sit on.

"I'm sorry," he said, rubbing at his eyes again. "I'm okay. Really. Just... Something's seriously off about this place."

"No shit. I hadn't noticed."

He chuckled a little at this. "I mean besides the..." He gestured at a skinny woman wearing nothing but thigh-high leather boots who was spanking the pale, hairy backside of a heavyset middle-aged man in one of the partitioned sitting areas.

She wrinkled her nose at the kinky couple and then immediately turned her attention back to him. "Forget them and talk to me. What's wrong? You've been acting weird."

"It's hard to explain. I don't know if I quite understand it myself."

"Just try," she urged.

But before he could say anything, a phone rang.

The two of them looked around, confused. It wasn't the musical ringing of a cell phone. It sounded more like those old-fashioned landline phones. (Although you could set your ringtone to those, too, Albert recalled. His brother-in-law's phone sounded something like that. It was quite jarring when it went off.)

But this wasn't a cell phone. When they looked up, they found that there was a small table in front of them. On it sat an old desktop rotary phone that looked like it had come right out of some old movie.

"Was that there before?" asked Brandy, pointing at it.

"No. It wasn't."

Both of them glanced around the room, but no one else

seemed to be concerned about a ringing phone. No one had stopped what they were doing. No one seemed to be expecting a call.

"You think it's for us?" she wondered.

There was only one way to find out. He stood up and walked over to it.

Brandy leaned in to listen as he lifted the headset to his ear.

Before he could say, "Hello," the shaman's sleazy voice spoke up in their ears: "You should both know that you're failing this task miserably."

Chapter 13

"We're not joining your nasty orgy!" snapped Brandy.

"No one said you had to," countered Shanzer. "I told you, sex magic isn't about sex. It's about the emotional energy *associated* with sex. The last thing you're going to want to do is waste that energy. You need to *seize* it. *Redirect* it. *Use* it."

"We don't know how to do that," said Albert.

"You can start by using your natural psychic abilities to your advantage."

He frowned. "What?"

"That weirdness you've been experiencing?" explained Shanzer. "Those feelings of things changing and time skipping?"

Brandy looked up at him, confused.

"That's you tapping into your surroundings. Your psychic sense is tied to your environment. It's why you were able to navigate that labyrinth five years ago. You can sense things that aren't as they appear, things hidden to others."

He recalled having strange moments of intuition inside the Temple of the Blind. He wasn't able to explain exactly what it was, but sometimes things just seemed a little off, even though they didn't look any different from anything else down there. They just seemed…*significant* somehow…prompting him to look closer. That was how he discovered that the dead end deep inside those old tunnels wasn't really a dead end. The stones had merely been stacked there, without anything to hold them in place. He only had to reach out and push it over. But he thought that stuff was just the Sentinel Queen or the Keeper giving him a psychic nudge, planting the thought in his head to keep pushing him forward.

"You're going to have to learn to focus that third eye,"

Shanzer went on. "As soon as you can do that, you'll be able to see what's *really* there."

He looked up at the room around him. It had been changing ever since he felt the first of those strange, vertigo-inducing shudders. There were twice as many chandeliers hanging over the room as there were when he first arrived. And there were at least three more naked statues.

"And *you*, my dear," Shanzer added, speaking now to Brandy, "are psychically tuned into the *people* around you."

"People?" She glanced back at the naked party guests frolicking in the fountain and frowned. She didn't really want any kind of connection with *them*.

"It's a very handy gift. You're very fortunate. You can see the *truth* within people."

"The truth?" What the hell did that mean?

"Haven't you ever wondered what possessed you to venture into those tunnels that night with a man you barely knew?"

She glanced over at Albert. He wasn't wrong. She told herself that she had a little bit of a crush on her chemistry partner and wanted to get to know him better. She told herself she'd always been adventurous, ever since she was a child, and sneaking into the university's steam tunnels sounded exciting. She told herself that she was *prepared*. She had a can of pepper spray in her purse, just in case. But the truth was that none of those things really explained why she decided to do something so stupidly dangerous. It was chilling to think back on how easily things could have turned out *very* differently that night.

"You went with him that night because you knew, deep down, that he was *good*. You *knew* he wouldn't hurt you. You knew he'd protect you, even though you were just a stranger to him, too."

Was that true? Five years ago, the Sentinel Queen told her she was psychic, but she never explained how it worked. And yet, she'd always had a talent for judging people. She tended to know right away if she was going to get along with a new coworker. And sometimes she simply had hunches about people. Sometimes she could just sense that the scary looking man scowling at the bar would actually be quite kind if you just got to know him. Or that the polite man who smiled at everyone at the grocery store was actually a creep. But those were only hunches. Passing thoughts about strangers she glimpsed as she went about her life and nothing more. She could have been wrong far more than she was right, for all she knew.

"And it's also the reason you never felt the same sexual satisfaction from your first two lovers."

"Oh my god! How long have you been spying on me?" Albert wasn't her first boyfriend, regrettably. There were two before him. And neither of them were ever very enjoyable. In fact, by the time she met Albert, she'd begun to think that she didn't really even *like* sex.

"You could see the truth in those boys," he went on, ignoring her. "How selfish they were. How they only cared about sex, never about *you*."

She reached up and covered her face. She didn't want to think about that. Those times before Albert were a mistake. Her single greatest regret in life. But she was young and naïve and curious…

"Albert was different," said the pervert. "You could see his truth when you were with him. Whereas the other boys pretended to love you merely because they wanted to have sex with you, *he* wanted to have sex with you specifically because he truly loved you. Once they had what they wanted, you could feel their greedy satisfaction, their obscene sense of having *won*. But *he* never felt that way. He felt nothing but adoration and love for you."

She turned and met Albert's gaze. It was surprising to hear it put into words like that, but somehow she knew that it was true. There'd always been something different about the way he looked at her, something that made him so much more special than anyone else in her life.

"That's the truth you're able to see," he went on. "*Use* that connection to people. That's where the magic begins."

"But *how?*" pushed Albert. "This stuff is all completely foreign to us. I feel like you're trying to explain advanced programming to someone who doesn't even know how to use a computer."

"It's not that complicated."

Somewhere in the background, he heard a woman's voice.

"Just a minute, dear. Almost done."

"What?" asked Albert, confused.

"Just tending to a little spellcasting of my own," replied Shanzer.

"Ewwww!" groaned Brandy.

"Listen," he went on. "It's like learning to walk. Anyone can do it. Begin by simply focusing on the energy. Feel the *emotions* that are all around you. Let those emotions flow through your mind and body. Think of it as *fuel*. Recognize it and seize it. Together, you have all the tools you need to pass this lesson. You just have to stop running away from what makes you uncomfortable. You have to face it. You have to *embrace* it. You have to *feel* it in order to *use* it."

"Use it *how*?" asked Albert. "What is it you want us to *do*? We don't understand the lesson criteria."

"I think you do, actually."

And with that, the line went dead with a very final click.

"I don't like him," said Brandy.

Albert nodded and hung up. As soon as he placed the receiver back into its cradle, another shudder rolled through the building. In the very next instant, the phone and the table had both vanished and they found themselves sitting on the wall of the flower bed again, as if they'd never stood up to answer it in the first place.

Was it really ever there? Or was it some sort of bizarre illusion?

"That was weird..." said Brandy as she clutched at the bricks beneath her for balance.

He nodded. His stomach felt fluttery, as if he'd just gotten off an intense roller coaster ride. He looked up at the chandeliers again, at the grand staircase by which they entered this celebration of depravity, at the couple still going at it on those steps...

There was another cat up there, he saw. A little white one,

sitting on the railing of the second-floor balcony, watching all the people down below. As he watched, it turned its head and seemed to look right back at him.

Apparently, Shanzer was a cat person as well as a pervert.

"Was he...telling the truth?" asked Brandy. "About what we can do?" She couldn't stop thinking about what he said about her past lovers. Ben Anshen, to whom she gave her virginity at the tender age of fifteen and immediately regretted. And Kevin Lefreys, who she dated for a few brief months at the beginning of her freshman year of college. She'd wondered more than once how she could be so addicted to sex with Albert when she never really liked sex back then. But if she could really see the truth in people, and the truth was that Ben and Kevin never really loved her...that they only wanted the one thing from her... Well, it sort of made perfect sense, didn't it?

"It sure *feels* true," he replied. "I mean, it sort of explains some things, doesn't it? Like why certain places in the temple felt strange, making me take a closer look..." He nodded at the oblong medallion hanging from the chain around her neck. "How I felt so sure we needed to go back for *that*."

She reached up and touched it. She remembered the scare it gave them all. Albert felt a strange need to climb up into a little recess in the temple and found a human skeleton wearing it around its neck. The sight startled him. He slipped and fell, busting his knee, reinjuring his broken arm and sending the rest of them into a panic thinking there was something alive up there.

It was so strange, back then, that he was so insistent on someone going back for it. Even when he told them that he'd figured out what the symbol meant, that it helped him understand who their real enemy was, it didn't really make sense.

And now the perverted shaman had told them that they were going to need it for something...

Was it really his psychic sense telling him that it was an object of great importance, something they'd need years later, something that would have been lost forever if Nicole hadn't gone back to retrieve it?

And what he said about *her* rang true, too. She *did* feel like she could trust him that night, that he wouldn't harm her, that he was a genuinely good person... The real reason she joined him that night... The reason they were married now... It was a little eerie to think about what she might've missed out on if she'd never done such a reckless thing.

"So what do we do now?" she asked, pushing the thought away.

Albert was looking up at the ceiling again. He wasn't sure, but he thought another chandelier had added itself while he was looking away. And there were a lot more flower beds than there were before. But he thought one of the newly added statues had disappeared. Or maybe it only moved... He couldn't quite remember how it looked before. "I guess we start figuring out this magic thing."

"Magic..." She tucked a stray strand of blonde hair behind her ear as her gaze swept across the room again. "I can't believe we're seriously talking about *magic* of all things. I mean, for real?"

"I know." He watched a tall, muscular man with an intimidatingly large penis walk past them. "This is *not* what I thought Hogwarts would be like."

Another of those strange shudders washed over them. When he looked around again, the building seemed smaller, but strangely backward...as if he were looking at it in a mirror.

Again, he felt as if something were off about it all. Something he could *almost* see, but not quite...

You just have to learn to focus that third eye, Shanzer had told him. *As soon as you can do that, you can see what's really there.*

Brandy sat watching the people in the fountain, her thoughts swirling inside her head like an approaching storm. Did she really possess such powers? Could she really see their inner truths? She fixed her attention on a thin woman with long blonde hair and lots of freckles on her cheeks and shoulders. She wasn't participating in the orgy. Instead, she was watching another couple next to her. There was an expression painted across her pretty face that was hard to read. A mix of keen interest and greedy envy, perhaps? But what was her *truth*? What did it mean? She couldn't tell anything about the woman beyond the fact that she clearly wasn't shy.

Feel the emotions that are all around you, she thought. *Let those emotions flow through your mind and body.* The pervert made it sound so simple, yet she still had no idea how to make it work. She continued to watch the people in the fountain for a moment, the expressions on their faces, the looks in their eyes as they gazed upon their partners…

(You have to face it. You have to embrace it. You have to feel it in order to use it.)

She closed her eyes for a moment…took a deep breath…let it out slowly. Then she stood up and turned to face her husband. "Fine."

He stared at her, confused. "What?"

"Just shut up," she told him as she took his face in her hands and kissed him.

Chapter 14

It was strange. The feel of his lips, the taste of his breath, the texture of his tongue...all so familiar, so comforting...and yet it was also so *alien*. It wasn't as though they'd never made out in public before. She often got a little handsy with him at parties and at the bars. Especially when she'd had a few drinks. But this was different. She could almost feel the lewd shaman's leering gaze washing over them. And everyone else at this perverted party, too. It made her uncomfortable. It made her self-conscious. She reached back and tugged at the hem of her dress again.

Albert pulled away from her. "Don't force yourself to do anything. He doesn't tell us what to do."

"I know," she assured him. Then she kissed him again. "But we both know he won't let us leave until we get whatever sick point he's trying to make."

She tried to clear everything out of her mind but him. There was no dirty shaman. There was no mansion. There was no party. There weren't strangers having group sex in a *very* unsanitary fountain not twenty feet away. There was only Albert. There was only her lover. There was only her *husband*.

This wasn't anything dirty. She *loved* him. She'd loved him since that night they first ventured down into that monstrous temple. She might have even loved him before then.

He was so cute that first day they paired up as lab partners. She could tell he was very smart. He knew the material. But he was visibly flustered throughout the entire lesson. He wasn't the first guy who acted like that around her, but somehow he was by far the most charming. He never tried to hit on her like all the other guys did, for starters. And there was just something so *endearing* about him. She was only in that class to fulfill a requirement. She was majoring in Psychology. But for some reason, he made her look forward to Chemistry more than any other class.

Nicole insisted that they never needed the temple to bring them together, that a love like theirs would have blossomed on its own in that classroom. But it broke her heart every time she thought too much about it. The very idea that maybe, in some other universe or some other timeline, she never went down that rabbit hole with him. He might never have worked up the nerve to ask her out. They might never have dated. And she never would've known this kind of happiness.

She pushed herself harder against him, kissing him deeper, probing his mouth with her tongue. She ran her fingers through his hair. She felt his hands slide around her, his warm palms against the skin of her exposed back. Her body was reacting like it always did, regardless of these twisted surroundings. That familiar heat inside her. The aching *longing*, as if they'd been kept apart for months, even though they'd barely spent a moment apart this entire past week.

Let those emotions flow through your mind and body.

She would've thought it impossible in such a setting, but Albert was everything to her. He was everything that was *comforting* to her. He was her happy place. He was her *home*. And being like this with him was utter bliss. It always had been.

Even that first time.

She lowered her hands from his head to his chest and closed her fists around the fabric of his shirt, clinging to him, holding onto him as she pressed even harder, kissed even deeper.

She opened her eyes and saw in her peripheral that the blonde woman in the fountain was watching them.

That didn't matter. That *couldn't* matter. They had no *time* for silly things like that to matter. The only thing that meant anything at all right now was Albert. She had to push everyone else away. She had to pretend they were alone.

She squeezed her eyes closed and kept kissing him.

Embrace the emotions. That was what Shanzer kept saying. If she understood him correctly, that meant she had to get into it. She needed those feelings. She needed to get good and turned on.

So why the hell didn't the old pervert just let them stay in that room? Why did he send them out the door and into this kinky party?

The first answer that came to her was simply that he was a creep. That he got off on the idea of humiliating them. But that couldn't be it. Albert would say that there had to be a real reason for it. She knew he would.

Shanzer also said that the last thing they'd want to do was *waste* that energy. That sounded like they were supposed to get heated up…but not actually go all the way? That almost made a sort of sense, she thought. She was familiar enough with sex to intimately know that breathless, exhausted sensation that came after. It really was as if they expended all that built-up energy in one blissful climax and were left completely spent.

(Sex magic isn't about sex. It's about the emotional energy associated *with sex.)*

Were they supposed to take that energy and do something *else* with it? Could they really do something like that? Could they take that great, heart-pounding energy and redirect it somehow?

If that was what the shaman wanted, then they needed more of that energy. She needed to be on the very brink of ecstasy.

She climbed up onto Albert's lap and slipped her feet over the wall of the flower bed he was sitting on, her naked thighs wrapped around his waist, her high heels digging into the mulch behind him. She was still clutching at the front of his shirt, yanking him closer as she slid onto his lap.

She was all too aware of how exposed she was with her legs open and no panties on and she struggled between feeling sexy and embarrassed.

Was her butt sticking out now? Again, she reached behind her and tugged at the dress again.

Stupid thing…

This wasn't enough. Her inhibitions were holding her back. She couldn't seem to fully ignore all those eyes she felt leering at her.

She pressed her flushed face against his shoulder and

sighed.

"Embrace it," the creep said… Like it was really that easy. How the hell was she supposed to do that in an environment like this?

"Just relax," said Albert. "It doesn't matter how many people are here. It doesn't matter what anyone else sees. It's just you and me. *Always.*"

She let out a huff of a laugh. She couldn't help it. He was always saying corny shit like that. Why the hell was it such a turn-on?

She kissed him again. He wasn't wrong. This *was* about them. She just had to focus on *him*.

She cast her thoughts back over the past few days they'd spent together. Their honeymoon… The beautiful resort in Wevenwert… So many breathless mornings and nights they'd spent together. Husband and wife at last. So many naughty little things they did…

That familiar heat was rising inside her again. She could feel her heart beating faster, her breathing quickening, her body opening up with quivering anticipation.

He was excited, too. She could feel him. That part of him was pressing against the front of his pants. She could feel him against that part of her as she thrust herself more firmly against him.

He was right. All those other people didn't matter. They were nothing. Let them watch if they wanted. Let them leer. She didn't care right now. All that mattered was the two of them.

Wife and husband.

A perfect pairing.

A perfect *fit*.

She reached down between her legs and touched him. She felt him gasp a little. For some reason, that always pleased her. She liked feeling like that…like she was in control.

Her body had begun moving on its own. Her hips were sliding back and forth, up and down, rubbing against that part of him.

His hands slid down her back, slipped under the dress and

squeezed her naked bottom, pulling her even closer in the process.

Another of those dizzying shudders swept through the building, but she barely noticed it. She was becoming entangled in these emotions.

God, she loved being with him like this. It wasn't just lust. It was a hungry feeling, too. A *greedy* feeling.

She felt his tongue inside her mouth and ensnared it, sucking on it, pulling it all the way into her, *capturing* him.

She unfastened his pants…reached inside…

The part of her that had been telling her she couldn't do this was fading into the background of her mind, slowly being buried beneath these urges. Of course she could do this. Who was going to stop them? What did she care if people saw them like this?

This was precisely why they were all here, wasn't it? This was why the pervert shaman lured them here. Because that was what happened. It wasn't by chance that she found that brochure in the hotel lobby. That was left there specifically for her. She knew it as sure as she knew the sound of her husband's voice.

Was it her psychic abilities that told her that? Or was it simple deductive reasoning?

She let go of his tongue and took a breath. She kept her eyes closed. She didn't want to see the people around them. She didn't want to see the hungry looks on their stranger faces. But she knew they were there.

Her dress was riding up again. Her butt was sticking all the way out. But she couldn't be bothered with that right now. She had her hands full. Literally.

She took that part of him out. She squeezed it. She stroked it. She rubbed it against that part of herself. Shivers of pleasure raced through her. She could feel her body responding with equal enthusiasm, begging for it, begging for *him*. She wanted him inside her again. She wanted it *so much*…

And he was so close…

But now wasn't the time for that.

This was what Shanzer was talking about. It wasn't about

sex. It was about *sexual energy*. It was about the *emotions* that drove this insatiable desire for sex. Giving in to those desires would *waste* that energy.

Now was the time, while her nerves were all alight with this intense, shivery sensation, her body enveloped in blissfully breathless anticipation.

She opened her eyes and turned her dreamy gaze toward the fountain. Her glasses were fogged up now, but she could see enough to tell that the blonde woman was still watching them. In fact, she was *enthralled* with them. She couldn't take her eyes off them. She wanted to see *more*...

(Truth...)

...but it wasn't the sex she was here for. Someone she cared about was in trouble. They were going through hard times. Depression. Anxiety. Fear. And so much alcohol... They were a danger to themselves. It was only a matter of time...

She was here for the shaman's magic. She was here to give them strength. Courage. *Hope.* The shaman showed her how to channel the energy into magic and send it on its way. She was feeding it to her loved one even now. All she needed was the raw emotion necessary to lift such a burden. And that young couple on the flower bed wall in front of her... They reminded her of better times. They brought memories flooding back. A better past, before all the troubles drowned away the happiness.

Brandy closed her eyes again and pressed her face against Albert's shoulder.

Was that real? Could she actually know such a thing? Was all this sexual energy really giving her such a power?

She looked the other way. A man was sitting alone in one of the partitioned rooms, watching everyone, enjoying the show. His gaze swept from one couple to the next, taking it all in. A voyeuristic paradise of so many people doing so many dirty things...

(Truth...)

...but he wasn't here for the show. He didn't have a partner because he already had one. His wife... The love of his life... His best friend... She was ill. Cancer. She needed healing magic.

He kept turning down invitations to join in the activity around him because he was true to her, but he needed the stimulation of the party to fuel the magic he hoped would heal her.

Brandy took a shuddering breath and looked away, unable to bear the heartbreaking emotion that she suddenly felt welling up inside her.

How could she know such a thing? It wasn't possible. This had to be some kind of trick. An illusion dreamed up by that wretched pervert.

A woman with long, brown curls and a black cat face mask strolled past, drawing her gaze. She had a sexy, confident sort of walk. One foot in front of the other, her tall heels clacking against the marble tiles, like a goddess strolling toward her throne...

(Truth...)

...but she was terrified. She could barely keep her body from trembling. She didn't belong in a place like this. But her business was barely staying afloat. She needed help luring in customers. The café was all she had. If it closed, she didn't know what she'd do, how she'd put food on the table for her daughter, how they'd *live*... But if she could give it just a little push... A little subliminal suggestion poured into the consciousness of the people of her hometown... An innocent little plea to come to her...to eat at Henrietta's...*please*...

No... This wasn't one of the pervert's dirty tricks. Somehow she was sure of it. These people desperately needed something. And this might be their last and only chance.

She looked around again. Not everyone here was like that. Some of them really were just sex addicts and lonely perverts and thrill-seeking swingers here for the party. These were the donors, she realized. The ones pouring their sexual energy into the room, more fuel to stoke those passionate fires. But most of the people here had a story. And she could suddenly *see* those stories.

The couple making love on the bench over there was desperately trying to have a baby. The man with the intimidating tattoos all up his back was a doctor who was running out of time to find a way to save a little girl's life. And the woman in stiletto heels and waist-long ponytail was urgently searching for her missing brother.

What was this? Why did she know these things?

"Is it working?" she asked in a breathless voice. "Is this what he was talking about? My psychic power to see the truth in people?"

But when she turned her gaze on Albert, he wasn't looking back at her. He was staring up at the ceiling above them.

"I see it…" he sighed.

She straightened her glasses and looked up, but there was only the ceiling and those same fancy chandeliers. "You see *what?*"

His eyes were wide with wonder. He seemed to be taking in something astounding. "*All of it,*" he replied. "I see *all of it.*"

Chapter 15

Where am I?

That was the question Albert focused on as he felt his body rising toward climax. *What's really there? What is this place?*

It felt almost *hydraulic*. Like when you squeezed a water balloon and all the water rushed to the other side. All that stimulation, all that sexual energy that was building toward blissful orgasm seemed to change direction somehow. It shifted to a different part of his consciousness. It became...*something else...*

A strange awareness blossomed somewhere inside him. There was something *significant* about the space around them. And when he opened his eyes, he saw that the shaman's manor wasn't what it seemed.

It was sort of like an optical illusion, not entirely different from those sidewalk art pieces he'd seen on the internet, the ones that looked like a realistic image of some deep and fantastic chasm when viewed from a specific angle. Except it took far more than simply moving around to break *this* illusion.

It was still a large house, still roughly the size and shape it was when they first arrived. But everything was weirdly twisted. The hallways leading off this room didn't go straight, as they appeared to do, but curved. He couldn't quite picture exactly how it was all laid out—trying to wrap his head around it made him feel almost queasy—but he understood somehow that all those corridors circled back to this main hall. That was why the lengths of the hallways kept changing.

And it was why time seemed to be mixed up. Now that he could see that the shaman's manor was laid out different than it appeared, he could remember things more clearly. The queer lapses in his memory weren't lapses at all. It was the building rearranging the *order* of his memories to account for the differences between the distances they'd walked and the time it took them to get from one place to another.

He looked up at the ever-changing chandeliers. That was an illusion, too. There was only one. It was the way the room presented itself to them that made him see more than that. Like cleverly arranged mirrors, it presented the illusion that the space was much larger than it actually was.

"What is it?" asked Brandy as she watched his gaze sweep across the ceiling and walls.

But he wasn't sure how to explain it. He could grasp it, but he wasn't sure how to point it out. She didn't have the same perception he did. That was why she didn't seem to notice the changes. She wasn't attuned to the space around her like he was. She was attuned to the *people* around her. She simply saw it the way it wanted her to see it. Without that same strange sense of *significance* that he felt, her mind simply didn't question the illusions it was presented.

But somewhere inside, *he* could feel that there was a difference between what was there and what he was seeing, breaking the illusion enough to confuse his brain. The shaman's magic struggled against his psychic sensitivity to his physical environment.

All these things made perfect sense to him now. It was almost as if he'd been wandering around in a sleep-deprived haze before and now he'd fully awakened. Everything seemed so much clearer.

Was that really the power of his psychic brain?

"Albert?" pressed Brandy. "You're kinda scaring me, babe."

He blinked and met her gaze, distracted. "Wha...? Oh... Sorry. I just..." He looked up at the room again. "I think I get it now."

"Get what?"

He realized she was still gripping him down there. It was such an odd sensation. He'd felt her touch countless times these past six years, but never like this. He glanced around at all the people watching them. They weren't even being sly about it.

They were just blatantly staring at them, as if they were performers on a stage.

Not that they were trying that hard to stay hidden. They were pressed close together when they started, sort of shielding each other from view, but they'd both become distracted. She'd leaned back a little. Most of them could see that he was standing at full attention down there. They could see the way her delicate hand was closed around him, gripping him. And *everyone* could see her bare bottom sticking out as she sat straddling his lap. The ridiculously short dress had ridden all the way up to her waist.

Was it weird that it wasn't an instant and complete turn-off? Not that it was a turn-*on* by any means. It didn't excite him in any way to realize that strangers were treating this intimate moment with his lovely young wife like a spectator's sport. Not even a little bit. This wasn't the start of some new and illicit fetish. But it also didn't hit him like a bucket of ice water. It simply *didn't matter*. They didn't come here to get freaky. They came here to complete the job the pervy shaman forced upon them. That was all. It felt like a visit to the doctor. They came. They took off their clothes. They let some people have a good look at them. And that was all there was to it.

He reached down and pulled her hand away. "The stairs…" he whispered.

She'd realized how much everyone could see, too. Her pretty face had flushed bright red. She reached behind her and tugged down the stupid dress. "Stairs…?" she muttered, distracted. "What?"

"How many staircases can you see?"

She slipped off his lap, still tugging at the dress, and looked back at it. "Just one…isn't there…?"

He fastened his pants and stood up. "No."

"Huh?"

"Come on."

There only appeared to be the one when they first entered this room. They descended from the second floor, seemingly traveling straight down. But there were *two* staircases. One on the left and one on the right, both of them curving slightly so that they ended at the same point in front of the statue of the absurdly hung Greek god and his starstruck angels. It was impossible to know which of the two they actually walked down when they first entered this party. And it didn't matter. What mattered was the *third* staircase. The one *between* the other two. The one leading *down*.

It was a little bit like a stereogram. Somehow their brains took the two staircases and overlapped them so that they looked like only one, essentially hiding the third one.

They walked past the blonde, freckled woman. She'd stepped out of the fountain and was sitting on the ledge there, watching them as they walked by, her knees spread casually, her hands propped beside her, completely exposed to them. Like Dolly back in the shaman's guest suite, she wasn't remotely shy.

She watched them as they walked away.

Brandy turned and looked back at her, holding her gaze for a moment longer. Then she faced forward again and squeezed his hand. "The pervert said I could see people's truths..." she whispered. "I feel like I understand why they came here."

"Truth, huh?" muttered Albert, thoughtful.

"They're not bad people," she decided. Then she caught sight of a rather sweaty, overweight man leering in the doorway of one of the partitioned rooms, watching two women make out while he pleasured himself. "Well...not *all* of them..."

"It's fuel," he deduced. "Sexual energy. Everyone's giving it off like crazy. Shanzer wanted us to tap into that energy and use it to more fully activate our psychic abilities."

"Not just us," she corrected. "Lots of people here are using it. It's like a community bread oven or something. Everyone brings a little wood and adds it to the fire, making it hotter than any one of them could make it on their own, letting them do so much more with it..."

He nodded. "That makes a certain amount of sense."

Again, she glanced back at the blonde woman, recalling what she felt from her back there, about the loved one she was trying to save.

Albert reached the top of the hidden stairwell. He wasn't

entirely sure what made him think of it, but he instinctively slipped his arm around Brandy's waist and gripped her hand as he took the first step down. "Careful."

She let out a startled gasp and grabbed onto him, almost falling. "*What the fuck?*"

"Sorry."

"Where did..." She looked back the way they came and frowned. "Was that the same room we were just in?"

"Don't think too hard about it. It'll just make your head hurt."

"Okay..." She faced forward again, not daring to let go of him for fear of tripping over the stupid heels. There was a wide hallway stretched out beyond the bottom of the stairs. Everything down there was the same garish red and gold as everywhere else in the shaman's house. And the walls were decorated with the same sort of pornographic artwork. "Is this what the pervert wanted us to find?"

"I sure hope so. I really don't want to go back up there and look for any *other* secret stairways."

She nodded. Her, too. "Where do you think this goes?"

"Hopefully somewhere a little more family friendly."

She tugged at her dress again. "Not *too* family friendly," she grumbled. "I'm pretty sure my cooch popping out of this stupid dress would get us kicked out of any self-respecting Chucky Cheese."

The hallway at the bottom of the steps was wide, but not very long. A pair of heavy wooden doors awaited them at the far end.

Was this the shaman's basement? God, he hoped they didn't end up locked inside an S&M dungeon next.

"Do you think that's the exit?" asked Brandy.

"I sure hope so." He hurried onward, quicker now that they were off the stairs and less likely to fall and hurt themselves. His mind was still racing. Looking back on it, he now realized that there were no *false* memories of that place, only *displaced* ones. All the things he recalled seeing were real (right down to the creepy man in nothing but a dog collar promising to be a "good doggy"). His mind had reorganized the order of things in an attempt to match the illusion and when his psychic mind glimpsed the discrepancies between perception and reality, it resembled two different chronologies.

It was kind of fascinating, really. A part of him was immensely curious about that place. That part of him almost wanted to go back and explore it more. But it was only a small part of him. The much larger part of him wanted nothing more to do with that place and its skeevy owner.

But any chance of finding a quick escape vanished before his eyes when he yanked open the door only to find the devil, himself, standing in their path.

Chapter 16

"What do *you* want?" snapped Albert. Lucas Kneede was not, after all, really the devil. He didn't fear for his mortal soul when he looked into those pale eyes. But he also wasn't really human. He couldn't be. Besides refusing to die after being burned alive, he was able to navigate the Wood with all its deadly terrors, apparently coming and going as he pleased, and he displayed extraordinary telekinetic powers.

Kneede's mouth was twisted into a pinched sort of smile that expressed no kindness or warmth of any kind. It seemed perfectly clear that the feeling remained mutual. "Remus Molsk."

Albert blinked, confused. "Huh?"

"His name," said Kneede. "I want you to know it."

"What are you talking about?" demanded Brandy. She sounded fearless enough, but she was clinging to Albert's arm so tightly he could feel her manicured nails digging into his flesh through the silky sleeves of his shirt.

"I suppose it wouldn't mean anything to you, would it?"

"Why would it mean anything to us?" challenged Albert. "We don't even know what you're talking about."

Kneede stood there, blocking the way forward, that tight smile unflinching. "I'm talking about what you took from me that night."

He shook his head, confused. "*What?*"

Then Brandy abruptly let go of his arm and turned to face the old man. "What are you playing at?" she growled. Something about the way she said these five simple words sent a horrid shiver through his entire body. It was her voice, but he knew immediately that nothing about those words belonged to her. It was as startling as if she'd suddenly started speaking a brand-new language.

The old man's smile spread a little wider, but also became even tighter. It was an odd thing to watch. A strange mix of smug pleasure and burning distain. "Warner," he sneered.

Albert took a cautious step forward and peered at Brandy's face. Her pretty blue eyes were gone. There was nothing behind those familiar glasses but an eerie darkness.

"Relax," said Kneede. "Warner doesn't hurt the people he possesses. They're rarely even aware of him."

He wasn't convinced. He wasn't willing to take the old man's word for it. He wasn't willing to take *anyone's* word for it, much less the self-appointed "Father of Lies." He wanted to grab Brandy's hand and tear her away from this black-eyed creature, to take her and run as far from here as possible, but he doubted that would work the way he wanted it to.

How *did* one go about exorcising something like Warner Harr? What was he? Some kind of demon? A dark spirit of some sort? He claimed to speak for the Keeper, but could he really be trusted? He wasn't even sure how much he trusted the Keeper. Had anyone they dealt with all those years ago been honest with them in the end?

"This will only take a moment," promised Warner. Again, the sound of those alien words spoken from Brandy's lips sent an awful shiver through him. It was the same way the waiter and the bartender spoke when *their* eyes went black like that. It was the same faint, unfamiliar accent. The same not-quite-right tone.

He didn't like this. Not at all.

"Yes," agreed Kneede. "Hardly any time at all. In fact, why bother? You can't reason with a filthy *parasite* who only repeats his Keeper's lies."

"Stay away from these two," growled Brandy.

Except it wasn't Brandy at all. It was her voice. It was her breath. It was her lips forming the words. But it wasn't her. That wasn't what she sounded like when she spoke. And that expression on her face was disturbingly unfamiliar, too. Everything about her was different. Even the way she was standing was all wrong. Her very personality had completely vanished. Because none of it was *her*. This wasn't Brandy at all. Everything that was her was *gone*. This was entirely *Warner*. It was as if everything beneath her skin had been erased. Something black and monstrous had taken her place. And something about that sent a sickly quaking sensation through his every nerve.

He wanted her back. There was a desperate sensation welling up inside him. A rapidly rising panic. He could feel his heart beating faster and faster as he stared into the empty abyss of those alien eyes.

She'd come back. He knew she would. Tanner came back. The waiter with the short hair and all those piercings. When Warner was done with him, those black eyes disappeared and the man inside returned, a little confused but perfectly fine. As did the attractive bartender. Neither of them stayed gone. Everything he'd seen about this "Warner Harr" suggested that Brandy was still in there somewhere, that she was perfectly safe, that she'd come back to him as if nothing ever happened. But he couldn't suppress the anxious need to see her pretty eyes again. Every second that she was gone was pure agony.

He wanted her back. He wanted her back *now*. But he didn't know how to get her back.

"Tell them the truth," growled Kneede. "All of it. None of the Keeper's self-righteous *rules*. None of his *games*."

Albert watched those obsidian eyes narrow between his wife's lids, not daring to look away, half-convinced that as soon as he did, this *thing* would snatch her away from him forever. But his ears remained wide open. A part of him continued to be very much aware of what these two monsters were saying. And these words stood out like a beacon in the dark. Truth? What truth? What was it with these two? He wanted to ask him what he meant by that, but he remained fixed on those black eyes. He didn't dare let down his guard. Not until his wife was back and whole and by his side again.

"I don't take orders from Tane's lapdogs," Warner growled.

Kneede remained unmoved. He stood his ground, still unflinching. "Tane has nothing to do with it. He's dead. You said so yourself."

"Then why are you here?"

"The same reason I've always had. I never needed Tane to tell me what the Keeper is. I saw it with my own eyes. I was there when the skies fell. As were *you*."

"What's going on?" demanded Albert, his eyes still locked with those empty black voids where Brandy's beautiful blue eyes should have been. "What are you talking about?"

"Armageddon," replied Kneede. "The End of Days. The inevitable hell on earth that awaits every world at the hands of the so-called 'Keeper of the Cycle.'"

"The end of the world..." murmured Albert. "Yeah... I remember you saying that. Back on that burning mountain. That's what you said would happen if we opened that door." Finally, he tore his eyes away from his bride and set his gaze on Kneede instead. "But we're all still here."

He expected the old man to glare at him, but instead he was surprised to watch his face melt into an expression of pained regret. "Not all of us..." he replied.

I lost a lot of friends that night, Albert recalled him saying as he sat slumped over his drink at the bar. *Their whole world was ripped apart... Everything... Every life... Every soul... All gone.* And then, only a moment ago: *Remus Molsk. His name. I want you to know it.*

"Everything has a price," said Warner. "The Oblivion Doorways are no exception."

Albert frowned. Oblivion Doorways?

(Do you think you can face oblivion?)

"A price?" growled Kneede, his expression darkening. "A *price*? An entire *world* wiped from existence is just a *price* to you?"

Albert stared at him, horrified. Something the Keeper said to him five years ago suddenly came rushing back to him: *By opening the door, you've brought about the end of an entire world, but perhaps the birth of another.* He'd thought that the strange little creature was speaking metaphorically, but by opening the door atop that mountain that night, did they actually destroy a world? Could they really be responsible for something like that?

I blamed you, of course, he recalled. *I mean, it* was *your fault.* You *opened that door.*

"All worlds die," replied Warner. "That is the unfortunate but inevitable flaw in every universe."

Albert stared into those oily eyes again. So it *was* true? An entire world...?

"Worlds die, yes," agreed Kneede. "But the Keeper doesn't leave those worlds to die in their own time, does he? He *murders* them."

"What would you do, then?" demanded Warner. "Take a page from your mentor's book? Force your selfish will into the workings of the cycle. Because you and I both know how well *that* worked out."

"I am not Janon Tane!" shouted Kneede.

"Are you sure?" Warner tipped Brandy's head to one side. The expression was probably supposed to look inquisitive, but it only ended up looking strangely *mad*. Like something straight out of a horror movie. The sight sent a jolt of terror straight through Albert's heart. "Because you sound just like him."

This was all so confusing. What was going on? They called him the Keeper of the Cycle. And the cycle was the mechanism by which humanity migrated to new worlds each time one died... Shouldn't that make him the good guy? But Warner wasn't denying what Kneede was accusing him of. He was only making excuses. Who was the good guy here? *Was* there a good guy?

"Remus Molsk..." pondered Albert.

"A very dear friend," said Kneede. "Gone now. Forever."

"A tragedy," agreed Warner. "But *there is no other way*. Following in Tane's footsteps will only lead to *more* tragedy."

"Tell them the truth," growled Kneede. There was something mad about him, too, Albert thought, watching the way his lips peeled back in a furious snarl as he spat the words at Warner. "Or *I* will."

Albert glanced back in time to watch as Kneede vanished. It was just like back then, when he appeared before them as little more than a charred corpse. He didn't walk away. He didn't even *fade* away. He just sort of... *blew away*... like ash in the wind...

He stared after him for a moment, then turned to face Warner again. "What truth?" he demanded.

But those empty black eyes were gone.

Brandy blinked back at him, confused. "What?" Her voice had returned to normal, as had her posture and her expression. All the familiar things were back as they belonged, as if she'd never left. "Where'd the old guy go?"

He stepped forward and embraced her, relieved.

"What's happening?" she asked, her wide eyes staring down the empty hallway. "Why do I feel like I nodded off for a second there?"

"Come on," he said, taking her by the arm. "Let's keep moving. I'll catch you up while we walk."

"Catch me...? What?" She looked back the way they came, more confused with each passing second. "Did I miss something?"

Chapter 17

"Ew..." groaned Brandy. "I can't believe that thing was *inside me...*"

Albert winced. "Please don't say it like that."

Everything had changed again. They were making their way down a concrete corridor. Gone was the garish red and gold of Shanzer's perverted mansion. The floors here were concrete. The walls were concrete and cinderblock painted in a dull, off-white shade. The ceiling was tiled and fitted with fluorescent lights. But there hadn't been any doors up until a moment ago, when they turned a corner. It was less a hallway than a tunnel, merely connecting the points at either end. But now it was starting to look like somewhere public. There were doors on either side. There were emergency lights, fire extinguishers, sprinklers and heating vents. There was even an exit sign up ahead. A way out at last.

"Oh, so *you* can gawk at the slutty bartender's tits, but god forbid I get fucking *possessed?*"

Albert scrunched up his face, confused. "*What?* How are those things even connected? And who was gawking? I wasn't gawking! *You* were gawking!"

"I was not!"

"Oh, so you weren't completely distracted by the *Brokeback Mountain* scene in the pervert's garden back there?"

"That was different."

"How's that different?"

"Because I don't care who you are, that was fucking *hot.*"

Albert frowned. "Double standard!"

"Wife's privilege."

"You're just making shit up now!"

The exit sign was pointing to a set of stairs. Wherever they were, it couldn't possibly be far now. They just needed to avoid any more run-ins with Shanzer's party guests…

"I don't get it," said Brandy, circling back to the confrontation she'd missed. "Are we supposed to open these doors or aren't we? Whose side are we supposed to be on?"

"I don't know. I don't get it, either."

"Who do we trust?"

It was a good question. On one hand, Lucas Kneede was prepared to kill them all five years ago. The Keeper, however, had managed to bring all six of them home.

But what did they really know about the Keeper?

By opening the door, you've brought about the end of an entire world…

Those words sent another shiver through him.

"We don't know anything about any of those people," decided Brandy. "Or *whatever* the fuck they really are." She clung to Albert's arm as she climbed the stairs in her heels, her free hand still tugging at the hem of the stupid, slutty dress. "For all we know the old drunk, the black-eyed freak and the pervert are all working together just to fuck with our heads. The fucking Keeper, too, probably."

"It's possible," he agreed. It might even be likely. Everything that happened five years ago… None of them were ever anything more than puppets. The Keeper, himself, called them his *tools*. They were just rats in a maze, trying their best to stay alive long enough to find a way out.

They reached the top of the stairs and pushed open the door that was waiting there.

"All I know for sure is that the next time I see that pervert, I'm shoving these stupid fucking heels…right…up…" She trailed off and frowned at the hallway stretched out before her, then turned and looked the other way. "Wait…"

"This looks *really* familiar…" said Albert, his eyes washing over the gray carpet and the blue walls, the room numbers printed on the doors. This wasn't the shaman's manor. This was a hotel. And not just any hotel…

A housekeeper stepped out of one of the rooms and set off down the hallway. They'd seen those brown uniforms dozens of times this past week.

Albert scratched at the back of his head, baffled. "Are we…?"

Brandy set off down the hallway, following the signs toward the hotel lobby, and Albert hurried after her. There were people coming and going, the sounds of voices and ringing phones and the ding of the arriving elevator.

"Maybe there's more than one," reasoned Albert. "Owned by the same people, so they all look the same?" But even as he suggested this, he recognized this hallway. Straight ahead was the first of the hotel's five luxurious pools. Guests were walking that way in their swimwear and flipflops. The two of them had been among those guests quite a few times these past few days.

And why *wouldn't* they be back where they started? If that hidden staircase in Shanzer's sex mansion could lead them to *any* hotel, why *not* the very one where this bizarre day started?

They stepped out into the busy lobby and looked around. There was a line of people checking in at the front desk. A phone was ringing. Rolling carts piled with luggage glided past them. There were children playing in the sitting area, running around the chairs, looking full of sugar and ready to start their vacation.

A middle-aged woman in a pair of oversized sunglasses gave Brandy's short dress a very disapproving look as she passed by on her way out the door. An old man in a Panama hat and a FedEx delivery man pushing a dolly piled high with packages, on the other hand, seemed to share a different opinion. Both of them took a double-take and then collided, sending both hat and parcels flying.

"The Lucianna Mysteria…" sighed Brandy, too distracted to notice the chaos she'd caused. It was their honeymoon resort. They'd spent the past five days here.

People were checking in, not out, meaning it was probably mid to late afternoon. He squinted at the brilliant sunlight pouring through the glass doors of the main entrance. The last time he looked out a window was back in Shanzer's mansion and it was pitch black outside. And the party started at the stroke of midnight. But that wasn't that long ago. Was it?

In his mind, however, he suddenly heard Warner speaking to him with the waiter's voice: "The kind of party where time, space and reality become distorted, transposed and intertwined."

(Sometimes they go on for days.)

He felt a shiver race through him at the memory.

So was it Friday afternoon now? Or might it already be the weekend? Just how long did the pervert keep them prisoner in that twisted place? He wished he still had his phone.

Brandy turned to face him. "What do we do now?" she asked. "The pervert took your car. We're stranded here." Those pretty eyes had grown wide at the realization of just how screwed they were. They had no ride. No money. No phones. No change of clothes. She suddenly felt very self-conscious standing here in this crowded lobby in this stupid dress. It felt like one of those nightmares where you found yourself locked out of the house in nothing but a bath towel.

He wished he had an answer for her, but he didn't know what to do. He glanced around, uncertain. Was this part of Shanzer's plan? To strand them here like this? Was this all some kind of joke to him?

No… That didn't make sense even in the context of all this weirdness. But it might be another of the pervert's "lessons" he was going on about back there.

He needed to stay calm. Think it through. It wasn't as if they were stranded in the wilderness. The front desk was right there. They could ask to use a phone. They could call Nicole. She was there five years ago. She knew about the temple and the Keeper and all that was possible in this big, strange world. They wouldn't even have to make up a story to explain how they ended up in this mess.

But as he turned to survey the crowd gathered at the front desk, wondering how long it would take to even get up there, he found his view blocked by a very rotund old woman in huge, rhinestone-studded sunglasses and a brilliant orange and green flower-print dress. Her long hair was woven into two thick, iron-colored braids that hung over her shoulders.

"*Here* you two are!" she exclaimed, as if she'd been looking everywhere for them.

"Um...hi?" said Albert, confused.

"I was wondering where you were going to pop up!"

"Do we know each other?" he asked. He was fairly sure he'd never seen this woman before in his life. He found himself squinting at those sunglasses, wondering if her eyes underneath might be empty and black. She didn't *sound* anything like Warner Harr, but that didn't necessarily mean anything. He knew virtually nothing about the creature. Perhaps this was another of his kind. There was no telling how many of them might be lurking out there. And each one might talk and act differently for all he knew.

But Brandy recognized her. "You were at our wedding," she realized. She was wearing a bright yellow dress that day, and that huge, floppy hat, but the sunglasses were exactly the same. It was the woman who appeared from the crowd and began gushing over how lovely she looked.

(God, but that felt like so long ago!)

"She was there?" asked Albert, still confused.

"I was, indeed!" the old woman giggled. "I hope you'll forgive me for crashing your beautiful party. I just can't seem to behave myself whenever there's a wedding!"

Albert still wasn't sure what this woman wanted from them, but she was considerably more pleasant than anyone else they'd met since they checked out of this hotel. It was rather refreshing, even, in comparison. But he couldn't help wondering how long it would take for this to turn into some new and equally unpleasant nightmare.

"You and him both..." recalled Brandy. "That perverted old man... You were *both* at our wedding reception."

The woman's bright smile shriveled for a moment, as if she'd suddenly tasted something foul. "Yes... Well, I assure you I don't make a habit of keeping *his* sort of company."

"Both of them...?" wondered Albert.

"In all truth, dear," said the woman, "there were *quite a few* uninvited guests lurking about that day."

"What?" gasped Brandy. "Who? *Why?*"

The old woman gave her a very girlish sort of giggle. "No-body you have to worry over, I promise you."

She stared at the woman, frowning. Something about the way she said that somehow struck her as meaningful. Or maybe it wasn't the way she said it so much as…something else? Some feeling that this person was here to protect them… Was that her psychic ability again? Or only her imagination? She didn't know how to tell the difference.

"Who are you?" asked Albert. He didn't really want to be rude to this woman. She seemed nice. But also, if she knew Lyle Shanzer then she wasn't just any ordinary woman. She was a part of whatever was happening to them.

"Oh, of course!" she exclaimed. "I never properly intro-duced myself, did I?" She pressed one pudgy, hand against her heart and laughed. She had rings on every finger and lots of bracelets that dangled and jangled from her wrists with every flourish of her arms (which was a lot). He couldn't help being reminded of Andrea. She was fond of wearing lots of jewelry, too. She was always joking about how much she liked shiny things. And she had the same kind of energy, too. "I've been watching over you both for so long, I forget sometimes that *I'm* still a stranger to *you*!"

"Watching over us?" asked Brandy. She recalled this woman saying something like that at the reception, now that she was thinking about it.

(*I still can't believe how much the two of you have grown up!*)

She remembered thinking that the silly old woman had simply confused her with someone Albert grew up with… She'd even felt a brief spark of jealousy at the idea that there may have been some other girl in his life once. Someone he'd never told her about for some reason, no less!

"My apologies again!" giggled the woman. "I'm Lucianna Estrane."

"Wait…" said Brandy. "Like…the Lucianna of *this hotel?*"

"The very same! The Lucianna Mysteria is *my* hotel. I own it." She reached up and pulled down her sunglasses, revealing not the empty blackness Albert had suspected, but perfectly human eyes that were deep and dark and surprisingly lovely. They seemed to shine with the energy of a young girl in spite of the wrinkles that surrounded them. "And I've been waiting a *very* long time to meet the two of you."

Albert and Brandy exchanged a concerned look.

"Oh, don't be like that!" laughed Lucianna, pushing her glasses back up again. "I'm here to help!"

"The Keeper sent you?" asked Albert, his voice hushed. He couldn't help it. He glanced around at the people walking by, many of whom were eyeing the three of them with obvious curiosity. And he could hardly blame them. They must have been quite the sight standing here, all of them dressed so out of place in this crowd.

She crinkled her nose at this, as if considering the question very carefully. "Perhaps he did," she replied. Then she laughed, "I certainly wouldn't put it past the old fossil!" She grasped the gray braids hanging over her shoulders and twiddled with them, still smiling that strangely joyful smile. "But the short answer is no. I don't take orders from *him*. This is *my* hotel. And it has been for a *very* long time."

Something about the way she kept saying that gave him a strange sort of shiver. Just how long did she mean? How old was she? *Who* was she?

Brandy stared at the woman, her thoughts racing. *Good luck on your new adventure, dear*, she recalled this woman telling her. *And whatever may get thrown at you, always remember that the two of you together can accomplish* anything. She wasn't talking about their new life as husband and wife. She literally meant *this adventure*. This *mess* they were in now. Starting with that sleazy museum. She knew it was going to happen. She knew they'd end up here in this place, at this very time. And she couldn't help feeling irritated by this realization. "What do you want from us?" she demanded, determined to get to the point.

"Yeah," said Albert. "Why are we here?"

He expected her to be evasive. But instead, she told them quite bluntly, "You're here to seek out and open the second doorway."

Brandy groaned. *"That* fucking thing again?" Just as the pervert shaman told them they'd be forced to do?

The Oblivion Doorways, thought Albert. Warner mentioned them. What did it mean? What was Oblivion? He and Kneede both made it sound like a real place, rather than a mere expression. Was that another name for the Wood? That huge, zombie-infested forest that was supposed to surround every living world?

"The road that will take you there is waiting for you here in this very hotel," explained Lucianna. "All you have to do is find it."

"Find it," repeated Albert. "And we're supposed to believe it's that easy?"

"No. It definitely won't be easy," she replied. "Mysteria isn't just a name I gave to this hotel on a whim." She leaned forward a little, her cheerful smile spreading ever-wider. "There's so much more here than what people see. You'll find that there are things just beneath the surface of these many walls that are *quite mysterious.*"

"What kinds of things?" pressed Albert. He glanced around at all the people. Should they really be talking about this stuff out in the open like this? They were still drawing curious looks from everyone.

Lucianna smiled a playful sort of smile. Then she turned and looked toward the main hallway.

Albert and Brandy followed her gaze. There was a couple approaching the elevator. They'd been to the pool and were on their way back up to their room, their hair still wet. Albert recognized the clothes they were wearing. The man's swim trunks and tee shirt...the woman's wrap and bikini top...even their flipflops... And not just the clothes. He'd know that woman anywhere. Her shape. Her posture. The color of her hair. The way she was hanging on the man's arm.

A feeling of such surreal surprise washed over him that he actually felt weak in his knees for a moment.

"Albert…" squeaked Brandy, her pretty eyes wide with shock as she stared at the lovers standing with their backs to them. "That's *us*!"

Chapter 18

"This hotel is not what it appears to be," explained Lucianna as she watched the other Albert and Brandy from across the lobby floor. "It sits on a crossroads, a nexus of sorts, where multiple points in the spectrum intersect, where it becomes possible to travel places that would otherwise be unreachable. These walls are designed to control what moves through those conduits."

"Am I supposed to understand any of that?" wondered Albert. He couldn't quite follow what she was saying. He was still staring at his own back, his mind still reeling from the shock of seeing himself from such an impossible angle. He couldn't wrap his head around *that*, much less crossroads, spectrums and conduits.

Brandy was staring at herself, too. "I remember that…" she breathed. Albert had poked fun at her for packing so many clothes, asking her if she ever intended to leave once they were checked in. Swimwear was no different. She brought enough to visit the pools twice a day throughout their stay and never wear the same suit twice. Among them were several brand-new bikinis that she'd never worn before. That other her was wearing the black and pink top that she'd only worn once. "That was our first full day here… That was *Monday*…"

"A little past four in the afternoon, to be exact," confirmed Lucianna.

"This is last Monday?" stammered Albert.

"Well, for most everyone in this hotel, it's only *this* Monday," she explained. "But for some of us, it might be any number of Mondays, and maybe not for the first or even second time."

He wasn't even sure how to process that.

"It's confusing, I know," sighed Lucianna. Then she giggled

again. "To be perfectly honest, I really don't understand it myself!"

Brandy watched that other her press close to that other Albert, nuzzling the sleeve of his damp tee shirt. She remembered that day clearly. She was hoping to get the elevator car to themselves so she could tease him a little on their way up to the fourth floor, but there was another couple going up to the second floor and an overweight middle-aged man who rode all the way up with them. In fact, she could see the other couple now, standing to one side, out of the way of the passing foot traffic.

"A lot of strange things are possible in Mysteria," said Lucianna. "Even *time* loops back on itself through some of the peculiar passageways hidden on these floors."

"That's…" began Albert, but he didn't know how to finish that sentence. It was *what*? Preposterous? Impossible? *Inconceivable*? Did any of those words even have any meaning left after all he'd witnessed inside and beyond the Temple of the Blind? But was she really standing here telling them they'd traveled *back in time*?

He recalled that time had behaved strangely there, too. Their watches were off when they returned. And he remembered feeling as if he'd been gone much longer than the amount of time that had passed. But the slowing down of time was one thing. Scientists theorized that black holes were said to distort time, making it slow to a crawl as one approached their event horizons. But to go *backward*? To be able to stand here and stare at his own back?

Brandy watched as the overweight middle-aged man who was also going up to the fourth floor appeared. He was wearing the same colorful swim trunks and baggy, sleeveless shirt. His thinning hair slicked back in the same unflattering style. If she wasn't looking at him again now, she wasn't sure she would have remembered exactly what he looked like. It wasn't like she took a very close look at the time. But it was the same man. Every detail was there. It was like watching a home video she didn't know someone was recording.

And did he just blatantly rock back on his heels and check

out her ass? What was with all the perverts today?

Albert didn't notice the man. He was staring at that other him, distracted, trying to remember that day. That *moment*. Standing there waiting for that very elevator, probably feeling impatient about how long it was taking. He remembered feeling impatient *every* time they went to use it and it didn't open up right away. Especially when they were going up. Because if they were going up, they were going back to their room. And every time they went back to their room... Well, it *was* their honeymoon, after all.

He *could* remember that moment, he realized. Once his spinning thoughts calmed a little. It wasn't so long ago. She was so *playful* all during their stay. That particular time, she was kind of handsy with him on their way up, in spite of the other three people in the car.

Back then...in that very moment...*this* very moment... If he'd only happened to turn and look behind him, back across that busy lobby, would he really have seen another him and Brandy staring back at him?

The very thought sent another of those surreal feelings washing over him.

The elevator doors slid open and several guests stepped out. Brandy watched as the *other* Albert and Brandy stepped inside. They were going up to their room. They were going to take a shower together. Wash off the chlorine from the pool. And while they were in there, they'd... Well, they'd do *honeymoon* stuff, of course...

Was it weird how much she envied herself right now?

"Come!" exclaimed Lucianna as the elevator doors slid closed between then and now. "Let's go to my office and talk things over properly."

She didn't wait for them to agree or refuse. She twirled around, her great, flowing dress billowing outward and trailing after her.

Albert and Brandy, still shaken from what they'd just witnessed, followed her.

Lucianna's office was located just behind the front desk, accessible through a short corridor located to one side. It was a surprisingly large room. It almost looked like the sort of executive office you might find the villain of the movie sitting in while grinning maniacally over his evil scheme, complete with a great big, meticulously tidy desk and floor-to-ceiling bookshelves on the back wall. But there were paintings of wildflowers hanging up and potted ferns in front of the windows and a little table to one side that appeared to be set for a quaint English tea. Half a dozen chairs were arranged around the room, all of them the sort of overstuffed armchairs Albert remembered being in both his grandmothers' living rooms, complete with colorful throw pillows and hand-knitted blankets draped over their backs. Curled up on the plump cushion of one of them was a small gray cat that didn't seem bothered in the slightest by their presence.

"Have a seat," invited Lucianna, gesturing at the two chairs already pulled up in front of the desk. "Make yourselves comfortable." She floated around and sank into her own chair, that cheerful smile never faltering.

"You seemed to be expecting us," recalled Albert as he seated himself on the edge of the chair cushion. He was leaning forward, curious. "How did you know when we'd arrive? Especially if time is really what you say it is here."

Lucianna smiled. It was a surprisingly girlish smile. Bright and energetic. "Being here to meet you is my job. I wouldn't be very good at it if I didn't know when you'd be arriving, would I?"

He stared at her, unsure how to respond to that. It wasn't really an answer to his question. It didn't explain anything.

"It's your job…" pondered Brandy. She sat back in her chair, but stiffly, ready to spring back up if something unexpected happened. "But the Keeper didn't give it to you," she added, remembering how she'd already said that the Keeper didn't send her here, that she didn't answer to him.

"He did not," she replied, still smiling. "The Keeper gave this job to *someone else*. But he wasn't very good at it. He disappeared a long time ago and left the channels unguarded. It was causing quite a lot of trouble when I found it. So I took over."

Albert frowned. "Took over?"

"That's right. I had this hotel built on top of it. It acts as a pressure cap of sorts. Or maybe 'gatehouse' is a better description. It controls what passes through the nexus that was left unprotected when my predecessor vanished." She frowned thoughtfully for a moment, then threw her hands up and laughed. "Truthfully, though, I didn't have much to do with that part. A friend arranged all that for me. But I was the one who *found* the nexus. I was the one who cleaned up the Keeper's mess. And I'm the one who's been protecting it all this time."

Again, he found himself wondering just *how much* time she was talking about. Why did he get this feeling deep in his bones that she was talking about much longer than any ordinary old woman should've been running any hotel?

"I don't work for the Keeper, but we both share the goal of protecting the cycle. I don't know what he intended to do about my predecessor's disappearance. I might have stepped on his toes by taking it upon myself like I did, but I couldn't leave the nexus open. Things had been getting out. People were getting hurt. And as I said before, very little happens under his watch that he hasn't foreseen, so I suspect that he always knew I'd come along, the clever little goblin. And that's pretty much the history of it." She flashed them a huge, girlish grin. "Now here we are!"

"Easy-peasy," he scoffed. She spoke about it as if it were nothing. Like she just happened to stumble across an empty roadside stand and decided to open a business on a whim. And there was nothing easy about these concepts. Dimensional crossroads? Time-distortions? Were they in an episode of *Dr. Who* now?

And just who was this woman? If she knew about the Keeper and Shanzer, she couldn't just be some random woman. Was she like the Sentinel Queen? Or Warner Harr and Lucas Kneede? Was she even human?

"Why *us?*" blurted Brandy. "Haven't we been through enough already? Why can't someone else open the next fucking door and let us get on with our lives?"

Albert reached over and squeezed her hand.

She looked back at him, a fine shimmer of tears welling up in those pretty blue eyes. "I mean, come on! We're finally married and we immediately have to deal with *this* shit?"

She wasn't wrong. Ambushing them on their honeymoon, even at the very end of it, just seemed like a rotten deal. It wasn't very fair. And somehow, after five years of nothing, it seemed downright *intentional.*

Lucianna's smile was gone, replaced with a gentle expression of sympathy that Albert, for one, wasn't sure he entirely believed. This woman—or whatever she might really be—*acted* very kind and understanding, but they still knew nothing about her. They knew so very little about so very much. How could they be expected to know who to trust?

And it wasn't as if they were being given any kind of choice in all of this. She wasn't asking them for their help. She was telling them what they were here to do.

"No one truly knows the mind of the Keeper," she explained. "His designs are beyond comprehension, even among those who can understand the secret workings of the universe. And his will is inescapable. If he intends something, it will be done. If he decides that someone's death is necessary to ensure the survival of the cycle, then they *will* die. I won't pretend like it isn't a terrifying concept. Placing trust in a being with so much power requires incredible courage and faith." She leaned forward and peered over her glasses with those dark, youthful eyes again. "But I can promise you that it is *well-founded* courage and faith. Whatever else the Keeper may be, the truth is that he's kept us alive far longer than even *gods* can remember."

Albert stared back at her. Gods? Did she really just say "gods"? That was a thing, too?

"I don't care!" snapped Brandy. She didn't want to hear about gods or the cycle or the Keeper's stupid plans. "Make someone *else* do it!"

"But it's possible that no one but you *can* do it. Have you thought of that?"

"Right," she scoffed. "Billions of people in the world and *we're* the only ones who can open a fucking door?"

Again, Lucianna flashed them that girlish smile. "Well, you *are* quite unique, after all. Two people with so much potential, so perfectly aligned, not just physically and emotionally, but *psychically. Spiritually.*"

"I don't know what you're talking about," she groaned.

"No. I suppose you wouldn't. But I'd wager that you can *feel* it. Somewhere deep down inside. You *both* do. Each time you look into each other's eyes." She was still peering over the top of her sunglasses. Those dark eyes slid back and forth between them as she spoke, a strange dreaminess in her expression. "That feeling like there's no one else in the world? That you were always meant to be together? A truly *perfect fit.*"

Brandy reached under her glasses and wiped at her eyes, frustrated. A perfect fit… She remembered thinking something very much like that back at that party, when she was trying to convince herself that it didn't matter if all those creepy party goers were staring at them. But still… "That's great. Real fucking romantic, yeah. But what does it have to do with the Keeper and his fucking doors?"

"Shanzer…" sighed Albert.

Lucianna leaned back in her chair, her smile spreading ever wider. "Exactly."

Brandy frowned. "You mean that gross sex magic stuff?"

"He said we were extremely proficient with sexual energy, or something, remember? That we feed off each other?"

"He's not wrong," said Lucianna, grimacing a little as if it pained her to say so. "But that unpleasant man makes absolutely *everything* about sex. It doesn't have to be about sex. Sexual energy is only part of the complex emotions that bind the two of you together." She took a breath, as if resetting herself, and then smiled again. "He is right about one thing, though. Sexual emotions might be the *fastest* way for the two of you to grasp the true extent of your powers. It might be the *easiest.* But it doesn't define you. It doesn't make you like *him.* You love each other dearly and completely. *That* is the true source of your strength. That's where your bond starts and where it is strongest. And that's what will carry you through this trial and keep you together forever."

Brandy looked over at him, distracted. That sounded so much more romantic than anything the perverted shaman said to them back there.

"That being said, though," added Lucianna, "your sexual energy output is, to be quite honest, simply *astounding*."

"Oh!" gasped Brandy, embarrassed. She really hoped this woman hadn't been spying on them, too. Did every mysterious stranger in the whole *universe* have a live feed directly into their bedroom?

"The reason you two are here right now," she explained, "is to find the entrance to the road hidden deep within the Lucianna Mysteria. But the passages leading there are barred by certain... *locks*."

"Locks?" said Albert. He glanced at Brandy again. *Magic can open doors that can't be unlocked*, he thought.

Brandy was thinking the same thing. "Let me guess," she groaned. "The kind of locks that require *sexual energy* to open."

Lucianna's smile was sympathetic this time. "You'll likely have to use what Shanzer taught you in some way, yes."

Brandy whimpered at the thought of having to relive what they went through back in that disgusting party. Hadn't they been humiliated enough?

"The world is different than it used to be," sighed Lucianna. "Sex is much more taboo than it once was. But sexual desire is no less *legitimate* than any other emotion. And remember that it's the *emotion* that is the key, not the act, itself."

Shanzer said that, too. *Most of the time, there's no actual sex involved at all*, Albert recalled. And that *was* how it happened at the party. They allowed themselves to feel the emotion, but they didn't actually have sex. He remembered feeling as if all that pent-up energy suddenly went somewhere else...and then he was finally able to see that place for what it was.

"And when it comes down to it..." Lucianna shrugged her shoulders and grinned. An adorably youthful gesture, Brandy thought. "Don't forget, this hotel *is* one of the region's top honeymoon destinations."

Albert nodded, his eyes widening a little as those puzzle

pieces clicked into place inside his head. "Not entirely unlike Shanzer's party. This is a place where sexual energy is already present."

"Exactly, dear. And I doubt it was any coincidence that this is happening immediately after your own honeymoon. I suspect the two of you are positively *bursting* with sexual energy at this point."

"That…sort of makes sense," he realized.

"I still don't like it," grumbled Brandy, pouting.

"So… What?" pressed Albert. "What're we supposed to do? Just go poking around the hotel until we find one of these locks?"

She shrugged. "More or less, I suppose. To be perfectly honest, I have no idea where they're hidden."

"You don't know—?" He stared at her for a moment, confused. "But you just said you *built* this place."

"I *commissioned* it to be built," she corrected him. "I told you, I left all the boring technical details to my friend. *He* was the genius behind the secrets of Mysteria. I honestly don't understand how it works at all."

He and Brandy exchanged a concerned look.

"All that's known about the methods he used was lost the day he died," she sighed. "He believed it was better that way." Those youthful eyes drifted upward, her gaze sliding thoughtfully across the surrounding walls and ceiling. "It's more than just a building," she said, lowering her voice as if it might be listening in. "It changes sometimes. Certain rooms have a strange habit of moving around. People occasionally complain of unsettling dreams about being lost in hallways that don't exist. And sometimes when the wind blows through the forest outside the westernmost rooms, it sounds like moaning voices." Her wondrous gaze shifted from the ceiling to Brandy, then to Albert. "It's *alive*," she whispered dramatically. "And it's been waiting for the two of you since this universe was new. Down there somewhere is a seal that only you two can open."

"With our *sexual energy*?" asked Albert. He couldn't help wrinkling his nose a little at the thought. It still sounded like a feeble plot device for a bad porno.

She actually giggled a little. "No, dear. With the key you brought with you."

"What key?" asked Brandy.

Lucianna pointed at her. "The one hanging around your neck, of course."

She looked down at the medallion hanging in the plunging neckline of the shaman's slutty dress.

"That's a key?" asked Albert.

"Not just any key," she informed him. "Yggdrasil's seed… One of the Three Whispers. The key to unlocking the path that lies hidden deep inside Mysteria."

Chapter 19

Lucianna opened one of the desk drawers in front of her and pulled out a black plastic card. "This is a master keycard," she explained, holding it out for Albert to take. "It'll open any door in this hotel."

Albert took the card and stared at it. It was the same size as the keycards they'd been carrying around all week, but was completely blank. It didn't even have the name of the hotel printed on it. "You can just give us something like this?"

Brandy was thinking the same question. She certainly wouldn't have liked the thought of such a card floating around out there every night when they were fast asleep in their room. But it wasn't as if she didn't know that such cards existed, if she'd only stopped to think about it. Of course the hotel had access to all the rooms. It only made sense. The housekeepers and maintenance let themselves into people's rooms every day. It was the idea of watching this woman hand such a card over like it was nothing to someone who didn't even work here that felt wrong.

"I know I can trust you both," Lucianna assured him. "You're free to use it any way you feel necessary. The security staff has already been informed that you have business here, so you won't be bothered."

He nodded and closed his hand around the keycard. "Okay, I guess."

"You'll do fine," she insisted. "It's not like you haven't done this sort of thing before, after all."

"Don't remind me," grumbled Brandy. She was holding the medallion up, still staring at it, remembering the night Nicole retrieved it for them from the one-armed skeleton. She still had nightmares about being lost in the endless black labyrinths of the Temple of the Blind. She *really* didn't want to go through that again.

"So we literally just…wander around the hotel?" asked Albert. He didn't want to do this. He didn't want to drag Brandy into another nightmare like five years ago. But what choice did they have? According to the pervert, they didn't have the luxury of simply refusing. Trying to walk away would only delay the inevitable and possibly make it all that much worse.

"Pretty much!" Lucianna replied, shrugging her shoulders and giggling again. She seemed to be enjoying herself.

"I mean, what are we even looking for? How will we know if we find it?"

"No idea!"

He stared at her, bemused. "If *you* don't know, how the hell are *we* supposed to figure it out?"

"Don't underestimate yourselves. You have everything you need. I know you do. Just think of it as a…" She made a flourishing gesture with one hand as she tried to think of an appropriate description, her bracelets jangling with the motion. "A *puzzle box* of sorts, you might say."

This caught Albert's attention. A puzzle? He sat up straight in his seat at the mere mention of the word. His love of puzzles was how he got himself into that temple mess in the first place. The wooden box with all those mysterious clues carved into the side… A complex map to something *amazing*.

But in his peripheral vision, he saw Brandy turn and glare at him and he forced himself to relax again. She knew him all too well, after all. It was because of that love of puzzles and mysteries that they were both nearly *killed* down in that dark labyrinth. More than once. But then again, it was that same love of puzzles and that same place that brought them together in the first place. And he wouldn't give *that* up for anything.

"It's a special kind of enigma," Lucianna went on, "designed to turn back anyone who isn't deserving of finding its answer. In fact, I'd wager it was likely built specifically for the *two of you*. The Faceless Ones were known for that sort of thing."

"Faceless Ones?" asked Albert. He sat up again at this, surprised.

"The architects responsible for the gateways like the one we're sitting on right now," she explained. "A race of mysterious, faceless giants that were said to have possessed sacred knowledge of all future worlds and who once acted as the Keeper's personal engineers."

"You mean the sentinels?" asked Brandy. "Like all those statues back in the temple?"

"Call them whatever you like. No one knows much about them, where they came from, where they went. It's believed that they all died out around the time of the last cycle, but no one knows for certain." She spread her hands in front of her, those bracelets jangling again. "*I* certainly don't!"

Albert stared back at her, intrigued. The sentinels were just one of many mysteries that had captivated him since he first set foot inside that enigmatic temple. He'd originally assumed that they were only stone representations of some deity or a personification of guardian spirits or perhaps even simply some kind of metaphor. But then he met a real one. Or, more accurately, a half-breed. The Sentinel Queen was a living, breathing female sentinel with the same sort of strangely elongated body as those statues, with a face that was *almost* the same smooth, featureless plane, but with just a tiny slit of a mouth and a subtle bump of a nose. She claimed that her mother was one of fourteen pregnant human women who migrated to this world through the temple when it was still new, and that her father was a real, full-blooded sentinel.

This really was about that, then? The Temple of the Blind? There was so much about that place that he still didn't understand, so much that still sometimes haunted his dreams even after all this time. A subtle tingle was slowly creeping up his spine. How many nights had he lain awake in bed with Brandy snuggled peacefully against his chest, wondering what other mysterious things might still be out there?

And now he was here…

"You're making it sound like we've totally got this," said

Brandy, "but you already said it wouldn't be easy."

"I did say that," she admitted, her smile never faltering.

"What's the catch?"

"There's always danger in the unknown," she replied. "And there is *much* unknown about Mysteria."

"Yeah," said Brandy. "It sort of sounds like you don't know shit."

This, too, made her giggle. "Because I don't!" she exclaimed, sounding positively delighted to be so utterly unhelpful. "I can't tell you how deep the crossroads go. I can't tell you what may or may not be living down there. I can't tell you what nightmare realms the crossroads open onto. I can't promise you won't get lost in the splintered flow of time that courses through it." Her smile had withered away while she said this, but now she paused and a deep frown creased her gentle features, making her look even older. "And most disturbing of all... My predecessor... Chosen by the Keeper, himself, to guard these crossroads... I still don't know what became of him. How or why... What it could mean..." She reached up and lowered her glasses again. Those dark eyes regarded each of them closely in turn. "Something's not quite right in Mysteria. You'll have to be on your toes. There are forces at work that oppose the Keeper. And places like these aren't unknown to them. There are things watching. I control this hotel, but not the other entry points within the crossroads. You'll need to beware."

"Well I know *I'm* fucking excited to get started," groaned Brandy.

Lucianna giggled. In an instant her serious expression was gone. "That's the spirit!" she jested. Then she stood up and spread her arms, her bracelets jangling as she did so. "Now off you go! I wish you only the very best of luck!"

Neither of them stood up. They sat there, looking up at her, uncertain.

"That's it?" asked Brandy. "You really think we can just...walk out there and do all that?"

"Of course I do. The Keeper personally chose you."

"You said the Keeper personally chose your predecessor,

too," she reminded her.

"Oh yes. That's a good point." She lowered her arms, still smiling. "But I'm still quite sure you'll do just fine."

"Fucking…?" Brandy looked over at Albert, pleading. "*Seriously?*"

He stood up and met the old woman's gaze. "What about Lucas Kneede?" he asked.

Lucianna frowned at this. "Lucas…? Is he poking around again?"

"Uh…*yeah*," replied Brandy. She sprang to her feet as well. "And some weird, black-eyed demon-looking thing that kept *possessing people!*"

"Warner Harr is entirely loyal to the Keeper," she assured her. "He's an ally. You can trust him. But Lucas…" She reached up and twiddled the ends of her iron-colored braids. More to herself than to them, she said, "I thought he might stay away now that Tane is gone… I wonder what he intends to do."

"Who *is* Tane?" asked Albert. "They both mentioned that name. Something about him being Kneede's boss or something?"

"Something like that," she replied. "Janon Tane wasn't a man at all. He was one of twelve siblings, all of them incarnations of an immensely powerful manifestation of a very ancient and very *unnatural* consciousness. They spread their influences throughout the world in various ways, maintaining an unbreakable grip to prevent the worlds of the natural and the supernatural from pushing them out of the equation."

Albert recalled Shanzer mentioning those three things as well… The natural, the supernatural and the unnatural… He still didn't fully understand it. It sounded like some D&D-themed twist on rock-paper-scissors.

"Tane's role was specifically to maintain balance between those three powers in the carrying out of the cycle, itself. But he became disillusioned with the process. He claimed that the Keeper's methods were too brutal and fought for a better way, but his influence only resulted in the near annihilation of mankind. Lucas Kneede was sympathetic to Tane's cause. If he's still out there, it could be problematic."

"He demanded Warner to tell us the truth," Albert recalled. "If Warner wouldn't, then Kneede *would*. That's what he said."

Lucianna smiled again. "Is that so? Intriguing…"

He and Brandy exchanged another glance.

"Well, I'm sure it'll work itself out," she insisted. "Hurry off now."

The two of them hesitated again. Was that really all they were going to get?

"You have everything you need," she assured them. "Just be sure not to let your past selves catch sight of you. We wouldn't want any time paradoxes complicating things."

"Is that a thing, too?" asked Albert. Then he shook his head. "Right. Of course it is. Why wouldn't it be a thing?"

For some reason, this made Lucianna giggle, too.

Albert turned and walked back to the door, his thoughts churning with all the new information he was processing.

But Brandy hesitated a bit longer. There was still something on her mind. "That pervert shaman…" she said, her gaze fixed blankly on the desk in front of her.

Again, Lucianna grimaced. "Oh, don't bother about him anymore. He knows he's been banned from this hotel."

Albert started to ask what he did to get himself banned, but decided maybe he didn't want to know.

"That's good," replied Brandy. "But…" She looked up at her. "There was a girl…"

"Oh, *her*." Lucianna twirled around, the fabric of her great dress billowing in her wake, and circled around the side of the desk, practically floating. "Let me guess, he offered to give her to you."

Brandy took a step back as the old woman strolled right up to her, almost into her face. She recalled the way she rushed up to her at the wedding and felt a subtle wave of déjà vu. "He said he'd release her from her contract if I agreed… I thought maybe…"

"Listen to me. That girl is nothing like she appears to be. She's an incredibly powerful *witch*. And she's immensely *evil*."

Brandy stared at her, shocked. She wasn't particularly fond of Dolly, but she hadn't thought for a second that she was *evil.*

"She possesses powerful psychic abilities. She can manipulate people, force them to do whatever she pleases, turning them into helpless puppets."

She looked over at Albert. Back in the pervert's reconstructed sex room, she remembered being unable to keep her eyes closed. Her mind kept filling with frightening thoughts of something dangerous stalking them, forcing her to peek, even though she knew what would happen. Sometimes, it even felt as if her eyelids opened of their own free will…

"She's dangerous and cruel," Lucianna went on. "She lies as naturally as she breathes. The terrible things she's done has earned her a rightful eternity in a place far worse than any hell you could imagine. Shanzer holding her prisoner by way of his contract is literally the only thing anchoring her soul to this world and delaying that fate."

Brandy stared at her. "Wait… So if we'd accepted his offer and tried to take her away from there…"

"A terrible karma would have immediately come to claim her."

She remembered the hateful glare Dolly shot at her as she considered the Shaman's strange offer. *(Don't you dare, bitch!)* No wonder she lost her composure when the Shaman threatened to shred their contract… The thought sent a shiver down her spine.

"But even so, she can't resist the urge to cause trouble," Lucianna went on. "She can't help herself. If she sees an opportunity to do someone harm, she'll seize it. Be wary of anything she might have told you."

Brandy frowned as she thought back on those interactions. If what this woman was saying were true, then that whole encounter made a little more sense. Dolly was doing everything in her power to keep them from trusting Shanzer, almost as if she wanted to sabotage his efforts.

"It's a terribly unsavory agreement those two have," said Lucianna, her face drawn tight with disgust at the very thought. "But there are two things you need to remember about that man.

First: Lyle Shanzer, in spite of whatever else he may be, is one of the most powerful mages in existence. Very few would dare make an enemy of him."

"That's right…" recalled Albert. "That waiter… No, it was *Warner*… He called Shanzer 'one of the Seven Mages of Magreech,' whatever that means."

"It means a great deal," said Lucianna. "It means he can pretty much do whatever he pleases."

Something about that left a vile taste in Brandy's mouth. There was something very wrong about the idea of that man having such awesome power and being completely unrestrained, without any repercussions whatsoever for his actions.

"But the second thing you need to know about Lyle Shanzer," Lucianna continued as if resigned to admit it, "is that no matter what else he may be, no matter how filthy and wicked he may seem, he *is* one of the good guys. I don't know what his intentions are for that girl, but I truly doubt he only kept her as a personal plaything. He *must* have something planned for her."

Brandy nodded. "If you say so, I guess."

"That doesn't mean you have to like him, of course. No one does. He's a creep." Again, she flashed that youthful smile. "Just don't lose any sleep over that girl's 'pitiful me' act. Nothing about her is as it seems, not even her age. She's much older than she appears. And she's a raging sociopath with far too much blood on her hands to ever wash off."

Brandy shivered. Now she felt uneasy at the mere thought of being left alone in the same room with her…

"Anyway…" said Lucianna, beaming at them again as if she hadn't just been talking about an evil sociopathic sex slave witch. "Off you go!"

Chapter 20

Albert and Brandy stepped out of the office and back into the bustle of the lobby. It was less busy than it was when Lucianna led them back into her office, but not by a lot. There were still guests checking in. And a number of people were passing through on their way out the doors, most of them probably on their way to dinner.

"Was it just me?" asked Albert. "Or was she *really* unhelpful?"

"No shit," grumbled Brandy.

He reached into his pocket and ran his fingers along the edge of the keycard Lucianna gave him. The key to literally every door in the hotel... And yet they didn't have the slightest clue where they were even supposed to start. "She *did* say something about the westernmost rooms..." he recalled. Something about the wind sounding like moaning voices in the woods.

"All the more reason to stay the fuck away from that area, if you ask me."

He frowned. "Well we have to start *somewhere*..." It really didn't seem like they were getting out of this hotel until they did what the Keeper wanted.

An older couple eyed Brandy's skimpy dress with apparent disapproval as they walked by and then hurried out the door when she glared at them in response.

"The first thing *I'm* doing is getting out of this whore dress," she spat, stalking out of the lobby and into the main hallway.

Albert hurried after her. "Where are you going?"

"The gift shop. I don't care how expensive they are, I'm buying a tee shirt and some shorts."

"With what money?"

She jolted to a stop as she realized that he was right. Her purse and wallet had been taken along with their clothes and car. "*Fuck me!*" she shouted.

Two teenage boys on their way back from the pool stopped in in their tracks, startled by the outburst. Their huge eyes washed over her, both of them taking in the short dress and plunging neckline.

"In your dreams!" she snapped at them.

Both of the boys blushed and quickly fled back the way they came.

Albert took her arm and led her in the opposite direction. "Let's just hit pause and come up with a plan."

She growled, frustrated. "I *hate* this!"

"I know you do."

"If I ever see that filthy pervert again, I swear I'll kick both his droopy balls so far up his ass he'll *choke on them!*"

"Ouch. Yeah, I'd rather not witness that." He eyed the elevator as they approached it. Avoiding that would probably be smart. They used it quite a bit while they were staying here and the last thing they wanted was to have those doors open and end up face-to-face with themselves.

He couldn't help, however, wondering just what would happen if they did. Would the universe just immediately implode or something? What was the usual scenario for the birth of a time paradox? *Back to the Future* never really explained it… The two Jennifers just fainted. Totally anticlimactic.

It would be far safer to stick to the stairs. They didn't use those once while they were staying here. That would eliminate any risk, at least while moving vertically. In fact, thinking back, they didn't bother exploring very much of the hotel at all. They walked around the public areas on the first and second floors, but otherwise they only went to and from their room. Even the ice and vending machines were between their room and the elevator. It would probably be safe for them to go pretty much anywhere as long as they avoided those particular paths.

Brandy grabbed his arm and pressed herself against him. "I

don't want to do this," she whined. "I just want to go home."

"I know."

"It's kind of ironic, I guess. I was so sad to hand back our room cards. I didn't want it to end. I would've given anything to turn around and run back up to our room and crawl back into bed with you."

He nodded. He'd felt the same way. It was funny. For a while, he wasn't entirely sure why they were bothering with a honeymoon. It wasn't like they'd been saving themselves this whole time. They'd already had sex *twice* before they even started dating. And they'd been living together for *years*. They'd done everything there was to do together. But in spite of that, there was something almost magical about this trip. He felt it the moment they arrived. It was special. It truly did feel like the start of a brand-new life with her.

"And now, *ridiculously*, here we are again…" She looked up at the hallway around her, her lip curled into a grumpy sneer. "Not exactly what I asked for…"

"Yeah. I know."

"Stuck in this stupid dress… Probably going to turn an ankle in these ridiculous heels… No money. No car. No *room*." She laid her cheek against his shoulder again. "Fuck."

He stopped walking and turned to face her. "We're together," he reminded her. "That's all *I* care about. Whether we're going home or back to that scary-ass temple or all the way to hell and back. I just want to be with you."

She gave a snort of a laugh. "You're such a fucking *dork* sometimes."

Albert scrunched up his face. "Wow. Okay. Not exactly the reaction I was going for…"

She rolled her eyes and then looked out at the quiet hallway around them. "This is *so* fucked up. Isn't it? I mean just stop and *think* about it a minute."

"I know."

"We're in the past!" she whispered. "There are *two of me* in this hotel right now! And two of *you*!"

"Yeah."

"There's another fucking *door* out there somewhere…"

He nodded. "There's that, yeah."

"Oh, and apparently we're such a slutty couple of freaky *sex-addicts* that we're off the charts on some *epic pervert's* list of *horniest people in the world*!"

He made a face at that. "Not his exact words…"

"And you're really just going along with all this, aren't you?"

He blinked, surprised. "What?"

"You didn't even *try* to tell the pervert you weren't doing it."

"I think he made it pretty clear we didn't have any choice," he reminded her.

"You still could've tried!"

He wasn't sure what to say. Now he felt guilty. Yes, it was true that he was a little intrigued by the idea of learning more about why they had to do what they did five years ago, but he wasn't exactly diving in head-first. He was still processing it all. Things got really scary really fast down in that darkness. He broke his arm. He nearly lost *her* to that blood-thirsty Caggo monster. And they thought both Wayne and Andrea were *dead* for a while. And that wasn't the half of it!

He couldn't imagine going through any of that again. He wasn't sure he *could* do it. But what *else* were they supposed to do? Shanzer told them they didn't have a choice. And why shouldn't they believe him. They never had a choice five years ago, either. Not really. Those awful phone calls… The envelope with Wendel Gilbert's picture inside… Somehow he knew that this was going to be the same. They could try to refuse. They could find a way home. But something would happen. It would drag them back here. He was sure of it.

Brandy pressed her face against his shoulder again. "Promise me we'll make it home."

This caught him by surprise. "What? *Of course* we're going home. What kind of thinking is that?"

"It's perfectly *normal* thinking! This is the fucking *Keeper* we're talking about! Remember? That little wrinkled monster with its head screwed on loose that put us through all that hell five years ago? Does that ring a bell?"

"I remember. Kind of hard to forget."

"Psychopathic fucking Muppet…" she grumbled. "God, I lost count of how many times I thought you were going to die that night! I don't want to go through that again."

"We'll be fine," he promised. "This isn't the Temple of the Blind. It's just a hotel. All we have to do is unlock whatever door Lucianna and Shanzer want us to find."

"And *then* what? Lucianna said we were here to find some kind of *road*. What the fuck is *that* about? Where will we get sent *next?*"

It was a good question. Lucianna said something about a road leading to the door. Was she referring to a path on the other side of whatever they were supposed to find and open here? Or was the hotel, itself, the road to the door? He didn't quite understand it. And she wasn't very helpful when it came to explaining any of it. "I don't know," he admitted. "But we'll do what we have to do and then we'll go home. Together."

"You really think it'll be that easy?"

"Maybe. Maybe not. But we'll take it one step at a time."

"Make someone *else* do it," she whined. "It's not fair."

Albert felt awful. He wished they didn't have to do this right now, too. He wished he could just take her by the hand and lead her out of this weird, time-hopping hotel.

He still had so many questions about what happened five years ago. What did they really do that night? Did their actions actually have any effect on the world? Did they do the right thing? What other amazing discoveries were hidden out there? There were nights he couldn't sleep for thinking about all these things. But he didn't care about those answers more than he cared about her. He couldn't bear seeing her unhappy. It wasn't worth it.

Behind them, a door opened and another young couple stepped out into the hallway, their arms linked.

"Do you think this town has any seafood restaurants?" asked the woman in a slight southern drawl as they walked away from them. "I think I want seafood."

Brandy lifted her head and watched them for a moment, distracted, then turned and looked at Albert again. "Yeah, I'm starving."

He nodded. Him too. And it wasn't any wonder. Lucianna told them it was already past four o'clock. And that was *before* she took them back to her office. Plus, that was what time it was *here*. Back in Shanzer's sex mansion, it was after midnight. And he had no idea how long they slept between passing out in the sex museum's nasty back-room surprise and waking up in bed with Dolly the Psycho Witch. It felt like he hadn't eaten all day. He felt his stomach growl at the mere mention of food. "But we still don't have any money."

"I know." She pushed her mouth to one side, thoughtful. "I wonder if we'd notice if we billed it to our room."

He considered the idea for a moment. They *were* currently registered as guests.

"I mean it's not exactly stealing, is it? It's *our* money."

"Didn't they give you an itemized bill when we checked out?"

"Yeah…" She thought back, trying to recall it. "I remember glancing at it, but I couldn't tell you anything that's on it now."

"I feel like you would've noticed if there were charges you didn't recognize, though."

"Maybe… I mean I certainly *hope* I would…" She groaned. "I hate this." She looked down at her feet. "And these stupid shoes are killing me!"

Albert considered the matter for a moment. "We could go back and talk to Lucianna again," he suggested. "See if she'll open a tab for us or something."

"I don't wanna talk to her again." She stared down at the uncomfortable shoes for a moment, thinking. Then she looked up and met his gaze, her blue eyes bright with renewed energy. "I have a better idea."

Chapter 21

"Are you sure about this?" asked Albert.

"Just shut up and trust me."

"If you say so."

She pushed open the stairwell door just a crack and peered out onto the fourth-floor hallway. Everything was quiet. "We were coming back from the pool when we watched ourselves get on the elevator. Don't you remember what we did after that?"

Albert smiled. "Shower," he recalled. "That was fun."

"*After* the shower. We got dressed and went to dinner. We ate at that steakhouse on Main Street."

"Oh yeah. That was good, too."

"The food was good, but the service was a little slow, so we were gone a while."

He pressed up against her back and peered over her shoulder at the empty hallway. "But how do we know if we've left yet?"

"We should be able to hear us talking if we get right up to the door."

"Unless you've got your tongue in my mouth at the moment. That happened a lot."

A hint of a smile touched her face. "It did, didn't it?" She stepped out into the hallway and paused. This was the danger zone. Between the elevator and their room. If they weren't careful, they could be seen. And while she still couldn't wrap her head around what would happen, she was fairly sure it would be *very* bad.

"Lucianna specifically told us not to let our other selves see us."

"I know what she said. But I also know where we were that

day." Then she made a face at herself. "Which is also today? *So fucking weird…*"

"We have no idea what time it is," he reminded her. "We don't know how long we were in Lucianna's office. And neither of us remember exactly when we left for dinner."

"We were talking to her for a while after we got on that elevator," she reasoned. "I'm sure we've had time to be out of the shower. And I remember being hungry. Remember me rushing you out the door?"

"I think so, yeah."

"If we're not gone, we're still getting dressed. And if we're getting dressed, we'll be able to hear us talking."

"As long as you're sure."

"Trust me."

"You know I do."

Besides, if she didn't remember walking out of their room and finding another her and Albert standing in the hallway, then they couldn't get caught now. Right? Because if it didn't happen then, it couldn't happen now. Because then was now and now was then.

Or was that not how it worked? How was she supposed to know these things? Like, what happened if they did something this time that *didn't* happen when they were here the first time? What if they blatantly walked up and knocked on the door while they were inside, for example? Would it still happen now if it didn't happen then?

Fuck this is confusing…

She could see their door from here, the "Do Not Disturb" sign sticking out of the card reader. They pretty much left it there. They even turned down housekeeping for the duration of their stay, which was better for the environment, anyway, she'd heard.

If she could get right up to that door and listen, she should be able to hear them if they were still inside. It wasn't like they didn't talk to each other. They were almost *always* talking. Six years together and they still never ran out of things to talk about. So there should be voices.

At least, she hoped so…

But then again, she wasn't sure what she was going to do if it was quiet inside. Would that mean that they were gone? Or that they were just being quiet? They *did* spend a lot of time in there trying not to make too much noise, now that she was thinking about it.

She peeked into the vending and ice room as she walked by, paranoid that one or both of them might be in there, browsing the drink selections even though she had no recollection of doing such a thing. But it was empty.

"This seems like a bad idea," whispered Albert.

She didn't have a chance to argue the matter with him. Ahead of them, their door opened and the other Albert stepped out into the hallway.

"Shit!" she whispered, her heart leaping in her chest. She grabbed *her* Albert's hand and quickly ducked into the vending room.

This was bad. They were almost seen. They might *have* been seen for all she knew, although she was pretty sure that other Albert was looking back into the room as he stepped into view, probably talking to *his* Brandy.

It was lucky they hadn't gotten any closer. That was a serious miscalculation. Albert (*her* Albert) was right. This was a bad idea. And now they were trapped. There was no way out of here. And she could already hear voices approaching! She needed to think fast!

There was a space between the ice machine and the wall, just wide enough to squeeze into. She pushed Albert into it and tried to crowd in after him, but there wasn't room. There was a trashcan occupying the space that she hadn't seen, preventing him from sliding all the way back, which in turn left no room for her.

And there was no time for a plan B.

Their voices drifted from the hallway, just out of sight and getting closer.

The only thing stranger than hearing Albert's voice from outside the room while looking into his worried eyes was hearing her own voice respond. It was almost more than she could stand.

Again, she wondered what would happen. Would everything just end? Like pulling the plug on a television set? Just an abrupt darkness and silence? Or would it be slow and terrible? Or would the universe just rewrite itself in an instant, changing everything?

It was probably bold of her to think for a second that she could even hope to comprehend the repercussions of breaking the flow of time.

Unsure what else to do and completely out of time to think of anything else, she twirled around, turning her back to the hallway and simply crouched in front of the nearest vending machine, pretending to be collecting something from its tray.

It didn't matter if they saw her, she told herself, as long as they didn't *recognize* her.

Albert and Brandy—the *other* Albert and Brandy, the ones in the hallway, the ones from last Monday who still had no idea what unpleasantness the Keeper had in store for them at the end of their lovely honeymoon stay—walked on by. She heard their footsteps as they passed. She heard her own voice, cheerful and oblivious, saying something about the bars in town being open late.

She could almost recall that conversation. Almost. They talked about so much that week. It was impossible to remember it all.

As the other them continued on out of earshot, she glanced up at Albert. He was peeking out around the ice machine, his eyes fixed on the hallway. "Did they see me?" she whispered.

"*I* did," he replied. "You didn't. You never looked. But I saw you…"

Tugging at the dress with one hand and straightening her glasses with the other, she stood up and looked back toward the hallway, half-expecting them to come back for a closer look. But of course there was no way *that* Albert would have thought for even a second that some random woman rummaging around in a vending machine was a future version of the woman walking next to him.

They should be safe for now.

"I *remember* it…" sighed Albert. He stepped out into the open again as he processed it all. "I forgot all about it, but I remember seeing you there that day." He pointed at her. "I *knew* I saw a dress like that somewhere before!"

She turned and shot him a dirty look. "You were looking at another woman's *ass* on our *honeymoon?*"

He stared back at her, confused. "What? No! I was looking at *your* ass!"

"But you didn't *know* it was me!"

"But it *was* you!"

"Oh my god! I can't believe you!"

He opened his mouth to say something, but seemed to lose the words. He scrunched up his forehead and blinked several times as he struggled to process the argument they were having. "Besides, I didn't say I *ogled* you. I said I *saw* you. That's all."

She growled and stalked away. "Absolutely unbelievable!"

"I didn't do anything!"

Chapter 22

Albert slid the keycard into the slot and watched the light flash green.

So far so good, he supposed.

He opened the door and peered inside. It was weird. The room was so completely familiar and yet so queerly wrong. He'd spent the past four nights sleeping in that bed, and yet this wasn't how it looked when they last saw it. Their big suitcase was sitting open on the luggage stand with their first day's laundry inside, their clean clothes transferred to the dresser and closet. The bathroom counter was still cluttered with their toiletries and Brandy's makeup. The bed was unmade from the night before, as it would remain for the duration of their stay.

There was a nagging voice in his head that kept telling him that this could all be some elaborate practical joke, that there was no way they could have actually traveled back in time. That other them could have been body doubles, simple look-alikes with the aid of some clever makeup. Lucianna and her staff could have spied on them during their stay in order to perfectly replicate every moment. They only had Shanzer's word that he'd returned the Mustang and all its contents back to Briar Hills for them. He could have sent all their stuff here, instead, for someone to unpack and stage this scene, perhaps off photographs taken by someone who sneaked in while they were at dinner that night.

But that all seemed even more unlikely than the time traveling thing, honestly. What would be the point? Why would someone go so far for a stupid prank? And the pervy shaman's perfect replica of the sex room was certainly no joke. Nor was that sex party or his bizarre, shape-shifting mansion... And yet, in spite of all that, the stubbornly logical part of his brain was still trying to convince him that someone could have recreated this scene.

But that voice was getting quieter and quieter with each twist and turn of this bizarre adventure.

Brandy walked straight to the big suitcase and unzipped the inner pocket. "Thank you, me!" she sighed. Inside was a cheap, travel-sized first-aid kit with some very basic supplies, including a small box of generic adhesive bandages. And inside *that* were three hundred-dollar bills she hid in case of an emergency. They didn't need to get into it while they were staying here, so she wouldn't miss it until they unpacked at home. And by then, the other them would be *this* them. "Now we can get something to eat!"

"You're a genius," he told her.

"Damn straight."

He turned and looked at the map on the door, curious. According to Lucianna, the hotel was built on top of whatever was here before it. It sounded as if it still existed somewhere inside this building. But the hotel was huge. It could take *days* to explore the entire property.

"Oh my god!" Brandy gasped at the mirror. "I'm a fucking *mess!* Why didn't you tell me I looked like an escaped mental patient?"

"You look amazing to me," he told her.

"You *always* say that."

"It's always the truth." He leaned closer to the map, studying it. The hotel was huge, but the layout wasn't all that complicated. There was the main building at the center where the businesses and social areas were located, along with the two indoor pools. Stretching outward from that main building were three four-story wings where all the guest rooms were located. Two of these wings curved outward toward the east, partially encircling the grounds where the three outdoor pools were located. The third wing snaked its way west, with one side looking out over the sprawling greens of the resort's golf course and the other nestled against the peaceful Tennessee wilderness, which was where this room was located.

"Well you have questionable taste," she grumbled as she

stalked into the bathroom and grabbed her hairbrush.

"I disagree." What was it Lucianna said? There were rooms that moved around? Was that a thing? And *which* rooms? How would they know if they saw one? And something about people dreaming that they were lost in hallways that didn't exist? That wasn't helpful, either. The only thing she said that pointed them in any direction at all was that weird bit about the wind in the trees outside the westernmost rooms sounding like moaning voices... And that still didn't narrow it down a lot. Was it only the rooms at the far end? Which floor? Why didn't he press her for more details?

Brandy ran the brush through her hair until she was satisfied with it. Then she rummaged through her makeup, looking for her foundation. "This is fucking weird, right? It's not just me?"

"Definitely not just you," he agreed, still studying the map. "Try to leave everything like you found it. We don't want ourselves noticing someone was in our room while we were gone."

She glanced down at her scattered makeup. "Have you seen my bathroom organization? I'm a slob. Trust me, I'll never know I was here."

"I hope not."

"Besides, this already happened, didn't it? If we come back later and notice something off, we'd remember it."

"Unless it doesn't work that way."

"What other way *would* it work?" she countered. "Other than it *shouldn't at all* because it's not supposed to be possible to fucking *time travel*."

"I don't know. I guess it all depends on how time behaves if you change something in the past. Is it even possible to change something? Does changing something cause some kind of breakdown? Or does it just instantly change the present? Or does it create a brand-new timeline? Like, which movie plot are we supposed to be following here?"

"Time travel makes my head hurt," she complained.

"Yeah, mine too." He turned his attention back to the room. "This is just so weird." He walked over to the window and peered out at the surrounding woods. There was such a nice view of the forest over here. No sign of any other people. Very private. They left the curtains open throughout most of their stay. They even made love on that balcony the first night they were here.

Now, however, he found himself looking out at those trees a little more carefully. They were much closer to the central building than they were to the western end of this wing, but those were the same woods. If he'd known there was something unnatural about this hotel, he didn't think he would've trusted those shadowy trees. It was far too easy to imagine something unseen lurking out there, watching them...

He shivered and turned away from it. That kind of thinking wouldn't help anything. He needed to stay focused on what was right in front of him. The first thing he needed was a change of clothes. Something that wouldn't stand out so much. And Brandy packed more than enough for him to take something without the other him ever noticing.

Brandy put down her makeup brush and picked up her lipstick. "It's so *strange*. It's our room. But it's *not* our room. This is my makeup, but it's *not*. It's *hers*."

"But she's *you*," he reminded her as he unbuttoned his shirt. "Or she *was* you." Then he scrunched up his face, confused. "*Will be* you? I mean, you *were* her...and she's going to be you..."

"Oh my god! Just stop talking! You're giving me a migraine!"

"Sorry."

She put the lipstick down and walked out of the bathroom. She stepped out of the heels the pervert gave her, then, in one smooth motion, she peeled down the dress and dropped it to her feet.

Albert stopped what he was doing, his shirt half-off, and stared at her as she bent over and picked them up, wearing nothing but her everyday jewelry, her glasses and the mysterious medallion around her neck.

What was he doing again?

Was it normal, after six years together, for her to still be able to completely empty his brain like that every time he saw her naked?

"Good riddance to *this* stupid thing," she grumbled, turning toward the waste bin.

"Don't throw it away!" gasped Albert.

She raised an eyebrow at him. "Don't tell me you *like* this skanky thing."

"Well…" he replied, distracted. "Kinda, yeah. You're hot as hell in that." Then, before she could yell at him, he quickly added, "But think about it. What happens if we come back from dinner and find that stuff in the garbage?"

She frowned down at the trashcan. "Fuck…" she grumbled. "You're right…" It wasn't a very big bin, after all. And there wasn't very much in it. There was no way the other them wouldn't notice it there.

"Just…hide it in the suitcase with the dirty clothes. We never went through it. They won't even notice it until they get home and start laundry. And by then they'll be us."

"Still making my head hurt."

"Sorry."

She turned and looked at the suitcase. There wasn't much laundry in it yet. They'd only been here one night so far, after all. But between the clothes they arrived in, plus the swimwear from that first day (and a couple of little outfits she bought special just for the occasion) there was just enough to hide *these* clothes under. Albert was right, after all. She never went through it. It was basically their hamper. All week long, they tossed in whatever they took off and forgot about it. That was an *after* the trip thing. A problem for once they were back home. And when it was time to leave, she just shoved everything in there and zipped it up. It was only dirty laundry so she didn't bother trying to be neat about it.

She never thought she'd be grateful that she was such an unobservant slob…

"But I'm throwing the stupid thing away as soon as we get home."

"Whatever you want." He took off his pants and handed his

clothes to her. "You even packed extra shoes for us, didn't you?"

"In case it rained and they got wet. And you made fun of me for packing so much!"

"I never made fun," he insisted. "I said it was cute."

"That's the same as making fun."

"How's that the same?"

"It just is." She walked back to the dresser where she'd un-packed the clothes to make room for the laundry and carefully picked through them, trying to remember which ones she'd worn.

"It *didn't* rain," said Albert, "so we never needed them. That means we won't miss them."

"You're welcome."

He chuckled. "My wife's definitely a genius."

"Yes, she is."

"She's as smart as she is hot."

"Now you're just sucking up." She lifted up a green and black cropped halter top. "Huh...I was looking for this. I thought I forgot it at home... How did I miss it?"

Albert looked up at it, distracted. "Because you took it," he realized. "Right now."

She blinked back at him for a moment, confused. Then she realized what he was saying and her eyes widened. "I...?" She looked down at it again, her pretty face twisted in a rather adora-ble expression of bewildered awe. "I did that...*this*...already?" Her eyes grew wider as she processed the bizarre fact. "Whoa..."

"I know, right?"

"But wait... That's something we did that we noticed." She looked up at him, her eyes wide. "Isn't that, like, proof that we've already done all this? That we can't really change anything be-cause it's actually already happened?"

"Maybe..." The same was true of him remembering that red dress, although he wasn't going to bring *that* up again. But was it proof that this stuff already happened? Or did those memories only exist *after* they changed the future? Did they really notice these things at the time? Or did they only *think* they re-membered these things? He grimaced. "Now you're making *my* head hurt."

She tossed the shirt onto the bed and picked out a pair of shorts she didn't remember wearing to go with them.

"You know," said Albert, his gaze washing over her soft curves, "this is the kind of opportunity that doesn't come around very often."

"What opportunity?"

He winced. This was probably a bad idea...but he couldn't help himself. "Remember when we walked out of here that last time? You said you wished we had just one more night?"

"This wasn't exactly what I had in mind," she grumbled.

"Yeah. I know. But you remember what you said, don't you? You wished we had time to do it just once more before we had to leave? I mean..." He glanced around. "Here we are."

She turned and glared at him. That was the end of it. He knew he was pushing his luck even bringing it up. But he simply couldn't help himself. How *could* he? She looked so *amazing* standing there like that...completely naked...and *so gorgeous*... But of course she was still mad about...well about a *lot* of things that had happened. Waking up in that bed with Dolly... The tattooed cougar who handed him her room key at the party... And of course that way-too-friendly bartender... Even that nonsense about remembering seeing the red dress as he passed by in the hallway. He still didn't think any of those things were his fault, but that wasn't the way she saw it. She never stayed mad at him long, luckily. She had a sharp temper, but she liked his company too much to hold a grudge. Still, he was smart enough not to push his luck any farther than that.

But with a frustrated sort of growl, she tossed the shorts aside. "*Fine*. But I'm not doing this for *you*," she informed him as she shoved him backward onto the bed.

"Yes ma'am," he replied, surprised. "Understood."

"Shut up."

"Okay."

Chapter 23

"Hurry up!" hissed Brandy as she crept out into the hallway. "Before we come back!"

"Hold on!" he grumbled. He was looking in the mirror, craning his neck back and forth. "You got lipstick all over me."

"Marking my territory," she informed him. "In case you run into any more rabid skanks."

Satisfied that he wasn't going to be walking around with kiss marks all over him—no *visible* ones, anyway—he turned the lights back off and stepped out into the hallway behind her. "You know, jealousy doesn't suit you."

"Think so?"

"Yeah. I much prefer my badass wife who once told her best friend she could walk around our apartment naked all she liked because *I* knew you could run circles around her in the sheets."

"Huh..." She wrinkled her nose and tried to recall. "Was I drunk when I said that? Because that sounds like something drunk me would say."

"Probably. I'm sure she was drunk, too."

"Drunk Nikki does like to get naked."

"She does." After their return from the temple five years ago, Nicole apparently decided that since they'd all seen each other naked, she didn't need to be modest anymore. She frequently changed clothes right in front of him. She had a tendency to lounge around topless, not just in her own apartment but in theirs as well. And after a few beers, she almost always stripped down and made herself comfortable. It was as if she were still raging against those awkward feelings of embarrassment and vulnerability that being naked in the temple instilled in them all, as if she refused, even after all this time, to give them any kind of acknowledgement.

It was actually kind of strange, the way Brandy simply let it happen. She never said anything. She never seemed to get jealous about it, despite how mad she was about all the unwanted attention he attracted from the strangers at Shanzer's sleazy party. But he supposed it was different when it was Nicole. They'd been best friends since grade school. They were like sisters. They trusted each other completely. In fact, if it was only the three of them, Brandy would often toss aside her own shirt and join her, usually saying something like, "If you're gonna look at someone's tits, it better be mine." He was fairly sure she just liked the idea of him getting all turned on and unable to do anything about it. Both of them had always enjoyed teasing him.

As for him, he'd never complained about any of it. He didn't want to be rude, after all.

They quickly made their way back to the stairwell and then descended to the second floor. There was a restaurant on this level where they dined their first night here. It was pretty good, but not quite worth the extravagant prices, in her opinion. And as nice as a leisurely dinner sounded right about now, she had no idea how long they might be stuck here. With only the three hundred dollars from her emergency stash, she couldn't risk spending it too quickly. Instead, she walked past it and made her way to the bar instead, where there was a small selection of pub food available that was still a little pricy, but more affordable and much faster than the fancy stuff on the restaurant's menu. They each ordered a cheeseburger, fries and a beer. Then, drinks in hand, they made their way to the back of the room and slid into an empty booth.

"I'm fucking starving," groaned Brandy, rubbing at her complaining belly. The motion drew his eyes. He loved it when she wore shirts that let him see her piercing like that. He could stare at her all day. "How long ago do you think we last ate?"

He didn't know. But it was starting to feel like days. His own stomach was growling in anticipation of the meal it had been promised. "It's strange. We're not used to being without our phones, and that's how we usually keep track of time." He hadn't worn a watch since he was a kid. And he couldn't remember the last time he even thought to look for a clock. Did any place other than waiting rooms and classrooms even bother with those anymore? He supposed they probably did, but he had no idea when he last bothered to take note of one. "I mean, we're not only in the past," he said, lowering his voice so no one could overhear him and think he was some sort of nutjob, "but we have no concept of the passage of time *whatsoever*. It could have been hours since we checked out of this hotel or days."

Brandy curled her lip at him, an expression that said, "I don't want to think about it that much," and took a sip of her beer. "The least the pervert could've done was left us our phones, don't you think? That guy was such an asshole."

"I don't know…" He leaned forward, thoughtful. "I mean, think about it a minute. What if we *did* have our cell phones right now? The *other us* have theirs, too. And they're the *same phones*. How would that work?"

She made another face at him. "Would that be a problem? Like with the cellular company?"

"Maybe. They might think someone hacked our phones or something. I'm not sure how all that works. But I do know you took a lot of pictures between then and now. Wouldn't those all automatically upload to the cloud? I mean, the next time Past You checked her phone, there'd be pictures she didn't remember taking. Like of her posing in front of a *giant vagina*."

She scrunched up her face at the thought. "That *would* be a weird thing for Past Me to see…"

"If the pervert knew we were going to be dealing with time stuff, it could explain why he'd take our phones away."

"Maybe… But he's still a pervy asshole."

"Well, yeah. I mean, obviously."

She looked out across the bar. It wasn't very crowded but there were quite a few people here. She even recognized some of them. That woman in the flowery skirt and bikini top was at the pools on several occasions. And she remembered seeing that cute older couple at breakfast the other morning.

It was strange seeing familiar faces in the crowds again. In a *normal* world, she'd have been back home by now, back in her ordinary life, the only differences a shiny new wedding band nuzzled against her engagement ring and a different last name and prefix. From Miss Brandy Lynn Rudman to Mrs. Brandy Lynn Cross. This place would have already slipped into the past and all these faces would have already faded from her memory.

Albert stared out the window at the sun-soaked parking lot and the lawns beyond. "The only place Lucianna mentioned was the westernmost rooms…" he recalled.

Brandy took another drink of her beer and then wrinkled her nose at him. "Can we at least finish a meal before we start thinking about that shit?"

"Yeah." He picked up his beer and lifted it to his lips. "I was just thinking."

"You're not supposed to be able to think right now," she informed him. "I just finished fucking your brains out."

He coughed, surprised and set his drink back down.

She propped her elbows on the table, rested her chin on her enlaced fingers and gave him that familiar grin, clearly pleased with herself.

He glanced around the bar, embarrassed at the thought of someone overhearing her and even more embarrassed at the realization that he might have blushed a bit… (Seriously, how was she still able to do that to him after all this time?)

"I don't want to do any of that scary shit," she sighed. "It's literally our honeymoon again. We actually got to rewind and go back. Who gets to do that? Why do we have to spend that amazing opportunity doing *scary shit?* It's not fair."

"No. It really isn't." He wasn't sure what else to say. What could he do about it? He could refuse. He could tell Lucianna to find someone else to explore her mysterious hotel. But everyone kept telling them that they had no choice. It was possible they were lying, that they could just say no and go home and nothing would ever come of it. But it was just as possible—and probably far more likely—that they'd only end up right back here again, wishing they'd just gotten it over with the first time.

He just kept thinking of those ominous, dead-air phone calls…

They sat there for a moment in silence, sipping their beers, staring out the window.

Brandy turned and looked back toward the bar. "Ugh. Where's our food. My belly won't stop growling."

"I don't think we've eaten anywhere in this town that wasn't at least a little slow," he recalled. "I think the theme of Wevenwert is 'sit back and relax,' not 'shove it in your face and go.'"

"Tell that to my tummy. It's the one complaining."

Albert smiled and took another sip of his beer.

Brandy turned her gaze back to the window and twiddled with a lock of her hair. The sun was shining brightly out there. She could see heat waves rising off parked cars. Birds swept by in the sky. It looked for all the world like any other day. "I wonder if the other us is still eating dinner."

He had no idea. There still weren't any clocks to be seen. And even if he *did* know the time, he couldn't remember how long they spent at dinner that night. It was a while, though. The service there was really slow. But they didn't mind it. They were enjoying each other's company.

"Mmm… I had the blackened tuna."

"I remember that."

"Lucky bitch."

Albert chuckled.

She flashed him a tired smile and took another sip of her beer.

They sat in silence for another moment, during which he found his gaze drawn to the golden medallion hanging from her neck.

Yggdrasil's seed, he thought. That was what Lucianna called it. She said it was the key to whatever was hidden here. But it didn't look like any kind of key. He supposed it *did* look sort of like a *seed*, though. Just a little. It was sort of oblong, smaller at one end than the other, sort of flat. A little bit like a sunflower seed, maybe? But fatter. And rounded rather than pointed at the end.

Or maybe he was just looking too hard.

He remembered the first time he laid eyes on it. Brandy begged him not to climb up into that little crevice, but he didn't listen. He still couldn't say exactly why. He simply felt *compelled*. And when he reached the cramped space at the top, he was so badly startled by the sight of the grisly skeleton crouched there that he slipped and fell, startling everyone. They grabbed him and dragged him out of there. But he made them go back. There was something about that flash of gold in that terrifying instant that felt so utterly…*significant*.

There was a symbol carved into one side of it. That symbol was turned away from him right now and was lying against Brandy's chest, but he didn't need to see it. He'd never forgotten it. It was an ancient symbol for the word "devil" in a long-lost language. A clue about the true identity of the monster that was stalking them up those burning slopes.

He thought that was all there was to it. But there was far more to the curious medallion. Apparently, it was some kind of ancient and mystical key.

A young waitress with her long blonde hair tied back into cute twin braids appeared beside them, delivering their plates.

"That looks *amazing!*" gushed Brandy. "Thank you!"

"Yes," agreed Albert. "Thanks."

"You're wasting too much time," warned the waitress.

They both looked up to see that her eyes had turned black as tar.

"Warner…" realized Albert.

"There's a strange energy building in these walls. Something dangerous is stirring. It grows stronger by the hour. The longer you take, the less likely you are to leave alive."

He and Brandy's eyes met, a worried look passing between them.

But when they looked up again, those black eyes were gone. The waitress was blinking down at them, distracted. "Um…? Sorry. Another beer?"

Chapter 24

They didn't talk much while they ate. They were hungry, after all. And these burgers were *delicious*. Brandy didn't think it was just because she hadn't eaten in who-knew-when. The meat was thick and juicy and well-seasoned, flawlessly cooked. The bun was soft and sweet. The cheese perfectly melted. The vegetables cold and crisp. And the fries were piping hot with just the right balance of crunchy outside and soft, fluffy inside. It was quite simply the best burger and fries she'd had in a long time.

But good food was only part of it. She was also plenty worried. Why did stupid Warner have to turn up *right then* of all times? As soon as they were getting ready to eat? Really? After all they'd been through, the black-eyed freak couldn't have waited for them to finish their meal before delivering an ominous warning about the task ahead?

And what the hell was he going on about, anyway? How were they wasting too much time when *nobody would tell them what they were supposed to be doing*? And what did he mean by a strange energy and something dangerous? Was he just trying to spook them into picking up the pace?

(*The longer you take, the less likely you are to leave alive.*)

What an asshole.

The least he could've done was told them where they should go next. This hotel was *huge*.

They finished eating, drained the last of their beers and then left.

"Let's make our way toward the far end of the western wing," said Albert, pointing down the hallway. "Maybe we'll stumble across whatever Lucianna wants us to find on the way." He supposed they'd put it off long enough. Was it any wonder that Warner made a point of scolding them for not making any progress?

But Brandy pouted. She didn't want to go. She very much doubted that they were going to find anything *good* waiting for them in this hotel.

"Unless you have a better plan," he added.

"Yeah. It's called going the fuck home and letting someone else deal with this shit. I never agreed to any of this."

"Sorry."

She rolled her eyes and started walking. She knew it wasn't his fault, but she knew him. She knew he spent sleepless nights lying beside her in bed, pondering over the answers to endless questions that were buried beneath the rubble of the temple when it came down. He didn't admit it because he knew it upset her to think too much about it, but she could tell it weighed on his mind every day. And she could hardly blame him. They were given a tantalizing peek at a world far more enormous than the one they knew before. A world filled with mysterious creatures and terrifying monsters and endless forests and people without faces and psychic powers and just *so many things...*

The truth was that she wanted to know those answers, too. But she was afraid of what they might cost her. Lucianna assured them they could trust the Keeper. She assured them they could trust the black-eyed Warner monster. She even assured them they could trust the pervert. But trust was far more easily assured than accepted. And she couldn't stop thinking that everything could go horribly wrong at any second.

Ahead of them, two women stepped off the elevator in their swimwear, their hair still damp from their afternoon swim. She envied them so much. She wished she could just go back to enjoying the hotel's amenities.

She *hated* this! Why did it have to be them?

Albert slipped his arm around her waist and gave her a gentle squeeze. "Whatever's going to happen, we can handle it."

"You don't know that."

"Of course I do. I'm psychic, remember? I can just tell these things."

"I'm psychic, too," she reminded him. "And unlike you, I can see the *truth* in people. So I know when you're full of shit. So there."

"I'm full of shit, am I?"

"*Very* full of it."

He stopped walking and turned to face her. "Then stop and look at me. Look me right in the eye. Tell me I'm full of shit."

She squinted at him.

He stared defiantly back at her.

"You've got ketchup on your face."

"Not the point," he replied. But he reached up and wiped at his mouth, embarrassed.

"You missed," she said, reaching up and wiping it away with her thumb.

"You're not answering my question. If you can see the truth inside perfect strangers, then surely you can see the truth in your own husband. So tell me I don't know with every fiber of my being that we can handle this."

"You. Don't. Know. Shit," she told him, poking him in the chest with each word she spoke. "You're just stupidly and *adorably* optimistic for some weird-ass reason."

He gave her that oddly charming grin he always had whenever he thought he'd made his point.

She jabbed him in the chest again. "You'd better be right about this."

The two of them continued walking.

"It just doesn't feel like we *can't* do this," he went on. "I mean, think about last time. All the times things could have gone wrong but they *didn't.*"

He *did* have a point about that. He'd often said that they couldn't help but succeed that night, that the Keeper made sure the six of them made it home. Because even after being separated—and against all odds—they somehow found their way together again. Even Wayne and Andrea, who they were sure were gone forever. And together, they made their way home. Not just to their old lives, but to *brand-new* lives that they shared as dear friends. Three of them went from complete strangers to people she cared about so much that she begged all of them to be in her wedding.

"Wasn't it like someone up there was looking out for us?" he asked. "Didn't it feel like we were *meant* to come back?"

"Tell that to Beverly," she countered.

Albert frowned. "Yeah… I guess that's true." Beverly Bridger didn't get a happy ending. In fact, her ending was downright gruesome. For as long as he lived, he'd never forget the morbid sight of her lifeless body lying in that monstrous pit, her blood pooling around her…

"I mean, yeah, she was batshit crazy and all," Brandy added. "But to die like that… It was…"

"Senseless."

"Yeah. Senseless." Brandy was lucky. She and Nicole both. They never actually saw Beverly's body. They were walking in front of the group, crossing that seemingly empty chamber, heading for the next passage, when she started screaming at something the rest of them couldn't see.

But they didn't need to see it to know what happened. They saw the deadly pit in that room, filled with all those wicked stone spikes. They heard her screams turn to silence in a sickening instant. And they saw the ashen looks on Wayne and Albert's faces when they returned without her.

She didn't need anyone to describe that horrific scene to her. She could imagine it just fine.

"But she wasn't supposed to be a part of any of that. It was that old man. Kneede. He manipulated her. Fed her obsession. Put ideas in her head. Made her lure us all to Gilbert House."

"I still don't understand all that." And how could she? According to the Sentinel Queen, Kneede used Beverly to lure them all to Gilbert House in hopes of getting them killed and that Wayne was some kind of backup plan. If she interfered with him, he'd use him to undermine their trust in her. Kneede, on the other hand, claimed that it was the Sentinel Queen who sent Olivia and Wayne to Gilbert House specifically to get rid of them and that he sent Albert and Brandy there to protect them from her. But Albert discovered that they were *both* lying about things.

And the bizarre game the two were playing with all of them as pawns was even *more* confusing and convoluted.

She never could entirely wrap her head around it all. Something about the whole ordeal just never quite made any sense. Albert had always said that there were still pieces of the puzzle missing, that there were still plenty of things no one had bothered explaining to them. There had to be.

A woman in a flowing white dress walked past them.

"We're not like Beverly," insisted Albert. "She wasn't a part of it. Not like we were. We were different. We *are* different."

But Brandy wasn't listening to him anymore. She'd stopped walking and was staring at the woman in the white dress as she walked away, her eyes wide and distracted.

"What's up?" he asked.

"She's not supposed to be here…"

"What?" He watched the woman as she walked away. "Not supposed to be here *how*? What do you mean?"

Brandy shook her head. "I don't know. Just… She's not supposed to be here. I don't understand it. I can just…tell…"

Albert stood there a moment, processing it. Then he gripped her hand and started after the woman. "Then let's see where she's going."

Chapter 25

The pervert said that she had the ability to sense things about the people around her. He said that was the real reason she decided to go down into those steam tunnels with Albert that fateful night. Because she could see that he was a good person, that he wouldn't hurt her. Perhaps even that he would *protect* her.

But was that really a thing? Five years ago, the Sentinel Queen told them they were both psychic, but she never explained how it worked. In the months that followed, Albert tried on a few occasions to test it. He shuffled a deck of playing cards and they took turns trying to guess what the other was holding. Sometimes he tried the same trick using random words and pictures on their phones. Every now and then one of them would guess something right and they'd get a little excited, but it didn't happen nearly enough to prove it was anything more than dumb luck. After a while, even *he* grew bored with it. And she'd all but forgotten about it until just now.

She remembered the people back at the shameless shaman's gross sex party. The struggling café owner and single mother… The husband desperate to save his sick wife… The couple who only wanted to have a baby…

This was like that.

The woman in the white dress. One look as she walked by and Brandy knew without a doubt that she didn't belong here. But unlike in that strange moment of enlightenment in the midst of that depraved party, she couldn't read this woman like she did those guests. She couldn't see her story. She couldn't see her *whole truth*. All she could see was that one little fact.

She just didn't belong here.

But what did it mean? Didn't belong *how*? Was she not a

guest of the hotel? Was she an intruder? Was she up to some-thing? She *looked* like any other guest. That dress was exactly the sort of thing she'd seen plenty of women wear over their bathing suits at the pools. Her hair wasn't wet. It flowed down her back in perfect, auburn curls. But that didn't mean anything. Plenty of women spent time at the pool without getting their hair wet. Some didn't get in the water at all. They just liked to lounge in the sun. And she was barefoot. Why would she be barefoot if she weren't a guest?

But she didn't belong here... The more she watched her, the more certain she was of it.

The hotel was huge. There were thousands of rooms. And the hallways seemed to stretch on for miles. But there was noth-ing in this direction but guest rooms. If she wasn't a guest head-ing back to her room, then where else *could* she be going?

The woman wasn't behaving suspiciously in the least. She wasn't glancing around at all. She never once looked back over her shoulder. She looked perfectly at home, like she had every business being here, like it didn't cross her mind that anyone might be following her. The few people she passed in the hallway didn't spare her a glance.

Brandy was the one who felt suspicious. Stalking some poor woman through the hallways like a creeper... She linked arms with Albert and tried to look more casual, as if they were merely strolling back to their room after a nice date.

"Are you sure about this?" she whispered.

"You're the one who said she didn't belong here," he whis-pered back.

"I don't know how any of this works! What if I'm wrong?"

Seriously, why was she doing this? What if her so-called psychic senses weren't what the pervert claimed they were? What if she was just stalking some poor woman who was merely on her way back to her room? She reached up and tugged at her hair, twirling it around her finger, anxious. She didn't even want to be here. She didn't care what anyone said, she didn't want to be a part of this weirdness. To hell with the Keeper and his stu-pid doors. She just wanted to go home and get on with her new life as her husband's wife.

And yet there was something about that woman. The more she looked at her, the more she felt that she didn't belong.

But what the hell did that mean?

Ahead of them, the hallway curved to the left and the woman disappeared from view. Albert tried to pick up his pace, but she pulled him back. She might notice them if they followed any closer. And she already felt icky enough about this. The last thing she wanted was to have to try to explain herself.

But when they turned the corner, the woman was gone.

Both of them stopped, surprised.

"Where'd she go?" she asked, confused. They weren't following that far behind her. They only lost sight of her for a few seconds. It didn't seem long enough for her to have entered one of the rooms. And even if she *did* have time, neither of them heard a door open or close. She was sure they would've noticed that. She turned and looked behind them, confused. "That was weird, right? Like, that shouldn't have happened?"

"It was weird," he agreed.

She reached up and adjusted her glasses, as if maybe *they* were the problem, and gnawed absently at her lower lip. This was all so confusing. *Did* she only step into one of these rooms? Was she only another guest after all?

A bald-headed man with a long beard pushed a luggage cart past them, reminding her that they were just standing there in the middle of the hallway and she stepped aside, embarrassed.

"So what now?" wondered Albert.

"Well, we can't just stand around out here all day. Someone's going to think we're being weird."

"We *are* being weird," he reminded her.

"But we don't have to advertise it!" She pulled at his arm, urging him back the way they came. "There was totally something strange about that," she said again, as if deciding once and for all.

"Yes, there was." He looked back as they rounded the corner. "What did you mean when you said she wasn't supposed to be here? What did you feel when you saw her?"

But she couldn't quite explain it. She didn't understand it, herself. "I just…" she began, shaking her head. "Maybe I was wrong. I don't know how this shit works."

He looked forward again, his expression thoughtful.

"Just forget it," she decided. In fact, she wanted to forget *all* of it. She just wanted to go home.

But Albert stopped walking and looked back again. "It doesn't feel wrong," he said.

She blinked up at him, confused. "What?"

"You thinking there was something about that woman… It's not like you have feelings like that about people every day."

"No…" In fact, she'd never felt anything like that before in her life. "But we don't do shit like *this* every day, either," she reminded him. "It's been kind of a fucked-up day, in case you haven't been paying attention."

"Yeah, I know, but…" He turned and walked back the other way again. "Somehow, I just don't think it was a coincidence."

"If you say so," she grumbled, still clinging to his arm. "But I don't know what you expect us to do. She's gone, remember?"

But he didn't stop. He retraced their steps back around the curved hallway, then stopped. "She was right about here when we lost sight of her."

Brandy nodded. She wasn't sure where he was going with this. The key words, as far as she could tell, were "when we lost sight of her," which sort of summed up the whole part where they lost her. Meaning she was gone. Either she slipped into one of these rooms in that brief moment before they followed her around the corner, or she'd simply vanished into thin air. But she looked up at Albert and kept her mouth shut.

She knew that look on his face. He was thinking. Something about all of this had set his wheels turning. And when it came to weird shit like this, she knew it was often best to just wait and see where it was going.

"Lucianna called it a puzzle, remember?" He swept his gaze across the walls and ceiling, as if searching for something out of place. "If it's a puzzle, then there must be a solution. And if there's a solution, there must exist a means of *finding* said solution…"

"Unless the woman who called it a puzzle was batshit fucking crazy," she interjected.

"True enough…" he admitted. "But you don't really think she was, do you?"

She didn't respond. He was right. Maybe if there was *only* Lucianna, they could write the whole thing off as the delusions of some nutty old woman, but there was Shanzer and Warner, too. All of them knew about the Temple of the Blind. All of them said the Keeper was summoning them to open another door. And then there was this freaky time-slip they were in. The pervert's twisted orgy mansion. They'd even resurrected the *sex room*. This was happening whether she liked it or not. (And she didn't.)

"My point is that I don't think it was a coincidence that you felt what you did when you saw that woman."

"But we *lost her*."

"Yes. We lost her *right here*." He turned and scanned the hallway around them. "So why did she lead us to this particular spot?"

Brandy frowned and looked around, too. Was he saying the woman in the white dress *intended* for them to follow her? So she could specifically lead them to this spot? That was his logic? "You think this is where we're supposed to be?" She wasn't convinced. It was just a hallway. There was nothing here. "You mean in one of these rooms or something?"

"I don't know."

She didn't know, either. They had the master keycard, so getting into any of these rooms wasn't a problem. But they didn't know which ones were vacant. They couldn't very well go knocking on doors and asking people if they could poke around their rooms.

"I don't think so," decided Albert. "If she'd wanted us to go into a room, she would've let us see which room she went in, wouldn't she?"

"How should I know what some ghostly bimbo would and wouldn't do?"

"Seems more likely to be the hallway, itself," he went on. He turned and looked the other way again. "But why? Is there something here? Something we can't see?" He examined the hallway walls, searching for anything out of place.

Brandy glanced back the way they came. There were people coming this way with their luggage. It was still too busy to be loitering out in the hallway like this. People were going to start thinking they were up to something.

"It *does* feel like there's something here," Albert decided.

She turned her attention back to him, curious. "Where?"

"I'm not sure. Something's just...*off*, I guess?" Then he frowned and scratched at his neck, frustrated. "Or I *think* there is... But *is* there? Or am I just trying too hard to feel something? I don't even know anymore."

"You're supposed to be the one tuned into your environment or whatever."

"That doesn't mean I know how to *use* it." He reached up and rubbed at his temples, frustrated. "I don't get. I mean, is it like Shanzer's sex mansion? Can we only see it using what he taught us or something?"

She made a face at this. "What, like I have to get you horny for you to find it? Because I'm *not* jerking you off in the middle of the hallway."

"I wasn't asking you to!" He glanced back and forth, embarrassed at the thought of someone overhearing her say that to him. "I'm just saying," he whispered, "maybe we need more energy than we have right now."

"And *I'm* just saying," she whispered back, "how the fuck are we supposed to get more of *that kind* of energy in the middle of a *busy hallway*?"

"I have no idea! That was my point!"

"Wanna go back and ask that bartender? She seemed eager to help you out."

"Oh my god, what is with you and that bartender? She surprised me was all! I wasn't expecting—"

One of the nearby doors opened, startling both of them.

Brandy grabbed his arm and continued walking as a muscular man with tattoos covering his arms and neck and a very skinny woman with a deep and frankly unhealthy-looking bronze tan stepped out into the hallway behind them and headed back toward the lobby.

She glanced back at the two of them as they walked away. They didn't seem to notice them, which was good. But as she watched them, she realized that there was something oddly unsavory about those two. It wasn't a strong feeling, like she had with the woman in the white dress. It was subtle. Easy enough to dismiss as her imagination if not for what the pervert told her about her psychic abilities. It wasn't even an unfamiliar feeling. She'd had occasional feelings like that about people all her life. Sometimes she just immediately didn't like someone. And if she was around those people long enough they *always* turned out to be complete assholes. Those two were like that. They were selfish and unkind people. The kind of people who took advantage of others for their own benefit. The kind of people who weren't capable of loving anyone, not even each other...

She looked forward again, her thoughts swimming inside her head. Did she really know all that stuff? She always thought she was just a decent judge of character. But could she actually see the *truth* in people? Was she really able to see what people were inside? It seemed wildly unrealistic...but then again so did *everything else*. So why not?

But did getting herself turned on really dial up the power? Could it actually give her the ability to see so much *more* about people? That seemed so...*stupid*. What the absolute *fuck*? There was no way that was a real thing.

And yet, even Lucianna, who clearly detested the pervert, admitted that sexual energy might be the fastest way to unlock their full potential.

"This isn't like Shanzer's party," reasoned Albert, his voice lowered so that no one overheard him. "If we just start making out and getting horny, we won't exactly be blending in."

"No shit." She seriously doubted that was what Lucianna meant when she said to do whatever they had to do. That was just a good way to get security called on them.

"That means we must be able to utilize that energy in other ways. Lucianna pointed out very specifically that this was one of the area's leading honeymoon destinations, remember? There's sexual energy all around us. We just have to figure out how to access it."

"There's a big difference between the pervert's party and a popular honeymoon resort," she reminded him. "A little thing called *privacy*. Which is something everyone here has *except us*."

"I know." He glanced around at the surrounding doors, thinking hard. "If we really need sexual energy to boost our psychic potential, then we must be able to access that energy without being physically surrounded by people actually having sex."

Ahead of them, a couple who appeared to be in their early sixties were walking toward them. They were clearly on their way to the pool. She was wearing a sunhat and a lacy black swimsuit cover up. He was wearing trunks and a Chicago Bears tee shirt. Both of them were in flip-flops.

Brandy watched them as they approached, her thoughts swimming.

They weren't like that other couple at all. That other couple was utterly self-serving. They didn't even really care about each other. They saw each other as only tools. Thinking about them now, she found herself sure of it. They weren't true to each other. They weren't honest with each other. She only cared about his money. And he only cared about sex. But these two… These two were in love. They only had eyes for each other. It was right there in the way she looked at him…in the way he smiled at her…in the way she hung on his arm…not unlike she, herself, was hanging on Albert's right now…

And as the older couple passed them, she felt an odd flutter in her chest and stopped walking, surprised.

"You okay?" asked Albert.

She nodded. She was fine. But she felt her cheeks grow warm with a faint blush as she processed what she just felt. It wasn't just a random thought. It wasn't her imagination. She *knew* it. It was the absolute truth.

That couple was on their way to the pool now, but only

moments ago they were in their room making love. She could *feel* the breathtaking emotions they'd shared. She felt them as clearly as she felt them each and every time she and Albert made love.

It was as if a switch had been thrown. Her body tingled with the intensity of an electric current. The hairs on her arms stood up.

What came next was like a flash flood inside her brain.

Chapter 26

It was their anniversary.

Forty years, they'd been married. And they'd never been happier. They drove down from their home in Illinois to celebrate in a way they never did on their honeymoon. They could never have afforded it back then, after all. But things were better now. Things were easier. They had more time to spend together. The kids were all grown up and moved away, which made the house feel lonely sometimes, and that had been a little hard. But they had each other. And that was all that ever really mattered.

So many years... Brandy could actually feel them. She didn't know it was possible to *feel* time, but there it was. It was like a weight settling deep inside her, on her very *bones*, weighing down her entire body. So many weeks... So many *days*... Every hour. Every *second*.

She was so nervous on that first date. She felt so out of place. She was always so awkward, after all. That silly way she had of giggling when she was uncomfortable. That nail-biting thing that her mother always told her was such a disgusting habit. And this dress... She never dressed like this. She felt so ridiculous. So *fake*. This was such a bad idea. Why did she agree to this? He worked upstairs in the offices and she was...well she was *nobody*... Maybe she should just leave...

She was so concerned that she was embarrassing herself that she didn't even notice how nervous *he* was until he fumbled and knocked all the silverware off the table, then spilled his water glass trying to retrieve it.

And she never would have guessed that it was that silly giggle that made him ask her out in the first place. He found it endearing. Refreshing. The very sound of it made him feel happy in ways he didn't know were possible. Even after all these years, he never grew tired of making her laugh. It was his favorite sound in the whole world.

It was a whirlwind romance. Warm and fuzzy and passionate and steamy and breathless at all the right times. He took her by the hand and he never let go. They went everywhere together, did everything and anything and nothing together. They couldn't bear being apart.

They were married barely more than a year later. Their son was born. Their daughter followed. Their first dog was a golden retriever. Happiness filled every nook and cranny of their life together.

There were rocky patches, of course. Sick leaves and unexpected expenses. Overtime and missed dinners. Growing pains. Little arguments here and there. All the worries and struggles that life threw at everyone from time to time. Yet their love never faltered.

Changing jobs. Moving homes. Buying cars. Saving money. Always hoping they were doing all the right things, but never certain.

Birthday parties, little league games and dance rehearsals. Graduations, weddings and babies. Bad news, sleepless nights and funerals. Happiness endured, even when peppered with worry and frustration and grief. A life filled to bursting.

Their lives were different from hers and Albert's, but their love was very much the same. She could feel it. It radiated from them. And it felt like *home*.

"What's wrong?" pressed Albert.

Brandy turned and blinked back at him, dazed. "Wha…?"

"You okay?"

She nodded. "Yeah. Sorry. I just…" But she wasn't entirely sure how to explain it. She felt as if she'd just spent a lifetime in those people's shoes. And yet it had only been a few seconds. "Um… I'm okay."

"You sure?"

She nodded again, more assertive than before.

"Because you're kind of stabbing me with your nails right

now."

"Huh?" She looked down at his arm to find that he was right. She was clutching his arm tightly, her manicured French tips pressed hard into his skin. She snatched her hands back, startled, and clasped them over her mouth instead. "I'm sorry!"

"It's fine," he assured her, looking down at his arm. She'd left deep little crescent marks in his skin, but he wasn't bleeding. "I mean, when have I ever complained about you scratching me with your nails?"

"Shush." She grasped his arm again, more carefully this time, and snuggled closer to him as she peered back at the couple walking away from them.

Was that real? She felt as if she suddenly knew them. Intimate details of their life had flooded her mind. She felt like she knew the layout of their home. Their favorite meals. The shows they watched together on television. Even the games they liked to play in the privacy of their bedroom. But that couldn't be real. Her imagination must have gone wild.

She didn't even know their names.

You can see the truth within people.

Truth... She remembered the people at Shanzer's party. The woman in the fountain. Her desperate desire to save her loved one.

(Haven't you ever wondered what possessed you to venture into those tunnels that night with a man you barely knew? You went with him that night because you knew, deep down, that he was good. You knew he wouldn't hurt you. You knew he'd protect you, even though you were just a stranger to him, too.)

She knew things about people.

Looking back on her life, she realized that she'd *always* known things about people. It had nothing to do with being a good judge of character or simply getting a bad vibe off someone. She could *see inside people*, to the parts of them they kept hidden from the world.

And as much as she was loath to admit it, the pervert seemed to be right. Sex, of all the stupid things, seemed to be the key to unlocking a much clearer picture of those truths. One look at that first couple told her what sort of people they were, but even just the lingering sexual energy still hanging over the second couple was enough to open a window through which she was able to perceive glimpses of their intimate *past*.

But she couldn't help grimacing a little at the thought of just how *voyeuristic* this ability was. Given the right circumstances, just how much of a person's life might she be able to see? If she wanted to, could she peek inside someone's head and see, for example, their most intimate desires? Their deepest regrets? Their most embarrassing moments? What dirty secrets could she find?

There was something both grotesque and weirdly alluring about the idea... What an intrusive power. Deceitful. *Dirty*. And yet a part of her was intrigued by the possibilities of such a thing. To be able to see into someone's most closely guarded thoughts and feelings. Their buried desires. Their fetishes. Their kinks. There was simply something enthralling about the idea. The thought of sneaking around in someone's most private memories, like her own secret peephole. She wanted to try it. But at the same time, she was horrified by the thought of just what kinds of evil such a power could reveal to her. What if she found out someone she cared about was being cheated on? What if she discovered that a dear friend secretly hated her for some reason? What would she do if she discovered a family member was some kind of closet pedophile or something? Or what if she laid eyes on some stranger on the street and discovered, quite by accident, that he had a dozen mutilated bodies buried in his back yard?

"Babe...?" worried Albert. "Seriously, are you okay?"

She met his worried gaze and snapped out of it. "Yeah. I'm sorry. I'm just..." She turned and looked back after the couple once more. "Those people..."

"What about them?"

"I *felt* them. Like I did back at that creepy party. I *knew* things about them." She turned back and met his gaze again. "I think I'm starting to get it. If I'm really turned on...or full of sexual energy, I guess?" She rolled her eyes. She didn't want to think about the pervert or his stupid magic lessons, but it didn't seem like they were getting out of this mess until they did what the creep wanted. "Something about that makes my...*ability*, or whatever it is...work better. It lets me see *more*."

He nodded. "Yeah. Like when we stopped running and tried it Shanzer's way. I felt that, too. Like, there was a point where all that built-up energy just...became something else."

"Yeah... But it's not just *me*. If the person I'm looking at has a lot of that energy, I can do it, too!"

He stared at her for a moment as he let that sink in. Then he turned and looked back toward the people she was distracted by. "Wait... So those people were—?"

"Not the point," she snapped.

"Right."

"But...yeah." She glanced back again, but by now they were out of sight. It was embarrassing to admit, even to Albert, that she'd been given a glimpse of something so private. She felt guilty. Perverted, even. It wasn't any different from creepy Shanzer telling them he was watching them the night they found the sex room. "They're here on a romantic getaway. Just like we were. They..." She bit her lip, uncomfortable. "They had a lot of energy, too," she said, leaving it at that.

He nodded. "Good for them."

"Yeah. But that means we really can access the energy of this hotel, doesn't it?"

"Well, *you* can. It's like you said a minute ago. The Shaman of Creepsville said you were sensitive to the people around you and I'm sensitive to my physical environment." He reached out and placed his hand on the wall. "As far as I can tell, this hallway isn't horny at all."

She squinted at him, frowning. "I seriously can't tell if you're joking right now or just being dense."

"Little of both, honestly. My point is, if we're supposed to find something that's *physically* hidden somewhere in this hotel, then won't we need *my* abilities to find it?"

"We're supposed to work *together*, sweetie. That's what the crazy lady downstairs told us."

He chuckled. "Okay. So how do we get *my* psychic abilities

charged up so I can see if there's something here that vanishing woman wanted us to find?"

She rolled her eyes again. "Why is it always about the *man?*"

He blinked at her, confused. "What?"

"You're all the same. Get your rocks off and you're done, never mind us women. But God forbid we don't finish *you* off. Then we're fucking *teases.*"

He stood there a moment, trying to process this abrupt turn of topic.

She turned and looked around. By now, the lines for check-in at the front desk had probably thinned considerably, but it was still a busy time of day.

A young couple walked by, pulling their rolling luggage behind them. A woman wearing the hotel's brown employee uniform passed them going the other way. Several doors back, a middle-aged man in damp swim trunks let himself into one of the rooms. Two shapely, bikini-clad women were approaching from the other direction.

That strange insight had faded. She could grasp only bits and pieces from these people. The young couple was eager to get unpacked and start having fun. The hotel employee was weary and irritable. It was well past her time to go home and she wasn't happy about it.

An older man in a rather silly looking cowboy hat was walking toward them who she immediately decided she didn't particularly like. It wasn't that he was a bad person, she didn't think. But she sensed somehow that he'd be unpleasant to talk with. Condescending. Arrogant.

And they just kept coming. It was hardly crowded, but it was a constant stream of people. It was going to be hard to nose around searching for whatever it was Lucianna wanted them to find, and even harder if they needed to find privacy to utilize the pervert's "sexual energy" nonsense. They probably already looked like a couple of weirdos loitering in the hallway like this.

Hopefully they just looked like they were waiting to meet someone.

"I try to make sure you're done," said Albert.

Down the hall, one of the doors opened. Another couple in bathing suits stepped out of their room and headed for the pools.

It wasn't as strong as the last couple. She wasn't flooded with flashes of their life together. But it was a much more intense connection than the other people passing through. She knew in an instant that they, too, were here on their anniversary. She knew they were in love. She knew they were enjoying their time alone together. And she knew they were looking forward to a long evening drinking and lounging at the pools.

"Don't I try to make sure you're done?" pressed Albert.

"Come on," she said, tugging at his arm. She glanced back and forth. There were still several people in the hallway, but no one was paying attention to anyone else. They were all on their way to somewhere. That was what hallways were for, after all. They were how you got from one place to another. Unless you were being a weirdo, like the two of them.

"I mean, you know you can always tell me if you're not done, right?"

"Yeah, whatever, just move it."

"Should we talk about this? Because if we need to talk—"

"Later. Just come on." But she couldn't help smirking a little as she tugged him along. She was only toying with him. She might not have had a ton of experience with men before she met him, but she knew well enough that he was a wonderful lover who did, in fact, care tremendously about her satisfaction.

But he was so damned *cute* when he thought he'd done something selfish!

She'd make it up to him later. That was a promise.

Chapter 27

Albert's head was spinning. Now he was distracted. He thought he was a considerate lover. He was fairly sure she was only messing with him. She did that a lot, after all. And it was so hard to tell when she was joking. Her deadpan delivery was absolutely epic. But now he was worried. He couldn't help it. This was kind of a serious subject.

But Brandy didn't give him a chance to discuss it. She led him to a nearby door and then turned and snuggled his arm. She smiled up at him and batted those pretty blue eyes. "Open the door, sweetie."

"Huh?"

She did that thing where she widened her eyes for just a second. That universal signal for "take the hint, stupid," and then giggled. "You have the key, remember?"

"Right…" He reached into his pocket. "We aren't going to knock?" he whispered.

"There's no one inside," she whispered back. "Just hurry and open the door."

"It's right here," he said, withdrawing the card. He slid it into the lock and watched the light flash green. He couldn't help feeling a little anxious. What if she was wrong? What if they opened the door to find themselves face to face with some angry hotel guest?

But she opened the door and pulled him inside without hesitation.

She was right. No one was here. But it also wasn't vacant. He stood there as the door swung closed behind him, staring in at the messy sheets and the laundry strung about the room. "Is this okay?" he wondered.

Brandy let go of his arm as soon as they were inside and walked to the middle of the room, looking around. "The people staying here just left for the pool. I saw them go."

"Lucky there was no one else in here…"

"Luck had nothing to do with it. I could tell they were here alone."

He rubbed at his neck, confused. "Psychic?"

"Yep." There was a frilly, sheer negligee lying on the bed. She picked it up by its straps and raised an eyebrow at it. "Nice. You *go*, girl."

He stared at the lingerie for a moment, surprised. "That's…probably not something we were supposed to see." Never mind the shaman. Now *he* felt like a pervert. "Seriously, you couldn't have found us a vacant room? There *had* to be some."

"I can't tell which rooms are vacant." She walked to the window and peered through the curtains. "But I know the couple who just left here were heading for the pool. They won't be back for a while."

"You're sure?"

"Mostly."

"Mostly?" He turned and peered through the peephole. "What if they forgot something?"

"They didn't." She closed the curtain and then turned and faced him. "You said there's something hidden in that hallway out there. Something we need to find."

He frowned at her. "I mean, I don't *know*. I could be wrong. What do I know about *any* of this? But that woman just *vanished*. That's not normal." He glanced back at the door again, thoughtful. "And I just feel like it wasn't a coincidence."

"Okay." She crossed her arms and cocked her head, staring at him. "So *find it*."

He stared back at her, confused. "In here?"

"It's all the same, isn't it? I mean, do *walls* block psychic powers?"

"How should *I* know?"

"We're out of sight now. It's nice and quiet. You can take

your time without people gawking at us. So do it. Make the weird pervo magic work."

He frowned at her. "I'm not sure it works like that…"

"Just do it. Close your eyes. Try…I don't know…feeling the space around you, or something. The pervert said you have some kind of connection to your environment. You used it way back then, too. When you knocked down that wall blocking the entrance to the temple. That was before we ever even found the sex room, so it didn't have anything to do with sexual energy."

He gave his head an indecisive wobble. "Maybe. Although I was hanging out with a really hot girl, so I wouldn't say there wasn't *any* sexual energy involved…"

"You're sweet," she told him. "But I'm being serious."

"So am I."

"There's something out there. Something *significant*. That's what you always called it."

He nodded.

"So find it. Close your eyes. Concentrate."

He glanced around at the room that didn't belong to them. He didn't like being in here. It felt wrong. But he trusted Brandy. If she said it was fine, then it was fine. And it wasn't as if they were going to steal anything. "If you say so," he sighed. He closed his eyes and stood there a moment, wondering exactly what the hell he was supposed to do next.

"The pervert was right about me, I guess. I've been getting weird glimpses into people's lives ever since he told us that shit. So I'm sure he was right about you, too."

She had a point, he supposed. But this wasn't like the temple. When they reached the end of that last tunnel and found the stone wall blocking the entrance, he remembered noticing that something was off about it. He couldn't put his finger on what it was. He told himself afterward that he simply noticed the stones weren't mortared into place. It was so gloomy down there, after all. It wouldn't have been blatantly obvious, but he could've noticed the gaps. But the truth was that there was something about that wall. It just *felt* different. It felt *significant*. It made him take a closer look. It made him test it. But the main difference was that he was standing right in front of that wall. He was staring right at it. He had no idea what might be hidden here, much less *where* it was hidden. What if he needed to be in front of it to see it?

Or what if he was wrong from the start? What if the woman in the white dress didn't disappear at all but merely entered one of these rooms at just the right time? What if it was just a coincidental illusion?

But Brandy said she wasn't supposed to be here... Why would she say that? Something about that woman was meaningful. She was *significant*.

He recalled standing there, gawking down the hallway that she suddenly was no longer walking in. He pictured it just as he saw it in that moment. The doors on either side. The color of the carpet. The brightness of the lights.

And...something else?

No. There wasn't anything else. It was an empty hallway.

Wasn't it?

"Anything?" she asked.

He frowned. "I don't..." *Was* there something else? He was quite sure he would've noticed anything out of the ordinary while he was standing there. But thinking back on it now, it seemed as if he could almost remember there being something. Something...*else*? What did that even mean? What kind of something? It didn't make sense.

Then Brandy was there. She slipped her arms around one of his and pressed herself close to him. "Here. Try this."

"Try what?" he asked, distracted. But then he felt her teeth close gently on his earlobe, surprising him and sending a shiver down his body.

God, it always set his nerves on fire when she did that.

"Okay..." he gasped.

"Shut up and focus," she whispered as she nibbled at him.

Focus. Right. Shanzer and Lucianna both said that emotions were the key to unlocking their psychic potential. But could the answers really be found so easily? It still seemed so ridiculous. What part of getting *turned on* made your psychic abilities stronger? How were the two things even related? Besides, it wasn't as if they weren't used to being intimate together. They'd been lovers for years. And they had sex a *lot*. Shouldn't they have noticed before now if getting aroused made them super psychic?

But what other option did they have at this point?

He closed his eyes and felt her tongue flick against his earlobe. Like every time she did that, it felt like every hair on his body stood on end. Goosebumps prickled up and down his arms.

Slowly, she slid her tongue upward, licking the rim of his ear all the way up and around the helix.

Yeah, if anything this seemed like it was making it *harder* to focus on the task in front of him.

But maybe he'd let her keep trying for a little bit. Just in case.

She slipped one hand under his shirt and lightly dragged her manicured nails slowly up his bare belly, sending a fresh shudder through his tingling body. At the same time, he felt her tongue slide across the middle part of his ear.

This sensation… He felt as if he were melting.

"Is this helping?" she whispered, her breath tickling his skin.

"If I say no," he whispered back, "will you stop?"

"Yes."

"Then yeah, it's totally working. I've almost got it."

"Be serious." She pulled away, then leaned in and kissed him behind his ear. Then again a little lower. Slowly, she made her way down the side of his neck. At the same time, she slid her hand farther up his shirt, her nails lightly dancing across his chest.

He closed his eyes and felt himself drifting away. There was a familiar warmth spreading deep inside him. God, he loved when she touched him this way. It was utter bliss. Everything else in the world always melted away.

What was he supposed to be doing?

She kissed him again and again, tracing a shivery trail along the side of his neck beneath his ear and to the base of his jaw.

Under his shirt, those nails began sliding downward, painting five electric lines down the front of his abdomen toward the fly of his shorts and wrenching a surprised gasp from him.

His knees went weak. He pressed his free hand against the wall to steady himself.

She pressed her body closer to him and squeezed his arm tighter. He could feel the swell of her firm breasts against his bare arm. The denim of her shorts was grinding against the back of his hand. He could feel the heat from her body, so warm, so wonderfully familiar.

Slowly, she slid her tongue back to his ear and flicked it across his earlobe.

This was heaven. He didn't want her to stop. Not ever.

But it was also a little weird. This was someone else's room, filled with someone else's belongings. Other people had slept in that bed. They were intruders here. It even *smelled* like a stranger's space. Unfamiliar perfume and cologne. A different brand of sunscreen than what Brandy bought.

And yet, the layout was so familiar... This room was just like their own, after all. They'd spent the past five days in a space exactly like this.

She touched him like this when they first arrived, too, he recalled. She grabbed his arm as soon as he'd placed the suitcase on the luggage stand and nuzzled his neck almost exactly like this.

It was like being all the way back at the beginning of their honeymoon...

And there was something positively *blissful* about it.

But something was happening. Slowly, everything shifted. The shivery, tingly feeling in his skin seemed to fade away. That warmth inside his belly seemed to sharpen to a fine point somewhere higher up in his chest. And that building pressure in his shorts softened and was replaced with an odd sensation somewhere inside his head that he couldn't quite describe.

There was something odd about the shape of the room. He couldn't quite put his finger on what...but something wasn't exactly the same as it was in their own room.

He opened his eyes and stared at the wall behind the headboard of the bed. Was there something...*off*...about it?

No. His imagination?

And yet...

Brandy was still nibbling at his earlobe, but those shuddery sensations had faded. He felt practically numb to her sensuous touch. And something about that felt incredibly wrong. He didn't like it. It bothered him. Nothing in this world—in *any* world—should tear his attention from his beautiful bride. But he couldn't help it. There was something *significant* in front of him. And it was as if this curious *significance* were overwhelming his senses, pushing everything else out.

Realizing that something had changed, Brandy let go of his earlobe and straightened her glasses. "What's up?"

He didn't answer her. He *couldn't*. His thoughts were racing.

The layout of the room... The layout of the space all around them...

Back in the hallway...

He turned and stepped through the door. There were still people walking back and forth, but he paid them no attention. He was too distracted by the fact that there was more than one hallway.

Chapter 28

"It's like Shanzer's mansion," Albert realized.

"What?" Brandy looked back and forth from his face to whatever it was he was looking at, but she couldn't see anything different. It was the same hallway that was there before. Nothing had changed.

"You don't see it, do you?"

"Apparently not. Wanna let me in on it?"

He took her hand and led her forward. They seemed to be heading back the way they came, toward the bar. But before she could ask him where they were going, he tugged her in a weird direction and made her stumble. She let out a startled gasp and grabbed his arm to steady herself. Then, suddenly and inconceivably, they were in *another* hallway.

"*What the fucking shit?*" she gasped.

"I know, right?"

She blinked at the scene before her. It was a lot like the hallway they were just in, except that it was narrower and there weren't any doors. It was the same gray carpet. The same blue walls. It looked for all the world like just another part of the hotel. Except for the fact that it simply *wasn't here a minute ago.*

They turned and looked behind them. The other hallway was still there. This one branched off it at a rather awkward angle. There were still people there, going on about their business with no indication that they were aware of this hallway's existence. No one even glanced this way.

Were they unable to see them?

When she was out there, she wasn't able to see this one. Not until Albert pulled her into it, nearly knocking her off her feet in the process. Was that how it still was? Could those people not notice them here, even though they were standing right out in the open?

"*So* weird..." she sighed. "I'm never going to get used to this."

He nodded. "I wonder how it works. Like, is it just clever optical illusions? Or is there really some kind of magic at play? I can't wrap my head around it."

"Yeah, let's not think about it too much," she decided. "This'll make my head hurt even worse than the time travel shit."

He nodded again as he watched a group of hotel guests pushing their luggage cart. Several of them were glancing around, looking at all the door numbers, searching for their room, but not one of them glanced this way. "Agreed."

Still clinging to his arm, Brandy turned and started down the new hallway, the voices of the other hotel guests fading behind them.

She didn't like this. What purpose did a mysterious hidden hallway serve? This wasn't like the Temple of the Blind. They never dealt with magical illusions down there. They never had to learn to utilize *sexual energy*.

Or did they? Thinking back now, she recalled the pervert saying something about how getting trapped inside the sex room was the only reason they were able to find the way forward. He said if they hadn't fallen into that insane trap, they would only have found a dead end waiting for them beyond.

Could it really be that they used some kind of sex magic that night? Did they really alter the path before them just by losing control and fucking each other like crazed animals? It still sounded stupid. Who would even come up with such an idiotic thing?

Except here they were. They were walking in a mysterious, hidden hallway that they only found because she got all slutty and made her husband horny.

God, this was ridiculous!

"The layout of the hotel is another illusion," observed Albert. "Like at Shanzer's place. That's why the one wall in that room looked off. It was canted at an angle. But something about the perspective made it impossible to see under normal conditions."

"Fascinating," she grumbled. She didn't recall noticing anything odd about any of that room's walls. It looked just like every other room, as far as she could tell.

She was still clinging to his arm. It wasn't so much that she was frightened, although she was, a little. But she didn't need him to protect her. It was that jarring transition between that last hallway and this one. If that happened again and she wasn't holding onto him, she might fall flat on her face. "Don't you think this is kind of creepy? I mean, *where are we going?*"

"It shouldn't go *anywhere*. The hotel isn't shaped like this." He looked back the way they came. "Given the size of the rooms on either side of us, we should be out past the balconies by now."

"How the fuck does *that* work?"

"More illusions, I guess."

"How does an illusion hide the fact that this hallway *sticks out the side of the hotel?*"

"No idea. Maybe we're at some kind of odd angle?" He looked up at the ceiling. "Between floors, maybe? Clever architecture? I don't know. It's so complex."

"It's so *stupid*. What kind of psycho would even dream up something like this?"

He glanced over at her. "Lucianna said she had it designed by some friend of hers. The hotel is just the face the world sees. I guess *this* part... This is the other side she was talking about. The Mysteria part of the Lucianna Mysteria. And all of it to hide whatever was *originally* here."

"What was here before..." She pursed her lips and wrinkled her nose. "Meaning what the *sentinels* built."

Albert nodded. "She called it some kind of gateway."

She remembered. She also referred to it as a road of some sort. It was all so confusing. "I was really hoping we wouldn't have to deal with any more of the sentinels' shit ever again. We already played their stupid game."

"Yeah..."

She glanced over at him, her mouth drawn tight. He said,

"Yeah," like he agreed with her, but she knew him too well. A part of him was enjoying this. It gnawed at him that they never found all the answers last time. She was well aware that he secretly hoped something like this would happen. And as much as she loved him, there was a small part of her that wanted to punch him right in the face for that.

Just a small part of her. Tiny, even. But it was there.

Ahead of them, the hallway made a sharp right turn. As they rounded this corner, they found that it continued on in this new direction for about a hundred feet, then turned to the right again.

There, at the far end, the woman in the white dress stood staring back at them, as if she'd been waiting for them there this whole time.

"It's her again," whispered Brandy. Even from here, she felt it. That overwhelming sense that this woman wasn't supposed to be here. And after all, if she was here, in this mysterious, hidden hallway, then she certainly wasn't just another guest.

The woman seemed to smile at them. It was an odd sort of smile. It was difficult to tell from that distance, but it seemed to Brandy that there was something unpleasant about that smile.

Then she turned and strolled out of sight.

"Come on!" gasped Albert, tugging at her hand and hurrying after her.

"Hold on!" she hissed. "We don't know anything about that woman!"

He stopped and looked at her, an impatient expression on his face. "She's the only reason we found this hallway," he reminded her.

"That doesn't mean she's friendly! Seriously, there's something not right about that woman. I can *feel* it."

He looked forward again, uncertain.

"I know you want to solve this stupid puzzle, but we have to be careful."

He nodded. "Yeah... But what else are we supposed to do?"

That was a good question. She looked forward, her lower lip poked out a bit. What else *could* they do? The woman in the white dress was the only one who offered them any kind of clue about where they were supposed to go. Lucianna and that black-eyed Warner monster were of no help whatsoever.

"We'll be careful," he promised, starting forward again, slower this time.

"You'd better not get yourself killed doing this shit," she warned him.

They made their way toward the far end of the hallway.

She very much didn't care for this part of the hotel. There still weren't any doors in this hallway. There was only straight ahead or back the way they came. It felt less like a hallway than a tunnel. And she didn't like tunnels. Tunnels were scary.

"Whoever she is, she must know something," reasoned Albert.

"You're right. She knows how to get you to follow her down a creepy-ass hallway."

He shrugged. "If you've got another idea how we should go about finding whatever it is we're here to find so we can hurry up and go home, I'm all ears."

She had no such ideas, of course. He was right. If not for the mystery woman in white, they'd probably be wandering the hallways all night, never knowing where to even start looking.

But when they turned the corner, they found that the hallway came to an abrupt end.

The woman in the white dress had once again vanished.

Chapter 29

"Where'd she go?" asked Albert, confused.

Brandy looked back the way they came. "What the fuck is the point in having a hallway that doesn't go anywhere?"

"Doesn't make sense," he agreed. There wasn't a single door. It served no purpose whatsoever. There was no reason for it to exist.

"I don't think *I* can do anything," she reasoned. "There aren't any people here."

He walked to the end of the hallway and placed his hands on the wall. It didn't appear to be any different from the walls on either side of them. "Is it another hidden opening?"

She wrinkled her nose at him. "Is this what it's going to be like now? Every time we find a dead end, you're gonna say, 'Maybe we just can't see it,' and use it as an excuse to try to feel me up?"

He frowned at her, distracted. "That was kind of a leap, wasn't it? I just said it might be something hidden."

"Which, according to the pervert, means we have to get all *sexy* to see. Meaning you're just thinking with your dick. You men are all the same. Only one thing on the brain."

"Says the biggest nympho I've ever met! How many times have you ever *seriously* tried to stop me from feeling you up?"

"At least two," she replied, staring him down with a straight face.

She was so much better at that than he was. He couldn't help laughing. Even after all this time, he never knew what might come out of her mouth. And he was never quite sure when she was being serious. "Okay then," he sighed. "But seriously. I mean, I don't know what we're supposed to do. Shanzer went on and on about that sexual energy stuff, but how're we supposed to know when to use it? When are we 'tuning into our psychic energy' or whatever and when are we just being that weird, pervy couple making out in some random hallway?"

"I'm not making out with you in *this* hallway. It's creepy here."

"Yeah, not exactly romantic, is it?"

"Seriously, though," she said, "this is going to take forever if I have to stop and stick my tongue in your ear every couple of minutes."

"Yeah, not very efficient." He looked at the walls on either side of them. He looked up at the ceiling. He looked down at the carpet. Nothing appeared out of place at all. But nothing appeared out of place in the last hallway, either.

Sexual energy… Brandy was right. Shanzer couldn't possibly expect them to stop and turn each other on every time they found themselves unsure what to do next. It didn't make sense. It took too long, for one thing. The only logical explanation was if they were capable of finding that mindset on their own, and quickly.

"Okay," he said. "Let me try something."

It shouldn't be that difficult. Ever since that night, he was *always* finding himself turned on. At all times of the day. Whether Brandy was around or not. At night after she'd fallen asleep. While she was at work. While *he* was at work. It was an inconvenience, really. A distraction. A *frustration*. There were times when he found it almost impossible to concentrate. And there were few things as embarrassing as trying to hide it when he needed to work. Especially when someone asked if he was feeling okay because he was looking "a little out of it." He was always blaming it on a bad night's sleep. Everyone he worked with thought he had chronic insomnia. Betty Losnagger kept telling him he needed to buy a better mattress. And Jack Porasan was convinced he had sleep apnea.

There was absolutely no reason that he couldn't do this on his own.

He closed his eyes and tried to concentrate, like he did back in that other couple's room. He pictured the wall in front of him. The ceiling above and the floor below. The walls on either side of him and behind him.

"You better not be thinking about that bartender."

"Not helping," he informed her.

"Just saying."

Deep breath. Nice and slow.

The soft blue of the paint on the wall. Smooth and cool against the palm of his hand.

It was quiet, he realized. *Very* quiet. No voices reached this far from the last hallway. No murmuring could be heard through the walls. From here, he couldn't even hear the droning hum of the air conditioning blowing through the vents.

How far from the hotel had they wandered?

It even smelled a little different, he realized. Slightly musty, he thought. Perhaps the cleaning staff didn't even know this hallway was here. Although it also didn't appear particularly dirty. If no one ever cleaned in here, wouldn't the carpet be noticeably dusty?

He clenched his jaw and forced himself to clear his head. It wasn't getting him anywhere to analyze how the hallway *smelled*. He needed to focus on the *layout*.

Sexual energy. If that was the key, this shouldn't be that hard. He had only to think about his beautiful wife. The times they'd spent together. Hell, only the past *week* they'd spent together.

She'd been so *playful* throughout their stay, embracing the experience to the absolute fullest. Everywhere they went, she teased him with little flashes of her lovely body, reminding him again and again that she didn't pack any underwear. She kept reaching over and touching his thigh when he was driving somewhere. And whenever they were walking around somewhere together, she kept reaching up and whispering naughty things she wanted to do with him when they were back in their room again.

He remembered the way she looked on their wedding night. Sitting there in front of him in her lovely gown, her hair and makeup so pretty. That mischievous glint in her eye as she slowly pulled up the dress and spread her naked thighs apart for him…

Yeah. He could definitely conjure up plenty of sexual energy on his own.

Maybe even a little too much of it… He shifted his weight, suddenly uncomfortable, and tried to focus on the space around him.

"Did you find it?" asked Brandy. She was standing close to him, watching his expression, waiting to see what he discovered. He could smell her perfume. He could feel the warmth radiating from her body. He found that he could even tell, with his eyes closed, that she was playing with her hair again, twirling a lock of it as she waited to see what he would find.

A part of him wanted to grab her right there and kiss her. But he needed to focus. He needed to *use* the energy, not expel it. That was what the shaman had taught them. That was why their psychic abilities didn't manifest in any significant way while they were living together. They didn't direct that energy. They didn't funnel it into the psychic part of their minds. They aimed it at each other instead. They never knew they could consciously direct it anywhere else. As much as he wanted to take her in his arms right now, he had a job to do. He needed that energy. He forced himself to focus. On this moment. On these surroundings. On this environment.

What was *really* here?

He opened his eyes and frowned. Something wasn't right. A restless sort of unsettling feeling was rapidly swelling inside him. "This feels wrong."

"What?"

He turned and met her gaze. "I don't think we should be here."

She stared at him a moment longer, a deep expression of concern slowly overtaking her pretty features. Then she nodded. "Okay. Then let's go back."

"Yeah."

They turned and hurried back the way they came. Around the last corner and back to the *real* hallway.

Albert breathed a sigh of relief as they turned and headed

back toward the main building. "I have no idea where that woman went, but you were right. That wasn't somewhere we should've been."

"What did you feel?"

"I'm not sure how to describe it. It was like…" He shook his head. "It just felt *bad*. Like *everything* in that hallway was wrong. Like *nothing* was what it seemed."

"That definitely sounds like somewhere we shouldn't be," she agreed. She glanced back, half-expecting to find the mysterious and apparently very *dangerous* woman in the white dress chasing after them. "Stay out of the bad hallway. Got it. But what do we do now?"

"I have no idea." He reached up and rubbed at the back of his neck. He felt tired. Did utilizing sexual energy take a toll on him? Or had it just been a really long day? "Maybe we should go find Lucianna again. See if she knows anything about that woman."

"I seriously doubt that airhead is going to be any help. She pretty much told us she had no idea how this place worked."

Albert stopped walking and frowned at an intersection in the hallway ahead of them. "I…don't remember this…"

"What?" She looked back the way they came. "Did we go the wrong way?"

He shook his head. "No…" They turned right when they exited that hidden corridor. That should have pointed them back toward the main part of the hotel. But there shouldn't have been any intersections between here and there, except for the stairways and emergency exits. But there were no stairways. There were no exit signs.

He continued walking, slower now, more cautious. When he reached the intersection, he stopped and looked both ways. The hallway continued on for some distance in each direction, then curved left, out of sight, just like the one behind them, limiting how far he could see. It was the same straight ahead. They were each the same length, with the same number of visible doors. Four strangely identical hallways that he was quite certain weren't there before.

Brandy turned all the way around, looking in every direction. She didn't like this. It didn't feel right. Albert wasn't the kind of person who got lost easily. He'd always been good at finding his way around, no matter where they were. Thinking about it now, after what the pervert told them, she realized that it could be because of that psychic connection to his environment. Someone like that might naturally be good at not getting lost.

But if that were true, then what kind of messed-up place could trip him up like this?

He turned and looked behind them again. "Seriously, where are we?"

Brandy looked up and frowned at the hallway in front of them. Then she looked behind them. "Where did everybody go?"

He looked forward again, his eyebrows scrunched together. "What?"

"There were lots of people walking around before. Where'd they all go?"

He turned and looked. "Oh yeah…" In fact, he couldn't remember seeing anyone roaming the halls since they returned from that dead-end where they lost the woman in the white dress.

And now that he was paying attention, he realized that it still had that strange, musty smell about it. It was a little stronger now, even.

Brandy didn't like this at all. The longer they stood here, the more she felt that it wasn't merely the hallways that were deserted. There were no voices drifting from behind any of these doors. No televisions were on. She felt strangely alone. As if there weren't another human being for miles.

But that made no sense. Of course there were other people here. They were inside a crowded resort hotel.

Right?

Albert grasped her hand and started forward again, continuing straight for no good reason he could think of, only that this was the direction they were walking when they first realized they were lost.

"I have a bad feeling about this," whimpered Brandy.

Albert said nothing, but she knew he felt it too. She could feel it in his grip as he held her hand, in the way his eyes flitted from doorway to doorway as they passed them.

As soon as they turned the corner at the far end of the hallway, they found themselves at another dead end.

They stood there a moment, clinging to each other's hand, staring at the empty wall ahead of them.

Chapter 30

Albert turned and looked back the way they came. Was it his imagination, or had something changed? He wasn't sure. It was very subtle. Something about the lighting, maybe? Everything looked just a little...*duller* than before...

Whatever it was, he couldn't help feeling that it was bad news.

He took Brandy by the hand and started walking again. He didn't like standing around. He wanted to keep moving. If the pervert was right about him having some kind of connection to his physical environment, then there was something wrong about this particular place, something he *really* didn't like.

This was starting to feel like the labyrinth down in the depths of the Temple of the Blind.

Was that what this was? Were they in another maze?

They returned to the intersection and he turned left, choosing entirely at random. It didn't seem to matter. Somehow, he didn't think it made any difference which way they went. Every hallway led to the same dead end.

But it wasn't *exactly* the same, he realized.

It wasn't his imagination. Everything *did* look duller. The carpet. The walls. The doors and ceiling. None of it was as clean and bright as it was before. The floor looked dusty, especially along the walls on either side. The blue paint was cracked and peeling in places. Even the doorknobs were starting to look tarnished.

Brandy looked back the way they came. "There has to be a way out, right?"

He glanced over at her. Did she not see what was happening around them? He was more observant than she was. He'd always been good at spotting little changes in things around him. Even growing up, he was always the first to notice when his mom changed something in the house, when she put up new decorations, when she did something different with her hair. (It used to infuriate Becca because Mom and Dad always teased her about being so oblivious.) And he was pretty sure it helped him at work, too, with web design code. But this was more than just a subtle change in the lighting or the hue of the paint. How did she not notice it? It couldn't just be him, could it?

"I mean we got *in*. We should be able to get out."

"I'm not sure this place works like that."

"Well it *should*."

"I know it *should*. I just don't think it *does*."

They turned the next corner and found another dead end, exactly like the last one. He wasn't exactly surprised.

Brandy uttered a very unladylike curse.

He nodded agreement. It would probably do no good to go back and try the last hallway. Something told him it was all going to be the same, no matter how many times they tried it. But what else were they supposed to do? The longer they were here, the more wrong this place felt.

But when he turned and looked back the way they came, he found that everything had changed even more. The carpet looked old and worn. The paint was peeling from the walls. The doors were faded and discolored. And several of the light fixtures were out. It looked as if it had aged a decade instead of mere seconds since they came that way.

"What's happening to the hotel?" squeaked Brandy.

"Oh good," said Albert. "You *are* seeing it, too. I was worried I was just going crazy."

"*Yeah* I see it! That did *not* look like that a minute ago!"

It was changing faster now. It was as if they were moving forward through time, picking up speed as they went. From weeks and months to years.

Brandy glanced around, uncertain, then let go of his hand, walked to the nearest door and beat on it.

"Okay then…" was all he could think to say.

"We're obviously not getting anywhere running around out here. Maybe the way out is in one of these rooms." She tried the knob, but it was locked. "Use the keycard. Open it."

Albert hesitated. He didn't care for the idea of just opening a locked hotel door. But if nobody was answering... He withdrew the card from his pocket and stepped closer. He knocked again for good measure. "Housekeeping?" he called, uncertain.

"There's obviously nobody there," she told him.

"I'm just being sure."

There was still no answer, so he slipped the card into the slot and opened the door.

He expected to find an empty room. Perhaps one that appeared to have been sitting neglected for years, but a room, nonetheless. Instead, the space behind the door was dark and empty. There were no lights, no windows, no furniture. That musty, disused smell wafted out at them, stronger than ever.

And the room was far bigger than it should have been. It stretched well beyond where the hallway lights reached. The far side looked like nothing more than an empty black void.

"That's fucking creepy..." whimpered Brandy.

He nodded. It was indeed.

"I'm *not* going in there."

"Me neither." He closed the door and made double-sure it was latched. Then they turned and looked back down the hallway.

It had changed again. The carpet was in rotten tatters. There were gaping holes in the drywall. The ceiling tiles were crumbling. And one of the few remaining fluorescent lights was flickering on and off in perfect horror movie fashion.

At this rate, the place was going to start falling apart around them any second.

Brandy turned on him, her pretty features twisted with mounting fear. "What're we supposed to do?"

Albert stood there a moment, his thoughts churning in his head. It was a lot to process. So much had happened in such a short amount of time. From the moment they found the brochure for Shanzer's absurd sex museum, it had been one thing after another. And between the wedding and the honeymoon, it felt like forever since he'd seen his normal life in his normal home with his normal job sitting in front of a normal computer screen. And now they were trapped in this rapidly aging dead-end hallway with no way out.

The only thing he knew for certain was that they were no longer in the Lucianna Mysteria. This was someplace else.

Gilbert House showed him without a doubt that there were worlds other than this one out there. That entire building was a doorway into the Wood. But it was an actual doorway. Somewhere between the cellar door and the stairwell at the far end of the basement was a point where you passed from one to the other. He didn't pretend to be smart enough to truly understand something like that. The actual physics of it were beyond his understanding, but he thought it must be some kind of wormhole. An Einstein-Rosen bridge, scientists called it. A gateway between the two realities.

This was like that. Except when they wanted to leave Gilbert House, they simply walked back out the way they came. How the hell did they get out of *this* place? He had no idea how they even got here.

He squeezed his eyes shut and rubbed at his forehead, frustrated. This was all so damned confusing.

"Hurry up and think of something!" she whimpered.

He opened his mouth to say he was trying, but before he could begin to form the words, something struck the other side of the door he just closed and locked, startling a scream from Brandy.

Albert grabbed her arm and backed away from the door as something began clawing at the wood on the other side.

"What is that?" she cried.

Something struck the door behind them next, startling another scream from her.

They spun around, terrified, as the unseen thing let out a chilling hiss.

"Albert!"

But he didn't know what to do. Within seconds, there were

things clawing and hissing at *all* the doors.
    They were surrounded.

Chapter 31

Brandy couldn't breathe. The last time she felt this kind of crippling panic, she was plummeting to what she believed was her death in the heart of the crumbling temple.

Somehow she didn't think Andrea was going to open up a magic portal and spirit them away to safety this time. Andrea was lucky. She was still back in the normal world, where monsters weren't trying to break down the door, pervert shamans didn't lecture her about sex magic and time didn't circle back on itself.

She and Albert were on their own this time.

He set off back down the decaying hallway, pulling her by the hand. He meant to check the last hallway, she realized. Lucky number four, he was probably thinking. But why would there even be a way out? It was becoming more and more obvious that something intended to trap them in this place.

The woman in the white dress? Was she trying to get rid of them?

There's a strange energy building in these walls, she thought, recalling the ominous words Warner spoke through the oblivious waitress' lips. *Something dangerous is stirring. It grows stronger by the hour.*

Her gaze flitted from one door to the next as they rushed down the scary corridor. Whatever was behind them was clawing and banging and hissing. It wasn't like the snorts and snarls of the hounds back in the temple. This wasn't *those* horrors. There was none of that almost mechanical clattering/rattling noise of their slashing scales. This was something completely different, but probably equally as dangerous.

As Albert pulled her through the intersection of the two hallways, she could hear the same, awful noises from both directions. She could even see some of the doors shuddering against their frames, threatening to break open.

The longer you take, the less likely you are to leave alive.

She gripped Albert's hand a little tighter and found herself reaching for the medallion hanging over her heart with her free hand.

Were they really going to make it out of this one? Because it was starting to seem less and less like the Keeper really had their backs this time.

It was getting darker. Less and less of those fluorescent lights still worked. The floor was littered with flakes of peeling paint and broken tiles. The carpet was little more than tattered rags beneath their feet.

Some of the doors were barely hanging on their hinges. They wouldn't last much longer.

Ahead of them, the fourth hallway dead-ended just like the other three. Albert cursed and turned to look the other way. "So much for that…" he muttered.

Brandy pressed herself closer to him and hugged his arm. "What now?"

But he didn't have an answer for her. Nor had she expected him to have one. This wasn't some silly puzzle for him to solve. This was an attack. Something was trying to stop them.

The sounds of whatever horrors were behind those doors were getting louder. Whatever they were, more and more were gathering there.

She didn't even realize they were backing away until her heel struck the wall behind them. A stark reminder that there was nowhere left to go.

Somewhere around the bend in the hallway, a loud crash announced that one of the doors had finally failed. A strange and unnerving scuttling noise was rushing toward them, like hundreds of sharp claws skittering across the rotten carpet.

She turned and buried her face against Albert's shoulder, terrified.

He wrapped his arms around her, as if he stood any chance of protecting her from whatever was coming. It was a sweet gesture, at least. Somewhere deep down, beneath the raging terror that was enveloping her, she could appreciate that much.

Was this it? Was this where the Keeper's stupid puzzle brought them?

Something large and shadowy rounded the corner and charged toward them. She saw it from the corner of her eye as she pressed herself against her husband. Something big and low to the ground, but not bulky like the hounds. It was a dark red color. And she thought she glimpsed a multitude of long, spindly legs. But she didn't dare look any closer.

She closed her eyes and screamed…

Chapter 32

Brandy screamed…

…but nothing happened.

As she stood there, her face pressed against Albert's shoulder, her jaw clenched against the inevitable agony of her violent impending death, it slowly sank in that everything had gone silent.

"What…?" muttered Albert, confused.

She opened her eyes to find that the dirty, disintegrating hallway with its vicious pack of monsters was gone. They were instead standing in their own living room. "Uh…? When did…?"

"This isn't right…" said Albert, glancing around.

"No shit. Why are we suddenly *home*?" She straightened her glasses and looked down at the coffee table, at the television remote sitting there, waiting for them to return to their normal lives. Suddenly, all she wanted in the whole world was to snuggle up with him on the couch, turn on Netflix and forget that any of this nonsense ever happened.

But Albert was shaking his head. "This isn't home."

"What?" She glanced around. It *looked* like home. This was their apartment. This was where they'd been living for the past five years.

Wasn't it?

But now that she was looking, something didn't seem quite right.

"We didn't leave it like this," he recalled. "Everything's too tidy. Remember how busy we were those last few days leading up to the wedding?" He pointed at the chair. "Where's your overnight bag?"

He was right. She'd worn her regular clothes to the country

club and changed into her gown in the bride's room with the girls. She brought those clothes home in her bag and left them in the Mustang overnight because unpacking wasn't part of her wedding night itinerary. The next morning, while packing up the car, he brought the bag in for her and left it on that chair, right where he was pointing. But it was gone.

"We left stuff on the table," he recalled, glancing around. "Dishes in the dish drain. There were empty beer cans on the coffee table."

"But this is our furniture, isn't it?"

"Is it?" he wondered, looking at the couch. "It looks newer, doesn't it?" None of the living room furniture was ever new. Most of it came second-hand from his Grandma and Grandpa Narwit when they bought a new living room set. He pointed at the cushion on the right. "Where's the stain from when we spilled that wine?"

"Okay, I get it," she sighed, looking around. "How do you always remember that kind of shit? I know you're psychic, but *fuck*."

"It's not just our stuff," he observed. "It feels like the living room's bigger than it should be, too. There's more space between the door and the table."

She looked around, trying to remember. It looked normal to her. But had she ever really taken the time to pay attention to the exact dimensions of their apartment? She couldn't think of any reason why she would ever bother.

He turned and looked across the kitchen, then tipped his head to one side, confused. "Also, we don't have a cat."

"Wait, what?" She walked over to where he was standing and followed his gaze to the top of the fridge where an elegant calico sat staring back at them with big, yellow eyes. "Yeah, he's new."

"Weird," he agreed.

"Okay... Why would someone send us to an *almost* perfect replica of our home? What kind of sense does that make?"

"I have no idea. But something's definitely not right." He remembered that stubbornly logical part of his brain trying to rationalize being back in their hotel room exactly as it looked three days ago. He even constructed a convoluted scenario as to how someone could have tricked them. That same part of him was still hard at work now, trying to convince him that it was still happening. But why would *that* part of the illusion be so perfect and *this* part be so flawed?

Brandy groaned. "Is it too much to ask that we're just dead and this is heaven?"

He glanced over at her, eyebrow raised.

"What? All the shit we've been through? At this point, I'd take never leaving our home for eternity."

"What, you mean like *this* is our afterlife? Like that couple from *Betelgeuse*?"

"Why not? You don't like the idea of spending eternity alone at home together?"

"Point taken." It *did* sound like heaven, now that she mentioned it. "But I really don't think we're dead."

"Shit. I was hoping we could be done."

"Sorry to disappoint you...I guess..."

Something moved in the window. They both turned to see another cat—white this time—step out from behind the curtain and stretch.

Brandy pointed at it, then to the calico on top of the fridge. "Are you going to tell them that pets aren't allowed in this building or do I have to?"

A soft cry alerted them to the presence of a third cat, this one a gray tabby that emerged from beneath the chair. At the same time, an orange and white longhair lifted its head and yawned beneath the television.

Were they there this whole time? She felt like she should've seen the one under the television before now. It wasn't the slightest bit hidden.

"Where are they coming from?" wondered Albert.

But before she could ask him why the fuck he thought *she'd* know, they were startled by a deep growl from the gloom of the hallway.

A *huge* black cat was sitting there staring back at them, the tips of its ears nearly three feet off the floor.

She grabbed Albert's arm and crowded close to him, startled. "That's the second biggest pussy I've seen this week..." she whispered.

Albert nodded.

It wasn't a panther. It didn't have the distinctive face of any big species of cat. It looked like any other ordinary housecat. It was just *really* big.

As they watched, it stood up and walked away. There was something odd about its movements. It sort of flickered. It was like watching a camera glitch. It twitched to one side, doubled for a second, then slid back again.

Before they could quite wrap their heads around what they were seeing, the enormous feline had vanished into the darkness.

It was only now that Brandy realized just how long and dark the hallway had become. In their real home, it only led to the bedroom and the bathroom. But this hallway seemed to reach back into a strangely vast and empty darkness, not unlike that room they peeked into back in the disintegrating hallway.

But the darkness wasn't empty at all. Something was there. She could feel it. A strange and somehow unsettling shape lurking just beyond her sight.

Then a voice called out. It was soft, almost a whisper, yet it carried like a scream, sending shivers down her body. "A longing gaze between two lovers... A hollow man in hollowed earth... Follow the pipes to find his tomb..."

Then, without warning, they were no longer standing in the queer, not-quite-right version of their living room. Instead, they were standing inside a blue canvas tent, surrounded by the loud murmur of voices and the soothing drone of music. The air was hot and humid and there was a strong scent of chlorine in the air. Her glasses began to fog up.

An overweight man with an abundance of body hair was stretched out in a poolside lounge chair in front of them, snoring loudly.

Brandy stared at the man, too confused to find any words.

Albert, however, was already turning around, taking in his

surroundings. "I know this place."

She did, too, now that she'd had a moment to process it all. This was one of the hotel's poolside cabanas. They spent an afternoon in one of these, themselves, just the other day. They had some amazing sex on one of those lounge chairs. It was awesome. But that wasn't exactly the point...

They were back at the hotel!

But how the hell did they get to the pool? Weren't they on the second floor?

Brandy pointed at the overweight napper, but still couldn't seem to find any words. What was happening? None of this made any sense!

Albert gave her hand a firm tug and the two of them hurried out of the cabana before the man could wake up and catch them standing over him like a couple of weirdos.

Chapter 33

Brandy gawked at the bustling poolside as Albert led her through the crowd, blinking in bewilderment. "Okay, so...? Just...? What the *fuck*?"

"Don't ask *me*. I don't know what the hell's going on." He was making his way toward the first set of doors he saw, eager to get back inside and away from the noisy crowd. Everything was happening so fast. He felt like he barely had time to breathe.

"I mean, what're we doing *here*? Weren't we on the second floor before all of that? And what the fuck was up with that weird version of our apartment? And those *cats*?"

"That was weird," he agreed. That definitely wasn't their apartment. But where was it? What was with that huge cat? And that voice... Two lovers? A hollow man? Follow the pipes? *What* pipes? What did it mean? Who was speaking to them?

"And when did it get so dark?" she asked, babbling on. "Wasn't it just daytime?"

She was right. It shouldn't be this dark out yet. He still didn't have his phone to tell him the time, but it hadn't been that long since they were sitting in the bar, looking out the window at the early evening sunshine. He looked up into the dark sky overhead. Looking out over the forest from their room, there would be stars shining in the sky, but here in the glare of the hundreds of flood lights illuminating the pools and surrounding grounds, there was nothing but a washed-out darkness that reminded him a little too much of the empty sky that loomed over the Wood. "It gets dark around eight this time of year," he recalled, pushing that frightful forest from his thoughts. "If it's full dark, it's probably closer to nine at the earliest."

"Well it can't be any later than midnight," she reasoned.

"Because that's how late the pools are open."

He nodded. "That's right. I remember. And it doesn't look like there's a lot of people leaving yet. My best guess is somewhere between nine and eleven-thirty." But then he frowned. "That seems like a lot of time we lost, though, doesn't it?"

"Well, Lucianna said time was fucked up here. Maybe we lost a couple hours."

Even time loops back on itself through some of the peculiar passageways hidden on these floors, he recalled. It seemed like Lucianna was expecting an awful lot of them. "Remember when they at least gave us a box full of random junk and convoluted clues to tell us where to go? Because I'm really missing the random junk and convoluted clues right about now."

He slowed down as he approached the doors and looked out over the pool. "Oh, I know where we are now."

"You should. That swim-up margarita bar was like my second home while we were here."

"Right…" It was still so surreal to be back here again. As much as they'd enjoyed their stay, this was all supposed to be just memories by now. They should be at home, safe and sound, living their lives, beginning their marriage.

"Actually, if we're going to be doing this shit much longer, I might need another one of those," she added, looking longingly at the bar.

"Put me down for one, too." He turned and scanned the surrounding walls of the hotel, trying to remember where they were in relation to where they found that mystery hallway.

"Wait…" Brandy pointed at the big chalkboard sign advertising their daily special. "That two-for-one deal…" she recalled, confused.

"What about it?"

"That wasn't Monday. That was *yesterday*."

Now he turned around, distracted. "What?"

"They had a different deal every day. I remember. This is Wednesday night."

"Are you sure?"

"Uh, *yeah*. I don't forget two-for-one margaritas. Just ask

Nikki."

"I'll take your word on it," he muttered as he stared at the sign. If she was right, then they'd not only moved down a floor and out into the hotel's pool grounds, they'd also skipped ahead more than two days. That meant that they'd traveled through time *again*. Forward this time, but still in the past. The other them would be checking out tomorrow morning. God, it was hard to wrap his head around that. Just the idea of the other them being here somewhere... "Wait..." He stopped and glanced around as something occurred to him. "Where were we this time Wednesday night?"

"Fucking like monkeys," she replied without thinking about it. "That many margaritas *always* makes my clothes fall off."

"Right..." he replied, looking around again, this time to make sure no one had overheard her. She was always blurting stuff like that out and she was long overdue for some surprised looks.

Was it any wonder the Keeper chose their honeymoon as the time to launch phase two of his stupid plan? Lucianna was right. They'd been building up sexual energy all week.

"We went back to our room right around sunset," she reminisced. Then she scowled at him. "How do you not remember? It was like, *last night.*"

"It's coming back to me! A lot's happened since last night, in case you hadn't noticed." He scratched at his head, confused. "Besides, it wasn't last night. Last night was the pervert's midnight sex party."

"Which was, like, two *hours* ago," she reminded him.

He was pretty sure it had been longer than that, although probably not *much* longer. Instead, he said, "See? *Confusing.*"

She stood there, squinting at him, as if trying hard to make out some tiny detail she couldn't quite see.

"Are you trying to use your psychic power on me?"

"Why? You feeling guilty about all the other women you've been ogling lately?"

"I wasn't ogling *anything*! What's up with you today?"

She turned and looked out at the busy pool, her lips tightly pursed. It was the look she always had when she was irritated with someone. It was usually reserved for bosses and coworkers, but she gave him his share, too.

But Albert didn't think he quite deserved the look. Not this time. He didn't ask for any of this stuff to happen. He was just trying to get through it all so he could go home with his wife.

And wasn't it *her* idea to go to that stupid sex museum in the first place?

He rubbed his eyes, weary, and tried to focus on the task before them. The good news was that right now their past selves were...*preoccupied*. They didn't have to worry about running into them. He remembered clearly now that they kept to their room the rest of that night. They were safe to go wherever. At least until they jumped to some other random day and time. But then again...if they were going to be bouncing around in time very much, they might have to worry about bumping into their *future* selves as well... Was he going to have to keep track of where and when they were at all times until they were done here?

God this was a lot to process.

He took her hand again and led her through the doors, into the much quieter and pleasantly air-conditioned hallway.

"Let's see..." he muttered, pausing to reorient himself. Two heavyset men in obnoxious Hawaiian shirts passed them on their way outside. An older couple was letting themselves into their room a few doors behind them. And two middle-aged women were talking a little more loudly than Albert thought was strictly necessary in the hallway up ahead of them.

When they were still guests here, they would have gone that way, following those women toward the lobby and that main elevator. But it wasn't their room they needed to get to this time. In fact, he had no idea where they should go next. That hallway they found obviously wasn't right.

They seemed to be right back where they started.

"Have you done it?" asked a deep, gravelly voice from behind them.

They turned to find a man standing in the open doorway of one of the rooms. He had black, thinning hair, ridiculous-looking sideburns and a broad, flabby chest covered in a patchwork of graying hair. He was wearing nothing but a skin-tight speedo that was barely visible below the sagging bulk of his huge, swollen beer belly. Warner's strange, soulless eyes stared back at them from behind the man's face.

Brandy wrinkled her nose and gestured at the scene before her. "Just so you know, that is *not* a good look for *either* of you."

Warner cocked the man's head slightly to one side. Without human eyes, it was difficult to tell if it was an indication of confusion or impatience or both at once.

"It's been, like, *ten minutes* since we saw you in the bar," Albert informed him. "What do *you* think?" It was another exaggeration, of course. They took longer than that finishing their dinner. But he still didn't think it could have been much more than an hour. They left the bar, caught sight of that woman, located the hidden hallway and then everything turned *really* weird.

Those black eyes narrowed. "You're from before."

"Before?" asked Brandy.

Albert stared at him. "You've talked to us before now..." he realized. "Your past but our future..."

"What?" She scrunched up her pretty features as she tried to process this. "The fucked-up timeline..." she deduced. When they first arrived back here it was last Monday afternoon. Now it was Wednesday night. Was Albert really saying that they were going to travel to some time between then and now and have another conversation with this thing?

Two young women walked through the hotel, their pool bags slung over their shoulders, and looked over at the man in the doorway.

"Ew!" gasped one of them.

"Gross!" agreed the other one.

Both women hurried off in the other direction.

"See?" said Brandy. "Told you it wasn't a good look."

Warner didn't look remotely embarrassed, though. And she supposed he wouldn't. What did he care what two random women thought of his unfortunate host's even more unfortunate fashion sense?

"Help us," urged Albert. "We don't know what to do."

"I'm not allowed to help," said Warner. "The Keeper forbids it."

"Well the Keeper's a *little bitch*," snapped Brandy. "You can tell him we said that."

"There's a woman wandering around," said Albert.

"An enemy of the cycle prowls the depths of Mysteria," warned Warner. "Be on your guard. Beware the Ruin."

"The Ruin…?" pondered Albert.

"But the cats are your allies," he added. "That is all I can offer you."

"Cats…" pondered Albert.

"So that voice in that fucked-up version of our apartment…" reasoned Brandy.

"That stuff about the lovers and the hollow man and the pipes…" agreed Albert, nodding. "But that doesn't tell us where we're supposed to go from here."

The man in the speedo blinked and Warner was gone. He stood there, staring back at them, confused.

"Typical," grumbled Brandy.

"Disappointing," agreed Albert.

The man looked down at himself, his cheeks flushing red with embarrassment. Then, without a word, he took a step back and shut the door between them.

Chapter 34

"Cats…" muttered Albert as the two of them wandered up the hallway. The first thing that came to mind was obviously that really big one. He recalled how strangely it had moved as it turned and withdrew into that ominous black hallway. It was as if it weren't a cat at all, but some kind of imperfect impersonation of one. *A longing gaze between two lovers…* he recalled. *A hollow man in hollowed earth… Follow the pipes to find his tomb…* Was that what Warner was talking about? Was that what they needed to focus on? In addition to the big one, there were at least four other cats in that not-quite-right version of their apartment, too. But there were more. "There was a cat in Lucianna's office," he recalled. "A little gray one."

"Oh yeah…" recalled Brandy. "I remember that."

"And there were several at Shanzer's party, too."

"Were there?"

"There was one in the windowsill in the foyer."

"Really?"

"There was also one in the bar and another one up on the balcony at one point, too."

"Hm. Well the whole time I was there, I was a little preoccupied with wanting to *not be there*. So maybe I didn't notice."

Even if she hadn't been preoccupied, he wasn't surprised she missed them. It wasn't as if the cats had been standing in their path, yowling at them. Most of them were just sitting quietly in some little out-of-the-way place, doing their own things.

He was used to noticing things other people didn't. He'd always been keenly aware of his surroundings. It was just how he was. Which, as it turned out, was *psychic*.

"That's at least three at Shanzer's place," he went on. "And there was even one outside of his sex museum."

"The first of *so* many pussies…" she sighed.

Albert ignored her. "Warner said the cats were our allies. Maybe they've been trying to tell us something the whole time."

"They're cats. Last I checked, they don't *say* anything. They just demand food and knock shit over."

"And that other thing he said…" he went on, thoughtful. "About an enemy of the cycle. He said, 'Beware the Ruin.'"

"Yeah, which made no fucking sense, like usual."

"I don't know. That place we ended up after we tried following that woman… That hallway that was falling apart. All that *decay*. And he said that to us right after I mentioned the woman."

"There was definitely something wrong about that place. And how the fuck did we get out of there, anyway? I mean I closed my eyes for a second and we were just…somewhere else."

He nodded. "Suddenly we were with the cats."

"It's so *frustrating*," she growled. "I don't understand *any* of this. Why won't they just tell us what they want us to do so we can get it over with and go home?"

He stared at the floor in front of him as he walked, going over it all in his head. A longing gaze between two lovers… This was a honeymoon destination. He was quite sure there were lovers casting longing gazes at each other pretty much *all the time*. How did that help them find what was supposed to be hidden here? Was it a reference to the sexual energy built up in these rooms? Were they supposed to keep using that? No… That didn't feel right…

A hollow man in hollowed earth… That one made *no* sense at all. Was it a metaphor for something? What was a hollow man? What constituted hollowed earth? Had he misheard it? Was it supposed to be "*hallowed* earth"? Like a graveyard? A church? Did this hotel have a chapel? No… Again, that didn't feel right.

And what pipes? What *tomb*? *Whose* tomb?

This was all giving him a serious headache!

They reached the end of the hallway and entered the main area of the hotel. To the right was the way back to the lobby. Straight ahead took them to the spa. And the passage to the left took them to the back of the building and the indoor pools.

He was starting to turn right and head back toward the lobby, but Brandy grabbed his sleeve and tugged on it. When he turned to see what she wanted, he saw it, too. At the end of the hallway on the left, a small, white cat was sitting there, staring back at them.

"Pussy," she whispered.

"You really like that word today, don't you?"

"Yes," she replied in the same whisper. "It amuses me."

As they stood watching, the cat stood up and vanished around the corner.

Albert grabbed her hand and set off after it.

"Okay," she gasped. "This is what we're doing now?"

"I don't want to hear any cracks from you about chasing pussy."

"Oh, I'm gonna make cracks," she informed him. Then she gave a snort of a laugh and chuckled, "Pussy cracks…"

Albert shook his head. "It's hard to believe sometimes that *you're* the mature one here."

"I know, right? You seriously need to grow up."

They turned right and spotted the cat just as it disappeared again to the left. But when they reached the place where it turned, they found the path blocked by a locked door.

"What the shit?" gasped Brandy. "Where'd it go?"

Albert had no answer. There was nowhere for the cat to go. It was a dead-end. He pressed his nose to the glass and peered into the darkness on the other side in time to catch just a glimpse of a small, white shape darting out of sight.

"How'd it get over there?" asked Brandy, her own face mashed to the glass next to his.

"Hell if I know." He turned and searched the door, looking for a hidden flap or something, but there was nothing. There wasn't so much as a noticeable space beneath the door.

"The art gallery…" said Brandy, staring at the sign on the glass. "We walked through on or first day here, remember?"

He definitely remembered that. It was beautiful. There were exquisite marble statues and dozens of bright, colorful paintings and lots of quiet benches to just sit and enjoy the scenery. In fact, the benches were the whole point of the exhibit. Spaced apart from one another, backed into little semi-private corners crowded between large, planted ferns, ivy-covered trellises and lush hedges, each one facing a meticulously curated selection of artistic beauty, they were a place for couples to get away from the bustle of the pools and other crowded amenities and snuggle together for a little while under the soft drone of relaxing music.

It definitely wasn't the artwork he remembered best about that brief visit.

"You stuffed your hand in my shorts while I was trying to admire the art," she reminded him.

"As I recall, *you* stuffed my hand in your shorts while *I* was trying to admire the art."

"Same thing." She pointed at the hours on the sign. "It's only open nine to eight."

Albert turned and looked around. "Dammit… What're we supposed to do now?"

Brandy cocked her head to one side and squinted at him. "You literally have a key to the entire hotel, dumbass."

He blinked back at her, embarrassed. "Oh yeah. That."

"It's a good thing you're pretty," she told him.

"Be nice to me," he grumbled, pulling the keycard out of his pocket. "It's been a long day."

She rolled her eyes and watched as he unlocked the door and stepped through it.

Almost immediately, the lights inside flickered on. Albert froze and stared up at them. "That's weird…"

"It's motion-activated lighting…" she told him, shaking her head at him as if he'd gone completely stupid. "God, we've got to stop sending so much blood to your dick. I swear your brain's being starved."

He turned and looked at her.

She smirked back at him. "It's okay. You're still pretty."

"What I found weird about that wasn't the motion-activated lighting," he informed her. "I found it weird that the lights *didn't come on for the cat.*"

That smirk melted away. "Oh..." Then she frowned. "Oh, yeah... That *is* weird, isn't it?"

"Yeah. Like, a *lot* weird."

"Sorry." She reached up and tugged at a lock of her hair. It was her turn to feel embarrassed. "But it's okay 'cause I'm pretty, too, right?"

"Gorgeous," he assured her. "As always."

"You put up with me so good."

"Of course I do. I love you. But seriously, how does a cat pass through a solid door and then not activate a motion sensor?"

Brandy stared at the room before them, her eyes widening a little. "Ghost pussy..." she whispered.

"It wouldn't surprise me at this point." He found himself reluctant to go on. He stood there, staring at the winding path before them. In order to achieve all those little semi-private, lovey-dovey benches, the layout of the gallery was essentially a big maze. He couldn't help being reminded of the temple and all those dark, winding corridors.

This was nothing like those black depths, of course. This place was bright and colorful and beautiful and comfortable. It was designed for privacy, not befuddlement. There was no chance of them going in and not finding their way out. But there *was* a certain eeriness about being here at this late hour, all alone, with the skylights dark and the music turned off...

Brandy felt it, too. He could tell by the way she was still clinging to his arm. She wasn't comfortable here. And it wasn't any wonder after the scare they had upstairs in that awful rotting hallway.

"Cats are supposed to be the good guys, right?"

"Don't ask me," she replied. "I don't trust *any* of those weirdos."

He nodded. That was probably best. But trust didn't seem to have much to do with it. Like it or not, there was no way back but forward. All they could do was play the Keeper's enigmatic game and hope to eventually find their way home again...

"So are we doing this?" asked Brandy. "Or are we going

home. Because I'm still all for going the fuck home."

"We're doing this," he grumbled.

Chapter 35

The Lucianna Mysteria's art gallery wasn't your typical small-town collection. It, alone, had drawn visitors from around the world. The artwork was made up of hand-selected pieces from around the world. Each and every one of them was beautiful, thought-provoking and moving. And all of it fit together seamlessly to create a visual mosaic of beautiful love stories that embodied a romantic atmosphere truly worthy of a world-class honeymoon destination. There was an elegant calmness about each and every piece. And Brandy, for one, felt as if she could sit down in front of any one of them, snuggle up to her beloved husband and stare at them for hours.

In other words, it was nothing at all like the god-awful pornography that was on display in the gallery in Lyle Shanzer's manor of perversions. Everything in that place was mere smut dressed up like art. This, on the other hand, was tasteful, mature and deep.

It was also quite large and filled to bursting with lush, indoor greenery designed to resemble a beautiful indoor hedge maze that also brilliantly allowed for all those quiet little, semi-private places for couples to sit and cuddle together. It was breathtakingly lovely in the daytime with the sunshine pouring through the skylights above and the soft, romantic music playing, but under the night sky, empty and in utter silence, it felt a lot creepier.

They walked straight through the sprawling gallery, glancing down every aisle they passed, but the ghostly, white feline was nowhere to be seen.

At the far end of the central aisle was a pair of glass doors overlooking the Lucianna Mysteria's award-winning gardens.

During the day, couples could take an extended stroll through both areas. But like the gallery, the gardens were gated off early in the evening and these doors only overlooked empty, lamplit walkways bathed in eerie shadows.

They both half-expected to find the cat sitting on the other side of the glass, mocking them, but there was still no sign of it.

Had they lost it? Or was it still in the gallery somewhere, waiting for them to find it?

Albert turned and ventured deeper into the gallery. "I'd say it has to be here somewhere," he said, peering into the various nooks and crannies a cat could feasibly squeeze itself into, "but I think we're well past that kind of thinking."

"You think?" she grumbled.

"But I really doubt it was random." He fixed his gaze on a painting of three women hard at work in an old-fashioned kitchen with several children frolicking about their feet. It reminded him for some reason of holiday dinners at his grandmother's house growing up, despite the fact that it was clearly set in a time well before he was ever born. "I really feel like it wanted to lead us somewhere."

"Or maybe it was just fucking with our heads," suggested Brandy. "Cats are kind of assholes, you know. My cousins had cats and I'm pretty sure they were actively trying to murder my uncle. He was always complaining about them trying to trip him on the stairs at night."

"My sister's allergic, so we never had one."

She raised an eyebrow at him. "I say we get one, then."

"Be nice."

"I'm *always* nice. But Becca's always been a bitch to me. I don't know what her problem is."

Albert moved on from the busy kitchen and turned his attention to a wide, panoramic painting of a peaceful mountain scene. "Yeah, I don't get it."

Becca had always been cold to her, from the moment Albert first took her home to meet his family. At first, she thought maybe it was the fact that she smoked. She was always nagging her parents to quit, after all. But Brandy quit smoking several years ago and nothing had changed. She couldn't figure out what the woman had against her, but she never felt welcome in the same room with her. It was always weirdly uncomfortable.

Albert turned the corner and pointed. "Cat!"

"What?" She turned, distracted, and glimpsed just the tip of a white tail disappearing from view.

"This way." He hurried to the next aisle and around the corner in time to watch it jump into one of the ferns framing two tall paintings.

Brandy looked back and forth. If the little beast was just going to jump right through the decorations, then they had no chance of catching it.

But Albert had already forgotten the cat. "Look..." he breathed.

She glanced up at him, then followed his gaze to the paintings in front of them. They were very clearly a matching set. The backgrounds looked like they went together. In one, a man stood with one hand pressed to his heart and the other reaching out toward the other painting. In the other, a woman was turned away from him, one hand raised as if in protest, but with a strangely flirtatious smile. "I remember these." She admired them when they were here the first time. *Juliet, runneth away with me*, she imagined the man saying. *Oh, Romeo, but we mustn't!* she could almost hear the woman crying back at him. She pointed at the woman and said, "Yeah, she's acting all pure, but she knows what the fuck she's doing."

"Lovers..." said Albert.

"Leave her alone with him for five minutes and I guarantee they will be."

"No, I mean the thing that voice said, back in that place that was our apartment but wasn't..."

"What?"

"You know, the 'longing gaze between two lovers' thing."

"Oh, right. That." She stared at the two pictures for a moment, letting it sink in.

"But it's not right..." he added.

She stepped a little closer, examining it. Then she saw it,

too. "They're not looking at each other."

"Exactly."

There was longing in these paintings. That was undeniable. She could almost feel it. But the man's eyes were turned up to the sky and the woman was looking the other way entirely.

"A longing gaze between two lovers..." Albert recalled. "That was what the voice said. Is this not the right lovers? Why would the cat lead us right to this spot if the clues don't match?"

"Maybe the cat wasn't really trying to take us anywhere. I mean, what do you expect from a cat?"

"Warner said the cats were our allies."

"Warner's some kind of alien demon freak. We don't even know *what* he is."

But Albert was shaking his head.

She turned and looked around. "Well...do you *feel* anything? Like with your psychic shit?"

She watched as his eyebrows crinkled tighter and tighter. He was trying his best to process it, but was there even anything to be found here. Was this even really where they were supposed to be? It was just a cat. A *freaky* cat, yes... A cat that could phase through walls and slip undetected through motion sensors... But it was still just a cat. Right?

He closed his eyes and tipped his head to one side, thoughtful. "*Is* there something here? I mean, I feel like there's something...*near*...? Does that make any sense?"

"Nope."

"Didn't think so." He opened his eyes and stared at the paintings again.

Brandy sighed. "As much as I just want to say, 'Oh well, we tried,' and go home... Something tells me you're just going to keep telling me we don't have a choice."

He glanced over at her. "I mean, do you really want to risk going all the way home just to hear the stupid telephone ringing off the hook again?"

She scowled at him. He knew damned well that was the last thing she wanted. Those stupid phone calls scared the hell out of her five years ago.

He turned his attention back to the paintings. "I'm sorry," he sighed. "I know this sucks. I'm starting to wonder if I can really do this again…"

"Of course you can. You did it last time."

"Did I, though? Or was I just following the script the Keeper and the Sentinel Queen planted in my brain?"

She stared at him for a moment, surprised at how much it hurt to hear him talk like that. What happened to all that stupid and adorable optimism? As much as she wanted to wash her hands of this mess and just go home, there was something about the idea of *him* just giving up that made her feel kind of sick inside…

Somewhere in the back of her mind she remembered him carrying her out of that awful fear room because she couldn't go any farther…

"It's frustrating," she admitted. "But I know you've got this. It's like you said before, a lot's happened since last night. Just…I don't know… Forget the pervert and all that psychic shit and look at it like you looked at things in the temple."

He glanced back at her, uncertain. "Yeah. You're right." He looked back and forth between the two paintings. "Treat it like a puzzle. Or…a *riddle*, even…" He frowned. "Something hidden… Something easy to overlook…"

She stepped closer to him and seized two handfuls of his tee shirt. "And if that doesn't work…" she said, pulling him against her.

He stared back at her, surprised.

"We can try it the pervert's way. See if *that* helps."

He smiled at her. "It *might* help," he said.

"It might."

He leaned closer to her. "The guy may be a creep, but I don't exactly hate his methods."

"It's got its perks," she admitted. She closed her eyes as he leaned closer, anticipating his kiss.

But nothing happened.

She opened her eyes, confused, to find him staring over her shoulder, distracted. "Hey." She pointed at her mouth. "My lips are down here."

"Yeah…" he said. "Sorry." Then he gave her a quick peck on her mouth and let go of her.

She wrinkled her nose. "What the fuck?"

He turned to face a marble statue of a young woman standing among the greenery behind the nearby bench. "That's it…" he sighed. "A 'longing gaze'…"

Brandy crossed her arms, irritated, and looked up at the statue. But he was right, she saw. The woman *did* have a longing expression on her face. "But there's only one of her." Then she turned and looked around, expecting to find another statue hidden somewhere. "Isn't there?"

"It's wordplay." He stepped up onto the bench, placing himself at eye-level with the stone woman. He reached up and placed his fingertips just beneath her eyes. "'A longing gaze…'" He turned and looked at the two paintings across from her. "…'between two lovers.'" He pointed at where she was looking, which was the floor directly beneath the space between the two paintings.

Brandy stared at the place he was pointing. "Well that's just stupid," she decided, still annoyed at having been denied her kiss by some stone bimbo. "Who comes up with this shit?"

Chapter 36

Albert knelt down where the statue was staring and took a close look at the floor.

"There's nothing there," Brandy informed him, as if he couldn't see that for himself.

But he shook his head. "No… I think there is. I just can't quite…" He squinted at it. Was it another optical illusion?

Were those optical illusions? He supposed *psychic* illusions might be more accurate. Maybe even *magic* illusions, if there was any truth behind the shaman's freaky magic school.

"Is this another of those things you have to get pervy to see?" asked Brandy, looking up at the ceiling overhead. "Because there *are* cameras in here. Just so you know."

"Yeah, that makes sense." There were security cameras in most of the public areas of the hotel, after all. If any of this art was even remotely valuable, there would definitely be security cameras rolling at all hours of the day.

"I mean, there aren't a lot of them." She bit her lip and turned around, scanning the entire ceiling. "Like, I don't think they could see us where we were making out last time we were here… I'm pretty sure I looked before we…you know…" It wasn't as if anyone could see anything anyway. They were fully clothed. It was just a little playful heavy petting. She never even unbuttoned her shorts.

"I'm sure we were fine." Those cameras were mostly pointed at the exits. The benches were hidden behind the decorative foliage. Cuddling was encouraged in the Lucianna Mysteria, after all. It said so in all the brochures. It was their gimmick. They catered primarily to couples as a lover's getaway destination. It even had a special children's playland tucked away by one of the indoor pools manned by trained daycare staff to give a little well-needed romantic freedom to couples with kids. So he doubted very much that any of the cameras were pointed at the benches.

But now that it had crossed his mind, he found himself wondering about the security cameras. What had they seen? What might they reveal about this bizarre task they'd been given. Was it possible for someone to notice that there were *two of each of them* in the hotel at the same time? Was there footage of the ghostly white cat walking through a door?

He doubted if anyone was watching the cameras right now. The footage was probably being stored on a hard drive somewhere and only reviewed if something happened to warrant reviewing it. He doubted a luxury resort required live twenty-four-hour surveillance. Besides, Lucianna said that her security staff had been made aware of them, so if anyone *was* watching, they'd probably know what was going on.

It was also possible that she might cut the cameras completely while they were snooping around. She warned them that there were dangers in the nexus, after all. She might not want anyone else trying to figure out what they were doing here.

But of course he didn't care to think too much about that. After all, if it was *that* dangerous, what the hell were *they* doing here?

Right now, he needed to focus. There was something there. The longer he knelt here, the more he could feel it. Something about the space in front of him was…*off*…

"I mean, I can stick my tongue in your ear again if want me to…"

"I think I'm learning to find the right mindset. Let me try it."

"If you say so."

"But definitely hold that thought."

"Gotcha."

He closed his eyes again and tried to picture what was in front of him. If there was something here, and he was more certain there was with each moment he lingered, then it was *already* here. That's how these things had worked. He didn't *make* the basement steps appear in Shanzer's house. They were there the whole time. He only made himself *see* them. The same with the hallway where the woman in the white dress disappeared. It was *always* there. Focusing on that fact seemed to make it easier. It solidified his conviction that it was *real*.

Having done that, he just needed that special *push*, like the shaman taught them.

And it wasn't like he didn't have anything sexy to think about. All he had to do was cast his thoughts back on this past week, starting with their steamy wedding night. There'd been so many times these past several days that she'd done or said something that took his breath away. She'd always been an energetic lover, for as long as they'd been dating. She was almost always eager to play. But this week she'd been positively *insatiable*. And he'd loved every sweltering moment of it.

He closed his eyes and remembered the first night they were here, after they'd come back from the pool. She stripped off her little blue bikini and stepped out onto the balcony, stark naked against the midnight forest. "I want to do it *right here*," she told him. And something about her damp hair and the beads of sweat on her chest as she stood in the humid night air sent shivers of ecstasy down his spine. The way she leaned against that railing… The way she pushed her hips forward… The way she bit her lip and flashed him that mischievous grin…

He grimaced a little and shifted his weight, suddenly uncomfortable.

That might have been a little too much fuel for the fire, actually… It was suddenly getting really stuffy in here.

And yet, at the same time, he became aware of a strong, earthy smell wafting across his face, like the smell of an old, dank tunnel.

He hadn't noticed *that* before.

He opened his eyes to find that he was not, in fact, kneeling on an empty patch of tile floor, but rather in front of a set of concrete steps descending down into a dimly lit tunnel.

His first reaction, however, was not a, "Eureka!" kind of moment, but rather very much an, "Oh shit!" moment, as his startled mind dragged him back to a similar set of concrete steps, descending into a very similar dark, underground place.

He shot to his feet and took a step back, his heart suddenly racing.

"You okay?" asked Brandy.

He nodded. "I'm fine. Sorry. Just..." He shook his head. "Just didn't expect that."

"Didn't expect *what?*"

He had no intention of telling her that he thought for one terrifying moment that he found himself back at the entrance to Gilbert House. She didn't need that kind of fright. *He* could've done without that kind of fright. In an instant, a flurry of awful memories had come rushing back to him. Heavy footsteps creaking overhead. Shadowy things prowling an impossible forest on the other side of darkened window panes. Congealed blood smeared across dusty floors. Corpses rotting in the darkness.

But this wasn't Gilbert House. It was an ordinary staircase. The two paintings were hanging on either side of a doorway, even though the space between them was a fraction that wide *before* he was able to see it. It looked perfectly normal, as if there should be a sign hanging over it advertising that there was more artwork on display on the lower level. Except there were no lights on down there. The steps descended into a dark, concrete corridor.

"What is it?" pressed Brandy. "What do you see?"

"More stairs," he replied. He put his arm around her waist and pulled her close. "Close your eyes and hold on to me. We'll go down together."

"This is so weird," she gasped as he guided her straight toward what looked to her like nothing more than the wall in front of them. But she trusted him, so she closed her eyes and clung to him.

"Okay, we're right there. One step down, directly in front of you."

She let out a soft squeal of fright as she reached out with the toe of her sneaker and found an empty space where there should have been floor.

"Right there," he encouraged her.

She settled her weight onto the first step and opened her eyes. Now she could see it. He could tell. She looked around, wide-eyed, taking it all in. "Wow..." she sighed. "That is *so* weird."

"Isn't it?

But he could see in her expression that the wonder of it gave way quickly to fear. "Where are we going, though?"

It was a good question. "We'll find out together, I guess."

"Goody," she grumbled. "Can't wait. Why does it smell like a fucking *grave* down here?"

"Why would you find the most *morbid* way to describe the smell of *dirt*."

"Why would there *be* dirt?" she countered. "This is a fancy resort hotel! Not a barn!"

She had a point, he supposed. He continued down the steps and found that there was no sign of the Lucianna Mysteria's signature décor down here. There wasn't even paint or carpet. There was nothing but naked concrete.

"Hold on," he said, pulling her to a stop."

"What's up?" she asked, worried.

He reached a hand out and raked it across the passage ahead of him. "Spiderwebs."

"Ew!" She leaned forward, squinting. "How did you *see* those?"

He wasn't entirely sure, actually. He thought he just happened to glimpse a hint of shine on one of them, just another example of his excellent observational talents... He'd always thought he was *extraordinarily* observant. Everyone told him so. He always thought he was really good with directions, too. And he always thought he was super talented at solving puzzles and riddles and mysteries. But...maybe it was always just that he was psychic. And he was sort of starting to feel like being psychic wasn't nearly as cool as just being good at things. It felt a little like he'd been cheating all this time.

Brandy shuddered. "I don't like spiders..."

"Yeah. I know." He leaned forward again, scanning the dark

passage ahead, focusing on the task at hand. "But it's not exactly a *bad* sign. Remember the temple? Gilbert House? There weren't any spiders in those places."

She *did* remember that. It was one of the stranger details about those places. The steam tunnels under the university and the sewer tunnels they connected to were lousy with spiderwebs. And all manner of other creepy crawlies, too. She remembered seeing pill bugs, centipedes and slugs, among other things. Also *rats*. Lots of them. But as soon as they entered the actual temple, there was a complete lack of any of those things. In fact, the temple was *immaculately* clean for an ancient, subterranean labyrinth. "It didn't make sense, did it? I've still never been able to understand what was keeping them out."

"Me neither. I mean, I know the Sentinel Queen's children acted as caretakers for the temple. They kept it maintained. But there was only one of them left when we went down there. That's a lot of dusting for one guy. Even a guy who could walk on ceilings like Spiderman." And it *definitely* didn't explain the lack of spiders in Gilbert House, which had no such custodial staff and was covered in years of accumulated dust and grime. "My best guess is that it had something to do with the fact that both of those places were in that other world. That black forest. Maybe a lot of living things instinctively avoid places like that."

"Sounds like a *warning* to me," she grumbled. "One we probably should've heeded."

"Probably."

"Come on. I'll go first." Using his arm to clear a path for them, he started forward again.

There were no lights down here, which didn't exactly surprise him. If most people couldn't see the stairs leading down here, then who was going to maintain something like that? Instead, there were narrow slots in the ceiling that seemed to allow the lights inside the hotel above to reach down into the gloom.

Clever. And he was willing to bet that those slots were as invisible to most people as the rest of Mysteria's secrets.

He looked back at the steps, curious. Lucianna told them she had no idea what was hidden beneath the hotel. Was she really that clueless about these areas? Or was she only lying about that?

I'm not allowed to help, he recalled Warner telling them. *The Keeper forbids it.*

Was she only playing dumb in order to stick to the little monster's stupid rules?

The Keeper was a serious pain in the ass.

"I don't like it down here," said Brandy, hugging herself against a chill. "It's *super* creepy."

He squinted into the darkness ahead of them. The lights didn't go much farther. Did the tunnel turn? Or were they approaching a dead end? "I wish we had a flashlight…"

"*I* wish we didn't have to do this."

He struggled to see into the darkness beyond those last beams of light. Was there something there? It felt like there was a shape in that darkness.

Brandy turned and looked behind them. "Okay, this place is really starting to freak me out. Are you sure we should be here? This isn't like that hallway you dragged us into, is it?"

"I have no idea," he replied, exasperated. "I really wish someone would just *tell* us what we're supposed to do."

His eyes were adjusting to the darkness. There was definitely something there. Some sort of dark shape.

He stepped a little closer, squinting to see it better.

Then his brain pieced all those shadowy shapes together and he realized with a dreadful start that there was a man staring back at him.

Chapter 37

Albert had to stop for a moment. His heart was thundering. He'd barely managed to keep from screaming.

"You okay?" asked Brandy. She was clinging to his arm. He could feel her nails digging into him again. He'd managed not to scream, but he *did* let out a startled gasp, which of course startled *her*.

"I'm fine. Just… Thought that was a real person for a second there."

"Looks like some kind of statue," she observed. "But why's it down *here*?"

He crept closer, his heart still thudding in his chest. It only took a second to realize that what he was looking at was hard stone, not flesh and blood, but during that single second, he felt as if his heart had shifted into high gear.

It was a good thing they were doing this crap while he was still young.

The figure before them *was* man-shaped, but not very convincingly when he looked closer. It was too thin, less like a person than some kind of life-size doll. And it wasn't standing, as he first thought, but sitting, with its knees bent and drawn up to its chest and its long arms folded over his shins, meaning it was much taller than any man he'd ever seen.

He walked up to it and placed his hand on the thing's slender arm. It was cold and smooth.

And it was *familiar…*

"I know this stone."

Brandy met his gaze, a worried look in her eyes. "It looks like what the temple was made of, doesn't it?"

Everything down there, every surface, every wall, every *stat-*

ue in every chamber, was all crafted from the same smooth, gray stone.

She shook her head. "But why would there be one of *those* statues *here?*"

He leaned closer, trying to make out all the details of the thing's face. "I don't remember any statues like *this* down there, though." Everything they encountered in the temple was crafted with exquisitely realistic detail. The people down there, whether they were engaged in furious copulation in the sex room or howling with terror in the fear room, were so completely lifelike that he remembered wondering if they hadn't once been real people frozen in cold stone by some real-life Medusa. And even the horrors he glimpsed in the fear room, things without equal in the natural world, things he never could have *imagined* in his worst nightmares, were so incredibly realistic that it set his hair standing on end to glimpse even *parts* of them. This thing, on the other hand, was nothing like that. It looked like something a child might have molded from Playdough. Its limbs seemed to flex like rubber hoses rather than bend at proper, anatomical joints. Its fingers were like limp sausages. And in addition to these weird, doll-like proportions, its face looked like some kind of goofy mask. It had a triangular wedge for a nose, a great, grinning mouth of skeleton-like teeth and two huge, cartoonish eyes. It reminded him more of some silly tiki mask than of anything that he recalled seeing in the depths of the temple.

The only things it came remotely close to were the statues of the sentinels, themselves. They were also tall and weirdly elongated. But that was where the similarities ended. The sentinels' bodies were stretched all out of proportion, but they had distinct muscles, wrinkles, veins and even fingerprints. And then there was the fact that the sentinels had no faces at all. The fronts of their heads were utterly blank surfaces, without a single visible biological feature.

But the longer he stared at this bizarre figure, the more convinced he was that it was the very same stone. "Lucianna said the sentinels created all these places, remember?" He turned and scanned the space around the statue. "If we've found some of that stone, then maybe it means we're close to finding what we came here for."

But there wasn't anything else down here.

"I don't know," said Brandy. "Freaky tall dude is just kind of chilling out down here all by himself. Maybe he checked out the internet recently and just decided he was done with people."

"Maybe so," he chuckled. He stepped around the side and looked the statue up and down. Like the sentinels back in the temple, it even had a penis, he discovered, though it was like its fingers, little more than a limp protrusion dangling between its thighs. "But it really feels like this guy's important somehow. It's sort of like Shanzer's place…but different, you know?"

"Oh yeah," she replied, curling her lip at him. "Same but different. Makes perfect sense."

"It's hard to explain, sorry."

"Whatever." She stepped around the other side of the statue, looking for anything out of place. "Didn't that voice say something about a man in the earth?"

He looked up at her, surprised. "Oh yeah… 'A hollow man in hollowed earth.' This place…" He turned and glanced around again. "This tunnel is sort of hollowed-out earth, isn't it?" Then he frowned at the statue. "But what does 'hollow' mean? Is *this guy* hollow?"

Brandy pointed at the back of the statue's head. "Yeah, actually."

He leaned behind it and looked. There was a great, gaping hole in the back of the statue's head. "Oh. There you go."

"That was easy," said Brandy. "I helped."

"Yes, you did," he agreed, standing up straight and staring at the strange gaping hole. It was so gloomy back here that it was hard to see. "But what do we do now?"

"*I* sure as fuck don't know."

He looked back the way they came, thinking. A longing gaze between two lovers… and a hollow man in hollowed earth… The last of those bizarre clues was "follow the pipes to find his tomb"… But there weren't any pipes down here. There wasn't even electricity. "What does it mean?" he muttered.

"I don't know. Brainless man sitting alone in the dark? Sounds like a metaphor to me."

"Somehow, I don't think the sentinels were concerned with social commentary."

"They sure *acted* like they knew everything when they made *me* decide whether or not to open the scary *doomsday door.*"

"True…" He peered into the hole in the back of the hollow man's head, but between the gloom of the space and the dark color of the stone, it was impossible to see if it was only the head that was hollow or if the entire statue was empty.

Cautiously, he reached up and probed the rim of the hole with his fingertips.

"Careful!" hissed Brandy, cringing.

"I am."

"God, there's no end to the awful things I can imagine hiding in there."

He knew she was right. Countless gruesome possibilities churned inside his head as he reached deeper into the hollow man's empty skull. It was far too easy to picture a nest of deadly snakes curled up inside, just waiting to strike. Or perhaps it would be full of scorpions. Or a nest of killer ants. None of that made any *real* sense of course. Why would any living creature just stay inside a creepy statue and not skitter, crawl or slither up into the hotel above? What would they eat? But the images were persistent, nonetheless. And it didn't have to be something alive to be deadly. The cavity could be filled with flesh-eating acid. Stinging thorns. Syringes dripping with deadly diseases. Not to mention all the things that he couldn't possibly imagine.

He'd never in his life dreamed up anything as awful as those hounds down in the temple's labyrinths, after all…

He shivered and withdrew his hand, uncertain. Maybe he should take a closer look before taking any unnecessary risks.

He stepped back around to the front of the statue and studied its goofy, cartoon face. "Back in the temple," he recalled, "there were two types of statues. The first was the sentinels."

"I remember," said Brandy. "Really tall. No faces. *Huge* cocks."

He frowned. "Uh…yeah. Them."

"Like, *really* huge."

"Anyway…"

"*Giant* balls." She held out her hand, palm up, fingers curled, as if to demonstrate. "Like *oranges* or something."

"Yeah. Not really where I was going with—"

"*Scary* huge. Like fuck up my *diaphragm* huge."

"Seriously?"

She reached out and patted him on the arm. "Don't be jealous. Yours is nice too."

"I'm trying to make a point here."

"I *like* yours. It's *cute*."

He stared at her for a moment, waiting.

She stared back at him, straight-faced as ever.

"You done?"

"Adorable, even."

"This is still about those women at Shanzer's sex party, isn't it?"

"Yes."

"*So* not cool."

"And don't forget Dolly. *She* thought it was adorable, too. I could tell."

"You know, you're being awfully hurtful for someone who wasn't exactly keeping her eyes to herself back there."

"Girls are allowed to look."

"Again, double standard. Not cool. And Dolly was a *sociopath*. You heard what Lucianna said about her. I'm lucky she didn't cut it off while she was down there."

"Maybe that would've kept you out of trouble."

Albert rubbed his eyes, tired, then turned his attention back to the statue. "I was just trying to say that the sentinels never had any effect on us when we saw them. They either just stood there or they gave us clues about the areas ahead."

"You're so cute when you actually get mad, you know that?"

"All the *other* statues, though," he plowed on, "were all about emotions in one way or another. They either depicted people exhibiting extreme emotions or they were something that *caused* people extreme emotions, like those monsters in the fear room. Either way, they instilled those emotions in our own brains, overwhelming us with them."

"I can always tell because you just start ignoring me."

"But this doesn't depict anything. It's just...*this guy*. He doesn't even *have* an expression. And it doesn't give of any kind of emotion, either. It doesn't *say* anything." He paused for a moment, his thoughts churning.

"Well..." offered Brandy. "This isn't the temple, either."

He nodded. She was right, of course. This wasn't the Temple of the Blind. Even if the two places were related, the same rules didn't necessarily apply. This was an entirely new puzzle. The rules had likely changed.

He reached out and touched the hollow man's face. The triangle nose. Those unblinking eyes. Those oversized teeth. Then he felt around his arms. His hands. Those limp fingers. He could feel the grooves cut into the stone where its few features were carved, but there was nothing more to it. No hidden switches. No secret messages.

Nothing except that gaping hole in the back of his skull...

He walked around the hollow man again and stared into that darkness. "Whatever we're here for has to be inside," he deduced.

Brandy crinkled her nose at him. "Do not approve," she grumbled.

"I know." He leaned closer again, trying to see inside. He wished he had a light. He hadn't realized just how dependent he'd grown on his cell phone. He should be better prepared than this.

But then he remembered waking up naked in the shaman's gaudy guest suite and realized that being prepared was never part of the plan from the start.

"Hold on..." said Brandy. She reached up and touched the medallion hanging over her heart. "Are we maybe supposed to use *this*?"

Albert had forgotten about the key. He stared at it for a

moment, considering it, then turned and looked at the hole. "But it doesn't exactly look like a keyhole…" They weren't even close to the same size.

She lifted the chain up over her head and then held it in front of her, watching the dim light from behind them glint off its smooth, golden surface. "And this doesn't exactly look like a key," she reminded him.

It didn't at all. How did it work? It didn't have any teeth. He leaned closer to the hole, peering into the eerie darkness. "I mean, are we supposed to just…stick it in?"

Brandy gave a snort of a laugh. "Isn't that pretty much what *everything's* been about?"

He blinked back at her, confused. Then he realized what he'd said and chuckled. "I guess it has, hasn't it?" He stared into the darkness again for a moment, pondering. "I don't know. Maybe that's what we're supposed to do… But I just don't know how I'm supposed to use it." He leaned closer, squinting. "Unless maybe the keyhole is inside somewhere?" Cautiously, he reached into the gaping darkness again.

Brandy let out a pained squeal. "Be careful!" she groaned.

Nothing happened at first, so he slowly reached in farther, his hand disappearing into the darkness.

Was it his imagination, or was it a little *too* dark inside that hole? It was as if he were watching his arm disappear not just from sight, but utterly and completely, as if he were being devoured by the black void inside that mysterious stone.

But nothing bad was happening. Nothing grabbed him. Nothing bit him. Emboldened by this, he reached in farther, his arm disappearing all the way to his elbow. Then he frowned. "I don't feel anything…"

"You're kind of freaking me out. Get out of there."

But he wasn't listening. A deep, puzzled frown had creased his handsome features. "I don't feel the back of the stone." He kept reaching. His entire arm disappeared into that eerie darkness.

Brandy leaned over and peered around the front of the statue. His arm was considerably longer than the depth of the hollow man's head. If he wasn't screwing with her and bending his arm down—and she really didn't think he'd do something like that to her—then his hand should have been sticking out the other side. "That's...kind of concerning..."

He scrunched up his face and felt around. "It's like there's an entirely different space inside."

"Then maybe you shouldn't be sticking your hand in there!"

"That's pretty freaking weird..." He withdrew his hand and peered into the darkness again. Was it another optical illusion type thing? Or did this statue somehow distort space the way this hotel distorted time? Or had he just reached through a gateway into another dimension? Like whatever gateway was hidden in the basement of Gilbert House that allowed them to pass between their world and the Wood?

Brandy pointed at the statue. "I don't think I like this guy."

He reached out and took the medallion from her. "Let's see if this does anything."

She growled, frustrated. "Just be careful. You're freaking me out."

It would probably be bad if he stuck it in there and dropped it... Lucianna talked about it like it was pretty important. And he still had no idea where, exactly his arm went when he reached in there. He wrapped the chain around his wrist and gripped it tightly. Then he braced himself for anything unexpected and plunged his hand back into the mysterious darkness before he could lose his nerve.

He wasn't sure what he expected to happen. Maybe the hole would glow brilliantly. Give off a strange, alien hum, perhaps. A rumble. A click. One of those chimes you heard in video games when you figured out the puzzle and unlocked the door?

Instead, nothing at all seemed to happen.

He stood there, his arm swallowed up by the hollow man's impossible mind...feeling sort of stupid...

"Well *that* didn't work," grumbled Brandy.

"Guess not..."

"But congratulations on getting your whole arm inside that guy. I think you owe him dinner."

Albert cringed. "Don't do that. That's not cool."

"Not if it wasn't consensual."

"Stop." He started to pull his hand back but then stopped. "Wait...what's...?"

Something shifted. There was a change he couldn't quite describe. Something that made him feel a little shaky on his feet, as if the floor had moved slightly beneath him.

"Albert?" she asked, her amusement flushing away in an instant. Her pretty blue eyes went wide with worry. "What's wrong?"

He withdrew his hand with a startled gasp and backed away so quickly that he banged the back of his head against the wall behind him.

"*Are you okay?*"

He nodded. "Yeah, I think so..." But he was holding his arm up, staring at it. "But what the hell is *this*?"

"What's what?" But then she saw it. "Ew!"

There was a strange, viscous, bile-colored substance covering his arm. It was oozing down his forearm and dripping from his elbow in great, slimy globs.

She leaned closer, staring at it, confused, her mouth pulled down in an expression of disgust. "What did you touch?"

"I don't know. I wasn't touching *anything*. There was nothing *there*, not even the inside of the statue."

"Well *something* was in there," she reasoned as she watched a long strand of oozing goop trail from his elbow and plop onto the concrete at his feet.

"It didn't splash onto me," he recalled. It was nothing as simple as that. "It was just...suddenly there." He looked back at the hole, confused. "I can't explain it." He turned and looked around. "And is that all it did?" It felt like something else had happened, but looking around, nothing had changed.

"Fuck this place," decided Brandy, already turning away. "Let's go back and get that shit washed off you."

He nodded. "Yeah... Definitely."

Chapter 38

"It doesn't burn, does it?" worried Brandy as they made their way back to the gallery.

He was examining his soiled arm, distracted. "No. It doesn't seem dangerous. It's just…gross." He tried flicking it off the medallion, but it was too thick. All he did was send gloopy ribbons of it spattering onto the floor. Instead, he settled for wiping his arm on the concrete wall as they walked. It didn't do much, but it raked away some of the dripping excess, which was a start.

"It *looks* gross," she agreed.

He brought the back of his hand closer to his face and sniffed it. "Doesn't smell like much," he observed. It had a subtle sort of dankness to it, reminiscent of earthy, underground places. It seemed sort of familiar, but he couldn't quite put his finger on what it reminded him of.

"Fascinating," she grumbled. "Maybe don't taste it. I think we have enough to deal with without you poisoning yourself."

"You don't have to worry about that," he assured her, grimacing at the thought. "I just wish I knew exactly what it was I stuck my hand in."

"Something's asshole, from the looks of it."

He glanced up at her, unamused. "Thanks. I needed that mental image."

"You're welcome. Maybe it'll teach you not to go sticking things where they don't belong."

"It was your idea to try putting the key in there," he reminded her.

"Yeah, the *key*. Not your whole arm. Fisting the hollow guy was all your idea."

He grimaced. "Yeah, we're not gonna call it that."

The tunnel grew brighter as they approached the steps leading back up into the gallery. He took advantage of the growing light to take a closer look at the substance, but it didn't change much. It had a yellowish-brown color to it, which didn't help make him any less queasy about it coating his bare arm. It was even soaking into his shirt sleeve, staining it.

Why did he feel like he'd seen something like this somewhere before?

But as he turned the key around and wiped the excess goo off it, he became distracted by something unexpected.

He stopped walking and held it up. "Wait... Why is this different?"

"What?" Brandy stopped walking and looked at it.

He was right. Something had changed. She leaned close and peered at it as he turned it to one side, then the other. The carved symbol was gone, for one thing, as if washed away. But the shape had changed, too. It looked flatter. There were strange bumps along the sides of it. And the tip protruded out a little farther than before.

She looked back at the shadowy outline of the hollow man at the far end of the tunnel. "Did you drop ours and pick up a different one?"

But he shook his head. "I never let go of it." He held up his hand. "The chain's still wrapped around my wrist."

"But that doesn't make any sense. It's a piece of gaudy bling. It can't just...*transform* into *another* piece of gaudy bling."

"Can it?" he wondered. "Lucianna called it a *seed*, remember?"

"But it's *not* a seed. It's *gold*. Or something that *looks* like gold, anyway. We don't know what it is. But I'm sure it's not *alive*."

He shrugged. "I don't know. I kind of stopped believing in 'impossible' five years ago."

Brandy started forward again. "Fucked up is what it all is."

He set off after her, staring at the medallion. It felt different somehow. Almost as if they'd acquired an upgrade. The Seed of Yggdrasil two-point-oh? But that was probably just his silly imagination.

Was it the same medallion? It felt lighter somehow.

The hollow man…with the impossible space inside him. Had he perhaps *exchanged* the keys when he stuck it in there?

Whatever happened, he was sure he couldn't hope to understand it. It was probably far too complicated.

Or maybe not…

Maybe it wasn't complicated at all.

(Magic can open doors that can't be unlocked.)

He frowned at the thought. Magic wasn't an answer to anything. Magic was a word people literally used when they *didn't want to answer a question.* When anyone ever asked an illusionist how they did that trick, how they made that lady disappear in front of everybody, how they passed through that solid pane of glass: "It's magic." For ages, people used it to explain all the things they didn't understand. How did the sun rise every morning? How did birds fly? How did the ocean's tide roll in and out? "It's magic." Or even when someone's kid asked for the first time where babies came from and they didn't think the little guy was old enough to handle the messy and awkward truth of it all: "It's magic."

Shanzer's mansion of perversions wasn't magic. It was a funhouse. A maze of optical illusions. Tricks of light and perspective.

And yet, it wasn't his cunning that opened his eyes to the truth of that place. It wasn't a change in perspective. They were trapped there as long as they continued to resist what the shaman wanted them to do. It was only when they forced down their inhibitions and started playing the pervert's lewd game that the truth revealed itself.

And then there was that hidden hallway. He couldn't find what was hidden until Brandy took him aside and started nibbling his ear.

Sexual energy…

It was so frustrating! This wasn't how the temple worked. The temple was subtle. The temple was mysterious. They followed the map the Sentinel Queen gave them and it led them on a journey from the streets of Briar Hills to the eerily silent towers of the City of the Blind to the twisting depths of the labyrinth to the burning mountain rising up into the starless skies of the Wood. No golden keys. No sex parties. No magic books or time paradoxes.

Brandy climbed the steps back up into the gallery, thrilled to be out of that dark and spooky tunnel, but her relief was short-lived. She stopped just short of the last step, her heart skipping a beat as she realized that this wasn't where they were supposed to be.

Albert didn't ask her why she stopped. He saw it for himself.

The gallery had changed.

The plants were all long dead and withered. The floor tiles were buried beneath a layer of dead leaves and dirt. On either side of them, the paintings of the lovers had rotted into colorless tatters.

"We're here again..." he whispered, looking around.

She stared at the marble statue of the woman whose longing gaze told them where to find these stairs. She was stained and discolored and weathered. Her youthful face looked older. She looked strangely sinister now, as if all those mysterious years of yearning had withered her heart and left her cold and dead inside.

She shook it off and stepped out into the gallery.

It was just a stupid statue. She needed to get ahold of herself.

But the last time they found themselves in this decayed nightmare version of the hotel, they ended up surrounded by monsters.

Was that what was going to happen again.

"The Ruin..." said Albert. It was the word Warner used. "Apparently, it's not confined to just that one hallway. It runs through the entire hotel."

"Like Lucianna said," she realized. *I can't tell you how deep the crossroads go. I can't tell you what may or may not be living down there. I can't tell you what nightmare realms the crossroads open onto.* The memory sent a hard shiver through her. "We shouldn't be here…" she whimpered.

"No." He turned and looked around. "But how do we get back out?"

"I don't know!" She set off toward what should have been the door leading out of here. Or at least that was where the door was in the *real-world* version of this gallery. The one that *didn't* look like a horror movie set.

"Did the hollow man send us here when I used the key on him?" wondered Albert. "Is this part of whatever that was?"

Brandy reached the main aisle and stopped, distracted.

They were standing by the door leading out into the gardens. The glass was dingy and cracked, aged like everything else in the room. But on the other side of those doors, the world had changed.

It looked like a wasteland out there. The plants had long ago turned to dust. The sky was a sickly shade of red. She could see no sign of any trees or buildings. Dust whirled across an arid earth in a harsh wind.

But not everything was dead out there. There were things flying in that red sky. *Strange* things that didn't move like birds or insects or anything else that she'd ever seen before. They floated through the air in weird, curling patterns, leaving strange, warbling trails in their wakes.

"Yeah…" said Albert as he stared out at the apocalyptic nightmare spread out before them. "That definitely has a wrong turn kind of vibe about it, doesn't it?"

Chapter 39

Albert grabbed her by the hand and pulled her away from the doors. "That's definitely not the way back."

Brandy followed after him, but her thoughts remained glued to that scene. "Did you *see* those things flying around out there?"

"I saw them."

"What the fuck were *those*? They weren't birds. Did you see their *wings*? *Were* those even wings?"

"No idea."

"Are we really in another world? Is this place like the Wood?" She could feel herself babbling, but she couldn't seem to stop herself. Her heart was racing. She felt like she was going to throw up. "How are we supposed to deal with something like that? This is *so* fucked up!"

"That definitely wasn't the Wood," he replied. "I don't know *where* we are. But I don't like it."

"No shit!" The Wood didn't have a sky that looked like it came out of a nuclear holocaust. The sky there was clear and empty and black and endless. It was utter darkness in the Wood. And most importantly, it was the Wood. It was covered in *trees*. Huge, nightmare-inducing, *man-eating* trees...but trees. It also had hordes of zombies and freaky carrion eaters that shit all over everything and pushed teenage girls off cliffs and *who knew what else?* Five years ago, that world had far surpassed any horror movie she'd ever watched, any nightmare that had ever startled her awake in the dead of the night. It was a dark and twisted hellscape of horrors, to put it bluntly. But something about that place she just glimpsed through those cracked doors felt somehow even *worse*.

(Beware the Ruin.)

She shivered and looked back over her shoulder, half-convinced that something terrible was about to crash through those glass doors and come bounding after them.

But so far all those horrors remained on the other side of the glass.

Albert reached the other door and yanked it open. She hoped they'd simply run through it and magically find themselves back in the real world, but of course they had no such luck. The hallway was just as rotten and sickly as the gallery.

"This looks familiar…" he grumbled.

It was just like that last decayed hallway. Except this one was even more far gone. The ceiling was sagging dangerously in places, threatening to fall in on them as they crept under. And even worse, only a handful of lights were still working. Large portions of the hallway were bathed in eerie darkness.

"What do we do?" she squealed. "Last time we were here…"

"I remember."

"*Do* something!"

"Like what?"

"I don't know! Can't you feel something? I mean, we got *in* here. There must be a way out."

"Maybe if I knew *how* we got here. This place makes no sense!"

She bit back an urge to scream. She needed to get control of herself. She could feel an icy panic building inside her. Tears were welling up in her eyes. And that wasn't going to do either of them any good. She needed to get a grip. She needed to breathe.

They reached the end of the hall and looked to the left. The lobby should be that way. But a portion of the ceiling had fallen in between here and there. There was a pile of rubble on the floor and strands of rotten wires drooping from the ceiling.

But when they looked right, they caught a glimpse of something as it disappeared from sight around the corner.

"*What was that?*" she whispered.

Albert shook his head. He didn't know. But she could tell he saw as much as she did. Whatever it was, it was very large and had far more legs than she was comfortable with. It looked like some kind of giant insect.

Suddenly, left didn't seem like such a bad choice.

They tiptoed through the debris, around the rotten wires, and made their way through the ruined hallway.

"Here!" hissed Albert, suddenly tugging her toward a restroom sign.

"What? You have to potty now?"

"No, I want to wash this goo off my arm."

"Oh." She'd forgotten about that stuff.

But the restroom lights weren't working. Everything was dark.

"Hold the door for me, would you?"

"Sure." She pressed her back against it, propping it open, and peered out into the hallway while he tried the taps.

The sinks didn't work, either, which didn't exactly surprise her, but there were paper towels for some reason. They looked a little old and brittle, but they were useable. He pulled several from the dispenser and began wiping himself and the medallion clean.

"Is this some kind of possible future?" she wondered suddenly.

Albert glanced over at her, surprised.

She didn't dare speak above a whisper for fear of the thing in the other hallway hearing her, but now that the idea had entered her head, she couldn't bear it. "I mean, we already know time is fucked up here, right? Is this, like…" She shook her head, overwhelmed. "You don't think this is what could happen if we fuck this up, do you?"

Albert shook his head. "No…" But he didn't look certain at all.

"Or worse…" she added. "If we *don't* fuck it up."

"There's no way…" His gaze drifted toward the hallway as he recalled that eerie red sky, those ominous, churning clouds. "*We* couldn't do something like that."

"Are you sure?" she pressed. "I mean, that Kneede guy *did* say it would destroy the world if we opened that door last time."

"But it didn't. It was never going to. Why would it *this* time?"

"Why *wouldn't* it? Kneede said the Keeper *murders* worlds, didn't he? You told me he said that while I was possessed by that Warner creep." She looked around at the decay. "What if *this* is what he was talking about?"

"I don't know," he sighed at last. "I don't even know what's real and what's fantasy at this point."

"No shit," she murmured. Six years ago, her perception of reality was severely tested by the weird things they found down in that creepy labyrinth. They found the sex room and lost all control of themselves to a bunch of pornographic statues. They found the fear room and saw things that terrified them to the very limits of their endurance. And they had a close encounter with a creature neither of them could identify. And then they came face to face with a man with no eyes. Not a *blind* man. Not a man with no eye*balls*. A man who had no eyes of any sort. But the world was a strange enough place that for the next thirteen months, she brushed it all off as things that she simply didn't understand. The world was full of stories like that, after all. Drugs. Mind manipulation. Secret government projects. So many ways to trick the brain. It was frightening, but there was probably an explanation for it all.

But then the phone calls drew them back into that world. They found Gilbert House and its murderous troll. The endless black acres of the Wood. The Sentinel Queen. The Keeper, himself.

The real world was far stranger than anything she'd ever imagined. Far stranger, and far *scarier*. Now, after all this time, they were traveling through *time*, of all things!

Was there even such a thing as fantasy? Or did every nightmare that was ever dreamt exist out there somewhere?

Albert tossed aside the soiled paper towels and handed her back the cleaned key.

She slipped it over her head, forcing herself not to think too much about the gross stuff it had been covered in just a moment ago. Then the two of them stepped back out into the hallway.

Almost immediately, something crashed to the floor some-where behind them, startling them.

"That was closer than I like…" whispered Albert.

She had her hands pressed to her mouth, still holding back the scream she felt bubbling up when that noise frightened her, so she merely nodded.

They pushed forward again, stepping carefully, trying not to make any noise.

They weren't alone in this place.

He peered into an open door at the rotting remains of the fitness room, at the exercise equipment that stood like rusty skel-etons beneath piles of dust. "There's got to be some way back," he reasoned.

But Brandy wasn't entirely certain of that. She was starting to wonder if they'd ever see their apartment again.

Well…their *real* apartment, she supposed… They'd already been to a fake one…

They followed the decaying hallway deeper through the ru-ined hotel, careful to make as little noise as possible. But the floor creaked beneath their feet in places. Even worse, it *sagged* in places, threatening to fall right out from under them. Was there a basement in this building? Or more tunnels like the one with the hollow man? She didn't think she wanted to visit another of *those* anytime soon.

They passed a short corridor that led to a fire exit. She couldn't see the door from here, but she could see the eerie red glow of that frightful sky.

"We just need to focus on why we're here," decided Albert. "Shanzer said there was another doorway. Then Lucianna told us there was a road of some kind hidden here."

"Great," she grumbled. "Keep your eyes open. I'm sure there'll be a sign around here somewhere. 'This way to the spa and the gift shop.' 'That way to breakfast and the gates to hell.'"

They paused at an intersecting hallway.

"This isn't right," said Albert. "The layout's changed again."

Brandy groaned. The last time he said something like this they ended up surrounded by monsters. "I really don't want to do this anymore…"

Something fell in the hallway behind them. A heavy thump. A metallic clank.

They turned and watched, both of them holding their breath, waiting for something monstrous to appear. But everything remained silent.

"Just debris falling?" hoped Albert.

But the words were barely out of his mouth when another sound broke the silence. A long, ominous scraping sound, like something being dragged across the floor or wall.

"Or not…" he said through clenched teeth.

Brandy felt a little lightheaded. Something about that sound gave her such an awful sense of dread that she thought for one terrible moment that she might black out right there. Not that anyone would blame her, she didn't think. It wasn't as if she didn't have reason to be terrified out of her mind.

"Yeah, let's keep moving," whispered Albert.

They pushed forward, trying to put as much space between them and whatever was making that ominous scraping sound as possible.

Chapter 40

Albert kept looking back over his shoulder, expecting to find something awful chasing after them.

But the awful thing he was anticipating wasn't behind them.

He stepped out into the next intersection and right into its path. A huge, bristling coil of spindly legs and lumpy, scaly flesh was taking up the entire width of the hallway less than ten paces away, easily close enough to be within striking distance given its size.

He grabbed Brandy's wrist and yanked her back, clasping his hand over her mouth in the process.

They stood there, nose to nose, their shoulders pressed to the wall, staring into each other's wide, startled eyes.

Did it see them?

Seconds passed like hours, his heart hammering against his ribs with terrible anticipation. He felt weak in his knees. His stomach boiled.

But nothing happened.

It was still there. He could hear it now that he was listening for it. A hard scraping and grinding sort of noise. A steady pitter-pattering. An odd sort of soft, wet grunting.

But it wasn't getting any closer.

Slowly, Brandy pulled his hand down and mouthed, "What was that?"

It was a damned good question. He could barely comprehend what he'd seen. It happened so fast. And he could barely think straight through the terror that washed over his brain like a tsunami. It looked like it might have been the same thing they glimpsed a few minutes earlier. It had the same abundance of freaky, spindly legs. But if that was the same sort of creature, then they'd only glimpsed a tiny portion of it that first time because it was *huge*.

He pressed his forefinger to his mouth and then slowly turned and leaned toward the corner for a better look.

Immediately, he felt her fingernails dig hard into his wrist. A silent but crystal-clear message passed between them. Something along the lines of, "What the fuck do you think you're doing?" he was sure. And he could hardly blame her. Now was the time to run away, not take a closer look. But he couldn't seem to help himself. He *really* wanted a second peek at the thing. Was it an insect? Some kind of giant centipede? He couldn't quite wrap his head around it.

It was like that night in the temple, when he finally had the chance to see a hound. For over a year, that strange, almost mechanical noise had haunted his thoughts, driving him mad.

He *had* to look.

This was like that. He couldn't help it.

Carefully…*quietly*…he peered around the corner at it.

It seemed to be rummaging around in the plenum space above the rotting ceiling. Rooting for rats, perhaps? Were there still rats in this strange, post-apocalyptic nightmare?

There were too many legs to count, each of them about eight feet long, thin and bony. They looked like insect legs. But they were sticking out of the thing's body in every direction, without any symmetry that he could discern. And the body was at least as long as a city bus, but curled around itself in a grotesque sort of pile. Its flesh, strangely, looked both scaly and blubbery at the same time. It sort of wriggled, worm-like, but with hard, thorny plates that seemed to flex and contract. It also had at least a dozen long, fleshy feelers that were slithering blindly about the floor and walls and probing the space in the ceiling.

He couldn't see the creature's head from this angle. But he could hear some kind of teeth or mandibles grinding away at the metal and concrete up above.

The pitter-patter sound was debris raining down around it, he realized.

Brandy pulled on his arm, impatient, and he turned away

from the monstrosity.

She pressed her nose all the way against his, her glistening eyes wide behind her lenses. It wasn't a happy expression by any means. "Move it!" the look screamed.

And she was right. It was well past time to go. He took her hand and crept back the way they came, careful not to make a sound.

Although they hadn't exactly been sneaking when they came upon the thing, he recalled. If it didn't notice them when they stumbled right out in front of it, it probably wouldn't notice them now unless they did something stupid. It seemed completely preoccupied with whatever it was digging for in the ceiling.

Five years ago, they'd encountered the deadly hounds and the murderous Caggo within the walls of the temple, but they also ran across strange, hairy, squid-like creatures that spat a foul, nausea-inducing fluid as a defense mechanism. After they'd returned home, he found himself thinking about those things on a few occasions and he'd deduced that they probably weren't dangerous. He was fairly sure they were just local fauna. It was possible that these things were like that, too. They were just big, dumb creatures rummaging for food in the ruins of this building.

Of course, it was also just as likely that it would have attacked and eaten them in a heartbeat if it hadn't been too distracted to notice them.

He retraced his steps back to the previous intersection—careful this time to peer carefully in each direction, lest they find out the hard way how nasty the freaky alien monsters could be—then hurried across and tried the other way.

"This is *not* like last time," he grumbled as he stepped around a dangling light fixture and peered through an open doorway at what looked to be a decrepit conference room.

"No shit," she grumbled back.

Something creaked overhead, freezing them both in their tracks.

They listened, both of them holding their breath, their pulses racing. But no more noises followed.

"This is stupid," grumbled Brandy as they continued forward again. "We're going to get eaten by something. I just know it."

"We can do this," he insisted. But as they peered around the corner into the next hallway, he caught a glimpse of a familiar white dress disappearing from view.

"You saw that, right?" whispered Brandy.

He nodded.

"What do we do?"

But he wasn't sure. Did they follow the mystery woman? Or did they run the other way? Last time they saw her, things went sour *really* fast.

(An enemy of the cycle prowls the depths of Mysteria.)

Was she the one Warner was talking about? Was the woman in white the enemy of the cycle? Was she responsible for this apocalypse-themed version of the hotel?

Something fell over in one of the rooms somewhere behind them, startling them again.

"Whatever we're going to do," hissed Brandy, "we should do it *now*."

"Agreed." He fixed his gaze on the hallway down which the woman had disappeared and made his decision.

Last time, no good came from following the woman in the white dress, so he went straight across the intersection, avoiding her.

They hurried on, eyes peeled for monsters of any shape.

But they were getting nowhere. They couldn't go on like this forever. More and more, he felt like something was amiss. Was he making a mistake? Had he overlooked something important? He couldn't shake the feeling that this wasn't supposed to happen. And if he didn't figure it out soon, he and his dear bride were going to be in serious trouble.

But if there was something he needed to figure out, he was out of time.

He turned the corner and jolted to a stop.

The woman in the white dress was standing in their path.

"Wow she's fast!" gasped Brandy, looking back over her shoulder, wondering if maybe there were two of them.

The woman was just standing there, staring at them, an odd sort of smile on her face. It looked forced, as if she were using it to mask some other emotion. Those eyes were as dark and shining as Lucianna's, but there was none of her warmth or cheerfulness there. She looked strangely intense, almost strained.

"Who are you?" he demanded, trying his best to not look intimidated (and fairly sure he was failing miserably).

But the woman didn't answer him. She simply stood there, staring back at him with that unsettling smile.

"Albert..." whispered Brandy as she crowded close behind him. "Something's wrong with her."

"What do you mean?"

"I don't know. I don't know how to describe it. I can see her, but it's like she's not really there. She's just...*wrong*."

"Awesome," he sighed. Something *wrong* about her... That wasn't very informative. Nor was it exactly surprising. The very fact that she was here in this rotting version of the hotel was wrong. "What do you want?"

But still the woman didn't answer.

"We need to leave," urged Brandy.

"And go where?" he asked her. "We've been trying to leave since we got here. We're not just lost, we're trapped." He never took his eyes off the woman. "Is it *you*? Are you holding us here?"

But the woman only stared at him, that same forced smile painted across her face.

What should they do? He needed to think. There must be *something* they could do...

For the first time in a while, he recalled the book Shanzer gave him. A spellbook, he'd called it, full of pages he couldn't read that would reveal more when he was ready for it...whatever that meant.

It wasn't as if he had time to pull out a book and start reading, but something about it suddenly struck him as important.

No... Not just "important."

Significant.

His hand gravitated toward his pocket. Suddenly he wanted

to hold it. He wanted to look through it. He wanted to *read* it. Every page. Every word.

Was that where the answers lay? Was he carrying them in his pocket this whole time?

But he didn't have time to ponder it further.

The woman in the white dress lifted one slender arm and held her hand out toward him, her open palm facing him.

Albert stood there in the intersecting hallways, staring back at her. He held his breath and waited.

Brandy pressed her body against his back. He could feel her fingernails digging into his arms again. She made a frightened sort of squeaking noise deep in her throat that he only heard because she was so close to him.

Without speaking a word, she closed her fist again. At the very same instant, all four ends of the two intersecting hallways began to crumble. A wall of dust and debris raced inward toward them, illuminated by the eerie red glow that he'd seen through the glass doorways, the doomsday sky that hovered over the wasteland that surrounded this nightmare version of the Lucianna Mysteria.

"Albert!" shrieked Brandy.

But Albert didn't know what she expected him to do. There was nowhere to go. The Ruin raced toward them from every direction. They were trapped.

They watched as it swept past the woman in the white dress, swallowing her.

Brandy screamed and pressed herself against him.

He closed his eyes as the churning clouds of debris bore down on them, bracing himself.

Then everything changed.

Chapter 41

Brandy stood there a moment, staring down a long, empty corridor of familiar gray stone. "Wha...?" she gasped, her brain struggling to comprehend what just happened.

She turned and looked behind her, but there was nothing there, either. The corridor stretched on in both directions, endless, featureless.

She knew these walls... This gray stone had haunted her dreams for months. This was where her life was changed forever. This was where she felt the *true* power of lust and fear for the first time in her life, where she learned that there were still plenty of strange and incredible secrets waiting out there in the real world.

This was the Temple of the Blind.

But the temple was gone. It was destroyed five years ago. She saw the wall of rubble that buried the entrance with her own eyes. It was impossible to be back here.

And yet here she was...

And why was she alone?

"Albert?" She looked forward again, her heart pounding with mounting fear. Where did he go? He was right here just a moment ago. "*Albert?*"

She began walking, pushing her way through the gloom. *Was* that just a moment ago? Now that she was thinking about it, she couldn't quite remember how she came to be in this place. Or even precisely *when* she came to be here.

She remembered being lost in those creepy hallways... But what came next? Did they get separated?

Why couldn't she remember anything that came after that?

She quickened her pace to a jog. She had to find him. They

were supposed to do this together. They *needed* each other. Luci-anna told them so.

Now she was running.

She *had* to find him. She couldn't do this on her own. She didn't have the courage. Not for this.

Where could he be?

Chapter 42

Albert sat atop his bar stool, blinking down at his whiskey glass, trying to gather his thoughts.

His head felt foggy. He couldn't quite remember what he was doing before this. In fact, he couldn't quite remember how he arrived at this bar. Or when.

Wasn't he supposed to be doing something else?

He reached out and picked up the glass. He held it up in front of his face and examined the ball of ice inside.

"Magic..." he muttered to himself, though he wasn't entirely sure why. He didn't believe in magic. Had he *ever* believed in it? He was sure he probably did at one point. *Every* child believed in magic at some time in his life, didn't he? At least until the weight of all the responsibilities and harsh realities of the real world inevitably crushed that pure innocence and forcefully transformed him into a properly dysfunctional adult?

Would life be easier if he believed in magic? Would that make it easier to believe in other things? Because sometimes he had trouble deciding what he did and didn't believe in. Growing up, his older sister had always done her best to spoil things for him. Santa Clause wasn't real. The Easter Bunny was a lie. Only babies believed in the Tooth Fairy. She seemed to decide for herself that refusing to believe in things like that was how you finally began to grow up. And he could never understand for the life of him why she was in such a hurry.

He wasn't even sure if he believed in God, if he were being completely honest. He *wanted* to believe. He rather liked the idea that there was someone out there keeping everything moving, holding everyone accountable.

But five years ago, the Temple of the Blind proved that

there were plenty of strange things hiding out there. There were monsters. There were entire worlds just beyond our sight.

He frowned at the glass. The temple… That's what he was doing. He was supposed to be looking for the next doorway. That's how he came to be here.

He turned his head and looked down the bar.

Wasn't someone sitting just a couple seats down from him? Someone he knew from back then?

(You never did answer my question.)

Before he could quite piece it all together, he felt a hand reach around from behind him and slide up his shirt.

He closed his eyes and smiled.

That's right. He was here with Brandy. How could he forget that?

He felt her warm hands slide up his belly and chest. He felt her breath on the back of his ear as she leaned over his shoulder.

But when he turned to look into her pretty blue eyes, he found himself instead staring at the blank, featureless face of the Sentinel Queen.

Chapter 43

Brandy reached out and grasped the door knob.

She couldn't quite remember when she arrived at this door. The last thing she remembered was running through that temple corridor. But that was then, she supposed. This was now. And now she was here.

She was looking for somebody, wasn't she? Or was she? She couldn't quite remember...

She turned the knob and stepped through the doorway.

A part of her was surprised to find herself in Nicole and Andrea's apartment, although she wasn't sure why. Wasn't this where she was trying to go?

But she couldn't quite remember *why* she needed to come here... Was it something important?

She stepped through the room, her gaze drawn, as it always was, to the many pictures hung all over the walls. She remembered when Nikki decorated her bedroom walls like this back when she still lived with her parents. She used to say that when she moved into her own place, she was going to decorate *all* the walls like this. And she did.

She crossed the room, looking at all the pictures. There was one of her and Albert. And one of her and Albert with Nikki. And that was a nice one of Albert with Andrea.

Albert with Wayne...

Albert with his parents...

Albert with Nikki and Olivia...

Albert...

She frowned. Albert? Where *was* Albert? She felt like she was forgetting something.

She turned around, confused, and walked out of Nicole's

bedroom and into the hallway, then down the stairs and into the living room. She'd always liked Nikki's parents' house. It was big, but cozy at the same time. And the back yard was huge. They used to spend hours playing out there when they were kids.

But they weren't kids anymore... And Nicole didn't live here. She had her own apartment she shared with Andrea...

Wasn't she just *there*?

It was hard to think clearly. She wanted to go outside. There was something going on out there... Something she'd forgotten.

She stepped out the back door and into the bright sunlight and stifling July heat.

"Make sure you drink enough water," her mother reminded her again.

"I'm fine," she assured her.

It was so hot. She loved her wedding gown, but she wished she could catch a breeze under it. Her thighs were sweaty.

(Don't let her deceive you.)

She'd been smiling all day, but now she frowned. What was that thought just now? Something familiar? Something...ominous...?

Was it a thought? Or did someone say something to her?

"You okay?" asked Nicole.

"Huh?" She turned and looked at her. For a second there, she had the strangest feeling like she should be surprised to see her here. But...why would that be? Of course she was here. She was the maid of honor. "Yeah," she said, pushing the odd thoughts away. "I'm fine."

And she *was* fine. How could she not be fine. This was her special day, the one she'd been planning for five years.

She reached up to straighten her glasses, but she wasn't wearing them. Just a habit. But for some reason it struck her as odd, as if she couldn't understand why she wasn't wearing them, as if they'd been on her face only a moment ago.

Only the heat and the excitement. It had been a long and wonderful day. And yet she was in no hurry for it to end.

She cast her gaze across the sunny lawns and all the people who'd turned out to help her celebrate. But as she looked out toward the lake, she saw the Shaman of Wevenwert standing there in his obnoxious red suit jacket, gaudy tie and great, over-sized glasses, his pale, splotchy bald head glistening with sweat. He was staring right at her, that perverted leer painted across his homely face.

She could almost hear Dolly's voice in her head, reminding her that, "He likes to watch."

She shuddered with revulsion and turned away as if she didn't notice him.

No. She didn't want to go back to that. She wanted to stay here.

She reached back and took Albert's hand.

That's right... *Albert*. She was trying to find Albert. She felt a wave of relief wash over her.

But then she heard Albert's voice from somewhere to her right.

"Wevenwert," he said. "In Tennessee, yeah."

She looked over at him, confused. She thought he was standing right next to her, but he was over there...talking to his aunt and uncle...

"Oh it's *beautiful* there!" exclaimed his aunt. "Which resort?"

But if Albert was over there...? She looked down at her hand, at the slender fingers gripping hers. Then she looked up to find herself face-to-face with the woman in the white dress.

Chapter 44

Albert was lost.

Somewhere deep inside, he felt like there was something he was supposed to be doing, but it was hard to think about anything else right now. It was *always* hard to think about anything else when he was making love to his beautiful wife.

Why would he *want* to think about anything else?

He pulled her close to him and kissed her, savoring her. God, how he loved the softness of her lips, the warmth of her body, the feel of her silky skin pressed against his.

To him, heaven wasn't a place he might reach someday if he lived a good life. It was right here in her arms, lost in her breath, enveloped in the steamy embrace of her flesh. Every time their bodies merged like this, the world, with all its confusing and difficult and frightening things, simply melted away.

She pushed him onto his back and rolled on top of him. She kissed him hard, pressing her face against his. She sucked at his lower lip. He felt her tongue probe his mouth.

Why did he have so much trouble believing what the shaman told them? No such thing as sexual magic? What *was* this feeling if not magic? What else could fill him with such immeasurable bliss?

If anything in this cold, unforgiving universe could grant them power, why wouldn't it be this feeling right here?

She lifted her head and moaned, her heavy breasts swaying sensually above him, her long, black hair pooling around his face.

He was getting close… Just a few seconds more…

(You have to take control.)

A twinge of pain passed through his head, making him wince.

What was that? Did someone just say something? Why did his heart stammer for a second?

He glanced around, but there was no one else here. They were alone in their bedroom, undisturbed.

Why did he feel like there was something he was supposed to remember? Something important...

She grasped the sides of his face in her warm hands and kissed him again. Those strange thoughts melted away. All he could think about was *her*.

Her hips ground rhythmically against his. She was so warm down there...so soft... Like an angel's embrace... He'd been in her arms like this countless times. It was such a comforting, familiar feeling. The feeling of home. The feeling of *love*. The feeling of *her*...

...so why did something feel so *wrong*?

(Look at her.)

He frowned. He *was* looking at her. He was looking right into those lovely brown eyes. Her beautiful face. Her long, black hair with the bright red streak running down one side...

...wait...

That wasn't right.

He felt the approaching orgasm melt away. At the same time, a sort of eye peeled open somewhere deep inside him.

Where was he?

What was this place? This wasn't home. In fact, it didn't feel like *anywhere*. There was nothing here. It was like he'd found himself adrift in the cosmos, floating through an endless void.

Why was the bartender from Shanzer's sex party straddling him? He'd never do this with her. He didn't even *know* this woman!

What the hell was happening?

The sexy bartender bent over him and kissed him again.

He tried to turn away, but she was surprisingly strong. He grasped her wrists and tried to remove them from him, but although those hands were small and soft, he couldn't budge them. It was like fighting against a machine.

This was *really* bad. How did he end up like this? What did he miss?

And where was his *real* wife?
Where was Brandy?

Chapter 45

Brandy stood alone in the darkness, her heart pounding in her chest, fear worming its way through every cell in her body.

This wasn't real. She couldn't be here again.

And yet the scene before her didn't waver.

Pillars of fire belched from cracks in the stone, illuminating a barren, winding path. Night trees swayed in the undulating light, their deadly, toothy tendrils probing the shadows for prey. Overhead, carrion eaters swarmed the skies.

Just like last time, she stood naked and vulnerable, wearing nothing but her glasses and her jewelry. Just like last time, she was filled with an awful, creeping dread.

But unlike last time, she was all alone.

Albert was gone.

Nicole and Andrea and Olivia were all gone.

No… There was no way she could do this alone. She wasn't strong enough. She wasn't *brave* enough.

(Look for the truth.)

She frowned. The truth? What did that mean? And where did those words even come from? Was it only her imagination playing tricks on her? Or was someone trying to talk to her?

The path to the top of the burning mountain was haunted, she recalled. Were the spirits trapped here trying to deceive her?

No… That didn't feel right. She was missing something. She'd *forgotten* something. Something important. She frowned and looked back at the path behind her. None of this was right. How did she get here? Wasn't the temple…?

(Truth.)

She winced at a sharp and sudden pain in her head. It was hard to think clearly. Had something happened? What was she doing before this?

And where *was* everybody?

Where was *Albert*?

She opened her eyes, a sense of sudden alertness overtaking her.

Albert. She needed to find Albert. That was what she was supposed to be doing. That was what mattered right now. The *only* thing that mattered.

But *how* did she go about finding him? She didn't even know where she was. What was this place? It couldn't be the temple. The temple was gone, reduced to smoldering rubble.

Looking around again, she found that the fires had died away. Darkness enveloped her.

An illusion of some sort? Like back in the pervert's filthy mansion?

But that didn't feel quite right, either. There was something deeper about these tricks. She felt so *lost*. She couldn't remember how or when she first arrived on the burning mountain... Or back at her wedding... Or at Nicole's apartment...

It reminded her of...

(Dreams.)

That was it! It reminded her of her dreams. How she could never remember how they began.

But...what did that mean? Why was everything behaving like a dream? That made no sense. Wasn't all this supposed to be about stupid sex magic?

She was so confused.

"There you are!" sang out a familiar voice.

Brandy turned and watched as Lucianna stepped from the darkness, a bright purple dress billowing out around her wide hips. "You..." she gasped.

"It's okay, dear," Lucianna assured her, holding out a chubby, bejeweled hand. "You've shaken off the worst of it. You'll be all right now."

"Why are you here?" she asked, struggling to grasp any tiny part of what was going on.

"You've stumbled into a trap," Lucianna explained. "It's

done a number on your head."

"A trap?"

Lucianna took her hand. It was warm. It reminded her of the chill she felt. She looked down at her still-naked body. Was that not one of the illusions, too? Had she really lost her clothes? When did that happen? What had she missed?

"Albert…?" she asked, her head still reeling.

"He's fine," Lucianna assured her. "You were separated from each other in the confusion, but he's safe, too. I knew you were both strong. I never doubted you for a second."

She nodded. Albert was safe. That was good. That was all she wanted.

But why did she still feel so uneasy? Was it just because he wasn't back at her side yet? Or was there something else? Something she was still missing?

Chapter 46

Albert struggled to fight off Shanzer's freakishly strong bartender, but he was helpless against her. It was like being pinned under a block of concrete. He couldn't even budge her.

Why was she doing this? Who was she? What did she want from him? Because he was quite sure no one would go to this sort of trouble just to have sex with him.

But when the bartender finally released his sore lips and sat up again, she was no longer the bartender. Instead, it was Dolly who stared down at him, her black lips spread into a wicked sort of grin.

She's an incredibly powerful witch, he recalled Lucianna warning them. *And she's immensely evil.*

His heart was pounding with fright now, rather than lust. Was this *her* doing? Had *she* orchestrated this trap somehow? Had she cast some sort of curse on them while they were alone with her in Shanzer's twisted mansion?

She kept the heels of her hands pressed against his cheeks, holding him in place, but she curled her fingers up over his face, revealing that her black nails had grown long and sharp.

Why was she so strong? He was prying at her wrists with all his strength, but he might as well be trying to bend solid steel.

He could feel the tips of those nightmarish nails pressing into his skin, lightly at first, then harder. They felt like cold needles in his skin. Was she going to carve the very flesh from his skull?

The terrible things she's done has earned her a rightful eternity in a place far worse than any hell you could imagine.

He didn't understand. What did he miss? How did she get her literal claws in him?

(Not real.)

He closed his eyes as another twinge of pain passed through his frightened brain.

Not real? Was that what he just heard? *What* wasn't real? Dolly? This place?

But he couldn't focus on that. Dolly's face descended on him again. He felt those black lips against his own. Her dainty hands squeezed his face with impossible strength, preventing him from clenching his teeth as her tongue forced its way inside his mouth, a little at first, then deeper...and deeper...probing his cheeks and the roof of his mouth, then slithering toward his tonsils.

How long was her tongue? It filled his whole mouth. He couldn't breathe!

A renewed panic welled up inside him and overflowed. He kicked and bucked, but although her body *looked* small, she didn't move at all.

He dug his own fingernails into her wrists, but it had no effect on her.

He felt her tongue wriggle past his tonsils and into the back of his throat, gagging him.

Tears sprang to his eyes and streamed down his face.

His chest spasmed. His stomach tightened.

What would happen if she made him throw up like this? Where would it go? He tried to resist it, but that awful tongue just kept going deeper and deeper. It filled the back of his throat. It slithered down his esophagus. He could feel his neck bulging as it wormed its way deeper inside him.

His head was pounding. His furious pulse echoed through his skull with each beat of his frantic heart. He could feel his face burning.

He was going to black out.

Worse, he was never going to wake up again. He was going to die here, choking on this foul witch's monstrous tongue like the butt of some perverse joke. And there was nothing he could do about it.

(Control the dream.)

The dream? What the hell did *that* mean?

But Dolly's body shuddered somehow. The inhuman tongue suddenly withdrew from his throat and mouth.

He sat up, gasping and coughing and gagging. He couldn't breathe. He couldn't see. He needed to regain control, but it was taking forever. Where did that witch go? What was she doing? How long did he have before she attacked him again?

But when he finally managed to open his eyes, everything had changed.

He was still naked, but he was no longer in his familiar bed. He was sitting in the dark on a floor of cold stone.

"Where…?" he gasped, looking around, confused.

There were no lights in this place. It was pitch black all around him, yet somehow he was able to see the area just around him.

Was he back inside the temple? Inside one of the larger chambers?

He rose to his feet and stood there, trembling, his heart still pounding, trying to listen over the ragged sound of his own rapid breathing.

(Open your eyes.)

That voice… He turned around, scanning the darkness. *Was* it a voice? It didn't seem to come from any direction. But he was sure it had been speaking to him this whole time. Was it Lucianna? Was she trying to reach him? Or might it be Warner? Shanzer?

(Open your eyes and see the truth!)

When he turned around again, the Sentinel Queen was emerging from the darkness, her freakishly long hand reaching out for him again.

Chapter 47

"Stay close," warned Lucianna.

They were walking through an empty hallway illuminated by nothing more than an eerie red glow that emanated from under each closed door. Were they back in that weird, apocalyptic nightmare again? Did they have to pass through the Ruin to get back to their own world? She supposed that would make sense. But since when did making sense make any sense? When it came to the temple, nothing *ever* seemed to make any sense.

"Once we're back in the hotel, things will go back to normal."

"And Albert will be there?" asked Brandy. She felt so strange walking through this nightmare world naked. Why was *she* the only one naked? Why did Lucianna get to keep *her* clothes? Not that she really wanted to see this woman naked. It just didn't seem quite fair.

"Of course, dear," she assured her. "You've both had a little setback, but you're doing wonderfully! You've already opened the first lock. The road is within your reach. You'll be there in no time!"

"No time..." she muttered. That was good. That was what she wanted. As long as she was reunited with Albert, everything would work out eventually. That's what he'd promised her. And he always kept his promises.

"Almost there," Lucianna assured her.

The end of the hallway loomed ahead of them. A heavy steel door waited there. She should have felt relieved, but something about that door felt weirdly ominous. It was such a heavy door, after all. From this side, it looked less like an exit than a prison door.

But that was a silly thing to think. Of course it was a heavy door. Lucianna probably put it there to lock out all those things prowling Mysteria.

Yet she couldn't shake the feeling that something wasn't right. This felt too easy somehow.

They reached the door and Lucianna pulled it open.

There, waiting for them on the other side, was the woman in the white dress.

Lucianna froze in place. Her grip tightened around her hand. "Impossible…" she sighed.

The woman in the white dress smiled a triumphant sort of smile and stepped through the doorway.

"You can't have her," said Lucianna, moving her formidable bulk between Brandy and the woman.

But then something burst through her back, spraying hot blood across Brandy's naked face and chest.

Lucianna collapsed onto the carpet between them.

And Brandy, filled with terror, fled back the way she came.

Chapter 48

Albert's head was spinning. Time seemed to be spiraling out of control, speeding up and slowing down, skipping ahead. He couldn't keep up. He felt lost.

The Sentinel Queen loomed over him, her featureless face hovering just inches from his own. And yet that couldn't be possible.

"You're supposed to be dead…" he breathed.

And yet, she didn't *feel* dead. Her hands were soft and warm, almost hot, even, against his bare skin. One hand was clasped around the back of his neck, her long fingers curled around his throat, her thumb pressed against his chest. Her other hand was curled around his waist.

"Things change in places like these," she explained. Although that didn't exactly *explain* anything.

It was so strange staring up into that face. She had no eyes at all, not even the faintest shadow to indicate any sockets in her skull. Nor did she have any nose to speak of. There was only a slight bump in the center of her face. And her mouth was nothing more than an empty slit. It was difficult to tell if there was even any sort of mouth inside there.

The rest of her body was no less strange. She was sort of squatting in front of him, her knees and back bent in order for her blank face to be that close to him. Her entire body was strangely elongated, much like the anatomy depicted by the sentinel statues back in the depths of the temple. Her neck was almost as long as his forearm. Her breasts were strangely shaped, too, more rounded on the bottom than the top, with long nipples that pointed almost straight up when she stood upright.

It wasn't merely that she was tall and thin. Her entire anatomy was strangely *alien*.

"What do you want from me?" he asked, trying to keep his voice calm.

The Sentinel Queen's empty face drifted even closer. Her forehead pressed against his. Her skin was so hot to the touch. She felt feverish. Was that normal? "Danger lurks in Mysteria," she warned him.

"Yeah, I kind of noticed." Something felt off about this, but he couldn't put his finger on it. He still felt lightheaded. It was hard to think clearly.

"You need to awaken your psychic powers in order to see the way forward."

"My psychic powers?" He frowned. But Shanzer said his psychic abilities were related to—

He shuddered hard as he felt her hand slide suddenly from his waist to his groin.

"*Oh no!*" he gasped, grabbing her arm with both his hands. "That's *really* not necessary!" But he wasn't strong enough to resist her. Like Dolly and the sexy bartender before her, she was impossibly strong.

With one hand she tightened her grip on his neck, holding him in place. With the other, she wrapped her long fingers around him and squeezed, sending a jarring shiver all the way up his body.

"Let the sensations of sex fill you to the brim," she instructed him. "As you did inside the emotion chamber six years ago."

"I'd really rather not!" he grunted, still trying to pry her arm away. "And who said we *let* anything happen?" He'd never felt anything like this before in his life. Her fingers were so strangely long that his brain couldn't quite comprehend what he was feeling. It was almost as if there were *several* hands grasping him at once.

Seriously, why the hell was everyone suddenly trying to get their hands on his junk? What was with all these cheesy porno situations?

"Fill yourself with wanting," she coached. "Teeter on the very edge of climax. Then cast your thoughts into your surroundings."

"This is *not* consensual!" he grunted at her.

Five years ago, this woman—or whatever the hell she really was—did this sort of thing to Wayne, too. In her desperation to postpone her impending death, she plunged her psychic conscience into his head and essentially raped him in order to impregnate herself.

Was that going to happen to *him* now?

No... She'd just told him to release his sexual energy in *psychic* form... If she was trying to get him to do the same thing he'd been doing, then she wasn't after his *seed*, or whatever you wanted to call it.

Besides, it didn't really work when she did that to Wayne. She was successful in her attempt to impregnate herself, but her time ran out well before she could give birth. Both she and the baby died.

Or so he thought...

Things change in places like these.

What did that mean? Did it have something to do with the time anomalies of Mysteria? Or was it something to do with that other dimension? The Ruin, or whatever it was called.

God, he wished he could think clearly.

"You must find the gateway. Show me the way to the road. It's the only chance you have of escaping Mysteria before it's too late."

"I got it! Just let go of me!"

"You must trust me," she told him. "Time is running out for us all. The enemy draws near."

"The enemy is already here," said a new voice from the surrounding darkness.

The Sentinel Queen threw back her strange head and let out an awful wail that echoed through the darkness. At the same time, she let go of him, allowing him to stagger backward, away from her, his hands immediately shielding his violated privates from another attack.

But the Sentinel Queen only dropped to her hands and knees on the cold stone. Blood dripped down her naked body.

"Traitor…" she rasped.

Lucas Kneede stepped from the shadows behind her and fixed Albert in his steely gaze. "Found you," he growled.

Albert didn't wait around to see what the psychopath was going to do next. He turned and fled into the endless darkness.

Chapter 49

The darkness swelled, enveloping everything until it was impossible to see *anything*. Running became futile. Fear thrived in the darkness. Fear of the known dangers behind. Fear of new and even more terrible dangers ahead.

Slow down... Listen to the silence... Listen for dangers in the shadows...

But every step soon became weighted with weariness.

So very tired...

How long had it been? Time wavered like images reflected on the surface of a trickling stream, stretching and scrunching, rippling and bubbling, distorting everything perceptible into something only vaguely familiar.

And as consciousness sank into the murky depths of all that was known and unknown, a single sound rang out like a beacon.

It was the solitary cry of a cat.

Chapter 50

Brandy's eyes fluttered open and she stared at the furry face looming before her.

"Wha…?" She blinked hard, trying to clear her head and reached up to straighten her glasses. What manner of horror had she stumbled across now?

But it was only a cat. An orange and white tabby, to be exact, staring intently at her, as if it expected her to give it a treat or something. But for a moment there, as her mind swam back to consciousness, those bright, yellow eyes had looked far more strange and mysterious. They seemed to stare deep into her soul for some unfathomable reason.

"What the hell happened?" groaned Albert.

She turned, wide awake now, and threw herself at him, an explosion of relief filling her. "Oh thank God!"

Surprised, he wrapped his arms around her and held on tight. "What's…?" He looked around, bemused. "Where are we?"

It was a damned good question. They were sitting together on a couch in what looked like the most ancient living room she'd ever been in. Everything was hoary with cobwebs and dust. And it was *dark*. All the curtains were drawn tight, so that only a few slivers of gloomy light illuminated the space, leaving most of the room bathed in eerie darkness.

But she was no longer naked. Unlike when they awoke in the pervert's gaudy guest bed, they were still wearing the clothes they had on *before* everything went weird.

Was all that happened back there just another illusion? Some sort of hallucination?

The orange and white cat was sitting on the arm of the

couch, still staring at her. And it wasn't alone. She straightened her glasses again and looked around, realizing that there were cats *everywhere*. They were on the floor and on the furniture, all of them staring straight at them. Even where it was too dark to make out their shapes, shining eyes stared back. Cats of every color. Longhairs and shorthairs. Small ones and big ones.

There was something dreadfully eerie about all those eyes on her.

Why were they all staring so intently?

There was something otherworldly about them. Something *unnatural*.

She couldn't help wondering if anyone had ever been killed by a pack of cats before… (Or whatever the word was for a group of cats…she couldn't quite remember…she was too frightened to remember much of *anything* at the moment.)

"This is weird…" sighed Albert.

"Finally…" sighed a new voice from somewhere in the deep gloom in front of them.

The space before them was filled with little more than indistinct shapes bathed in shadow. But now that they were looking, they realized that they weren't alone. There was someone there. A small figure was sitting motionless in an old rocking chair. A woman, Brandy thought, draped in scarves, her face hidden. But she could see pale, bony hands resting on the arms of the chair.

"Who are you?" demanded Albert. "Where are we?"

"We…are friend," replied the voice. It was wispy and soft. It barely carried across the room to where they sat. "And this…is home."

"We?" said Albert, glancing around at all the cats. What a creepy way to introduce oneself.

"We've been here before," Brandy realized. Somehow she just knew this. She could *feel* it somehow. Something about this woman's presence. "But last time it looked like our apartment."

Albert nodded. He recognized it, too. "Cats," he sighed. But it wasn't the cats or the woman who felt familiar. Something about this *space* felt the same as it did then.

"Cats…" whispered Brandy, her gaze returning to the orange and white one that was still sitting on the arm of the couch next to her, still staring at her with those intense yellow eyes. Why did those eyes give off such an odd and mysterious aura? They felt like something from a storybook, the eyes of something ancient and wise, mysterious and powerful.

Seriously, what was up with these kitties?

"Perceptions vary," said the woman. Or at least, she *appeared* female. She *sounded* female. But it was difficult to tell from shadows and a pair of frail, bony hands. "Familiar spaces creep in…distorting truth…making hard to see what lies beneath. Such is the nature of dreams."

"Dreams?" said Albert, surprised.

"That's right!" recalled Brandy. "There was something about dreams when I was lost back there!"

Albert nodded. Dreams… He seemed to recall someone saying something… (*Control the dream.*) But it was so hazy…

Brandy looked down at her lap as she struggled to remember all of it. "I was in the temple… Then I was in Nikki's apartment and, like, every picture she had up on her walls was of *you*. It was *so* weird! Then it wasn't her apartment anymore, but her room back when she still lived with her parents. And then I was at our wedding again and that woman in the white dress was there! And she attacked Lucianna!" She turned her pretty blue eyes on Albert. "Did that happen to you, too?"

Albert stared back at her, distracted. "Uh… I…can't really remember…"

"Really? I feel like mine were *super* vivid. You don't remember *anything?*"

"Something about the Sentinel Queen," he replied, looking uncomfortable. "It was…*weird.*"

"Dreams are slippery by their very nature," explained the mysterious woman. "Difficult to grasp. Even more difficult to mold into something that fits coherently into neatly organized flow of time and space in waking world."

There was something about her voice that Brandy didn't like, but she couldn't quite put her finger on what it was. Something about the way she enunciated her words. It reminded her for some reason of the hissing of a cat. It made the hairs on the back of her neck tingle a little to listen to her.

"This place, as in all dreams…is temporary. Paper thin. It exists somewhere between worlds of living and dead…accessible only from deep within subconscious."

Brandy glanced around the room. Why did her voice seem to travel around as she spoke, even though the woman never moved? There was something immensely creepy about it.

"You are real," explained the woman. "As are we. But this place…this *time*…this *conversation* we are having…all of these things…nothing more than a dream within a dream."

Brandy frowned. "A dream…*what?*" She looked at Albert, but he only shrugged. He didn't understand it, either.

"In dreams…human mind is capable of creating temporary realities…entire universes, complete with their own physical laws…unique flow of time. Everything that happens in a dream is real…but only for duration of dream. The moment it ends, it not only ceases to be real…it ceases to ever have *been*."

Brandy scrunched up her face, confused. "Huh?"

But Albert nodded. "I think I get it."

"Really?"

He shrugged. "I mean, a *little*. It's still kind of hard to comprehend."

The orange and white cat on the arm of the sofa had been staring at Brandy this entire time. It hadn't once taken its eyes off her. But now, it suddenly turned its head and stared into the darkness behind an open doorway.

Two or three other cats did the same, as if something out there had drawn their attention. The rest, however, kept their creepy eyes fixed on them.

Something stirred in the darkness surrounding the woman. Brandy realized she could make out shapes around the eyes shining back from there. It was the really *big* black cat they saw in that imperfect replica of their apartment. It appeared to be curled up at her side.

And now that she was looking, she realized there was more than one.

All of those creepy shining eyes belonged to impossibly big cats...

"So if this place is only accessible from the subconscious, like you said," pondered Albert, "does that mean we're dreaming right now?"

"You are," replied the woman. "And are not."

Brandy frowned. "Um... Which is it?"

"Usually, one can only reach us in dreams. But you two are currently in *unique* state of existence."

"Unique...?" pondered Albert.

"Awake and asleep at same time."

Brandy looked over at him, surprised. "Wait...does she mean the *other* us? The ones asleep in the hotel?"

It was already after dark when they were outside by the pool. Wednesday night's Brandy and Albert had already had some drinks and returned to their room. There were nights when they stayed up late, but she remembered very well that on that night they made love in their room and then immediately fell asleep in each other's arms.

"Correct," replied the woman. "It is only reason you are able to speak to us like this. And it will only remain possible while your other selves remain in sleep. The moment they awaken...which will be *soon*...your connection to us will be severed."

Only when their other selves were asleep... Brandy thought back to the last time they were here...back when it looked like their own apartment... That was still Monday night, wasn't it? She remembered going out to dinner. After that, they came back with the intention of going to the pool. But they became...*distracted*...while changing. They had sex. Then they cuddled together. If she remembered right, they fell asleep for a little while. A little afternoon nap before they dressed and went back downstairs.

"We won't be able to help you again...as long as they are awake," warned the woman. "It is likely we will not have this chance again."

Two more of the room's mysterious cats turned and stared at the open doorway.

The white and orange one jumped down and ran in that direction.

Brandy stared after it, surprised. "Did that one have two tails?" she asked, confused.

"Cats with two tails…" repeated Albert as he stared into the darkness where the cat vanished.

"Wait…" She furrowed her eyebrows and tried to recall something. "Isn't that supposed to be a thing? Cats with two tails? Some kind of… You know? A *thing*?"

"There's an old Japanese superstition about cats turning into monsters if they live long enough. Or if they're abused by humans."

"Better not be anyone abusing kitties!"

"Enemies of the cycle are near," explained the woman. Although for a moment, her voice seemed to be coming from the doorway where the orange and white cat disappeared, not from the rocking chair. "They swarm halls of Mysteria," she went on, her voice shifting back to the gloom in front of them. "They seek to deceive you. They hope to make you reveal hidden road…and steal your fate from you."

"Kneede…" breathed albert. "I saw him. In my…*dreams*? I guess? Before I was here. The Sentinel Queen was…" He glanced at Brandy. "Telling me to hurry and find it," he finished. "Then Kneede showed up and literally stabbed her in the back."

Brandy nodded. "That woman in white," she recalled. "She attacked Lucianna." She looked down at herself, remembering the blood that spattered on her face and chest. But there was none on her now, which wasn't very surprising considering that she was naked at the time and fully dressed again now. "But that was only a dream, right? She's okay?"

"I mean, the Sentinel Queen's been dead for five years," reasoned Albert. "I mean, hasn't she?"

"Up is down and out is in."

Albert and Brandy stared back at her, confused. "What?" they both asked in unison.

"Things in Mysteria are not what they seem," said the woman. "Be careful who you trust. Truth is being distorted. The one you call 'Lucianna' is especially not what she claims. You must beware."

"Not what she…?" murmured Brandy. What did *that* mean? Was she lying to them? But didn't Warner *send* them to her?

Although…thinking about it, what *was* it Warner wanted from them? Did he ever really say?

Several more cats turned their constant gazes away from them and toward the darkened doorway. Then, one by one, they each set off across the room and out the door.

But many eyes still remained fixed on them.

Were there more than there were before? It was hard to tell.

"What's going on over there?" wondered Albert, staring through the darkened doorway.

"This realm is vast," said the woman, her voice again seeming to not come from the direction it should be coming from. It sounded like the words were spoken from one of the pairs of shining eyes in the darkest corner of the room. "We have much business. Many tasks."

"We?" squeaked Brandy. She glanced around the room. Why did she keep saying that? Did she consider herself and all her feline companions as a single person? Talk about crazy cat lady…

And yet…there was that odd habit her voice had of drifting about the room…almost as if it weren't her talking at all…but *them*.

She stared at the figure before her, at those pale, bony hands that hadn't once moved since they awoke here.

"Our time together draws short," said the woman. "In other world, other you are beginning to stir. Listen closely…before it's too late."

They exchanged an uncertain look, but said nothing.

"The journey you are on is not yours alone. Twelve are fated to gather in City Beyond Memory."

"In what now?" asked Albert. "And you mean like twelve *people?*" Or was she talking about those twelve brothers, or whatever they were that Lucianna mentioned, the ones that included that Janon Tane guy Warner and Kneede kept arguing about?

"Twelve will go…" she went on, "…fated to open way to second doorway. Twelve to do Keeper's bidding…but only ten to return."

"Wait…" gasped Brandy, squeezing Albert's hand. "Why only *ten*? What's going to happen? To *who*?"

"The Keeper's heart is stone and ice," she went on. "But the task he demands is necessary. The doorways must be thrown open…or all will end."

Albert shook his head. "No… We didn't agree to that. We didn't agree to *any* of this!"

"Sort through the lies," said the woman, ignoring him. "Embrace your abilities. Follow the pipes. And beware the Ruin."

Again with that? Warner said the same thing to them. "What does that mean?" pressed Brandy. "*Who's* lying? How do we know?"

"What pipes?" asked Albert.

But what little light there was in this room was fading. Darkness swallowed everything until there were only the shining eyes of the cats remaining.

"Together…" said the woman, her voice sounding more and more like the hissing of a cat as she drifted into the distance, "…you are strong enough."

And then even those glowing eyes vanished into the gloom.

Chapter 51

Brandy took off her glasses and rubbed her eyes, confused. Everything was suddenly so bright. What happened? She returned them to her face and then squinted at her new surroundings, confused. They were back in the hotel lobby, sitting together on one of the sofas as if nothing strange had happened. The sun was shining through the glass doors, glinting off the brass fixtures. People were walking by in the hallway. Someone was checking out at the desk.

"How're we…?" she started to ask, but she sighed and shook her head. What was the point in asking? The answers never came.

"That was weird…" sighed Albert.

"*You think*? I mean, what the fuck?"

"Twelve of us…" he pondered. "Did she mean like how there were six of us last time?" Although it started as just the two of them that first fateful night, six of them ended up in those dark depths that next year.

"Well, I haven't seen anyone else," grumbled Brandy. "We've been doing all this shit by ourselves."

"True…" He squinted at the brilliant light pouring through the front doors. "How long were we in there?"

But Brandy didn't bother guessing. She stood up and stalked toward the front desk.

"What're you doing?"

"I'm going to see our *gracious hostess*," she replied, spitting those last two words as if they were curses. "I want some fucking answers."

He jumped up and hurried after her. "Hold on!"

But she had no intention of waiting. This woman had hijacked the last day of their honeymoon and turned the best week of her life into an absolute nightmare. And now some spooky crazy cat lady said Lucianna *wasn't what she claimed?* She was done being denied answers.

"It doesn't make any sense, though," he said. "Why would she send us to look for this thing if she wasn't who she said she was?"

"How the fuck should I know?" She marched up to Lucianna's office door and knocked.

Albert caught up to her. "Calm down," he urged her. "I get it. I'm frustrated, too. But there's something about her. I really feel like we don't want to piss her off."

"Well *I* feel like I'm done with her shit!" she retorted. "I want some answers."

She knocked again, harder this time.

"Guess she's not here," Albert reasoned.

"Or is she just ignoring us?" She reached up and hammered her fist against the door hard enough to rattle it on its hinges, but still there was no answer. "Use the card," she said, turning to face him.

He looked up at her, surprised.

"What?" she challenged. "She said *anywhere we feel necessary,* didn't she?"

He shrugged. "I suppose so..." He pulled the keycard from his pocket and slid it into the slot. The light flashed green. "Huh..." he said. "Sort of didn't expect that to work."

She reached past him and opened the door.

But Lucianna wasn't in her office.

The room was empty. Even the cat that was sleeping in the chair last time they were here was gone.

She growled, frustrated, then turned and stalked away.

"What're you doing?"

"The front desk is right here. Someone's bound to know how to get in touch with her."

But the girl manning the desk had stepped away. There was no one in sight.

Why couldn't anything ever be easy?

There was a bell at the far end. She walked toward it, determined. But as she was reaching for it, the elevator doors slid open and the *other* Albert and Brandy stepped out of the car.

"Oh shit!" she hissed.

There was a large potted plant next to this side of the desk. Panicking, she turned and crouched in front of it.

Albert darted back toward Lucianna's office door and ducked out of sight. A far better hiding spot than this one. She was barely hidden at all! What if they saw her? What would happen? And the more conspicuous she was, the more likely they were to stop and gawk at her. She knew for a fact that's what *she* would do because…well because she *was* her.

Her heart thudding in her breast, she turned away and pretended to be fumbling with her shoe.

They were so into each other all during their stay. She sure as hell wasn't paying much attention to anyone else that whole time. She spent most of the time trying to find new and exciting ways of making Albert not take his eyes off her. But she was fairly sure that if she saw herself hiding behind a bush, she probably would've stopped for a second look.

It worked last time. She turned her back and simply pretended to be getting something out of the vending machine. They walked right on by. Although Albert did apparently stop to ogle her half-exposed ass on his way by. (She made a mental note to yell at him again about that later.) But it worked. And why wouldn't it? It wasn't like they'd ever expect to run into another version of themselves. Especially dressed like she was, with her butt crack probably sticking out.

Except now she wasn't wearing the pervert's slutty dress. What if the other her recognized her outfit? What if that was all it took to make her take another look?

But it was too late now.

She could hear her voice drawing closer.

She was almost upon herself…

Please, don't let me be the one who fucks up and breaks time, she thought, cringing in anticipation of whatever happened when you did just that.

But the other her walked on by.

She lingered a moment longer, her heart still pounding, then dared a peek. She half-expected them to both be standing there, staring back at her, confused. But they were already heading out the door, completely oblivious.

She saw Albert peer out from around the corner, too. Then he turned and looked back at her. "That was too close!" their eyes said to each other.

"Can I help you?"

She looked up to find that a woman was peering over the top of the desk at her.

Brandy stared at her for a moment, unsure what to say. Then, somehow, she regained her composure and stood up, glancing back at the other them walking out into the sunlight. "Sorry... Um..." She lowered her voice and said, "That was my *ex.*"

"Oh!" said the woman, complete understanding settling into her expression. "I see."

"Thanks."

"No problem," the woman assured her, then retreated back behind the desk.

Brandy glanced at the door again, making sure the other them were safely out of sight, then she stood up and hurried the other way.

Albert caught up with her in the hallway. "Your ex?" he asked.

"Yeah. I *was* dating him, now I'm dating *you.*"

"Huh..."

Chapter 52

"So it's Tuesday morning now…" grumbled Brandy. "Fucking confusing."

Albert frowned at her. "How do you know?"

She looked at him as if he were dense. "The other us back there?" she said as if that were supposed to answer anything. When he only stared stupidly back at her, she said, "You didn't see what they were wearing? Today's the day we spent checking out the sights in Wevenwert."

"Oh." He wasn't really looking at their clothes. He was far more concerned with whether or not they were about to create some sort of doomsday time paradox. Maybe that was just a guy thing, though…

He turned his attention on the hallway before them. "Well, Lucianna doesn't seem to be around. And I have no idea where we're supposed to go next."

"It really pisses me off," she growled. "Was she lying about everything? The whole time?"

She was really stuck on what the crazy cat lady said about Lucianna… "Let's just take things one at a time," he tried. "We'll figure it out."

"We have to figure out what she was lying about as soon as possible," she argued. "How else do we know if we're even getting anywhere? I mean, what if she's got us looking in entirely the wrong places? What if she's luring us into traps and that's why we keep running into that bitch in the white dress?"

She *did* have a point. "But we don't know where to find her. She could be anywhere. And if she figures out that someone told us she's been lying about something, there's a good chance she'll be avoiding us."

She stopped and leaned against the wall, frustrated. "I *hate* this," she growled.

"We can do this," he assured her. "We just can't let our frustrations get the better of us." He turned and looked up the hallway ahead of them. "Maybe I can get a feel for the place again. Find something hidden."

"I'm *so* not in the mood for that shit right now," she grumbled.

"I wasn't asking you to help. I managed it before. Shanzer was right. It's not about the sex. It's a mindset. Something about feeling the emotions and then converting them into psychic energy."

"Energy," she spat, disgusted. "Psychic shit. I'm *over* it."

"I know." He focused his attention forward and tried to clear his head. It wasn't easy. It was always hard to concentrate on *anything* when Brandy was upset about something. He hated to see her unhappy. All he wanted to do was make everything better. And much of the time he could do just that when they were home alone. Sometimes just giving her a little extra attention was enough to do the trick. Not even *sexual* attention. Just fetching her a blanket and making her a treat, sitting down and letting her vent about things. Sometimes all she really needed was a little quiet cuddle time.

He was pretty good at making things better, usually. It was one of his better talents, he thought. Far more useful than his silly puzzle-solving skills. But what could he do for her *here*? He didn't blame her for being pissed off right now. Everything was going to hell and he had no idea how to make anything better. The only thing he could think of was to finish this stupid job so she could finally go home. And the only way to do that was to find what needed to be found.

He took a calming breath and tried to find that mindset. Sexy thoughts...he guessed... Practically every memory of the time they spent together this past week was potential fuel. But it was hard to keep himself focused.

The truth, after all, was that he was pissed off, too.

Seriously, what the hell was going on in this stupid hotel?

He reached up and rubbed wearily at his eyes. He hated this.

Brandy turned and looked back the way they came. "And where the fuck is Warner? He's literally some kind of fucking *alien* that can pop up inside people's *bodies*. I know we're bouncing around in time and shit, but where the fuck was *he* when we were lost in that nightmare world?"

It was a good question. He didn't have an answer for her. "I still can't wrap my head around that guy," he said. "I mean, what *is* he when he's not *inside* someone looking out with those scary eyes? Like, does he *have* a body of his own?"

She nodded. "Last time we saw him he didn't even know which us he was talking to. Is it weird that he doesn't seem to have a clue where we are or what we're doing?"

"It does seem weird that he won't help us."

Brandy was still staring down the quiet hallway when an attractive woman in a flower print cover-up skirt and a revealing bikini top appeared from an adjacent corridor and set off back toward the elevator.

"Lucianna said he was loyal to the Keeper but..." He shook his head. "I don't even know what to believe anymore."

"Hold that thought..." said Brandy, setting off after the woman. "I think *she* might be able to help us."

Chapter 53

Brandy kept her eyes on the woman in the skimpy bikini top as they followed her down the hallway. She was older than they were, in her late thirties or maybe even early forties, but she looked great. Very fit. Very attractive. She had long, toned legs and a cute fairy tattoo on her right shoulder. Her hair was a deep, sultry red, but that wasn't her real color. She couldn't tell by looking. She just *knew*. Her real color was a dingy shade of blonde that she hated. She'd kept it dyed since she was in college.

"What's up?" whispered Albert as she pulled him along by his hand. "Is she like the other woman? The one in the white dress?"

"No. Just shut up and do what I say."

"Okay…"

It wasn't the way the woman looked that made her stand out, however. It was her *mood*. She was practically *seething* with frustration.

He wasn't paying attention to her. This was supposed to be their chance to get away and spend some quality time together, but all he wanted to do was lounge around the pool and play on his stupid phone.

What was the point in spending money on this stupid, sexy bikini if he was barely even going to look at her the whole time they were here?

Brandy found herself staring at the woman's back. Everything else around them seemed to fade away. Her very presence overshadowed it all.

It wasn't the fact that she was angry. It wasn't the fact that she felt neglected and ignored. Those emotions were radiating from her like heat from a raging inferno, but that wasn't what caught her attention. That wasn't what was attracting her to this woman.

She was fucking *horny*.

She'd been in a sexy mood all morning. She couldn't stop thinking about sex. And that oblivious asshole of a husband couldn't care less! It was like she didn't even exist!

And it had been like this for *months*!

Brandy felt for the woman. She knew plenty well what it felt like to be frustrated. It happened all the time. Although it was almost never because Albert wasn't in the mood to play with her. Even if he was busy, he'd usually stop what he was doing the second she gave him that mischievous, lip-biting smile he loved so much and told him she needed him. She knew the feeling so well because it had a way of coming over her *all the fucking time*. At work. At family gatherings. In the middle of the grocery store. It even happened at a funeral once! (But it wasn't anyone she knew very well. Honest!) It only took one fleeting sexy thought and she was ready to grab Albert and run straight to their bedroom. But Albert never neglected her. She couldn't imagine having that kind of relationship with someone who didn't reciprocate those feelings. It sounded like sheer hell.

But then again, she and Albert were something of a special case…

The poor woman had finally had enough. To hell with him. She left the insensitive jerk at the pool and was headed back to her room on the fourth floor.

But in spite of her anger, all that pent-up sexual frustration was as strong as ever. It filled every cell of her body. She was burning up. And Brandy could feel it. She could almost *taste* it. Just looking at the woman was enough to stir those mysterious senses deep inside her brain. She could feel everyone around her. She knew how many people were behind every door she passed.

It was strange.

And it was strangely *exhilarating*.

But most of all, she could tell that it was only the tip of the iceberg.

The woman reached the elevator and mashed the button.

The car was already on the floor, so the doors slid open immediately.

"Follow my lead," she whispered.

"Whatever you say…" Albert whispered back.

"And keep your eyes closed after we start."

"Keep…? Huh? Start *what?*"

They slipped into the elevator before the doors could close. Brandy even thought to make a show of reaching for the floor button, as if she didn't already know which floor the woman was going to. Then she stepped to the back corner of the car and pressed herself against Albert.

The woman paid them no attention as the car started up. But that wouldn't last long.

She grabbed Albert's shirt and kissed him.

He stiffened, surprised, so she jabbed him with her finger. He seemed to get the message. He relaxed. He even slipped his arms around her waist. She opened one eye and peeked to make sure he was keeping his closed, but he'd always been a fast learner. He was following the script perfectly.

She didn't need to see the woman to know that she'd noticed them. Even with her eyes closed, she could tell that she was peeking back at them.

She felt a little bad. The poor woman was going through some difficult emotions. That sort of lull in sexual attention might even be the death rattle for her poor marriage. And here she was, exploiting her bottled up emotions to feed this weird sixth-sense that she didn't even know she had until some uber-creepy pervert told her about them…

But as ridiculous as lust-powered psychic abilities sounded, the fact was that this stuff was real. She wasn't behaving randomly. She *knew* what would get this woman's attention.

Right now, she was peering back over her shoulder at them, practically *seething* with jealousy.

That was all she wanted, after all. Was that so much to ask? Just a taste of that kind of passion again?

It *used* to be like that. Once upon a time. He used to be into her.

Brandy didn't dare let up. In fact, she needed to lay it on thicker. The trip up to the fourth floor wasn't going to take long. She reached up and grabbed his head, kissing him harder. She shoved her tongue into his mouth.

He was surprised, she could tell, but he managed to keep his cool.

Behind her, she could feel the woman raising an eyebrow.

That's so hot...

Was that only what she imagined the woman thinking, she couldn't help but wonder, or did her psychic brain just give her an intimate glimpse of her actual thoughts?

Was that a thing she could do? In addition to understanding people, was it possible to actually pick up their private *thoughts*? That was... Well, she wasn't entirely sure *what* she thought of that. It was kind of intriguing. But it also felt kind of *icky*.

But she couldn't think about that right now. How far had they already ascended? How much longer did she have?

This was weird. She *knew* it was weird. She was basically putting on a dirty little show for this stranger. But she could *feel* the sexual energy pouring off her. It was growing stronger with each passing second.

She'd gone this far. She supposed it was time to go for broke. She shifted her hips a little, making sure the woman could see, and then reached down and grabbed the crotch of his shorts.

The feel of him shuddering at her unexpected touch was almost more than she could handle. God, she loved when she made him react like that! But more than that, she could almost feel the woman's heart skip a beat at the unexpected sight. The heat in her belly spread like wildfire. She couldn't take her eyes off them. She was breathing faster and faster. Her hand closed around the fabric of her skirt, tugging at it.

God, she wanted that so *badly* right now.

It wasn't fair...

Brandy could feel him reacting to the aggressive touch of her hand. That part of him was wide awake, it seemed. And it was all for her. It had nothing to do with the voyeuristic gaze of the stranger in the car with them. She didn't have to trust him to know that. She could see the truth in him. He'd forgotten all about the woman. He was entirely enchanted by her touch.

The woman, on the other hand, hadn't failed to notice the bulge in his shorts as she squeezed him. She was looking right at it, no longer sneaking peeks at all, but blatantly staring, her eyes wide with the thrill of the spectacle before her.

Brandy should have felt embarrassed. Ashamed, even. She was practically performing a sex show here in this cramped elevator car. And maybe she *would* be embarrassed later, when she looked back on it. But right now, in this steamy moment, she was *exhilarated*.

The woman wanted to do more than watch, she realized. She wanted to feel that way. She wanted it *so* much... She was wondering if they'd like some company, perhaps... That would be a thrill. She'd never done anything like *that* before. She'd never even considered it. But watching these two now, going at it like this... So *hot!* And he was a cutie, too. *So* sexy!

Her imagination was running away with her. She barely realized that she was rubbing at the front of her skirt. Her knees felt weak.

The elevator came to a stop. The doors slid open.

But for a moment, none of them moved.

Brandy squeezed that part of him and pushed her tongue farther into his mouth.

The woman continued to stare at them.

It wasn't just the spectacle of the situation, Brandy realized. It was *sexual energy*. Just like the pervert said. They couldn't just *feel* it. They could *use* it. They could manipulate it. They could take it from their environment. And they could feed it into others, too. They could heighten those feelings within others without them even realizing it, thereby creating even *more* sexual energy for them to use.

The doors started to close again and the woman snapped out of it. She mashed the open button and hurried out, embarrassed that they might notice her, completely unaware that Brandy had known she was watching them the entire time.

As soon as she was gone, Brandy finally pulled away. For a

moment, they stared at each other, breathless, their faces flushed. Her glasses were fogged up and crooked. He had her lipstick on his mouth.

She was still holding on to that part of him.

"Wow…" was all Albert had to say.

She blinked and turned away, letting go of him. "Come on," she whispered, straightening her glasses.

"We're still doing this?" he gasped. He wasn't sure how much more he could take.

She leaned out the doors and caught sight of the woman entering one of the rooms just a short distance from the elevators.

"That was different…" muttered Albert.

"Shut up."

"Sorry."

She crept up to the door the woman just slipped into and leaned close to it, listening.

"Are we seriously stalking this woman all the way to her room?" whispered Albert.

"Shh!"

"Sorry," he said again.

She couldn't hear anything, but she didn't need to. Her psychic senses were alive. She could *feel* her in there. She was standing right on the other side of the door, her chest heaving, her hands pressed hard against the front of her skirt.

She couldn't stand it anymore.

Brandy's heart was pounding. She could feel the woman's frustration. She could feel her *desperation*. She pressed her hand to the door and closed her eyes.

Most of the rooms near here were empty. There was a man napping two doors down. And three doors past that a woman was at the desk, getting a little work done before she headed down to the pool. On the other side of the hallway there was a couple lying about, watching television. She could see them all. She could see for a *long way*. She could even see the people on the floor below.

Use that connection to people's truths, she thought, remembering the words the pervert spoke to her back in that icky sex party.

That's where the magic begins.

She could feel the truth within this woman. All her pent-up desires. All her sexual frustration. Alone in her room, unaware that anyone knew what she was doing, she threw herself onto the bed and shoved her hand into her skirt.

Brandy's heart was pounding in rhythm with the woman's. Their breath was synchronized. Their emotions flowed back and forth, in perfect harmony.

Without taking her hand off the door, she turned and grabbed Albert's tee shirt. "Touch me!" she whispered.

He stared at her, surprised, then glanced back down the hallway. "Now?"

"No one's coming!" she hissed. "Just do it!"

He didn't argue with her. He reached down and squeezed the front of her shorts.

She let out a hard, shuddering breath and bit back an intense moan of pleasure that he wasn't expecting. Surprised, he started to pull his hand away, but she grabbed his wrist and held him there.

"Don't stop," she breathed.

Inside the room, the woman reached her long-desired climax in record time.

Outside the door, Brandy did the same.

The pervert told them not to waste the energy, that they needed to convert it into something different. But this wasn't like that at all. This was *both*. A feeling of such utter physical pleasure washed over her that she would have fallen to her knees if she hadn't been hanging onto Albert's wrist. And at the same time, the *entire hotel* became visible to her.

She felt every person on the property. She could see each and every one of them as clear as if they were standing right in front of her. She knew who they were. She knew what they were doing. She knew their deepest desires and their darkest secrets.

She let go of the door and threw her arm around Albert, hanging on him as her legs trembled beneath her.

"Are you okay?" he whispered.

She nodded, breathless. "That was…"

"Kind of weird?"
"Fucking *awesome!*"
"Oh!"

Chapter 54

Albert led Brandy back to the elevator. He couldn't stop glancing at the doors they passed. It seemed to him that behind every one of those peepholes was some spying stranger who'd seen everything.

"So what happened back there?" he asked as the elevator doors slid shut behind them.

"You really need me to explain it to you?" she snapped, blushing. She was right. Now that it was over, the entire ordeal was embarrassing. *Mortifying*, even.

"Not *that* part." He could hardly blame her for looking uncomfortable. She was behaving so...*lewd* back there. It was almost scary how much she got into it. And the way she looked at the end there when she...

Well, that wasn't really important.

He didn't press the floor button. He didn't know yet where they should go next. Instead, he turned and met her gaze. "I'm assuming you did something. Sexual energy and all that." He reached up and wiped at the smeared lipstick on her face.

"Yeah." She crossed her arms and let her gaze drift into the distance. "That woman was *bursting* with...*that* kind of energy. I just... I don't know. *Fed off it*, I guess?" Her eyes grew wide as she remembered the feel of it all. "And it was *crazy*. I could see *everything*."

For a moment there, she was able to feel every single person on the property. *Intimately*. But *that*, thankfully, had almost immediately faded. And it was far too much too fast to even remember the vast majority of it. Now she only felt a strange, fleeting sort of sensation of having known a great deal of very intimate things...

But not *everything* had vanished.

Albert didn't dwell on the sexual stuff. He knew that wasn't important. He focused on the most obvious point. "So you know where Lucianna is," he deduced.

But she shook her head. "Lucianna's not here."

"Oh…"

"I couldn't see that woman in white, either." Now she looked up at him, her eyes focusing sharply. "But your old friend from the pervert's party is having himself a drink in the bar."

"Kneede…" he sighed.

She nodded. "I got the distinct feeling he's waiting for you."

He remembered the dream. The handsy ghost of the Sentinel Queen falling to her knees, her blood spilling around her.

(Traitor…)

"Yeah." He turned and pressed the button for the second floor. "I've got some questions for Old Man Lucifer."

The elevator gave a gentle lurch and started down.

"You okay?" he asked, noticing the distant look on her face.

"Yeah. Sorry. Just thinking about Trixie."

"Trixie?" He frowned. "You mean…?" He cocked a thumb over his shoulder, indicating the woman just now. "You know her name?"

Her eyes widened. "I know a *lot* of things…"

"Oh."

Then her expression changed. Her eyes narrowed. Her mouth tightened. "Her husband is a total douchebag. She needs to dump his ass."

"…okay."

Chapter 55

It felt strange returning to the hotel bar. It wasn't very long ago that they were just here. A few hours at most. And yet it was a completely different atmosphere now. The place looked deserted at first glance, and it wasn't any wonder given the time of day. Was it even open yet?

But as soon as they walked in, they saw him sitting there at the end of the bar, nursing another old fashioned. Except for the fact that he'd changed from his fancy tuxedo into a less fancy suit pants and dress shirt, he looked exactly the same as he did in Shanzer's bar.

Albert didn't hesitate. Brandy said she sensed that the old man was waiting for them here. And he could think of no other reason why someone would be sitting all alone in an empty bar. He walked right up to him and stood there.

"You've been on quite a journey," Kneede said without looking up. It wasn't a question. He knew exactly what they'd been doing. Had he been watching them this whole time? "Have you actually gotten anywhere after all that?"

"Maybe," said Albert, refusing to be intimidated. "You were there, weren't you? In that twisted dream world."

"I *was* there," he admitted. "The real question is, what exactly do you think you saw?"

He frowned. "What?"

"What did you *see*?" he repeated, impatient.

"I saw *you* murdering the Sentinel Queen. *Again*."

Now he glanced up from his drink, an eyebrow raised. "That *thing* looked like the *Mother* to you?" His bushy eyebrows scrunched together. "Huh."

Albert felt himself blush a little as he recalled just what the

Sentinel Queen was *doing* to him in that dream. "You killed her," he said again, eager to get to the point of the matter. (And hoping more than a little to not have to explain to his lovely bride just why he was having a dream about being jerked off by a dead, naked sentinel hybrid, because that was just something he wasn't remotely eager to discuss with *anyone*, much less *her*.) "But you did it with your own hand this time. I saw her fall. I saw her bleeding. I heard her call you a *traitor*."

He turned his attention back to his drink again, his expression softening. "Yes. That sounds about right. I cut that monster down. It did, indeed, call me that."

"You just admit it," marveled Brandy.

"Of course I admit it. I did it. The question is, do you really believe that the *thing* in your dream was the same creature I buried in that God-forsaken gatehouse five years ago?"

Albert's brow furrowed at this. "Um…"

"I'm not taking his side," said Brandy, "but it's kind of a valid point. The Sentinel Queen's supposed to be dead."

"Yeah… That part *was* bothering me."

And something else was bothering him about that entire ordeal, too. Something he wasn't able to put his finger on at the time, but now he thought he understood. The *real* Sentinel Queen didn't have a working mouth. She couldn't speak to them using a physical voice. Instead, she spoke directly into their brains. Telepathically. It filled their heads in a weird and intrusive sort of way that he remembered feeling uncomfortable, in spite of the soft and gentle way she spoke.

The Sentinel Queen in that queer dream world, however, didn't do that. She spoke in a voice that he heard with his ears.

That was what seemed so wrong about the situation.

(Well, *one* of the things that was wrong about it, he supposed…)

He felt stupid realizing that now. It should have been obvious from the start. But everything was so confusing back there. *Nothing* made any sense.

"That was *not* the Mother," said Kneede, lifting the glass to his lips and holding it there for a moment, "Or whatever silly name you want to give her. That was a bogey."

"A what?" Albert frowned. "What the hell's a bogey?"

"Didn't you get, like, a shit-ton of those when we played that game of mini-golf downtown?" asked Brandy.

"I do suck at that game," he agreed, but he really didn't think they were talking about golf, miniature or otherwise.

Kneede sighed. "Bogey. As in 'bogeyman.' A creature of the Ruin that sometimes finds its slimy way into our world to wreak havoc and spread terror."

"The Ruin?" pondered Albert. So it *was* a real place?

"They're responsible for hundreds of unsolvable murders and disappearances every year," Kneede went on.

"Holy shit…" breathed Brandy.

"Indeed," he said. "Worse still, they aren't simply blind killing machines. They serve a purpose, twisted as it may be. They're agents of an ancient god. They spread chaos and fear. Their goal is to undermine the order of the universe, something that the cycle embodies. In other words, they're sworn enemies of the Keeper. That thing was trying to trick you into revealing the gateway. Then it was going to kill you."

Albert felt Brandy press closer to him and he didn't blame her. How close did that thing come to actually killing him?

"*I* saved your life," explained Kneede. "You're welcome."

"You…?" Albert glanced back at Brandy. "Why would you save my life? What happened to 'if we ever meet again'? What about Remus Molsk?"

Kneede had lifted his glass to his lips again, but he lowered it without taking a sip. Those bushy eyebrows crept upward, surprised. "You remembered his name…"

"Of course I remembered. You said it was my fault. Who forgets something like that?"

The old man placed his glass back down on the table. "You'd be surprised," he responded softly.

Albert stared at him for a moment, processing it all. Was this self-proclaimed Father of Lies really telling him the truth? Did he really save his life back there? Was that vision of the handsy Sentinel Queen really some murderous monster merely trying to trick him into revealing the location of the hidden road? "She called you a traitor," he said again.

"Of course it did," replied Kneede. "I used to share a common goal with the Ruin. I wanted a better way than the Keeper's cycle. I saw with my own eyes the suffering the Keeper's way brings. He calls it a 'necessary evil,' but I've never been able to believe that those horrors were *ever* necessary in any way. But to make something better, you have to tear down what isn't working. I took a page from the Keeper's own book. A *necessary evil* of my own. I sided with the Ruin. I joined their cause." Again, he lifted the glass. "So yeah. From their perspective, I'm a traitor."

"And you just expect us to believe you?" challenged Brandy.

"No. Only a couple of bumbling idiots would take the word of someone who pointedly expressed a desire to kill them."

She scrunched up her face, confused. "Right... Like I...said..."

"The question is, I suppose," posited Kneede, "who *would* you trust? Lucianna Estrane? Warner Harr? Lyle Shanzer?"

"That woman we met in that weird dream-verse..." pondered Albert. "That crazy cat lady. What about her? Can we trust her?" Although he remained perfectly aware of the irony of asking someone he didn't trust whether he could trust anyone else...

"That is no woman or lady of any kind," said Kneede. "She's no more human than the Keeper." Again, he lifted his glass to his lips. It was almost empty now. "But perhaps. I've never known her to tell a lie. She has no need to."

"She said Lucianna isn't what she seems," recalled Brandy.

"And she's right," he replied, then left it at that.

Albert and Brandy looked at each other, surprised.

"And Warner won't be any help, I promise you that. He follows the Keeper's rules to the letter, for better or worse. He'll only intervene if someone breaks those precious rules. And by then, of course, it might be too late."

"That just leaves Shanzer," reasoned Albert.

"Ugh..." groaned Brandy. "Creep."

"He is that," agreed Kneede.

"But did he ever lie to us?" wondered Albert.

"Not once," replied Kneede. "And I'd wager that you haven't bothered to look at the gift he gave you since leaving his mansion."

"Gift?" He frowned.

"The book!" realized Brandy.

The book... He reached into his pocket and withdrew it. He *hadn't* looked at it since they left the mansion. But he'd *thought* about it. Back in the decaying hallways, just before that woman in white sent them to nightmare town. He remembered having a sudden and almost overwhelming desire to look in the book. But then everything went to crap and he forgot about it again.

Last time he looked inside, he could read very little of it. But they'd been practicing what the shaman taught them this whole time. They'd both been learning to use their sexual energy, just as he taught them.

It'll reveal more when you're ready for it, Shanzer had told him.

Now, as soon as he opened the book, he found that the mysterious, illegible symbols scribbled all over the pages were gone. In their place were words scrawled in plain English.

There appeared to be instructions for casting a number of spells, though he wasn't sure he quite understood them. They didn't have names like "healing" or "shield" or "fireball" or even so much as a "petrificus" or a "leviosa." In fact, they didn't have names at all. Each tightly packed paragraph was merely a complex and confusing description that was—not surprisingly—written with erotic language.

Something about fooling around under the covers in the dark. Something about embracing one's lover. A *lot* of stuff that sounded like perverted sexual activity and anatomy using unnecessary words like "steamy," "throbbing," "slick," "heaving," "engorged" and "humid."

"'...quivering kaleidoscope of fleshly pleasure...'" read Brandy, her nose wrinkled with distaste. "'...pulsating depths...dripping nectar...' Gross." She leaned a little closer. "'...trembling, sweat-soaked bodies breathless with exhausted satisfaction...' Ugh!"

"You know," said Albert, "in this guy's defense, if Ryan Reynolds said that to you, you'd probably melt."

"Well no shit. Flash flood warning. For sure."

He glanced over at her, surprised.

"But that *disgusting blobfish* isn't my Ryan, is he?"

"*Your* Ryan?"

"Yes."

Making a mental note to not bring up Deadpool again, he flipped forward. There were more tightly-packed notes about more advanced handling of sexual energy that he hoped wasn't relevant right now because he didn't really feel like reading all of it.

There were also more than a few rather lewd illustrations that he didn't care to look too closely at.

He flipped to the last page of the book. There, scrawled in big, bold letters, were the words, LUCIANNA WAITS WHERE THE WIND CRIES WITH LUST. FIND HER TO BREAK THE SEAL.

"Where the wind cries with lust..." said Brandy, her lip curling with distaste. "Does the freak have to turn *everything* pornographic?"

"Such a creep," he agreed. "But the wind..." He looked up at her. "Remember? Lucianna told us that the wind sounds like moaning voices in the woods outside the west wing!"

"Oh yeah!"

He'd forgotten all about that. It was where he intended to go first. But they kept getting distracted. He looked up from the book and stared at Kneede. "You knew what was written here, didn't you?"

"Of course I did," replied the old man. "Shanzer was the one who requested my presence at his party, remember? I guess he had a feeling you'd need looked after."

Albert looked back at Brandy, confused. The two were working together the whole time?

"I'd get going if I were you," said Kneede. He finished off his drink and then stared down at the ice in the glass, as if disappointed it was empty. "It's a long walk to the far end of the west wing."

Albert turned to leave, but he hesitated, his thoughts churning. He looked back at Kneede once more. "Aren't you going to tell us the truth?" he asked.

Brandy looked up at him, surprised. "What?"

"You told Warner to tell us the truth. If he didn't, *you* would."

"I did say that."

"Well?"

"I will if I have to," he replied, never taking his eyes off his empty glass. "But there's still time for the parasite to do the right thing. It should at least come from *him*, if not the Keeper, himself."

Albert lingered a moment longer, but he already knew the conversation was over.

He recalled the end of that night five years ago, this man's charred corpse standing in the dark tunnel, ribbons of foul smoke wafting from his burnt flesh.

(*If we ever…cross paths again…*)

The Keeper sent him away before he could finish that threat…but for the first time, he began to wonder if that really was a threat…or if he was about to say something different…something to reveal the Keeper's lies in some way…

But there were no more answers to be found here and now.

He took Brandy's hand and the two of them walked away.

Chapter 56

"Given how completely and utterly *fucked-up* everything is in this place," said Brandy. "I don't think it would've killed Beelzebub to give us an escort to the far side of this deathtrap."

"Personally, I think I feel safer leaving the temperamental old fart to his day drinking."

"Hm." He had a point there, she supposed. "I wouldn't have turned down a *ride*, though. My feet are tired."

"Mine too."

She glanced back the way they came. The main building was well out of sight by now. She wondered how much farther it was to the end of the west wing? Were they even halfway there yet?

It wasn't fair. She had such a great time staying here... So many wonderful memories. Now, would she ever be able to look back on her honeymoon without being reminded of nothing but the Keeper and his stupid schemes?

"So...that dream you had about him killing the Sentinel Queen wasn't really a dream at all. He was really there." But in *her* dream, she saw the woman in the white dress murder Lucianna... And *that* couldn't have been real if they were supposed to seek her out in the westernmost part of the hotel... "Confusing," she grumbled.

"This *whole thing* is confusing," said Albert. "The Keeper's the one calling the shots, according to pretty much *everybody*. And everybody pretty much told us that *he* sent us to the shaman."

"Pervert," grumbled Brandy.

"Yeah. Him. So he could train us. Or whatever."

"With his pervert magic."

"Yeah. So if *anyone's* telling the truth, then they *all* are."

"Or none of them," she agreed.

"Right. So what if *none of it* is true? What if this has nothing to do with the Keeper? What if they're *all* playing us?"

"That's what I've been saying since pretty much the beginning!"

"I know. But *if* that were the case... *Why*? What could they want from us, then?"

"To keep us from it?" she guessed. "To make sure we can *never* open the door?"

"But we didn't even know there *was* a second door before they told us about it."

"Unless they lied about that, too," she posited. "What if there *is* no door? What if *all of this* is a lie?"

"Then what's the point?"

She opened her mouth to reply, but no answer came to her, so she shut it again.

"Either they're lying and there is no door...in which case, what *do* they want from us? Or they're telling the truth...in which case, why won't they just let us do it and get it over with?"

"I feel like you're trying awfully hard to rationalize something we may not even be capable of comprehending. I mean, think about it. These aren't *people*, like in your mysteries. It's not *Scooby Doo*. There's no man in a mask. These are *monsters*. Older than shit old men pretending to be the devil? Some kind of alien parasite? A perverted fucking *wizard*?"

"Point taken."

"I remember you telling me once that mysteries can only be solved if the writer *lets* you solve it. If the writer doesn't give you all the clues, if he hides a critical piece of evidence, if he introduces new characters during the big reveal, if they *cheat*...then you never really have a chance. What makes you think *these things* are going to play by the rules?"

Albert stopped walking. A deep frown creased his handsome face. "Rules..." he breathed.

Brandy stopped and looked at him. "Um...?"

"The Keeper's rules... Everyone keeps talking about his rules. It was one of the first things Shanzer told us."

She remembered. *The next gear in the Keeper's machine is turning,* he told them, way back in that gaudy red room while that naked, psychotic little goth witch watched on. *These are* his *rules. And* everyone *is subject to his rules.*

"When Warner and Kneede were arguing," recalled Albert, "Kneede said to tell us the truth. 'None of the Keeper's self-righteous rules,' he said. And last time we saw Warner, he told us the Keeper's rules kept him from helping."

(I'm not allowed to help. The Keeper forbids it.)

Brandy nodded. "And Kneede said the same thing just now. About how Warner wouldn't help us because he follows the Keeper's rules no matter what."

"Yeah…" He stood there a moment, pondering it all. "But what *are* the Keeper's rules? Everyone keeps talking about his rules, but no one's explained them to us."

Brandy stared at him, letting that process.

He turned and met her gaze. "Are *we* bound to any rules?"

"The Keeper's rules forbid *interference,*" said a woman's voice from behind them.

They turned around to find an older woman in a one-piece bathing suit and sunhat walking toward them, her shoulders still damp from her morning swim. Her eyes were a familiar and eerie black.

"They are there to *protect* those who do the Keeper's work," explained Warner, "not to *govern* them. Your free will is an integral part of the process. It's what ensures that each new world belongs to mankind and not those who built it for them."

"Where the fuck have you been?" snapped Brandy.

Albert glanced over at her, surprised.

But she wasn't holding back. "That psycho woman tried to *kill* us! And you were no help at all!"

"I was doing my job," replied Warner. "You're not the only ones seeking the shadow road. I've been busy keeping the *other two* out of the enemy's sight."

"Shadow road?" asked Albert.

"Other two?" wondered Brandy. She glanced at Albert. The cat lady said there were others like them out there. Twelve of them, in fact. "What other two?"

"You'll meet them soon enough. First, you must confront the mistress of this hotel. She's waiting for you ahead, as you've already been made aware."

Brandy was confused. "Yeah, because the *other weirdos* basically told us so. The cat lady warned us that Lucianna wasn't what she seemed. And the pervert told us where she was hiding. Why can *they* tell us what we need to know, but not *you?*"

"The 'cat lady,' as you call them... They cheat. They can do that with little repercussion. That's the perk of being an elder deity."

"She's a *god?*" gasped Albert.

"For lack of a better word, yes. They are."

"They...?" wondered Brandy, recalling the way the woman's voice kept drifting around the room, as if it were really the many cats that were talking to them...and those pale, bony fingers...so like the frail hands of a cold corpse...

"As for the shaman..." Warner went on. "He made the book legible only to those who reached the goals he set. You *earned* the right to view those pages. *And* he only gave you information you already had. Lucianna Estrane pointed you toward the moaning wind when you first arrived. That's why she's chosen to wait for you there."

"I *did* say we should start there," Albert reminded her.

"I know you did," she grumbled. "What do you want, a cookie?"

"And in regards to the Keeper's rules," Warner added. "They state that you have to find your own way to the doorways. I can intervene when your path is blocked by an external force, but I must otherwise stay out of it. That means I can't answer any questions that aid you *directly*, but I can warn you when I think someone is scheming against you."

"Like you did when you told us there was an 'enemy of the cycle' in Mysteria," Albert realized. "And that 'beware the Ruin' warning. Because you knew those bogey things were prowling around the crossroads and that they wouldn't follow the rules."

"Exactly. And now that you understand the rules..." He tipped the woman's head to one side and waited for them to catch on.

Brandy looked over at Albert again, her eyes widening. "We're not obligated to *follow* them!" she realized.

The woman's mouth twisted into a smile. It wasn't a very charming smile. Warner didn't seem to be very good at doing it. It just sort of made her look insane… "The Keeper is wise beyond comprehension. He plans everything to the very last meticulous detail. It gives him the illusion of omnipotence. It gives him the illusion of *control*. But he isn't the one in control of what happens here. *You* are. You should remember that."

"Is that the 'truth' Kneede wanted you to tell us?" asked Albert.

"No. But it's the first step in finding the truth."

Albert and Brandy exchanged a confused look.

"What does *that* mean?" asked Brandy.

When they looked back at Warner, however, he was gone. The woman was staring back at them, bewildered. "Hello," she said, smiling a much more charming smile in her puzzled state than Warner had managed with the same mouth. Then she frowned and glanced around. "I think I forgot where I was going again…"

Chapter 57

They arrived at the end of the hallway and stood at the stairwell door.

Nothing seemed out of the ordinary here. Should they go down to the ground floor? Or up to the third or fourth?

Albert doubted it would be nearly as simple as just exploring the stairwell. The answer was sure to lie somewhere they could only find using his pervy psychic powers.

Brandy had come to the same conclusion. She crowded closer to him and whispered, "What do you need me to do?"

He glanced back down the hallway. It was a quiet time of day. There weren't many people around. The only guest in sight was a man dragging a rolling suitcase back toward the lobby. But there were two housekeeping carts parked within sight, both surrounded by bustling staff. A vacuum cleaner was droning away. "Can you tell if any of these rooms are vacant?"

"I was still sensing people when we were in the bar, but it's faded. I'm not really getting anything right now. I doubt if Trixie's gonna be any help again. She's probably gonna need a nap after *that* workout session…"

"What?"

"Nothing," she said quickly, blushing a little.

"Okay…" He looked back at the empty stairwell and sighed. "Is it weird that I'm not really in the mood for sexy stuff right now?" he wondered.

"I think that's called being *human*, you freak."

He chuckled.

"Seriously, it's a good thing we're *both* like this. You'd have *killed* a normal woman *years* ago. The fact that I can still *walk* is a fucking miracle."

He narrowed his eyes and considered that. "Can't decide if I should apologize or feel proud."

"Both, I think."

"Gotcha." He stepped into the stairwell and looked up at the ascending steps above him. Like all stairwells, it reminded him of Gilbert House...which wasn't exactly *sexy*... But it did have a hint of privacy to it. And it was quiet. They'd be able to hear someone walking up or down.

Brandy didn't need him to suggest a course of action. She pulled him to the side, away from the door, out of sight of the Lucianna Mysteria's housekeeping staff, and then pressed herself against him. "There's got to be something here, right? Something hidden? Like in the gallery?"

"I think so." He closed his eyes and tried to feel the space around him. He wasn't getting any of that strange *significance*. Did that mean they weren't close enough to it? Or that it was just well-hidden?

She laid her head against his shoulder and grasped the front of his shorts.

Albert looked down at her, the bored expression on her face, the distracted way she looked back toward the doorway, watching to make sure the coast remained clear. "You know, the shaman called it 'sex magic,' but this stuff feels like it's gonna take all the magic *out* of sex."

She giggled wearily. "No shit." She leaned back, peering back down the hallway, then pulled her shirt up, revealing her perfect breasts for him. "This better?"

"Always," he replied, smiling. Her body was so beautiful. He could stare at her for hours. But he reached up and tugged it back down again, covering her back up. "But I think I need a minute."

She frowned up at him, concerned. "Okay?"

"It's starting to feel like it's a *job* or something, you know?" He reached up and rubbed at the back of his neck. "And that doesn't feel *real*. Does that make sense?"

She nodded and pressed herself up against him again. "Yeah. It does." She looked up at him, those pretty blue eyes shining behind her glasses.

How did she always look so cute? Even when she was clearly exhausted and well past ready to go home?

"It gets harder when you kind of *don't* want to find what you're looking for," she said.

He nodded. "Yeah. I totally understand *that*." He glanced up at the stairs again. "But we can't check out of here for good until we find whatever it is."

She groaned and pressed her mouth against his sleeve. "Stupid…" she murmured into the fabric.

"I know." He took her hand from his shorts, then brought it to his mouth and kissed it. He held it there for a moment, his arm curled around her, savoring the feeling of her body pressed against him. "It doesn't have to be about sex," he reminded her. He kissed her forehead and then closed his eyes.

It didn't have to be about sex…. The Shaman said so. And why *should* it have to be about that? It wasn't really the sex that he treasured when he was with his wife. It was the closeness. The intimacy.

It was about the *love*.

He loved Brandy more than anything in the world. He couldn't live without her. He couldn't even bear the thought of trying. And it had nothing to do with the temple or the sex room. Somehow, from the moment they set foot in those steam tunnels six years ago, he knew she was the only one for him. No one else even came close.

Sex was only one way of expressing that love.

Most of the time, there's no actual sex involved at all, he recalled Shanzer telling them. *It's all about the* emotions *involved*.

He didn't say it was about *sexual* emotions. All he said was "*emotions*."

He closed his eyes and held her, focusing on *that*. On the *love* he felt for her. The way he felt when she laid her head against him like this. The way he felt when he made her laugh until she snorted. The way she always reached across the bed or the couch or the table when they were too far apart for too long, and brushed her fingertips across the back of his hand.

He remembered standing there at the wedding, staring into her beautiful eyes. The way she stared back at him. The way she smiled. The way she made him feel like there was no one else in the world...

It was happening right now. An entire universe surrounding them, and yet she was all there was. Never mind the stairwell. Never mind the housekeeping staff in the hallway. Never mind the Lucianna Mysteria and its sprawling grounds. None of that existed. All there was...was *her*.

She *was* his universe.

He pressed his lips against her forehead again. The feel of her skin... The smell of her hair...

Nothing else.

...except...

He frowned. No. There *was* something else. Something *below* them.

Brandy remained the center of his universe, but when everything else faded, *something* remained.

He opened his eyes and stared at the lower landing. "There it is," he whispered.

Brandy lifted her head, surprised. "What? How?"

He squeezed her hand and led her downward.

"You don't even need me now?" she asked.

"Exactly the opposite," he replied. "I couldn't have done it without you."

"That's sweet," she told him. "But I'm not looking forward to whatever it is you're dragging me into."

"Understandable." He held tight to her hand, focusing on the feel of her skin against his, clinging to that idea that she was the only thing in the universe that mattered.

It was the stairs, themselves. There was another floor below this one.

He couldn't see it, exactly. It looked like they were at the bottom. But there was another flight, hidden in the shadows. "Close your eyes," he warned her as they stepped onto the landing.

Brandy did as he said without hesitation. She trusted him.

He needed to be careful. One misstep and they could both take a dangerous tumble down to whatever horror-filled basement might lie beneath their feet. But if he hesitated, he might lose it again.

He held his breath and plowed straight toward the wall...

Chapter 58

It was jarring. Brandy felt the floor disappear beneath her feet and let out a startled yelp as she felt herself falling.

But then she was in Albert's arms again. She opened her eyes to find that they were still descending the stairwell, heading for an even lower level. "That's never not going to be weird!" she gasped.

The space before them wasn't a dark and dingy basement. Instead, it was bright and sunny. A pair of dusty glass doors awaited them at the bottom, leading out into an overgrown courtyard that neither of them had ever seen before.

In fact, she found herself quite sure as they stepped out into the hot sunshine that *no* guest of the Lucianna Mysteria had ever seen this place before.

On either side of them were tall stone walls almost completely overrun with ivy. The grass was knee-deep and bursting with wildflowers. Bugs leaped into the air as they waded through it. Birds and cicadas sang a chorus in the trees all around them.

"It's so pretty…" she marveled. She looked back over her shoulder. The hotel was there, its outer walls towering over them. She could see balconies and windows of the westernmost rooms, but somehow she knew without a doubt that anyone standing on those balconies or looking out those windows wouldn't be able to see them.

This was the secret side of the hotel. This was Mysteria. The Mysteria that *wasn't* infected by the Ruin.

What a nice change of pace!

Or so she thought for a moment. Then the wind picked up and a strangely ominous sound rolled through the forest, like groaning voices calling out. "That's kind of unsettling…" she whimpered, clinging more tightly to Albert's hand.

"That's the moaning Lucianna was talking about."

"You think?" she muttered. "God, it sounds creepy as shit..." It was a deep and strangely throaty sort of sound that did, in fact, have a lustful quality to it, breathy and longing, almost *desperate*. But she couldn't decide if she only heard it like that because the pervert put the idea in her head.

The path they were following curved to the left. The wind seemed to be coming from that direction, carrying the haunting moan from somewhere beyond, so they set off through the tall grass, pushing a path through it, sending scores of bugs springing from their feet in the process.

"Do you think this was some kind of garden, once?" wondered Brandy.

"Sort of looks like it might've been, doesn't it?"

She wondered if it was once a part of the regular grounds and then somehow *slipped away* into this other place, sort of like Gilbert House did. Or was this always a part of Mysteria? It seemed like a lot of work for something that no one ever saw.

The ivy-covered walls took them left, then right again, then curved back to the left. Then, barely a hundred yards from the door, they found the source of the strange moaning noise.

It was another hollow man.

Or, more precisely, it was *two* of them.

They stood in the center of a round clearing, surrounded by those same ivy-covered walls. They were long and thin, like their brother beneath the gallery, but instead of sitting on the ground, they were sort of squatting, their knees spread and bent. They were holding hands, their long, jointless fingers enlaced at their sides, and they were leaning forward, facing away from each other, with their butts pressed together for some reason. Those featureless, limp sausage penises were far more visible on these guys than it was on the first one. And strangely, she found that the lack of detail somehow made them look even more obscene than their sentinel cousins back in the temple.

Instead of in the backs of their heads, the holes were in the front, where their mouths should have been, making them appear to be yawning impossibly wide, pushing those basic, triangular noses high up on their heads. Their eyes were just two carved arches, giving them that silly cartoonish look again.

The moaning sound was, indeed, the wind. It entered one mouth, circled its way through their hollow insides, and exited through the other mouth so that one or the other of the hollow men seemed to be uttering the noise.

It didn't go unnoticed by her that this strange, anatomical arrangement meant that the breeze had to pass from one of these men to the other, most likely through their butts. "That's not cute art," she criticized.

"Let's just be glad the wind is blowing through their *mouths*," decided Albert. "Given some of the things we've seen today, I *know* it could be worse."

"Good point…" She reached up and grasped the medallion. "So you think we're just supposed to shove it down one of their throats this time?"

"I don't see anywhere *else* to stick it."

She giggled. It was a tired giggle, without much emotion, but it was a giggle. "Is it wrong that I kind of want to see you have to stick it up one of these guys' butts?"

"Yes," he replied, taking the medallion from her. "*Very* wrong."

Again, she giggled. No one else made her giggle like that. She supposed Lucianna had a point back in her office. They really were a perfect fit.

Albert faced the nearer of the two statues. On its feet as it was, even bent over, it was higher than the one under the gallery. He wasn't tall enough to stick his whole arm in there.

"Be careful," she groaned. "I still don't like this. It feels like that thing's going to come to life and bite your arm off or something."

"I know what you mean."

But of course they didn't have much choice. The hidden floor Albert found led straight here. There was no other place they could have gone. Like the stairs hidden in the gallery, it was a dead end. These bizarre statues were the only significant things to be found. And since they were specifically pointed toward the moaning winds outside the westernmost rooms, it stood to reason that this was definitely why they were here.

Albert wrapped the chain around his arm again, clenched the medallion tight and stretched up onto his toes. He didn't hesitate this time. He plunged the key into the hollow man's great, yawning mouth and reached as far inside as he could.

It was much more jarring than the first time, probably because they were down in that tunnel, where she didn't noticed everything change. Here, where she was out in the open, it felt as if the whole world shuddered around her. A wave of intense vertigo swept over her, making her sway on her feet and filling her belly with a sickly, nauseous sort of feeling. She closed her eyes and gasped, suddenly feeling as if she might throw up.

But then it was over. Just as quickly as the feeling swept over her, it was gone. She opened her eyes and found that the lush, green forest around them was gone. The walls were naked, dusty stone. The earth beneath them was barren and cracked. The sky was a sickly shade of red and churned with menacing clouds.

It was at least ten degrees colder here, and the wind was blowing harder now, whipping through her hair. The sound it made as it rushed through the hollow men was less a moan than an eerie and painful shriek. There was an unpleasant, rancid sort of smell carried on it.

Albert had felt the same thing she did, she realized. Having backed away from the statue in surprise, he'd stumbled and fallen onto his butt. He was sitting there, staring up at that poisoned sky, his arm dripping that foul, yellowish-brown goo.

"I was really hoping we wouldn't end up here again," she groaned, looking up at several of those strange flying creatures with the weird, warbling wings.

"The statues are some kind of gateway," Albert realized. He looked down at his arm and tried to shake away the filth, but like before, it didn't want to come off. "I guess we're *supposed* to end up in this horror setting, then?"

"What kind of shitty plan is that?"

Albert wiped the medallion on the ground, scraping as much of the goo off it as he could, then wiped it on his shorts for good measure. Then he held it up in front of him. It had changed again. It was longer, with a flair at the narrow end that wasn't there before. And those bumps along the edges had grown into dull spikes.

"Weird…" was all he had to say about it.

Brandy took it from him and looked it over. "How does it keep doing that?" It looked completely different now.

But of course he didn't have an answer.

She slipped the chain back around her neck and then looked up at the statues again. They were still pretty much the same as they were before, just dirtier. But while they looked mostly silly before, beneath that churning red sky they now looked incredibly creepy. Menacing, even.

And now that she was looking, she noticed that the foul, black sludge on Albert's arm was oozing from the hollow men's screaming mouths.

Did the first one do that, too? Thinking back, she recalled that it was too dark in that tunnel to have seen it if it did.

"What do we do now?" she asked, turning her back on the creepy hollow men so she wouldn't have to see them. It was bad enough she could *hear* them. The gusting of the wind made the sound swell and fade, almost as if the unfortunate pair were gasping for breath between each scream.

Albert stood up and backed away from the statues. "I don't think I want to linger out here," he decided. "Let's get inside. See if we can find a way back."

He'd get no arguments from her.

She followed him back the way they came, between the winding walls, back to the doors and the stairwell. She half-expected the hotel to not be there, that the way back had changed like the hallways from before. But she could see the towering walls from here. The building looked as creepy and menacing as the hollow men, like it had aged a hundred years since they'd come this way, but it was there. And when they rounded the last curve, they found that the door was there too.

But so was Lucianna.

She was standing in their path, her dress—the same purple dress she was wearing in that dream with the woman in white—fluttering about her ample waist in the wind. There was a great, bloody stain soaked into the fabric.

Albert stopped as soon as he caught sight of her and stepped in front of Brandy, protecting her as he surveyed the scene before him. "What…?"

But Brandy stepped around him. "I told you I saw her being attacked by that other woman in those weird dreams," she reminded him. "She looked just like that. Same dress. Same injury."

"I'm not going to lie," Lucianna chuckled wearily. "We've had a little hiccup."

Chapter 59

"I'm afraid I've lost control over the hotel," Lucianna bemoaned. "Things aren't quite going to plan anymore."

"No shit…" muttered Brandy, staring at the gaping hole in her belly.

"Don't worry yourselves about this," she assured them, flashing that sweet, charming smile. But there was nothing charming about those bloody teeth. "I'll be fine after a little rest."

"You don't *look* fine. You look like *shit*."

"Thanks for noticing, dear," she replied with a weak giggle.

"Crazy Cat Lady said she's not what she claims," Albert whispered.

"I know what Crazy Cat Lady said," she hissed back without taking her eyes off her.

"The truth in people," he reminded her. "What can you feel from her?"

"Nothing," she replied. "I already tried that."

It was weird. If she was supposed to be able to see people's truths, why couldn't she tell if she could trust Lucianna or not? Was she able to hide herself somehow?

"You've opened both the seals," Lucianna informed them. "Good job, both of you. You're almost done. We just have to open the gate within the nexus. We'll go together."

"I really feel like you should go and have that looked at," countered Brandy. "We can take it from here."

"Nonsense. The Ruin pervades Mysteria. The intruder knows you're close. She'll be watching. She wants to steal it from you."

Brandy stared at her, uncertain.

Albert took a step forward. "It's hard to tell which side everyone's on when both sides want the same thing, isn't it?"

She glanced over at him. "What?"

"Everyone loyal to the Keeper wants us to find the road so we can reach the second door. Everyone who wants us to fail, though…"

"…still wants us to find the road," finished Brandy.

"Right. There's more to it than just stopping us, isn't there?"

"You're so clever!" squealed Lucianna. "The followers of Ruin know the Keeper will only have planned for the fall of his champions. More will come. The only way to stop the doors from opening is to destroy the roads leading there."

"Which they can't do if we don't show them where it is," Albert finished.

Brandy frowned. "So everyone's motivated to help us right up until the time comes to cut our throats? What the fuck?"

"That's why it's important that we get you out of here as quickly as possible," pressed Lucianna.

"Unless you're the one we shouldn't be trusting," countered Albert.

"That's perfectly *silly!*" she laughed. But there was something in her eyes that Brandy didn't like.

"Yeah…" she said. "We *don't* trust you. We'll do it ourselves."

"You don't trust me…" she sighed. "Then who *will* you trust? The pervert? The parasite?" She took a step toward them. Something had changed about her. "The *devil?*"

"Maybe no one," said Albert, squeezing Brandy's hand.

Brandy nodded. "Yeah. No one."

Lucianna's familiar smile was gone. There was something deeply unpleasant about the woman now.

Albert turned and hurried back the way they came, pulling her along by her hand. "Come on!"

"Where? It's a dead end!"

"I know. But maybe if I shove the key back inside that statue it'll send us back to the other side."

It was worth a shot, she supposed. Anything to get away

from Bloody Lucy.

But as they approached the clearing where the hollow men stood, they found their path blocked again, this time by the woman in the white dress.

"*Seriously?*" shouted Brandy. It was one thing after another. Why couldn't they catch a break?

They turned to go back again, but Lucianna was already there.

"Why's her fat ass so fast?" she gasped.

"Hurry," pleaded Lucianna. "That woman is a monster. You'll die if you don't come with me."

"Up is down and out is in," sighed Albert.

Brandy glanced over at him. She remembered those words. Crazy Cat Lady said them. At the time it sounded like nonsense. But she was starting to understand.

She was telling them to reverse their thinking.

She turned her face defiantly toward Lucianna. "We're not going to trust you," she decided.

Then the woman in the white dress was there. She moved quickly and silently, practically floating. She glided past them and straight toward Lucianna, whose face had lost all its gentle kindness and looked positively monstrous with her bloody snarl.

The two didn't speak a word.

Lucianna's plump form leapt forward, twisting and stretching in weird ways. At the same time, the woman in the white dress seemed to unravel before their eyes and lurched forward as well.

There was a scream, although it was difficult to tell which one it came from. Blood splashed across one wall, then a tangle of monstrous, struggling flesh crashed through the other, leaving a crumbling hole.

"Time to go!" decided Albert, leading her back toward the hotel by her hand.

"You saw that, right?" gasped Brandy. "They both turned into freaky monsters and broke the wall?"

"I saw it," he assured her.

"That's good. I mean, I *think* that's good..."

So Lucianna was the bad guy all along? How did that make any sense? He thought she was the one who was protecting the sentinels' road this whole time.

They ran through the doorway and up the stairs to the hotel's ground floor, but as they set off down the first-floor hallway, she realized that they were still in the nightmare version of the Lucianna Mysteria.

"How do we get back to *our* world?" she asked.

"I have no idea! I'm pretty sure Cat Lady sent us back the last two times."

He was right. Both times they found themselves lost in Ruin, they stumbled into the cat lady's dream world. The first time was early Monday evening. The second time was late Wednesday night. But this was Tuesday morning. They spent the day in Wevenwert. They didn't do any napping. And if the other them wasn't asleep, they couldn't escape to the safety of the Cat Lady's spooky house.

Ahead of them, another hallway intersected this one.

That wasn't the layout of the real hotel. That was Mysteria's twisted nonsense architecture. They weren't even *close* to being out.

They stepped out into the intersection and spotted one of those huge, freaky monsters curled up in the hallway to their right, its countless legs rippling and bristling from its grotesque body.

The others never noticed them, but this one did. It turned its bloated head toward them, three sets of thorny mandibles opening and closing, a great mass of bulging black eyeballs staring back at them.

"Well that's just fucking great," she groaned.

Chapter 60

Albert hurried down the crumbling hallway, his mind racing.

How the hell were they supposed to find their way out of what was, essentially, an entire separate *dimension* from the one they wanted to be in. It wasn't as if they could just walk through a door. Apparently, he needed to shove some gaudy gold necklace into a statue's hollow head to get here. He was fairly sure there wasn't going to be a handy fire exit sign anywhere nearby.

"It's still following us!" squealed Brandy.

He looked back over his shoulder. A great mass of bulbous flesh and wriggling limbs was turning the corner, pursuing them down the decrepit corridor. Those long legs sticking out in every direction were working together, skittering not just along the floor, but along every available surface, propelling it forward in a surprisingly smooth and fluid motion for its otherwise bulky size and shape.

That strange mass of bulging black eyeballs stared back at him. Was it following them by sight alone? Or did it have their scent? Without knowing anything about these ugly things, he had no clue how to avoid them. If all those eyes meant that it was a visual hunter, they might be able to lose it if they could just get out of its sight, but if it had their scent trail, too, it very well could seek them out wherever they went. Attempting to hide could just end up trapping them in a corner somewhere with no hope whatsoever of escape.

What should he do? He was already exhausted. He felt like he'd been going nonstop for *days*. And he was sure Brandy was running out of steam, too.

But then he saw it. It was sitting in the middle of the hallway ahead of them. A small, black cat with bright yellow eyes that seemed fixed on him.

Brandy saw it too. "Pussy!" she gasped.

"Cats are our allies!" he recalled. Crazy Cat Lady wasn't lying about Lucianna not being what she seemed. It definitely felt as if she were on their side in all this, just as Kneede told them she was. The devil, the pervert and the parasite... He found himself thinking that of all the weirdos they'd met, Lucianna was the only halfway *normal* one of the group, and she'd turned out to be some kind of monster in disguise. *Up is down and out is in*, he thought. He was starting to understand what she was talking about. Everything here felt inside out and backwards.

The cat turned and trotted on ahead of them. He picked up his pace, determined to keep up with it.

"It's fast!" cried Brandy.

Albert looked back to see that the monstrous mass of flesh and legs was gaining on them. They wouldn't be able to stay ahead of it forever.

Ahead of him, the cat turned left and darted through an open doorway.

His heart sank. Was the cat really trying to help them? Because if they ran into that room and there was no way out...

Up is down and out is in, he thought again, and made the decision to trust the cat. He turned and ran through the door, into the room where their feline guide was leading them...only to find that it wasn't a room at all.

"What happened?" gasped Brandy.

He stumbled to a stop and stared down another empty hallway. When he looked back, he saw that the door they came through was gone. There was only more hallway.

Ahead of them, the cat yowled at them and disappeared through another doorway.

"Pussy says, 'Move your ass,'" Brandy translated.

"You speak cat now?"

"I thought it was pretty apparent from his tone, to be honest."

"I suppose so." He hurried forward and stepped through

the door, only to find himself in another hallway.

"Trippy," sighed Brandy.

The cat nudged its way through a partially opened door and vanished from sight again.

Albert pushed the door all the way open and stepped into yet another hallway just in time to see a black tail disappearing from sight again.

"Too many hallways," Brandy decided. "Not practical at all. Two stars."

"Not just one?" he wondered.

"Cute cat."

"Right."

He followed the cat through the next doorway. Not surprisingly, they found themselves in another hallway. But this time, the cat was there waiting for them. It was standing in the middle of the floor, staring back at them with its bright yellow eyes.

"Okay..." gasped Albert, out of breath. "What now?"

But the cat didn't lead the way. It just sat there, staring back at them.

"Um... Please?" he tried. "Exit? *Fetch*?"

"It's a cat, not a dog," Brandy reminded him.

"I don't know!"

Brandy stepped forward, her pretty eyes fixed on the curious feline.

"I mean, is *this* where we're supposed to be?" asked Albert, looking around. "Because it looks the same as everywhere else."

Brandy knelt down, still staring at those bright, yellow eyes. "It's here..." she said.

"What?"

"There's something here. We just have to find it."

"How do you know that?"

"I don't know." She looked back up at him. "I just kind of get this feeling like he's done leading us. The rest is up to us."

"Huh."

She stood up and faced him. "Meaning up to *you*, I think. You're the 'physical space' guy."

"Oh..." He turned and looked around. "I get it."

She smiled down at the cat. "He's a little slow, but he's cute."

The cat made a faint chirping noise at her, as if in acknowledgement.

Somewhere behind them, something crashed to the floor.

Brandy grabbed his hand and crowded closer to him. "I think you'd better hurry."

"Yeah..." But what was he supposed to do? He looked around, but nothing seemed out of place. Nothing felt *significant*.

More noises echoed down the corridor. Something slid across the tiles. Something else scraped against the concrete.

"It's coming..." breathed Brandy. As if this crap wasn't hard enough without being rushed...

He closed his eyes and took a calming breath. He needed to push those noises out of his head and focus on the space around him. He needed to find the *significance*.

"Albert..." she squeaked.

He opened his eyes to see a multitude of long, spindly legs creeping into the passage. His heart skipped into third gear.

"Any day, please!"

"I'm trying!"

If the cat brought them here specifically to find the exit, then they couldn't run. Chances were good this was the only place they could go.

"Hurry!"

The thing was rounding the corner, moving toward them, those huge, oozing mandibles twitching. Long, shiny feelers probing the floor ahead of it.

When he was looking for those stairs, he was able to make it work by focusing not on sexual thoughts, but simply on how much he loved her. That felt like a pretty major breakthrough in the shaman's magic training. But somehow he didn't think he was going to be able to do this the same way.

Lucianna might have been the enemy, but she didn't lie about how their psychic abilities worked. And she told them that sexual emotions might be the fastest and easiest way to activate them.

Ignoring the approaching horror, he grabbed Brandy and kissed her.

She stiffened, surprised, but didn't resist. She knew what he was doing. She understood how these things worked by now. This was just like all those other times. He just needed to clear his head. Focus on *her*. Find the sexual energy and focus it.

He could tell she was impatient, but she wrapped her arms around him and pressed her lips against him harder.

The honeymoon was full of sensual moments he could look back on. She was so into it the whole time. The way she kept flashing him little sneak peeks at her body everywhere they went. The way she kept reaching over and touching him whenever they were alone. The way she kept biting her lip and smiling that mischievous smile.

He could hear the monster drawing closer, but he refused to look. If he opened his eyes, he'd lose it.

She bought several sexy little outfits to wear. Skimpy lingerie... Revealing, see-through things... God, she looked amazing! And the things she'd said to him, dirty little whispers during dinner...naughty little things at the poolside...and the things she'd gasped into his ear in the midst of furious lovemaking...

A piece of plaster from the ceiling broke off and crashed to the floor, making her jump. The motion caused her to bite his lip.

Pain shot through him, a blinding sensation that washed away all his other thoughts.

She felt it, too. He felt her stiffen again. He felt her hands close around his shirt. He could even feel her heart thundering right through her chest.

And yet as soon as the pain numbed, he found himself not distracted, but instead *reminded*.

That first night in the hotel...steamy and breathless...caught in her greedy embrace...fingernails digging into his back...

She'd apologized profusely afterward, when she saw the welts on his skin. But he wasn't mad at her in the least.

That was *hot*.

The horror of the Ruin drew closer. He could hear the skittering of its countless legs. But they were unimportant compared to his beautiful wife.

He pulled her closer, kissing her harder. He focused on the taste of her lips. The feel of her heart pounding against his chest.

And somehow, she felt it too. In spite of the thing that was almost upon him, she seemed to melt into his arms.

Time slowed to a crawl.

Perhaps…it wouldn't be so bad to die like this…

A door opened.

Albert opened his eyes. Brandy was staring back at him through her crooked glasses. The light had changed. There were voices.

They looked over to see a young woman standing in an open doorway, staring at them.

"You're literally *in a hotel*," she informed them. "Get a fucking room."

Chapter 61

"Well *that* was fucking embarrassing…" grumbled Brandy as they walked together through the busy hotel hallway.

"Sorry."

"It's not your fault," she sighed. She took a breath and tried to shake it off. "So what now? Lucy the Liar said we were done. She said we opened the locks. It sounded like she was ready to take us to where the road was hidden."

He nodded. "If we were smart, maybe we would've played along, let her show us where it was before we pissed her off."

"You really think it would've worked out for us if we did?"

"Probably not."

They were back in the main part of the building, heading toward the lobby. Whatever they were looking for could be any-where. "I wish we knew who to trust," she sighed.

"We can trust each other," he told her.

She rolled her eyes at him. "Yeah, but neither of us knows what the fuck we're doing, so that's not very helpful, is it?"

"Oh yeah…" He glanced back the way they came. "I wonder if we've time jumped again. That's happened every other time we've come back from one of those weird places."

She glanced back. He was right. Everything looked pretty much the same as it did when they were going the other way, but it was hard to tell anything from inside these hallways.

Albert reached up and rubbed at his head, wincing.

"You okay?"

"Yeah. I think all this jumping back and forth is giving me a headache. Feels like there's an air raid siren going off right by my ear."

She frowned. "Want to go back to the bar? Get a drink? Sit

for minute?"

But he shook his head. "I don't really want anything. I still feel kind of queasy from all the excitement back there."

She understood that. "Well let's have a break anyway." The lobby was just ahead of them now. She took his hand and steered him toward it. "Maybe you'll think of something if you just stop moving for a bit."

"Yeah… Maybe…"

There was an older woman standing at the front desk, tapping at a keyboard. She let go of his hand and stepped up to it. "Excuse me. Can you tell me the time and date?"

The woman glanced up from her screen and offered her a polite smile. "Sure. It's ten-oh-seven. The twenty-fifth."

"Thank you."

"You're very welcome."

She grabbed Albert's hand again and led him to an empty couch in the far corner, out of sight. "You were right. It's Thursday morning." It had been two days since they had that close call with their past selves in this very lobby. That other them would be checking out in about an hour.

"Every time we've seen one of those places," he said, thinking. "It's like moving back and forth is what throws time out of whack or something."

"Don't think about it too hard. You'll make yourself as crazy as everyone else in this nuthouse."

He chuckled and sat down.

The couch felt so nice and soft. She hadn't realized how much time she'd spent on her feet. She couldn't remember the last time she felt this tired. Maybe not since returning from the temple that night.

Albert leaned back and closed his eyes.

She leaned back, too, but she kept her eyes on him. She watched him as he sat there.

Sometimes she did this. While he slept. While he read or watched television. When he thought she was preoccupied. She liked watching him. She was always trying to carve his handsome face into her memory, capturing him forever, so she could always see him, even when he wasn't around.

She hated the Keeper and all these stupid, scary things he'd put them through. But it was only because of the Keeper that they were together, that they had this life that she treasured. She wanted to believe that they would've ended up together anyway. They didn't *meet* in the temple, after all. They were lab partners first. And he *was* pretty charming, even way back then. If he'd asked her out, she probably wouldn't have turned him down. But... Well, she wasn't really sure, was she? They were different people back then. They hadn't been to the temple. They hadn't been to the sex room. What if, without that push, they never would've had any chemistry?

Albert opened his eyes and looked back at her. "What's up?" he asked.

"Just thinking," she replied. "Feel any better?"

"Nice to be off my feet." Then he closed his eyes again. "Still can't shake this headache though."

"Poor baby..." She wasn't being sarcastic. She actually felt bad for him. And she wouldn't be surprised if it was because of all that bouncing back and forth. She was surprised *she* didn't have a migraine.

"It's just..." He reached up, his eyes still closed, and pressed his hand against his forehead. "It's like I'm standing next to railroad tracks and there's this endless train roaring past me, rattling my brain."

She frowned. She really hoped he wasn't getting sick. This would be a lousy time for something like that.

Albert winced and turned his head to face her. Then his eyebrows furrowed. He frowned. He lifted his hand and held it over his head, as if he were feeling for something. Then he turned his head the other way... Then back again...

Brandy watched him, her face drawn into a worried frown. "Um... Whatcha doin' there, buddy?"

He opened his eyes and looked back at her for a moment. She could see something processing inside his head. "Interesting..." he said.

"Interesting how?"

"If that's inside my head…" he pondered, turning his face one way, then the other, "…then why isn't it moving *with* my head?"

"Huh?"

He jumped up and looked around. "Over here…" he said.

She stood up and followed him. "Did all our sexy times finally break your brain?" she asked.

But he ignored her. He walked toward the corner of the room, stood there for a moment, listening, then turned and walked back toward the desk and did the same thing.

The woman at the desk caught sight of him and tipped her head to one side, curious.

Brandy gave her a shrug. She wasn't sure what else to say. She didn't know what the hell was going on, either.

Then, suddenly, he turned and stalked out of the room.

"Wait up!"

"I described it as a train before," he said. He was walking down the hallway, his fingers dragging along the wall beside him. "But that wasn't quite right. It was more like the roar of rushing water."

"Okay…" she said, confused. "Do you need to use the little boy's room?"

"But it's not in my head…" he went on. "It's in the *walls*."

She grabbed the tail of his shirt and tugged him to a stop. "What are you talking about?"

He stared at her, distracted. "Don't you remember what the cat lady told us?"

"Up is down and down is out or some shit?"

"She said, 'Follow the pipes.'"

She stared back at him for a moment, letting that process. Then her eyes widened and she looked at the wall where his hand was pressed. "Pipes…" she whispered.

"We must've unlocked some kind of mechanism inside the hotel walls," he explained. "There's some kind of *energy* rushing past. Like water through pipes. And I can feel it."

"So we just follow the pipes!"

"Right!"

She scrunched her face up. "Well what're you standing around talking about it for? *Go!*"

He frowned at her, confused. "Right..." he said. "We'll... Yeah. Let's go."

Chapter 62

It really did feel like pipes. Not so much the sound, he realized now that he knew what it was. It was more like the way pipes in old houses shook and rattled when water was rushing through them. *That* was what he could feel.

His fingertips dragging along the wall, he made his way down the hallway and around the corner, past several doorways, though he wasn't entirely sure how the energy was moving around these doorways... Was it redirected over or under the frame? Or did it just sort of...jump across it?

Trying too hard to understand this sort of thing would probably be a mistake. He'd figured out that he was supposed to follow it. That was probably all he needed to know. And all his mere human brain might be able to comprehend anyway.

He walked past the spa and the fitness room, then stopped and frowned.

He backed up a few steps, his hand sliding across the blue paint.

"Is that it?" wondered Brandy.

"There's *something*," he confirmed, although he wasn't entirely sure how to describe it. He took a step back and looked it over. Then he closed his eyes and concentrated on the space for a moment. Then he nodded. "Yeah. There's something here all right."

Brandy turned and looked back. The hallways were significantly more crowded now. There were a lot of people moving around. "What do you need me to do?" she asked.

He glanced over at her, saw the embarrassed but determined look on her face. Making out in a busy hallway wasn't the most romantic thing she could think of, he could tell. But she was also determined to finish this unpleasant business and be done.

At least it was a honeymoon resort. They wouldn't be the first couple making out in the hallways, he was sure.

But he didn't think that was necessary this time. The pipes had already shown him where he needed to be. He leaned against the wall and then took her hand and pulled her closer. He didn't need to make out with her. He didn't need her to touch him anywhere inappropriate. He needed those sexy thoughts when that monster was bearing down on him, but back in that stairwell he found a better way.

He squeezed her hand and looked into her eyes.

"You gonna picture me dressed like Slave Princess Leia or something?" she asked him, smirking.

He chuckled. "I am *now.*"

"Me and my big mouth."

"Yeah, that one's on you."

She smiled at him. God, that was a pretty smile.

"You plan on telling me what you're thinking about when you do this stuff without my help?" she asked.

"It's a secret."

"You're not allowed to keep secrets from me," she informed him.

"No?"

"Nope. Spill it."

"Maybe later," he teased.

She puckered her face at him. "Not cool."

"I love you so much," he told her.

"Don't change the subject."

"I'm not," he promised, still staring into those gorgeous eyes. "That's the secret."

"What is?"

He smiled and put his arm around her, then turned and stepped onto the hidden staircase.

Those bright blue eyes flashed wide and she flung her arms around him, surprised. "Whoa!"

A long, shadowy flight of stairs descended before them.

He looked back at the hallway they'd just left behind. People were walking by, completely unaware of them.

How did that work, anyway? Even if they couldn't see these stairs, from their perspective, hadn't two people just disappeared through a solid wall? Did the queer magic of this place just make people ignore something like that? He didn't understand it.

But he supposed it didn't matter. He turned his attention downward and began to descend.

"All I know," grumbled Brandy, "is that you'd better have been thinking about *me* up there."

"You're *all* I think about," he replied. And it was the truth.

She squinted at him, suspicious.

Below them, a dingy concrete floor stretched away from the foot of the steps.

"Really not liking all the Gilbert House vibes this place has going on," said Brandy.

"I know what you mean. But hopefully this'll be the last time."

"We'd better find what we've been looking for down here or I'm going to be pissed."

There was a light down there, a soft, yellow glow that became visible as they approached the bottom. Maybe that meant there was electricity down here for a change?

But the source of the light turned out to be a propane camping lantern. And holding this lantern was none other than the woman in the white dress. She was standing in an archway of familiar gray stone, smiling that same strangely misplaced-looking smile at them. But now her familiar white dress was drenched in blood.

"You again…" said Albert. He stepped in front of Brandy, determined to protect her. "What do you want with us? Who are you?"

She tipped her head slightly to one side, as if she couldn't understand why he'd ask such a silly question. "I'm your host, of course," she replied. Her voice sounded vaguely familiar. Had she spoken to them before this? He was fairly sure she hadn't said a word, not even when she attacked Lucianna. "I'm the

370

Keeper of Mysteria."

He squinted at the woman as if she'd suddenly begun speaking another language. "What are you talking about?"

"For someone so clever," said Kneede, who was suddenly descending the steps behind them, "you're kind of slow on the uptake, aren't you?"

Albert grabbed Brandy's waist and pulled her away from him. "You…!"

But Kneede made no move to attack them. He stopped at the bottom of the steps and gestured at the woman. "I suppose I should introduce the *real* Lucianna Estrane?"

"What?"

Both of them turned to look at her, surprised.

"He's telling the truth," she assured them.

"Then who was that *other* Lucianna?" asked Brandy.

"Well, that's where things get a little *complicated*," said the woman. Then she laughed. It was a strange thing to hear, because it was an eerily familiar laugh. It was *Lucianna's* laugh. The same laugh they'd heard so many times since they arrived back here. The woman lifted the lantern higher, letting its light wash over her blood-spattered face. "I wasn't *always* so old and plump," she informed them.

Albert stared at her as it all fell into place. That was why this woman looked so familiar. She was a much younger and shapelier version of the woman who greeted them in the hotel lobby several hours earlier.

Lucianna waits where the wind cries with lust! thought Albert, remembering the words in Shanzer's spellbook. *Find her to break the seal!*

He wasn't talking about the other Lucianna. He was talking about this one. The *real* one.

Brandy looked over at Albert, confused. "You mean…like how there were two of *us* back there? Past and present?"

"The time anomaly…?" pondered Albert.

"Time doesn't remain constant across world boundaries," explained Kneede. "There's almost always a shift of some sort. And sometimes that shift is quite drastic. But the Lucianna Mysteria is a special case."

"*I* was the one who broke the flow of time within these walls," said Lucianna. She turned and walked through the archway, her lantern revealing a heavy, wooden door waiting in the gloom beyond it. "I created a paradox," she elaborated. "The very kind my future counterpart warned you against."

"You actually created a paradox?" asked Albert, surprised.

"Dangerous gamble," grumbled Kneede. "You should've been torn to pieces and erased from existence in the process."

Brandy looked over at Albert, her eyes wide with startled horror. She didn't need to say what she was thinking. He, too, remembered how close they were to coming face to face with their past selves in the convoluted chronology of this crazy hotel. Was that what would've happened to them if the other them had noticed them? Torn to pieces and erased from existence?

"I *was* torn apart, actually," said Lucianna. "That was the point, after all. But I promise I won't be parted from existence *that* easily."

"It seems not," admitted Kneede.

"What are you talking about?" asked Albert. Torn apart? She looked perfectly whole to him. A little bloody, but she was most certainly in one piece. Unlike the *other* Lucianna, it seemed… Then he frowned. "You mean torn apart into the two separate Luciannas?"

"That's exactly right," she replied. "One of me continued onward, blissfully unaware of the existence of another her, while *I* slipped into the fractured stream of time and made my way toward the two of you in the here and now."

Brandy frowned. "So…when I first saw you…and I got that super intense feeling that you *didn't belong here*… It meant you didn't belong here as in, *now*? That you were from a different time?"

"Also correct," she replied, beaming in that familiar way the *old* Lucianna had beamed at her. It was strange to see the same expressions on *this* face.

"That's…confusing…" decided Albert.

"And why are you working with *him*?" demanded Brandy,

thrusting a finger at Kneede.

"Because he's on our side, of course," replied Lucianna.

"For today, at any rate," grumbled Kneede.

"For today," agreed Lucianna.

"Shanzer's a creep," explained Kneede, "but he knows what he's doing. He foresaw what was happening here and sent me to keep things from going south while Warner was preoccupied with his main task."

"His main task?" asked Brandy.

"The other two…" recalled Albert. Two more like him and Brandy, seeking the road to the next doorway. He kept wondering who they were.

"I'm afraid not everything you were told when you arrived here was entirely truthful," said Lucianna. "My apologies for that. It was necessary, believe me. But you've accomplished your task now. You've earned the truth. And first on that list was my predecessor."

Her predecessor? As in, the guy the Keeper *actually* tasked with guarding the gateway she built her insane resort hotel on top of?

"The older me told you she had no idea whatever became of him. It wasn't a lie. She really doesn't possess that knowledge."

Albert frowned. *Older* her didn't possess knowledge that *younger* her did? How did *that* work?

"But when we first arrived here in Wevenwert and ventured into the crossroads," she continued, "back when we were still one, before we separated, we *found* him." She reached out and grasped the handle of the door. "He's right here. Still dutifully doing his job."

She pushed open the door, revealing a strange and ancient corpse.

Chapter 63

It was little more than a skeleton wrapped in leathery, mummified flesh, draped over a gray stone block roughly the size of a casket, clinging to it as if hanging on for dear life, even in death.

But no human remains had ever looked like that, as far as Brandy was aware. Every one of his bones had sprouted strange, petrified branches that spread outward from the body, reaching across the stone like creeping ivy, encasing it in a morbid, skeletal latticework. "That is fucking freaky…"

Albert nodded. It looked like some kind of monstrous mutation, something that might be imagined in some dark, post-apocalyptic comic book.

"He was already dead when I found him," explained Lucianna. "But even in death, he was determined to protect the gateway. His very corpse now embraces it, warding off the evils of the Ruin. He still fights to preserve the cycle."

"So he was employee of the month material," said Brandy. "Good for him."

"If only there were as many of us fighting for a *better* cycle," sneered Kneede, "instead of a *broken* one."

"Better a broken cycle than *no* cycle," Lucianna reminded him.

"Better for *some*."

Lucianna stepped closer to the strange corpse, a sad sort of smile spread across her too-young face, as if she were looking upon an old friend. "I knew the moment I found him that something had gone terribly wrong here. The Keeper's gatekeepers aren't so easy to kill."

Albert stepped closer to the stone, trying to get a better

look at the morbid scene, and Brandy gave the tail of his shirt a firm tug. "Don't," she begged.

"Was it one of those bogey things?" he asked, reaching back and giving her hand a reassuring squeeze.

"Impossible," replied Kneede. "There's nothing in the Ruin with that kind of power."

"This was something else," agreed Lucianna. She never took her eyes off the corpse. "Something that attacked him from *inside*."

Albert looked up at her, confused. "What, like a *disease* or something?"

"Similar concept," said Kneede. "Or maybe 'possession' would be a better word for it."

"Possessed...?" wondered Brandy. She and Albert exchanged a worried look. The same thought had passed through them both.

But Kneede sneered. "As much as I'd love an excuse to wipe that parasite out of existence...I assure you I'm not talking about Warner."

"No..." sighed Lucianna. "Nothing at all like Warner. 'Disease' was a closer description. This was an *infection*. But not of germs or bacteria. This was something entirely different. Something even I can't begin to comprehend. But I know it didn't come from the Ruin. And, even *more* concerning, I know that it didn't get here by itself."

"The only thing more frightening than something capable of killing a gatekeeper," said Kneede, "is something capable of *commanding* something capable of killing a gatekeeper."

"I didn't know what I was dealing with when I first came across this scene," said Lucianna. "But I knew in an instant that I was already infected. I could sense it. Somewhere deep inside me."

"You were going to end up like this guy?" gasped Brandy.

"Worse," she replied, turning to face them. "The primary goal was never to kill the gatekeeper, but to take its place. My predecessor wasn't strong enough to survive the attack, but he was strong enough to keep it from taking over his body. He *chose* death over becoming a puppet. I, on the other hand, am not that strong." She reached out with one slender hand and caressed the corpse's leathery skull. "Unlike him…I was going to be the tool it used to destroy the gateway hidden here and end the cycle forever."

"But strength isn't everything," said Albert. Already, he'd begun to put the pieces together.

Lucianna gave him a knowing smile. "True. I knew the thing inside me couldn't be removed, but it wouldn't take control until the time was right. So I did the unthinkable. I used the tenuous grip the crossroads held on time and shattered it. In the process, I broke *myself* apart. But not the infection. It was contained in a single timeline, completely unaware that there was more than one of me. The infected Lucianna's memories were altered. And *I* withdrew into Mysteria to watch and to wait."

"Altered memories…" pondered Albert. "So that's why she didn't know what became of her predecessor. Or where the locks were hidden."

"Exactly," she replied, beaming at them. The expression was so surreally like the other Lucianna that Brandy felt a little lightheaded with the realization that they really were the same person… "All she knows is that a dear friend designed and built the hotel for her, then passed away, taking the secrets with him. In reality, that friend was me."

"That makes sense," said Albert.

"It does?" asked Brandy, bewildered.

"I mean, as much as anything else we've had to deal with."

She rolled her eyes. "If you say so."

Lucianna giggled that eerily familiar giggle.

"The other Lucianna carried the infection, but it lay dormant," explained Kneede. "It had no effect on her whatsoever until it came forward and took control, which was sometime *after* your conversation in her office."

Lucianna nodded. "Yes. That was all me, with the exception of a few displaced memories to protect you. So please don't feel like she was trying to deceive you. I promise you she was doing the best she could."

"So not until she appeared in that dream was she being controlled by the infection," reasoned Brandy.

"Yes. By then, she was gone."

"But you showed yourself to us *before* then," recalled Albert. "You were in the hallway that went nowhere."

"I was trying to guide you," she explained, "but those nasty pests from the Ruin got in my way. They're clever. They dragged you out of Mysteria and into the Ruin, tried to make it seem like *I* was the one blocking your way." She glanced up at Kneede. "That's where Lucas came in."

"While you two were stumbling around like blindfolded kids looking for the piñata," said Kneede, "I was hunting down bogeys. You're welcome."

"Thanks," spat Albert.

"You know that shitty personality of yours is probably why only nutjobs are devil worshipers," decided Brandy.

Kneede actually chuckled a little at this.

"So how does that crazy cat lady fit into all this?" wondered Albert.

Lucianna flashed him that weirdly familiar smile again. "Who do you think sent me to Wevenwert all those years ago in the first place?"

Brandy frowned. "Wait… You're working for *her*?" She did recall the *other* Lucianna telling them that she didn't work for the Keeper, that they only shared a common goal in protecting the cycle.

"Only a god could've conspired to bring the infection here," reasoned Lucianna. "No one else possesses that kind of power. Naturally, only another god could stand against something like that."

"We do use the word 'god' rather loosely," grumbled Kneede.

"True," admitted Lucianna. "There are no adequate words to describe them. Their very existence is impossible to properly comprehend, even to remnants like us."

"The next time we saw you," recalled Albert. "It looked like you attacked us. When all those hallways exploded."

"That was a close one," she sighed, pressing her hand over her heart. She was wearing a few rings and a bracelet, but it didn't appear that the younger Lucianna had the same affinity for jewelry that the older one did. "I almost wasn't able to hold the Ruin back long enough for your other selves to fall asleep."

"You were protecting us?" asked Brandy.

She smiled that same sweet and charming smile. "Always."

Albert remembered the look on her face in that tense moment, that strange, strained smile... That was her using all her strength to hold back the power of that nightmarish apocalyptic wasteland?

This was making Brandy's head hurt. "Okay..." was all she could think to say.

"The infection," said Albert. "Is it gone? Did you destroy it? Or is that something we still have to worry about?"

"It's gone," she assured them. "I made sure it won't be back." A very sad look passed across her lovely face. "It was destroyed along with the other me. But without knowing where it came from, I can't promise there aren't more of them out there. And then there's the matter of who, or *what*, sent it here in the first place."

"Great..." grumbled Brandy. "Like I needed more nightmare fuel."

"So what do we do now?" asked Albert. "You brought us all the way here. What's next?"

Lucianna gestured at the stone. "The last lock is right here. All you have to do is insert the key."

Brandy frowned. "Insert it *where*? There's no hole."

"He's lying on it," said Kneede.

"*What?*"

"It's just like the others," explained Lucianna. She reached down and patted the corpse's back. "The hole is right under here. Don't worry, you can just plunge it right through the skin. It's paper thin."

Brandy made a gagging face and then took off the key and thrust it at Albert. "This is *your* thing," she informed him.

Albert took the medallion from her and stared at it, a look

of mild horror on his face.

Chapter 64

Lucianna wasn't lying about the brittleness of the corpse's flesh. It parted like paper when he thrust the key through the remains and into the hidden hole beneath. He half-expected to feel his hand pass through a mass of cold and slimy guts, but there didn't seem to be anything left of the old gatekeeper's innards. His hand sank all the way down into the open void waiting below.

The world seemed to lurch around him. He swayed on his feet and grabbed onto the strange, skeletal cage for balance. At the same time, the empty void surrounding his hand turned into something cold and wet. He yanked it out with a revolted groan and stumbled backward.

The corpse was gone. The stone stood unguarded, the gaping hole in its middle oozing the same yellowish-brown goo that was dripping from his arm.

The entire room had changed, he realized. Every surface was now made from the gray stone that had comprised the entirety of the temple. The door behind them had vanished. Instead, there was now another stone archway in front of them, leading into a gloomy tunnel that he didn't particularly like the looks of.

"I'm never going to get used to that," grunted Brandy.

Albert looked down at his dripping arm. "What *is* this stuff?"

"Ichor," replied Kneede. "It's what powers the portals you've been using. It comes from beyond the boundaries of all worlds and possesses unique, pan-dimensional properties. Coming in contact with it can, under the right circumstances, take you places otherwise unreachable. It's what connects the two sides of the Lucianna Mysteria."

"Oh," was all he could think to say. He wasn't entirely sure what to do with this information now that he had it. "Should I be concerned about being covered in it?"

"Not unless you intend to attempt any sort of spatial magic, fourth-dimensional traveling or deep-sea fishing."

Albert stared at him, bemused. "Not…on *today's* itinerary… I don't think."

"Then you'll be fine."

"Compliments of the hotel," said Lucianna, holding out a tightly rolled white hand towel.

"Where were you hiding that?" asked Brandy.

It was a good question, Albert realized. It didn't look like the bloody dress had any pockets. And it wasn't as if there were a housekeeping cart nearby.

But Lucianna only shrugged her shoulders in that charming, clueless way that the *other* Lucianna had done when she couldn't—or *wouldn't*—answer their questions.

"Um… Thanks," said Albert, taking the towel and wiping down his arm and the key.

It had changed shape again, he saw. It was surrounded by little dull spikes now, with a sort of double-sided barb at one end. And there were ridges running along the surface on each side that weren't there before.

"Are we going to need this again?" he wondered.

"Most definitely," replied Lucianna. "The Mysteria locks also double as an activation system for the seed. You wouldn't be able to use it to reach your final destination, even if you *could* get there without taking the road hidden here."

"Okay…" said Brandy, perplexed.

"You've finally arrived," said a new voice.

Albert looked up to see that one of the hotel staff was standing in the stone archway. A man with a young face and neatly combed black hair. Except it wasn't really one of the hotel staff, he realized. Even in the gloom, he could see that the man's eyes were empty and black.

"Did you have any trouble?" asked Lucianna.

"None," replied Warner. "As you anticipated, the infection remained focused on these two. It made no attempt to interfere with me."

"Excellent. Where are our other guests?"

"Ahead. Examining the carriage."

"Carriage?" asked Brandy.

"A relic from a past world," explained Lucianna as she began walking, her halo of lantern light sliding across the gray stone around her. "Waiting since the dawn of *this* world to carry the Keeper's chosen champions to the Denselands."

Albert followed behind her, unwilling to be left alone in this place in the dark. "Denselands?" he asked. He thought they were supposed to be going somewhere called the City Beyond Memory. Wasn't that what Crazy Cat Lady called their destination?

"An area deep in the vast expanse of the Wood," she explained. "A place where the forgotten remains of countless dead universes have piled up over the endless ages. A wasteland, where the very air is heavy with the weight of the inescapable atrophy that awaits all life." She flashed them another of those smiles that belonged on another woman's face and added, "Where everything is lost and nothing is ever found, except by the will of the Keeper."

"That sounds just fucking *great*," growled Brandy. "Just what I wanted to do next."

Lucianna giggled, but she wasn't trying to be funny.

"Everything has an end," said Kneede. "*Everything.*"

Albert looked back at him, but he wasn't talking to them. His pale blue eyes were fixed on the black voids of Warner's.

"Do you think the Keeper's cycle of cruelty is an exception?"

"Your job is done now," Warner informed him. "Your presence here is no longer needed."

"Perhaps," he replied, not budging. "Perhaps not."

"Behave yourselves, boys," sighed Lucianna without looking back at them. "We still have a job to finish." Then she glanced over her shoulder at Brandy. "Literally older than dirt, the both of them, and still acting like spoiled children."

Albert glanced back at the two of them. They were follow-ing them at a distance, barely within the reach of the lantern, si-lent, pointedly not looking at each other. They *did* sort of look like children, he realized. But that bit about them being *literally* older than dirt... "About that..." he said, curious. "What exactly *are* they, anyway? I mean, they're obviously not human."

"Technically, Lucas is," replied Lucianna. "He was born just like you. But unlike you, he found himself quite immune to death. He's lived through more than most people can imagine. Wars. Plagues. Famines. Even the death of our last world. And memories like those leave scars. That much time can harden an-yone's heart."

He recalled that strange conversation back in Shanzer's bar, before he realized who he was talking to. He said something about having been married a few times...

(*If you're really unlucky, you live long enough to find yourself all alone. Sometimes over and over again...*)

He found himself squeezing Brandy's hand. The very thought of such a life, of watching her grow old and pass on, knowing he'd never be able to join her... It was a terrible thought.

"Warner was born of a poisoned world several cycles past. One of many shadow races that prowled bygone worlds. The rest of his race disappeared eons ago, but he persisted and eventually pledged his loyalty to the Keeper. His job is to watch over people like you and make sure enemies of the cycle don't interfere."

"And *you*?" asked Albert. She, too, wasn't human. They saw her turn into some kind of monster when she confronted the other Lucianna. They *both* transformed. And then they crashed through that stone wall like it was paper.

Lucianna gave him another of those sweet and mysterious smiles. "That's a bit more complicated," she replied. "Let's save it for another day, shall we?"

He frowned. Another day? Would there ever *be* another day? He didn't exactly plan on keeping in touch. He was rather hoping they could wrap this nonsense up and finally go home.

Maybe do Vegas for their next vacation...

The five of them made their way down the long, stone corridor. It wasn't straight, Albert saw, but rather slightly curved, as if they were slowly spiraling deeper and deeper into the earth. Again, he found himself reminded of the temple and its pitch-black depths.

But after a few minutes of walking, he caught sight of a light. A moment later, another stone archway came into view. Beyond it was a space somewhat larger than the one they'd just left. There was another lantern, a modern, battery-powered LED one this time, sitting on the floor, illuminating more of the room.

Looming over the lantern was an unsettlingly familiar figure.

Ten feet tall. Stretched out of proportion. Naked and unashamed. His feet together, hands at his side. And no face.

A *sentinel.*

Or at least the stone likeness of one, just like those they first laid eyes on six years ago, back in the Temple of the Blind. After that place crumbled, he didn't think he'd ever see one of them again, and yet here it was, waiting for him, bigger than life.

The sight of it was somewhat exciting, a glimpse of a promise that there were still answers waiting for him out there. But even more so, the feeling that it sent settling into his gut like a ball of hot lead was of *dread.* It really was a sentinel... This really was about the temple... And there really was a second doorway waiting for them out there.

Brandy felt it, too. He felt her fingernails digging into his hand as they approached it. He knew that she, for one, had *hoped* to never encounter one of these guys again. But here he was...

He could hear voices from deeper in the room. And he could see shadows moving across the far wall. The others like them? Two more of the twelve Cat Lady said would be involved?

"The Denselands is extremely vast," explained Lucianna. "And the weight of all those fallen worlds breaks any semblance of natural law that the Wood allows. Reality, itself, is broken there, making it the perfect place to hide something invaluable."

"The second doorway," groaned Brandy. She still hated the thought of it.

"It can only be reached by way of one of three roads. *This* is the shadow road."

The shadow road… He remembered Warner calling it that, but he didn't know what it meant.

"And there…" Lucianna lifted a slender finger and pointed. "…awaits the carriage that will carry you to it."

As they rounded the corner and approached the illuminated archway, he saw that there was, indeed, some sort of vehicle awaiting them beyond the sentinel. It didn't look much like a carriage, though. It looked more like something someone built for a low-budget science fiction set. It was a roughly cylindrical metal box, rounded on each end, with dark windows running around the upper half of it. It was sitting in a recessed channel in the floor, looking more like a miniature subway car than a carriage.

Albert had *many* questions about the so-called carriage and the sentinels' mysterious shadow road, but his attention was drawn to the two people standing next to the strange vehicle, looking back at them.

"Hi!" said a small, thin woman with short-cropped, raven black hair. She was wearing distressed denim shorts, a black tee shirt with an AC/DC album cover on the front and clunky leather boots. "You must be our travel buddies."

"Um…?" said Brandy, glancing at Albert. "I guess so?"

"I'm Violet." Then she gestured at the man standing next to her, practically dwarfing her with his impressive size in his faded jeans, hiking boots and a blue and white tee shirt stretched over his ample gut. "This is Corey."

Chapter 65

"Your job was to unlock the carriage house," explained Warner. "Their job was to activate the carriage."

Corey was holding onto one end of a silver pole as if it were a walking stick. As soon as Warner said this, he raised it up, as if to show it off. "We brought the key."

"We don't know if it's a key," clarified Violet.

"*Might* be a key," amended Corey, frowning at it. "Important, though. Either way. Prob'ly."

"How did they get here before us?" wondered Albert.

Violet pointed at a second passageway leading out of the carriage house. "There was a hidden hallway leading to an underground room. Just a dead end, but Warner told us to wait there. Then, a few minutes ago, everything just sort of…"

"Went blip," said Corey.

"Went blip," she agreed, wobbling her head a little at the word. "Then it was a *different* room with a different passageway, leading *here*."

"When you unlocked the door back there, it brought all of us here," explained Lucianna.

"You were able to find one of the hotel's hidden passageways?" said Albert, impressed. "Does that mean you two know sex magic, too?"

"Sex magic?" asked Violet, looking shocked. "What? *No.* Ew. What the *shit?*"

Albert and Brandy exchanged a surprised look. Maybe they should've kept that to themselves?

"You guys get to use magic?" asked Corey, his bushy eyebrows raised.

Violet reached into the neckline of her shirt. "No. With

this." She pulled out what appeared to be a broken shard of blue glass hanging on a chain. "Piece of looking glass. Bought it from some super creepy street vendor in St. Louis a few years ago. Lets us see all kinds of hidden things."

Brandy pointed at the glass, her forehead scrunched up. "Why does *she* get magic glass?"

Violet mirrored the expression, except she scrunched up her small nose instead. "What the hell is *sex magic*? How does *that* work?"

Brandy snapped her mouth shut, a visible blush rising in her fair cheeks.

"Everyone has their own road to follow in the Keeper's machine," said Warner, walking the hotel employee's body to the carriage and examining it.

"For better or worse," growled Kneede.

"The carriage house is finally open," interjected Lucianna, smiling that charming smile. "And the carriage is made whole again. Everything is in place for your journey to the Denselands."

"Whoopie," grumbled Brandy.

"By the way, is…she okay?" asked Violet, pointing at Lucianna's blood-soaked dress.

Albert glanced back at her. "Um…? Yes?" It wasn't her blood, after all. Except that it *was* her blood…just not from…*her* her? From the *other* her? Was the other her going to *be* her someday? Did she kill her own future self? Or were they, like, time clones, from separate timelines? Was that a thing, too? That was probably a thing, too. Jesus this was confusing.

"The carriage requires that piece to secure the yoke," explained Warner, gesturing at the rod in Corey's hand.

"For the yoke," repeated Corey, looking down at it. "Not a key."

"Told you we didn't know it was a key," said Violet.

"Yoke?" asked Brandy, looking around. "Is this a horse-drawn carriage or something?"

"Something," giggled Lucianna.

Albert walked over and peered into the recessed channel the carriage was sitting in. It didn't have wheels, he immediately saw.

Instead, it was sitting on a set of wide rails, more like a sleigh than a carriage. And the bottom of the channel was covered in what appeared to be the same bile-colored fluid that filled those statues after he reached inside with the key.

Ichor, he thought. For some reason, the word made his skin crawl. He wanted to wash his arm. *Repeatedly.*

He counted fourteen lengths of heavy chain attached to a hollow bar resting in a set of hooks at the front of the carriage. The other ends of these chains remained unseen. They stretched out into the tunnel into which the carriage was pointing, making a mystery of whatever might be there.

"There's no point looking for them," said Lucianna, watching him strain to see what might be lurking in the darkness. "You could follow the chains, but they'd only go on forever. The Keeper's carriage is pulled from somewhere beyond."

"Beyond *what?*" wondered Violet. She was holding up her mysterious shard of glass, peering through it with one eye, but it didn't seem to show her anything because she only frowned and let it fall back to her chest.

Lucianna only beamed at her. "No one knows," she whispered dramatically.

"Oh…"

"Cool," decided Corey, nodding his head with apparent approval.

Warner removed the bar from its hooks and lined it up with the mounts on either side. "Insert it here."

Corey knelt down and did as he was instructed. There was an audible click when it was in place. Then a door on the side slid open, revealing an interior that looked considerably more comfortable than Albert was expecting. There were cushions of deep purple on the seats and a velvety carpet lining the floor. There were even curtains that could be drawn between the front and back seats, allowing for an option of privacy.

"That's it," announced Warner. "It's time to go."

"Awesome," said Corey, standing up straight.

There was a duffel bag at Violet's feet. She picked it up, straining with the weight of it, and stepped toward the carriage, but she only made it a few steps before Corey grabbed it from her and carried it off as if it weighed nothing. Relieved of this burden, she walked back and collected the LED lantern.

"That's all there is?" wondered Albert. "Just stick his pole in and go?"

Brandy sniggered at this. Why did he have to keep saying things like that? Was he doing it on purpose? Or could he really not hear these things before they came out of his mouth.

"Seriously," he pressed, ignoring her. "None of this makes any sense. Why did we have to go through all that?"

"It's the Keeper's way," replied Warner. He turned to face him as Violet and Corey climbed into the carriage, those empty black eyes fixed on him. "Everything is the Keeper's way."

He expected Kneede to say something at that. He seemed to have something snarky to say every time Warner mentioned the Keeper. But he said nothing.

Albert didn't like the way it felt looking into those black eyes. It was unsettling. But he remained determined to hold his gaze. "But you said he wasn't in charge of us. You said it was about *us*. Not *him*."

"I *did* say that."

"It's roomy in here!" Violet called back from inside the carriage.

"The choices are always yours in the end," Warner went on.

"A lot of good it does us if we don't understand the repercussions of the choices we make, though, don't you think?"

Warner tipped the hotel employee's head to one side in that not-quite-right attempt at looking quizzical. "True. If only someone had a tool to help with that. A useful *guidebook*, perhaps?"

Albert's eyes widened. His hand was drawn to the pervy shaman's spellbook resting snug in the pocket of his shorts.

"Something is different this time," said Warner. "Things are changing. I don't know what the future holds, but I know it rests not in the hands of the Keeper, but rather those like you."

Albert looked back at Kneede, curious. Again, he expected the old man to say something, but he only stood there, staring back into those empty voids.

Then, like he did back in Shanzer's basement corridor, he blew away like dust and was gone.

Warner let out an irritable sort of huff and then set off back toward the stone that brought them all here.

Lucianna let out a surprisingly girlish squeal. "The boys are getting along!"

"Don't get used to it," snarled Warner.

"Be a dear and put my employee back where you found him, would you?" she said, her tone serious again. "Preferably with a minimal amount of psychological trauma."

Warner didn't reply. He simply walked off into the darkness and vanished from sight.

"This thing has a *bathroom* in it!" exclaimed Violet from inside the carriage.

Brandy looked back, surprised. "Oh. It has a bathroom. That's a nice touch."

Lucianna giggled. "All the necessary comforts."

"Sounds like it..." said Albert.

"It's a long trip," said Lucianna. "You'll have plenty of time to rest up before you arrive." She pointed to two plastic coolers sitting near the back of the carriage. "And I've had my staff prepare you meals and refreshments for your journey. Your favorites, I assure you."

Their favorites... Albert remembered the *old* Lucianna saying she'd been watching them for a very long time and wondered if *this* Lucianna was also watching them all along. But he didn't care to keep asking questions.

"The shadow road will allow you to travel a vast distance in a fraction of the time it would normally take. It bypasses the countless dangers lurking in the Wood between here and there. But be warned, no one knows what dangers may await you in the unspeakable wasteland that is the Denselands. You'll need to be cautious." Then she flashed that bright and cheerful smile at them again. "Good luck!"

"That's it?" said Albert.

"That's it," she laughed.

"Fucking unbelievable..." grumbled Brandy as she turned

to gather up the coolers.

Albert stood there a moment longer, watching the young Lucianna smile back at him in her blood-soaked white dress.

Things are changing, he thought, pondering Warner's curious words. What did that mean? *What* things were changing? How were things different?

But if there were any answers to these questions, he was sure he wasn't going to find them here.

He took one of the coolers from Brandy, then climbed into the carriage and sat down beside her. Violet was right about how roomy it was. It almost looked bigger inside than outside. The seats were soft and comfortable, with plenty of room to stretch out. Two up front, facing forward, and two more behind them, facing backward, and a short bench behind those, facing forward again, with a space between it and the door to walk farther back. There was another bench against one side at the rear of the carriage, this one wide enough to double as a bed, allowing them to get some sleep on the journey, just as Lucianna promised. There was even a curtain that could be pulled closed around it, providing some privacy. And there was, indeed, a tiny little bathroom crammed into the corner next to it.

To Albert, it looked less like a *carriage* than a *camper*.

Beyond the layout, however, there was something otherworldly about it. There were soft lights running along the ceiling, illuminating everything in a pleasant, somewhat bluish glow. But these lights looked strange in a way he couldn't quite describe. It somehow felt neither artificial nor natural, as if it were an entirely different kind of light than any he'd ever seen before…which of course made no sense whatsoever. What kind of light hadn't he seen? Wasn't light just light?

Nothing made sense anymore…

There was another light out front, too, he saw, although he didn't remember seeing one when he was outside. It illuminated the tunnel in front of them, giving them a splendid view of absolutely nothing. Only the endless darkness and those creepy chains with nothing on the other end of them.

"Everybody ready?" asked Corey.

"Do we have any choice?" grumbled Brandy as the door slid closed, sealing them inside.

"Doesn't seem like it," said Violet.

There wasn't a handle to be seen. Were they trapped in here? Albert felt a sudden wave of claustrophobia at the idea of being cooped up in here for God only knew how long.

How did the door even work? He could see no moving parts. And how did it know when to close? How did it know exactly when they were ready to go? "Do you know how to drive this thing?" he asked. Looking between the two strangers in front of him, he saw that there didn't appear to be any controls.

"Looks like I don't have to," observed Corey.

Ahead of them, those chains had begun to move. Something in the ominous darkness up ahead was pulling on them, slowly taking up the slack. He could hear them jangling together out there. It was a surprisingly eerie sound in the otherwise silent tunnel.

"Are we sure about this?" Violet asked, looking over at Corey.

"Little late to ask that now, isn't it?" snapped Brandy.

"Yep," agreed Corey. "Too late."

"Okay then," sighed Violet.

The last of the slack came out of the chains and the carriage lurched forward, wrenching a startled gasp from both girls.

Albert looked out the window and watched as Lucianna and her lantern light slid backward, offering one last cheerful wave before she was out of sight.

He could feel a slight panic welling up inside him. This was really happening. They were really going back out into the Wood. To someplace called the Denselands, with no telling what kinds of horrors waiting there for them…

He pushed the feelings away and looked up at their new friends. "So the Keeper sent you guys here, too?"

"Don't know who sent us," said Corey.

"Yeah, details are a little fuzzy yet," agreed Violet.

"But you still came?" said Brandy.

Violet smiled. It was a pretty smile. Friendly. Disarming.

There was something about her that Albert immediately liked. She seemed *genuine*. "It's kind of our thing," she replied. Then she turned around in her seat and fixed them with her bright green eyes. "So what's your story, anyway?"

Brandy rolled her eyes and rested her head on Albert's shoulder. "Don't even get me started," she groaned.

"You're the one who said it'd be a laugh," Albert reminded her.

Chapter 66

Lucianna watched the carriage vanish down the black tunnel, speeding away toward the Keeper's inescapable will, until well after it was gone.

A large, black cat stepped out of the gloom behind her and sat down at her feet, its shining eyes turned up toward her.

"What lies ahead for them," sighed Lucianna. "It won't be easy."

"No… But they are ready. And they are not alone."

"They *are* stronger together," she agreed. "But someone is interfering. Someone strong enough to bring the Ruin to my hotel."

"Yes."

"And the Keeper. His actions this time. Something's changed."

"Yes."

Lucianna looked down at those mysterious shining eyes. "It's unsettling."

"Yes."

She looked back up at the dark tunnel where the carriage's light had already long faded into the unfathomable distance. There was nothing more she could do.

It was up to them now.

About the author

Brian Harmon is an independent author of horror fiction, suspense and dark adventure. He grew up in rural Missouri and now lives in Southern Wisconsin with his wife, Guinevere, and their three children.

For more about Brian Harmon and his work, visit
www.BrianHarmonBooks.com

www.ingramcontent.com/pod-product-compliance
Lightning Source LLC
Chambersburg PA
CBHW050024030726
47506CB00001B/102